PRAISE FOR THE REVEREND ANNABELLE DIXON COZY MYSTERY SERIES

"Delightful."
"I read it that night, and it was GREAT!"
"I couldn't put it down!"
"4 thumbs up!!!"
"It kept me up until 3am. I love it."
"As a former village vicar this ticks the box for me."
"This series keeps getting better and better."
"Annabelle, with her great intuition, caring personality, yet imperfect judgment, is a wonderful main character."
"It's fun to grab a cup of tea and pretend I'm sitting in the vicarage discussing the latest mysteries with Annabelle while she polishes off the last of the cupcakes."
"Great book - love Reverend Annabelle Dixon and can't wait to read more of her books."
"Annabelle reminds me of Agatha Christie's Miss Marple."
"A perfect weekend read."
"A wonderful read, delightful characters and if that's not enough the sinfully delicious recipes will have you coming back for more."

"This cozy series is a riot!"

THE REVEREND ANNABELLE DIXON COZY MYSTERIES

ALSO BY ALISON GOLDEN

Death at the Café

Murder at the Mansion

Body in the Woods

Grave in the Garage

Horror at the Highlands

Killer at the Cult

Fireworks in France

COLLECTIONS

Books 1-4

Death at the Café

Murder at the Mansion

Body in the Woods

Grave in the Garage

Books 5-7

Horror at the Highlands

Killer at the Cult

Fireworks in France

THE REVEREND ANNABELLE DIXON COZY MYSTERIES

BOOKS 5-7

ALISON GOLDEN

JAMIE VOUGEOT

The characters and events portrayed in this book are fictitious. Any similarity to real persons, living or dead is coincidental and not intended by the author.
Text copyright © 2021 Alison Golden
All rights reserved.

No part of this book may be reproduced, stored in a retrieval system, or transmitted in any form or by any means, electronic, mechanical, photocopying, recording, or otherwise, without express written permission of the publisher.

Published by Mesa Verde Publishing
P.O. Box 1002
San Carlos, CA 94070

ISBN-13: 9798722985866

Edited by
Marjorie Kramer

"Books are engines of change, windows on the world, and lighthouses erected in the sea of time. They are companions, teachers, magicians, bankers of the treasures of the mind. Books are humanity in print."
~*Barbara Tuchman*

For a limited time, you can get the first books in each of my series - *Chaos in Cambridge, The Case of the Screaming Beauty, Hunted, and Mardi Gras Madness* - plus updates about new releases, promotions, and other Insider exclusives, by signing up for my mailing list at:

https://www.alisongolden.com/annabelle

USA TODAY BESTSELLING AUTHOR

A Reverend Annabelle Dixon Mystery

HORROR IN THE HIGHLANDS

Alison Golden

Jamie Vougeot

HORROR IN THE HIGHLANDS

BOOK FIVE

The characters and events portrayed in this book are fictitious. Any similarity to real persons, living or dead is coincidental and not intended by the author.
Text copyright © 2017 Alison Golden
All rights reserved.

No part of this book may be reproduced, stored in a retrieval system, or transmitted in any form or by any means, electronic, mechanical, photocopying, recording, or otherwise, without express written permission of the publisher.

Cover Illustration: Rosalie Yachi Clarita

Published by Mesa Verde Publishing
P.O. Box 1002
San Carlos, CA 94070

ISBN-13: 978-1545398357

Edited by
Marjorie Kramer

GLOSSARY

cèilidh: a social event at which there is Scottish or Irish folk music and singing, traditional dancing, and storytelling.
cèilidhean: plural of cèilidh
eejit: idiot
kirk: church
wheesht: shush
fair reekin': furious
Haud yer wheesht: Be quiet
How ye daein?: How are you doing?
A dinnae ken: I don't know
Och, away wi' ye: Never mind

MAP OF BLODRAIGH

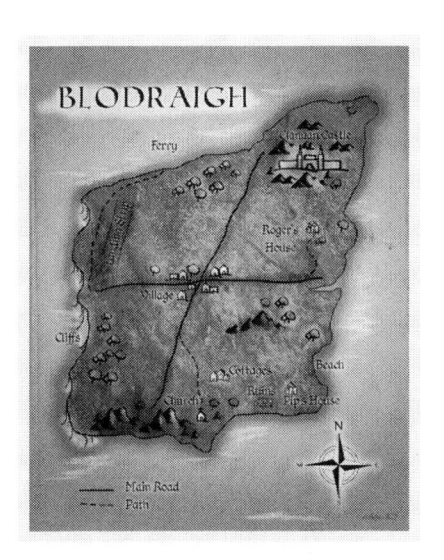

To see a larger version of this map, go to https://www.alisongolden.com/horror-in-the-highlands-map

CHAPTER ONE
FRIDAY

A SHORT, SHARP jolt woke Annabelle up, followed immediately by the queasy sensation of being gently rocked on her back. She found herself grasping wildly for something to steady herself, but succeeded only in banging her hand against the solid, cloth-covered wall next to which she lay. After opening her eyes, she went stiff with surprise, struck by the realization that this was not, indeed, her cozy bed in her cozy cottage in her cozy adopted parish of Upton St. Mary.

Her confusion only lasted a few moments, before the gentle chug of railway tracks and the sparse, old-fashioned decoration of the sleeper cabin reminded her of where she was.

Suddenly feeling entirely awake, Annabelle threw aside her sheet and leaped out of the narrow cabin bed, quickly turning to the window. She furiously rubbed at the light mist that covered the glass and gazed through it intently. Her breath stopped, her eyes widened, and her heart began to sing as soon as she saw what lay on the other side of the inch-thick glass. The beautiful Scottish Highlands!

Annabelle was on the Caledonian sleeper train on her way

from London to Inverness. She discovered the source of the rocky motions of her carriage when she saw that the train was winding itself along the crest of a riverbank, affording her an almost overwhelming view of the land that was unfurling ahead of her.

"Oh my!" gasped Annabelle, as magnificent, dark-green hills tumbled elegantly among the thick mists of the spring morning. Faint traces of winter snow graced their highest points. Silver-clear water glistened as it made its way over the craggy rocks that lay nestled on the riverbed. Even the gray clouds above, dense and heavy, that threatened to burst forth at any moment, somehow seemed joyous to her. It had been over a year since she last visited Scotland, and though she remembered well enough how impressed she always was by the Highland landscape, memories alone could not capture such magnificence.

She had grown rather accustomed to the quiet, natural beauty of her parish in Upton St. Mary. It was delicate and garden-like. Down there, spring was a time of blossoming color and light breezes that made the budding, sprouting, emerging flora dance cheerfully. Here, however, there was no light breeze. Thistles and nettles stood defiantly, sturdy and proud against the strong winds and heavy rains. One need only look at their surroundings to see why the Scots had a reputation for being a tough bunch. Demonstrations of courage and fortitude were all around them.

While Annabelle was basking in the glorious scenery, she said a quiet, humble prayer, and set about getting dressed. She still had rather a long way to go; yet another train journey, and two ferries to catch before she reached her journey's end.

Once ready, she picked up her heavy sports bag and made her way to the lounge car where she quickly secured herself a cup of hot tea and a comfortable seat from which to contemplate the view some more. It was an intimate carriage, and there were already a few early-risers enjoying their breakfasts. Annabelle glanced around and was greeted with quiet smiles and deferential nods, attracting instinctive respect despite wearing her regular clothes instead of her customary cassock or her black and white clerical collar.

It struck her that only a very particular type of traveler still took the train. A garishly-colored plane could take one most of the way in a tenth of the time for the same price. A leisurely drive while enjoying frequent pit stops and the company of friends or family, even unswerving solitude, was another alternative. As she sat at her table, it seemed to Annabelle that only those with a very contemplative, appreciative, and patient disposition would choose the train as their preferred mode of transport. It was this type of group that Annabelle was happiest to place herself among.

She sipped from her teacup and reached down into her sports bag for the oatcakes Philippa had prepared for her. As she pulled the foil-wrapped package out of her bag, she could almost hear the voice of her church secretary fussing.

"I don't care if they do serve food on the train! It'll be far too expensive and five days old anyway!"

Annabelle smiled as she nibbled delicately before furtively pushing an entire oatcake into her mouth and munching away. She brushed the crumbs from her fingers and sipped the last of her tea. Reaching once more into her bag, Annabelle pulled out the gifts she had procured for the two people who were the reason for this long journey; the two people she loved most in the world, her older brother, Roger, and his daughter, Bonnie.

The first gift was a hand-knitted scarf in red and white. These were the colors of Arsenal football club, her brother's singular passion during the time they had grown up together in the East of London. The scarf had been knitted by Mrs. Chamberlain, who lived just around the corner from St. Mary's Church, and who seemed to Annabelle to possess hands imbued with the dexterity of a concert pianist and the flight of a hummingbird. A computer analyst who worked from home,

Roger still kept himself abreast of every fixture and transfer dealing that his beloved team were involved in. Annabelle knew the gift would be appreciated, especially on the blustery moors of Blodraigh, the outer Scottish island where he and Bonnie lived.

Roger was a single dad, a widower. His daughter was seven years old. Annabelle had visited her niece almost every spring since the death of her mother when Bonnie was a baby. Now, as Annabelle watched the young girl grow ever more confident, energetic, and tall, the trips had become one of the highlights of the year for both of them. Annabelle adored her niece, finding in her a kindred spirit who loved sweets and laughter as much as she did, while Bonnie, growing up in the rather barren and isolated confines of the island, thought of her aunt as terribly exotic. Bonnie longed to hear tale after tale of what, to her, were the peculiar and far-off people and events of Upton St. Mary.

To the young girl, almost anything beyond the coastline of the island that she had grown up on was the source of mystery, excitement, and intense curiosity. She bombarded her aunt with question after question on the smallest of details. She asked about the types of plants and flowers that surrounded St. Mary's church, the shops that people frequented, and the fashions and foibles particular to those who lived on the south coast. Annabelle indulged her niece's inquisitions, finding Bonnie a rapt audience for her accounts of life as an English country vicar.

Though Annabelle did her best to temper the wide-eyed wonder that accompanied her answers to Bonnie's questions, it often seemed that Bonnie envisioned Upton St. Mary as a bustling metropolis of action and momentum; a place in which the people were determined and always in a hurry; where there was drama and excitement on a regular basis. Whenever Annabelle was tempted to dissuade Bonnie of these notions and convince her that Upton St. Mary was only slightly larger and busier than Blodraigh, she saw her stories through the young girl's eyes and quickly realized that her own life as the Vicar of the village was indeed rather hectic and often full of surprises.

Bonnie loved nothing more than adventure, and she thought constantly of escape from her narrow existence. It was for that reason (as well as a rather obvious hint in one of her letters) that Annabelle had brought with her a special, limited-edition copy of the latest and hottest children's fantasy series, *Celestius Prophesy and the Circle of Doom*. It had been released only a few days prior, and Annabelle had reserved it long in advance, already cherishing the moment she would hand it to her niece.

Annabelle set about wrapping the presents in the paper she had bought during her stopover in London. As she did so, she glanced at the passing lochs and mountains, a sense of satisfaction warming her insides like a glowing hearth. Upton St. Mary may not be a hive of activity and drama, but the persistent requests and quirks of her congregation still kept her busy. It was appealing, exciting, essential even, to squirrel oneself away from those demands every so often. As she always did, she had agreed to give a sermon at the church during her stay on the island, but it would be her only duty. For the rest of her week-long visit, she was determined to enjoy the rest and tranquility that her trip would afford. What could possibly be more pleasing than spending time with her much-loved brother and his daughter amid the serene and beautiful landscape of a Scottish island?

CHAPTER TWO

SEVEN HOURS LATER, much of Annabelle's cheerful spirit had ebbed away. She had virtually skipped off the sleeper when it arrived in Inverness, but another three-hour train journey, in a far less comfortable carriage, tested her patience. By the time she trudged off the ferry she had taken to the island of Fenbarra, not even the splendor of the Atlantic Ocean stretching out in front of her could raise her spirits. She stood, somewhat forlornly, in the small hut that served as the ferry station.

Her hips and legs were sore from the combination of sitting in one place or walking briskly to the next. Her shoulder was aching from the increasingly heavy sports bag hanging off it. The oatcakes were long scoffed. Even though the wind couldn't be felt in the rudimentary hut, there was no heating, and Annabelle shifted from foot to foot as she tried to circulate her blood to guard against the cold. Even this felt like a huge exertion. It was not even six o'clock in the evening, yet she already felt that climbing into a warm bed would be the only thing that she could manage.

The ferry ride from the main island of Fenbarra to the smaller one of Blodraigh was to be the final leg of her journey. Unlike the previous ferry, which had been as big and as busy as a cruise liner, the seafaring vessel that she could see chugging its way toward her was the size of a fishing boat. It was just about big enough for a car and a dozen or so people. As it neared the jetty, the skipper killed the engines and floated it into dock. Annabelle gratefully boarded along with seven others and made her way to the front of the ferry so that she would have first sight of land where she knew her brother and niece would be waiting. She settled herself down on a small bench situated against a railing that ran around the perimeter of the boat and that, most importantly, stopped her from falling into the sea. Only then did she allow herself the opportunity to look over her fellow passengers.

Across from her, on the other side of the boat, a young couple cooed and clapped their hands to entertain a pair of tots in baby carriers. It was behavior Annabelle was quite sure they wouldn't have anticipated or contemplated before they became parents, which by the look of it, was about six months ago. A little way behind her, the ferryman stood at the wheel, steady and comfortable on his sea legs, exchanging the occasional grunted word with an elderly passenger who seemed just as much at home. A middle-aged woman sat toward the back of the boat, adjusting her large, tortoiseshell glasses every few moments, while nearby a sullen youth draped himself nonchalantly over the railing, his eyes fixed upon the sea spray. All the passengers were thickly-clad in heavy raincoats, tightly-wrapped scarves, and various types of headgear, the colors of which seemed to camouflage them as they reflected the greens, browns, blues, greys, and purples of the landscape around them.

By now, all the passengers had claimed their spots for the duration of the journey. All, that is, except an excitable couple who were pacing about the boat, looking around as if it were a small museum. As they drew closer to Annabelle, she made out their distinct, American accents.

"Isn't this amazing?" the woman said.

"'*Och aye*'," her husband replied, mimicking a terrible Scottish accent. "Grander than the pictures. Look at that." With his hiking pole, he pointed to a crate of glass bottles full of milk, his face full of wonder.

"Let's sit down. I'm feeling all woozy with excitement." The woman flutter-patted her chest.

"Excuse me, ma'am, would you mind if we sat here?" the man asked politely.

Realizing that they were talking to her, Annabelle turned her head and took in the strikingly colorful figures of the American couple. They looked to be in their early sixties. The man was tall and broad-shouldered. He would have been intimidating were it not for his sparkling blue eyes. Beside him stood a small, blond, endearingly freckled woman who clutched a map in one hand and a large camera in the other. In their unnaturally bright clothes and with their loud exclamations of pleasure, they seemed larger than life, very different from their subdued and hard-to-spot fellow travelers. Both beamed at Annabelle with teeth so immaculate they seemed to emit their own light.

"Of course," remarked Annabelle, smiling as she shifted along the bench.

"Thank you kindly, ma'am," said the man in his booming voice.

The Americans flashed wide grins as they sat beside Annabelle, and she smiled back at them, in spite of her fatigue.

"Heck of a view, ain't it?" the big American said.

"It most certainly is," Annabelle replied.

"Where are you from? I haven't heard a Scottish accent like yours before," his wife asked.

"Oh, I'm not a Scot," Annabelle chuckled. "I'm from the South of England. I'm visiting my brother and his daughter."

"My, that sounds wunnerful!" the woman exclaimed. "So you've been here before?"

"Yes," Annabelle said, wanting to match her companion's enthusiasm but finding herself far too exhausted.

"Have you ever seen Clannan Castle?" asked the woman in a hushed whisper.

"Of course. You can see it from almost anywhere on the island."

This reply was met with excited nudges from the couple, as they looked at each other gleefully.

"Tell her, Mitch!" the woman said in a loud whisper as she elbowed her husband.

He turned to Annabelle and began. "We're—"

"—Laird and Lady of the Castle!" the woman blurted out, too thrilled with her news to wait even a second.

"Oh my!" Annabelle exclaimed. "It's wonderful to meet you! I'm Annabelle," she added, omitting the "Reverend" part. This was to be a holiday away from her responsibilities and she wasn't going to threaten it. Not this early, anyway.

"My name's Mitch Gilbert," said the American, holding out his hand warmly, "and this is my wife, Patti."

"*Laird and Lady* Gilbert, I presume," Annabelle said, smiling.

They laughed warmly.

"Mitch and Patti is just fine," giggled the woman. "We're not going to let it go to our heads!"

"So your ancestors emigrated from Blodraigh to America?"

"Oh, no," Mitch said, fishing in his coat pockets. "Nothing like that."

"We bought our lairdship online," Patti said, as her husband handed a carefully-folded sheet of paper to Annabelle.

Annabelle opened it up and saw that it was a photocopy of an ornately decorated document of some sort.

"The original is hanging in our great room, pride of place!" Mitch said, pointing a broad finger at the paper, "This certificate entitles us to three square feet of pasture in the castle grounds. It also means we have the title of Laird and Lady, fishing rights, and lifetime access to the castle."

"It also lets us wear the Clannan tartan!" Patti squealed, unzipping her orange raincoat to reveal the vivid red, black, and sky blue crisscrossed sash that she wore.

Annabelle gazed at the document for a few moments. She had never heard of titles being transferred in this way before and couldn't help thinking that the delight of the Americans seemed more than a few feet of land merited. Nonetheless, she handed the document back with a bright smile.

"It all sounds terribly thrilling!" she said, as the boat skipper turned off its engine and coasted to the ferry landing. "I sincerely hope you enjoy your time here. I feel rather privileged to meet such nobility!"

The Americans looked at each other and embarked on a fit of giggles and loud guffaws, clearly thrilled with their newly purchased status.

"Maybe we'll get to show you around our grounds!"

"I'd like that," Annabelle said, as they rose from the bench and bid each other goodbye before making their way off the boat. "That would be super."

CHAPTER THREE

ANNABELLE SCANNED HER surroundings for signs of her brother as she walked along the small pier that served as a disembarkation point as well as mooring for the ferryboat. Perhaps it was tiredness, her eyes were heavy-lidded with lack of sleep, but she caught no sight of him.

"Bumble!" came a high-pitched scream from behind, and a moment later a small body forcefully ran into Annabelle, almost knocking her flat on her front. Two slight arms wrapped themselves around her hips and squeezed her hard.

"Bonnie!" Annabelle cried, when she looked around to find her excited niece's cheek pressed against her bottom, her fatigue evaporating.

Annabelle set down her bag and knelt in order to take Bonnie in a tight hug, before pushing her away to see how much the young girl had changed since the last time she had visited the island. It was remarkable. Bonnie's wide brown eyes were even more searching and intelligent than before, while her body had stretched itself out, adding almost three inches to her height.

"How you've grown!" Annabelle exclaimed, knowing full well it sounded cliché, but that her words were no less true for it.

"Hi Sis," came the unmistakably warm voice of her brother.

"Roger!" she said, as she stood up and was immediately enveloped in a big bear hug.

"Was it a tiring trip?" he asked, as he always did. He picked up her sports bag and led the way back to the car.

"No journey's too tiring when there's two people you love waiting at the other end," Annabelle smiled, ruffling Bonnie's hair before taking her by the hand.

Moments later, the three of them sat in Roger's battered and muddy Land Rover as he weaved the car between dry stone walls and along the sloping roads of the island. It was already dark, and the swirling wind was making bushes and trees perform an ominous rain dance. Inside, however, the car was filled with Bonnie's sparkling tones as she regaled her aunt with all the news and tales of important events that had happened since she last saw her. The questions hadn't started yet, but Annabelle knew they would just as soon as Bonnie said her piece.

It wasn't long before they arrived at a large, low farmhouse that sat stoically between a pair of hills, a quarter of a mile away from the main village. A long, muddy road led up to it. As soon as Roger brought the car to a halt, Bonnie grabbed her aunt's hand and led her inside while Roger followed with Annabelle's bag.

Unlike her niece, the house itself was much as Annabelle remembered it. It was large enough for a sizable family, and every room was filled with furniture, pictures, and ornaments. With only Bonnie and her father living there, many of the rooms were rarely used, so they heated only the few that they did. But Annabelle's visit was a welcome exception to that rule, and the whole house was comfortably warm and inviting throughout. After Annabelle had taken her bag from Roger and dumped it in her room, the trio sat down to devour a hearty meal of thick vegetable soup and roast lamb that had been left warming in the oven. They voted to leave the washing-up until morning, and instead settled in the living room where Roger stoked a roaring fire in the hearth.

As the heat chased away all the chills from her body and the satisfying meal settled inside her, Annabelle smiled contentedly and watched as Roger and Bonnie unwrapped their gifts. Bonnie was delighted with her book. She squeezed her aunt once again before stroking the cover tenderly, savoring the moment before she opened it up. Roger showed his appreciation for his gift by holding his scarf aloft and performing the chant known to Arsenal fans the world over.

"Ar-se-nal! Ar-se-nal!" he shouted, much to Bonnie's and Annabelle's amusement, his voice dropping a note on the last syllable as is the custom. "Thank you very much indeed, Bumble. It's a wonderful gift."

Bonnie looked up from her place on the floor, still stroking her book, and asked, "Daddy, why do we call Auntie Annabelle, 'Bumble?'"

"Have I never told you?" Roger asked, with a frown.

"Your father has called me that since we were as young as you are now, perhaps younger." Annabelle said. "It's because I work very hard, like a bee. I've been fascinated by bees since I was a child. And I'm also very sweet. Like honey."

Bonnie beamed at Annabelle, then at her father, who wore a look of confusion on his rugged features.

"That's not quite true," he said, slowly.

Annabelle turned to look at him suspiciously. "What do you mean?" she asked.

"That's not the reason I've called you 'Bumble' all these years."

"Well if not that, what was it?" Annabelle asked, curious to know what the answer to her question might be.

Roger pressed his lips together to squelch a wry grin. "It doesn't matter now. I like your reason."

"Roger!"

"Yes?"

"I demand that you tell me this instant!"

Bonnie's wide-eyed gaze switched back and forth from her aunt to her father like someone watching a tennis match.

"Well..." Roger began, reluctantly, "I called you Bumble because... Well, you are, were, rather clumsy."

Annabelle opened her mouth wide in a gasp of horror.

"I was *not!*"

"You were," Roger continued, nodding regretfully. "Don't you remember when you climbed the fence because we were late for school?"

"Everyone's late at one time or another."

"Indeed, but most people would have remembered to take their skirt *out* of their knickers *before* they ran into the assembly hall in front of the entire school."

Annabelle huffed a little as she sought an excuse. "Still, Roger, one incident is no reason to call me—"

"And then there was the time you rode your bike straight up a ramp into an open delivery truck."

"There was an incredibly cute *puppy* tied to the lamp post, Roger. I told you."

"And then there were the numerous occasions you got your coat caught in the car door, tripped up when stepping off escalators, dropped your sunglasses looking over the balcony, sat on things, walked into things, got your hands caught in things—"

"Yes, yes! Alright!" Annabelle said, laughing at the memories. "I get it. Clumsy. But I like my explanation better. Busy. Bees. Honey. Sweet." She laughed again, looking at Bonnie who gave her another quick squeeze.

"So anyway, how are things down there in sunny Cornwall?" Roger asked, in between sips of his large mug of tea.

"Rather well, in fact," Annabelle replied. "We've finally renovated the cemetery, we have some interesting projects lined up for the young people in the village, and the congregation is as large as ever."

"And the Inspector?" asked Roger, disguising a smirk behind his hefty mug.

"I'm sorry?"

"The Inspector," repeated Roger. "You mentioned him in your last email. Several times."

Annabelle was flustered for a few moments, and had she not been rosy-cheeked from the warmth of the fire, would have found herself blushing profusely. "Well, he's a good man – a good detective. He's been very helpful whenever we've needed him. That's all."

"Okay," Roger conceded with a sly smile. "If you say so."

CHAPTER FOUR

"How have you two been?" Annabelle changed the subject to safer ground.

"Good, good," Roger sighed. "Bonnie's doing very well in school—"

"I've decided I'm going to be a pilot when I grow up!" Bonnie announced.

"Oh yes?" Annabelle smiled.

"Yes. I'll fly to every country in the world!"

Annabelle and Roger chuckled, but the Vicar detected an air of melancholy in her brother.

"That's all any of the young people on the island seem to care about," he said, sadly. "Leaving it."

"It's much the same in Upton St. Mary. Most of them can't wait to see the bright lights. It's the nature of youth," Annabelle said.

"I suppose," Roger sighed.

They sat in silence for a few minutes, listening to the crackle of wood in the fire.

"Do you still hire that lovely lady who I met last time? "

"Mrs. Cavendish? Yes. Even more so now that I have plenty of work. She still picks up this little scamp from school. She cooks and cleans. It was she who left the soup and roast for us."

"Well, it's nice to see things have remained pleasantly stable on the island. Rather that than the excitement of trouble and upheaval."

"Hmm, it's not all plain sailing. We've had somebody famous move to the island since you were last here. In that house by the ruins. Caused quite a stir, he has. A *Pip Craven*, would you believe?"

"*The* Pip Craven!?" exclaimed Annabelle, leaning forward so quickly she almost spilt her tea.

"You've heard of him?"

Annabelle put her tea down and sat back. She threw up her hands.

"Well, I was young once, you know! Are you sure it's him? He's one of the wildest rock stars this country's ever seen! Drugs, drink, women – why would someone like that come to such an out-of-the-way place as this?"

"Precisely because it is out of the way, I suppose. From what I hear, he's cleaned up his act. Apparently, he had a few too many brushes with the law. And probably close calls with death, I shouldn't wonder. He had to get himself away from the high-life. And you can't get much further away from it than up here."

Annabelle nodded, picking up her tea again.

"Of course, it hasn't stopped people talking," Roger said, brushing a hand through his short, brown hair. "Satanic rituals, magic, cults, that sort of thing. The villagers are letting their imaginations run wild. He seems to live quietly and stay at his house most of the time. We don't see him about much. He doesn't bother anyone, but that only makes the people around here even more enthusiastic to fill in the gaps for themselves."

Annabelle scoffed lightly. "Sounds familiar. The more you tell me of the island, the more it reminds me of Upton St. Mary."

"I guess some things are very much the same no matter where you are."

After a moment of silence, Annabelle once more put down her tea and leaned forward.

"That reminds me, do you know who lives at Clannan Castle?"

"Yes. Robert Kilbairn. Australian fellow. Keeps himself to himself, but you can usually find him in the pub if you want him. Why do you ask?"

"I met an American couple on the ferry – rather nice people. They told me that they'd purchased a title, and three square feet of land around the castle. It seemed a little…odd."

Roger frowned as he mulled this piece of information over.

"Interesting. I can't say I know anything about that, which is strange in itself. There are only a hundred and fifty people on the island, and it can be hard to keep a secret when there are so few distractions. Then again, when people do have business that they want to keep quiet, they tend to keep it very quiet indeed."

"Hmm," Annabelle said, as she watched the dying embers of the fire fade out in the hearth.

"Anyway," Roger said. He pushed himself out of the armchair, "It's time both of you ladies got a good night's sleep."

"Can Bumble read me a story, Daddy?"

Roger exchanged an apologetic look with his sister.

"Another time, Bonnie. Your aunt's had a long journey—"

"But you promised, Daddy!" Bonnie pleaded, her face at its most vulnerable and imploring. "I've waited *so* long for her to come. I don't want to go to bed without her reading to me!"

"It's fine," Annabelle said to her brother. "I've waited a long time to read Bonnie a bedtime story, too. I don't want to delay it a moment longer, either."

"Yesssss!" squealed the happy girl.

"Okay," sighed Roger, leaning over and planting a soft kiss on their foreheads. "I'll see you two mischief-makers in the morning. Make sure she cleans her teeth properly, won't you?"

"I will," Annabelle replied.

"I was talking to Bonnie," Roger responded.

Once they had readied themselves for bed, Annabelle tucked Bonnie into her patterned, very pink sheets. She gazed at Bonnie's well-stocked bookshelf.

"So what would you like me to read? Nothing scary, I hope!"

"The book you gave me! I can't wait to read it!"

Annabelle smiled softly as she pulled her gift from the bedside table. She nestled herself in beside Bonnie and opened the book to the first page. Quietly, she began to read the tale of young magicians, dragons, and terrible villains that commanded hordes of monsters. Bonnie beamed as she listened to her aunt give voices to the characters and describe the fantastic locations with flourish.

They were only a few pages in, however, when Bonnie noticed her aunt's voice slow down, pause frequently in all the wrong places, and begin to draw the words out in long, low slurs. Eventually, Annabelle ceased to speak entirely. Bonnie turned to face her aunt. Her lips were moving but weren't producing any sound whatsoever. Her eyes were completely shut.

Realizing they would make no further progress on her book that night, Bonnie gently pulled it from Annabelle's limp hands and climbed carefully out of bed. She grasped her quilt and pulled it over her sleeping aunt, smiling fondly at her slumbering face. The young girl quietly crept out of the room and padded down the landing. Tonight, she would sleep in Annabelle's bed.

CHAPTER FIVE
SATURDAY

"BUMBLE'S AWAKE!" BONNIE shouted. She jumped off the couch and gave Annabelle a big, warm hug.

"Morning, Bonnie!" Annabelle said.

Annabelle had awoken in a strange environment for the second morning in a row. It took her a moment to remember where she was. Bonnie's bedroom's walls were colored an inoffensive magnolia and were dotted with various artwork that she had done at school. They were stuck alongside photographs of Bonnie and her friends. On one side, next to her antique pinewood wardrobe, was a vast bookcase filled with colorful books, toys, and other bits and bobs familiar to parents of little girls the world over. On the other side, above a small desk with pens and paper neatly arranged on it, the particularly smoky light of a Scottish day peeked through the closed curtains.

Annabelle had shut her eyes again to enjoy the birdsong for a few moments, then pulled the quilt aside and got out of bed. Once she realized that she must have fallen asleep as she was reading to Bonnie, Annabelle smiled. She made the bed, stepped into the fluffy bunny slippers she had brought with her, and went to find the others.

A few moments following Bonnie's shout, Roger emerged. "Morning, Bumble. Sleep well? Bonnie told me you spent the night in her bed. Must have been a little cramped."

"Oh no," Annabelle said, "I was so exhausted I could have slept in a suitcase!"

"No doubt," Roger said, looking over at the ornate clock on the center of the mantelpiece, "It's well past eleven."

"Would you like some breakfast?" Bonnie asked sweetly.

"I'd love some, Bonnie!" Annabelle said. "Lead the way."

Annabelle sat at the kitchen table as Roger prepared some tea and toast. Bonnie sat beside her, pleased as punch to be in the company of her exotic aunt.

"Are there girls like me in Upton St. Mary?" Bonnie asked.

"Of course," Annabelle replied. "There are plenty of girls around your age there."

"And what do they do?"

"Hmm," Annabelle said, musing over the question, "Well... They play, they go to school, chat with their friends, and some of them go to church. They're really very much the same as you."

Roger placed a mug of tea and a jar of marmalade beside Annabelle's toast and butter. Then he said, "Speaking of church, or kirk as we call them up here, I hope you don't mind, but you'll have to check out St. Kilda's on your own this morning. I have some urgent work I need to do."

"Of course, I don't mind. I don't want to impose at all."

Roger turned around and slid open one of the kitchen drawers. From it, he took a large iron ring containing three keys and a small, battered notebook. One of the keys was big, black, and heavy. It looked very old. The other two were small, modern, and brass-colored. He placed them on the table in front of Annabelle.

"The keys," Annabelle smiled. "And the notebook. How is Father Boyce?"

"I imagine he's lying on a hot, sunny beach having the time of his life."

Annabelle laughed. "I always enjoy performing Sunday service here. It makes a nice change. I hope the islanders don't find it *too* different."

"Not at all," Roger said vehemently. "Frankly, you could turn up and give the service in Greek, and the locals would still appreciate the change. Father Boyce is a good man, but he does have a habit of repeating himself. As the only minister on the island, he can get pretty tiresome year after year. No, I think most of the locals look forward to your visit as much as Bonnie and I do. They wouldn't miss your service for the world. Harry told me on Thursday he's really looking forward to it."

Annabelle looked up at Roger.

"Harry?"

"Have you not met Harry before? He's the publican. He goes back and forth between his pub on Fenbarra and the one he has on Blodraigh. He's here at the moment. You'll meet him tomorrow."

"Can Bumble take me and Felicity out somewhere later?" Bonnie asked quickly. Roger looked at Annabelle for her reaction.

"Bonnie's friend comes over every other Saturday. Her aunt works from home – like me – so the girls often have play dates together so that at least one of us can get some work done," Roger explained.

"Please, Bumble, *please*," Bonnie implored. "It gets so *boring* at home."

"Well," Annabelle said, "how about you and Felicity take me for a walk around the island? We could get some fresh air and exercise, and it would give your dad a good opportunity to get some work done in peace. What do you say?"

"I say yes!" Bonnie squealed, clenching her fists excitedly.

They both looked at Roger, who nodded his approval.

"That's settled then," Annabelle said, before popping the last piece of toast in her mouth and drinking the rest of her tea. "I'll get ready and check on the church, then we'll go when I get back."

After receiving directions to St. Kilda's from her brother who, mindful of her nature, was worried she'd forgotten them, Annabelle set off in search of the kirk. She had been to the island many times, but the simple rolling landscape that stretched endlessly all around her was so different from that of Upton St. Mary that it was as unfamiliar to her as that of an alien planet.

With her fingers wrapped around the big iron key ring in her pocket and her other hand holding the notebook, Annabelle strode across the empty landscape toward the kirk. As she walked, dark grey clouds formed overhead. She looked up at them anxiously. They looked ominous.

Eventually, Annabelle saw the church, a simple structure made from local stone with a pointed roof, and the ground surrounding it littered with gravestones haphazardly planted in the earth. Now that she could see her destination, she relaxed. She slowed her step and gazed around at the view. The church stood isolated but proud on the edge of the island, close to the cliffs beneath which was a rocky beach and beyond that, the Atlantic Ocean.

She turned off the road to a path that wound its way up to the church like a long yellow-grey ribbon. As she got closer, she could see that it was set with loose gravel. Annabelle passed a small cluster of crofters' cottages, the one on the southern end distinguished by its overgrown garden and old apple tree to one side.

She took a rest and inhaled deeply as she soaked up the magnificent view from the upper reaches of the hill, savoring the crisp, fresh air. All around her were wide open, green, undulating spaces, dotted with trees, some clustered together, others standing in pairs or alone. They looked lonely, and they were certainly weather-beaten. The wind swished the ground covering, beating the tall weed grasses and rustling the heather. The dark blue ocean was empty save for choppy waves and a light gray, squally sky overhead.

Finally, she reached the large, wooden doors of the rudimentary kirk and took a second to marvel at their age and ability to endure the harsh weather. St. Kilda's was not as big as her own St. Mary's, but its impressive location made up for it. Annabelle could not resist taking off her glove to run a finger against the deep wood grain of the heavy weather-beaten door.

"Marvelous," she said to herself. Inside, she was struck as always by the diminutive size of the church. She estimated that no more than fifty people could seat themselves comfortably inside it. The pious sanctuary of this small space offered a far more intimate and private atmosphere for worship than the typically grander and more resplendent larger churches on the mainland. St. Mary's could seat around two hundred, although only rarely, perhaps on a particularly popular holiday or festival was it pressed into such service.

She made her way to the front of the church and stood, turning back to look at the pews. Two displays of heathers and bluebells had been placed at the front of the church and on either side of the door. Posies were attached to the end of each pew. She suspected these were touches that had been made in honor of her visit.

Tomorrow she would give a sermon here, one that she had been preparing for weeks. She had considered and discarded many topics before finally settling upon those of judgment and acceptance, but as she stood near the altar, she realized that anything she said in this tiny church would assume a sense of importance.

"How now brown cow," she said aloud, testing the acoustics. "The quick brown fox jumped over the lazy dog."

After giggling to herself and nodding approvingly at the timbre the church walls lent to her voice, she turned to her right and slightly behind her. As she did so, a loud, high-pitched squeak pierced the silence of the church. She fair leaped two inches into the air and let out a big yelp. She spun in the direction of the noise and to her surprise, a broad-shouldered man with scraggly red hair and wearing full Highland dress was standing at the back of the church. He cradled a set of bagpipes in his arms.

The bagpiper strode over to Annabelle with a big smile on his face. He clasped the bagpipes to his chest with one hand as he shook Annabelle's with the other.

"How ye daein?" the man said, his voice quick and loud.

"My, my! You gave me a fright!" Annabelle gasped.

The man bent over her, looking at her carefully, "Och, you'll be alright, just a bit of fun. No harm done. What was your name again?"

"Annabelle," she replied, gently trying to pull her hand from the man's grasp. He was wearing a black jacket with shiny silver buttons. Underneath it was a red waistcoat. A black and white sporran hung at the front of his green kilt while knee length socks with black flashes and brown lace-up shoes completed his ensemble.

"Aye. Good name, Annabelle. I'm Harry Anderson. I own the Pig and Whistle – best pub on the island. And the worst. Cause it's the only one! Ha ha!"

"I see. Well, pleased to meet you, Harry," Annabelle said, unsure of what to make of this lively man and still trying to calm her rapidly beating heart. "Is there anything I can do for you?"

"Nah. Thought I'd pop in to see you and say hello. I was just passing. What are you doing here?"

"I've just arrived on the island. I'm covering for Father Boyce who's on holiday. I'm checking on things in time for tomorrow's service. Will you be coming?"

"Wouldn't miss it for the world, Annabelle. Don't you worry I'll be there, large as life."

"I don't doubt that for a second, Harry. Will you be bringing your bagpipes with you?"

"Och aye. Go everywhere with them."

"Then I'll be on full alert. See you tomorrow."

"See you, Annabelle." The man put the blowstick, or chanter, in his mouth and took a deep breath before letting out a long, low drone on his bagpipes. Annabelle suppressed a wince and guided him out of the church. She listened as the noise got quieter and quieter as he walked away. She let out a sigh of relief.

At the front of the kirk was a doorway so small it required her to angle her body sideways in order to slip through it. Past the threshold, there was a tiny office, sparsely furnished. A recess that had been built into the wall, originally to display a church artifact no doubt, now housed a small safe behind a roughly hewn oil painting of Jesus Christ tending a flock of sheep.

Annabelle pulled the rattling keys from her pocket and peered at them. After some experimentation, she found that one of the two smaller keys opened the desk drawer. The other, she knew, opened a box that contained a crucifix necklace and ecclesiastical ring. That box was stored in the safe. Also in the safe were the goblets, candlesticks, and other valuables used during church services. Annabelle consulted the notebook in which Father Boyce left messages for her including the list of the safe's contents and its combination. She dialed the number and the safe door clicked open. She looked inside to check everything was present and correct. Satisfied, she closed it back up.

Annabelle took a minute to gaze out of the small window in the office. Three upright bars obscured her view, but she could see the cottages she had passed on her way. Happy that she had seen everything she needed and eager to get on with her day, she locked everything back up and left the church, using her long strides to hurry her way back home to Roger and Bonnie. There was no sign of her earlier visitor – neither sight, nor sound.

CHAPTER SIX

THINGS WERE IN full swing when Annabelle returned to her brother's home. Bonnie and Felicity had turned the living room into a classroom and were playing "teacher." Stuffed toys and dolls were lined up the length of the sofa facing a stool that acted as the teacher's desk. A magic wand served as a pointer. Bonnie and Felicity were standing in front of the "class," haughtily explaining why red was the best color of them all and the right way to combine white and red crayons to make pink.

Annabelle, recognizing the game instantly and in good spirits after her walk, slunk around the back of the sofa and sat cross-legged on the floor next to the other "students."

"Sorry I'm late, Miss!" she said, cheerily.

The girls giggled.

"Okay. Listen carefully," Bonnie said, pompously in between fits of laughter.

"Yes Miss, I promise I'll be— Ow! This unicorn just poked me with its horn, Miss!"

The girls once again fell about in uncontrollable bursts of giggles.

"And, oof, this giant rabbit poked me with his ruler, Miss!"

"That's it!" Bonnie shouted happily. "You're both getting put on the naughty step!"

Roger emerged from his workroom with a frown on his face.

"What's all this uproar?" he said, before noticing that Annabelle was sitting on the floor. "Ah. I see."

Annabelle stood with a mischievous grin.

"This is Bumble, Felicity. She's a vicar! That's what they call them in England," Bonnie said proudly, pulling Annabelle by the hand toward her friend. "I told Felicity all about you," she added to Annabelle.

"Hello," Annabelle said, looking down at the black-haired, delicately-featured girl. "We haven't met before, have we?"

"Hello. It's nice to meet you. I'm Felicity," the young girl replied, with a startling amount of poise for her age. She even offered her hand.

Annabelle shook it warmly.

"Can we take Annabelle out now, Daddy?" Bonnie said.

Roger looked at the eager expressions of the young girls, and then at Annabelle who looked out of the window at the sky.

"The dark clouds seem to have moved on, for now. I can even see a patch of blue," she said. "Why not? Let's risk it. We'll take our hats in case it rains."

"Okay, then," Roger said to the girls. "But go put on something warm. It's chilly. And no sweets while you're out. Mrs. C. will have prepared a good meal for us by the time you come home."

Without a word, Bonnie ran out of the room.

"That goes for you too, Bumble. Are you sure you want to go out again? It's rather cold."

"Of course," Annabelle replied. "I can't think of a better way to spend the day."

Roger nodded. "Try to get them back before six. Dinner should be ready by then. I'll ask Mrs. Cavendish if she'd like to eat with us."

"That would be lovely," Annabelle said, before frowning a little. "But will it be alright to go roaming the island with the girls? I don't want us to get lost."

Roger grinned. "Don't worry, the girls know the island like the backs of their hands. Navigation is Bonnie's second language, I always say. They couldn't get lost if they tried – and believe me, they certainly do try. You'll be alright."

Reassured, Annabelle watched as Roger returned to his workroom, and then accompanied Felicity to the front door in order to put on their boots and gloves.

"Vicar," Felicity said slowly, carefully smoothing her gloves over each of her fingers and once more surprising Annabelle with her maturity, "May I speak with you about something?"

Annabelle stopped pulling at her boot to look at her.

"Of course. What is it?"

Felicity opened her mouth, then closed it again, as if reconsidering her request. She glanced over her shoulder toward Bonnie's room anxiously.

"It's... I have something to show you. Will you be at church tomorrow?"

"Yes. I'm conducting the service."

Felicity nodded and walked over to the coat rack to retrieve her jacket, signaling that the conversation was over. Annabelle frowned for a few seconds at the bizarre exchange, before returning herself to the unexpectedly difficult task of pulling on her boots.

When they were ready, the three of them set off, each of the young girls clutching one of Annabelle's hands. To her right, Bonnie skipped with enthusiasm across the grass, while Felicity strode purposefully and gracefully to her left. Annabelle felt it was a wonder that these two girls had become friends. They seemed almost perfect opposites. Her niece, brown eyed, fair-haired, and round-cheeked, was rarely other than excited and smiling. Felicity, with her bright-blue eyes and dark hair, was much more serious and composed, although she was clearly prone to Bonnie's influence, falling into fits of giggles and utter silliness alongside her.

"So where will you girls be taking me today?" Annabelle asked.

Bonnie looked at Felicity, then up at Annabelle.

"Wherever you want, Bumble!"

"How about we give you a tour of the island?" Felicity suggested. "To the spots we like to go. We can get around the whole island in an hour and a half. We've got loads of time."

"Oh yes, that sounds nice. Lead the way then!"

"Let's take her to see where you live first, Felicity."

"Okay," Felicity nodded, as she quickened her step.

Pulled by the singing, dancing, inquisitive pair Annabelle found herself traversing paths and surroundings that seemed familiar, and after half an hour of brisk walking, the Vicar once again saw the elegant spire of the local kirk.

"That's my house over there," Felicity called out suddenly, pointing toward the small cluster of cottages that Annabelle had noticed earlier.

"Hers is the one with the apple tree in the garden," Bonnie added.

Annabelle looked again at the overgrown thistles, vines, and weeds surrounding the old apple tree, and the small, weather-beaten cottage that sat next to it. She found herself surprised to discover that the simple cottage was the home of this well-spoken girl. Something in Felicity's poised demeanor had led Annabelle to assume that she was from a more comfortable and privileged background than the modest cottage with its neglected yard suggested.

"It's lovely!" Annabelle said politely. "And so close to the church, too!"

"I go there every Sunday," Felicity smiled. "Sometimes even alone when my aunt has to work."

Annabelle smiled, though she couldn't help but feel a tinge of sadness at the idea of such a young girl going to church alone.

"But it's okay," Felicity added quickly, sensing Annabelle's concern, "my aunt watches me from the kitchen window. It looks out along the whole path."

"Where shall we go next?" Bonnie interrupted, already eager for a new distraction.

The girls looked at Annabelle.

"How about Clannan Castle?" she suggested.

"Yes!" Bonnie enthused.

"No," Felicity said, "that's all the way on the other side of the island. It's too far."

Bonnie shrugged, before lighting up with another suggestion. "I know! Let's show Bumble the abandoned house!" Her eyes were wide and her expression roguish.

"No!" Felicity repeated, this time quick and adamant. "I don't want to go there. What about going to Pip Craven's?"

"Yes!" Bonnie said. "Maybe he's doing something strange again!"

Without waiting for Annabelle's approval, the two girls darted off to the left toward the sea, pulling at her arms as if she were merely a delivery they had to make.

CHAPTER SEVEN

AS THEY RAN, marched, and occasionally rested under the cloud dappled sky, the girls threw numerous questions at Annabelle about the lives of the boys and girls on the south coast of England. Up and down the hills they went interrogating Annabelle before finally, and much to her relief, they reached the crumbling ruins of an old castle not far from which sat a large two-story house.

"Over there!" Felicity said.

Annabelle's gaze sauntered across the retired rocker's home that stood at the bottom of a dip. The front of the dark grey building was punctuated by four small windows and a peeling black painted door. On either end, two round turrets jutted out and rose above the main body of the house. Annabelle could see at least one more turret at the back. Black guttering ran underneath the uneven slate roof that, like the rest of the house, was in dire need of maintenance. A broken down pipe ended three feet from the ground. Next to the house were the remains of an outbuilding, broken down and left in ruins. A thick, dangerous jungle of tall thistles had taken over the garden. The property was small compared to the lavish homes of retired entertainers that Annabelle had seen in glossy magazine spreads, but the unkempt surroundings notwithstanding, she thought it possessed a certain gothic charm. It had potential, as a realtor might say.

"Shhhh!" Bonnie said quickly, ducking behind the waist-high remains of a wall. "Something's moving!"

Felicity and Annabelle followed Bonnie's lead and threw themselves behind the cover of the wall, giggling. For a brief second, Annabelle felt guilty for behaving like a seven year old, but she soon got over it.

The three of them slowly poked their heads above the top of the wall to peer in the direction Bonnie pointed. Annabelle recognized him immediately. About ten yards from the house, Pip Craven was engaged in some heavy digging. Annabelle studied the man intently. He still had the long, jet-black hair she remembered from the music magazines she had read as a youth, and she thought she could see a long silver earring dangling from one ear. The dark cloaks and skull necklaces, though, had been replaced by an entirely mundane set of denim jeans and a farmer's coat. It was also immediately apparent that the once-wiry frame of the singer had filled-out in the years since she had last seen him perform on a late night TV music show.

"What's he doing?" Felicity asked in a whisper.

"He's digging for treasure!" Bonnie hissed back, excitedly.

"Oh hush!" Annabelle admonished. "He's probably just gardening."

"Maybe he's done something terrible and he's hiding the evidence," Felicity said.

"Come on now, girls. Don't be—"

"Maybe he's going to bury somebody alive!" Bonnie could hardly keep still, wriggling and opening her eyes wide.

"Oh, now really!" Annabelle said. The girls clutched at her. "I'm sure that—"

"He's going to put *us* in there if he sees us!"

"No, he's not," Annabelle began, "He's—"

Suddenly, overwhelmed by the frightfulness of the thoughts shooting around their imaginations, the two girls looked over at each other and opened their mouths wide as they screamed like banshees at the tops of their voices. They bolted up the hill away from the house. Pip Craven looked up mildly and watched the girls run. Her cover broken, Annabelle, startled and confused, stood up nervously. She watched the two sprinting girls ascend the hill, then turned to look at Pip Craven who was eyeing her curiously.

Finding herself stuck awkwardly between the shrieking young girls and a confused, former rock star, Annabelle could think of nothing else to do but pat her clothes down, smile weakly, and offer a feeble wave before turning to run at full tilt after her screeching companions.

At the top of the hill, the girls rounded a tree and were already giggling and clutching each other, thrilled by the danger and excitement of their narrow escape. Annabelle, on the other hand, having run up the steep slope as fast as she could, bent over double, hands-on-knees, as soon as she reached them.

"That was... not very... nice..." she said, gasping to catch her breath. "I'm sure... he's a... very nice man..."

The girls paid absolutely no attention to what she was saying and immediately Annabelle found her hands grabbed once again. Her head flung back as her body was pulled forward and down the other side of the hill, the girls squealing their excitement as Annabelle tried to keep up.

Eventually, they fell into an easy stroll, and the girls steered Annabelle, who was feeling quite exhausted by all the drama, into the only village on the island. It was tiny. It sat at the intersection of two roads bisecting the island. It contained all the shops, many of the eating and drinking establishments, and most of the businesses that Blodraigh had to offer. About ten outfits in all. As they walked along, Annabelle was greeted warmly on all sides by villagers who recognized her from her earlier visits to the island.

"I think we should start heading back, ladies," said Annabelle, as they neared the pub at the very edge of the village. "We'll miss our supper if we don't."

The girls agreed. Both of them, tired and not a little bedraggled after their adventures, were hungry. Just as they were about to the turn the corner at the pub and begin the walk back home, however, they heard the creak of the pub's heavy door, and saw a tall man with sandy-blonde hair that stuck up at all angles barrel through it into the street. With the swaying, uncoordinated movements of a man who'd spent far too long in the darkness of a bar, he pulled an old, black bicycle from where it leaned against the wall. He mounted it clumsily. Wobbling, he began pedaling furiously back up the cobbled street, bouncing uncomfortably in his seat.

The three of them stared as he passed, but before the girls could exchange big-eyed looks, and exaggerated shoulder shrugs, the door to the pub was pushed open noisily once again. This time Annabelle recognized the two figures who emerged: Mitch and Patti Gilbert, the Americans from the ferry. They stepped out into the road so quickly that they didn't see the Vicar. They scanned their surroundings, frowning, throwing their arms out to the side in exasperation.

"Hello!" Annabelle called to the American couple.

"Oh, hey there!" Mitch said, flustered and out of breath. They walked over.

"Good to see you again, Annabelle!" Patti said warmly.

"Did you see a guy about this tall," Mitch said quickly, holding his hand up to his shoulder, "blonde hair, stubble?"

"Yes!" Bonnie said, eager to help. "He went *that* way." She pointed up the road that led away from the village center.

"Thanks," Mitch said, looking over their heads in the direction of her outstretched arm.

"I don't think you'll catch him, however," Annabelle said quickly. "He was on a bike. He looked rather precarious, but there's nothing much around here to get in his way as long as he can stay upright. He'll be well away by now."

"Damnit!" Mitch said.

"Mitch!" Patti said in a harsh whisper. "Language!"

"Oh, sorry ma'am," he apologized to Annabelle.

Annabelle smiled. "It's alright. So who is he? The man on the bike."

"Robert Kilbairn," Mitch said, defeated, "the man we're here to see. The Laird of Clannan Castle. We think."

"Ah," Annabelle said, before frowning. "You're not sure, though? Why don't you ask in the pub?"

"We did," Patti said, "but nobody seems to want to say too much. We were asking around when, all of a sudden, that guy jumped up and ran out. It was very strange."

"I'm sure that's him," Mitch said, more to his wife than to Annabelle. "He fits the description perfectly. And the guy at the post office told us we'd find him in the pub."

"It's all *so* not what I expected!" Patti sighed.

"Why not just go to the castle?" Annabelle asked.

"We were there all goddamned – sorry – we were there all day yesterday. The gate was locked, and the number we had for the castle isn't in service anymore."

Annabelle offered the couple a sympathetic look, and felt sorry that she couldn't give them any of the information they were so dearly craving.

"I'm sure it's just a mix-up. Are you staying on the island?"

"Oh yeah," Mitch said, with conviction, "I'm not leaving until I set foot on Clannan soil! *My* soil!"

"Well, I'm sure you will," Annabelle said. "And I hope I get to see you again once you do.

Annabelle watched them for a little while as the couple, deep in conversation, walked off in the direction the man on the bike had taken. She turned back to the girls.

"Shall we go to the pub?" Bonnie asked, eagerly.

"Bonnie!" Annabelle answered, shocked at such a precocious suggestion. "You're not allowed in pubs, are you? What on earth would you go there for?"

"To see Harry!" Bonnie responded quickly, as if the answer were obvious.

Annabelle frowned a little in confusion.

"The landlord, silly!" Bonnie said, smiling once again. "Remember Daddy said Harry was looking forward to seeing you."

"Oh yes. I've already met him, actually."

"Everybody knows Harry," Bonnie said. "He's so funny! And when we come to the pub, he always has some sweets for us – but only if we promise him we've had our dinner. Sometimes he gets his bagpipes out and plays for a bit, but we don't ask him to because he makes an awful racket." The girls looked at each other and giggled again.

"Hmm," Annabelle mused. "Well, I'm sure he's a fun person, but I don't think we have the time to see him now. We're already going to be late for dinner, and you girls don't want to disappoint Mrs. Cavendish, do you?"

The girls responded by grabbing Annabelle's hands once again and pulling her along. They skipped merrily in the direction of home, the prospect of a hearty dinner spurring them on. Annabelle had to trot to keep up.

CHAPTER EIGHT

B Y THE TIME Annabelle, Bonnie, and Felicity got back to the house, the smell of beef stew was enough to make them scramble to get their coats and boots off and rush to seat themselves at the table.

"Welcome back, girls. Good afternoon?" Roger greeted them.

"Brilliant," said Bonnie.

"Exciting," said Felicity.

"Exhausting," said Annabelle, patting down her hair and flopping onto a chair at the table.

"Excellent. And you're just in time for dinner. Mrs. C. is joining us," Roger added.

"Hello, Mrs. C.," Annabelle said as Roger's nanny-cum-cook-cum-housekeeper walked into the kitchen. Annabelle was fond of Mrs. Cavendish, who had been a lifesaver for Roger after his wife died. She was a hot dab in the baking department too.

"Och, there you are," Mrs. Cavendish said. "It's lovely to see you again, Annabelle. Hasn't the wee one grown?"

"She certainly has, Mrs. C," Annabelle replied. "I would

have hardly recognized Bonnie here. Three inches. Three! That must be some kind of record."

"Well, you all sit down now. You must be famished. I've made your favorite for afters, dearie." She looked at Annabelle and said, "Whisky marmalade pudding."

Annabelle swooned. "Mrs. C, you are simply too kind."

Mrs. Cavendish served the meal from a large ceramic two-toned brown casserole dish, ladling the stew into matching bowls and handing them to Bonnie who passed them around the table. Annabelle and the two girls devoured their meal hungrily and in silence, while Roger and Mrs. Cavendish ate slower, exchanging amused glances. It was only after a vigorous and intense bout of eating, the clatter of forks and spoons ringing out like church bells, that everyone relaxed, and replete with food, began to chatter as they ate. Bonnie recounted where they had been. Felicity told of their flight from Pip Craven's. And Annabelle informed Roger of the peculiar exchange she had had with the American tourists.

"I'm not surprised the people in the pub couldn't help them," Roger said, sitting back and patting his belly contentedly, "they probably know as little about Robert Kilbairn as those tourists. He keeps himself to himself."

"Do you think he might have swindled them regarding the lairdship?"

"I honestly don't know. But I will say that it's not uncommon to see him staggering out of the pub half-drunk or completely drunk in a hurry to get somewhere else."

"Is everyone finished?" Mrs. Cavendish said, standing up and beginning to stack the plates.

"Oh, let me help you," Annabelle said, starting out of her chair.

"Wheesht, sit down, lassie!" Mrs. Cavendish said. "You've only got one job to do now, and that's to try my pudding."

Annabelle settled back in her chair, unable to even pretend

she wanted to do anything but oblige. Mrs. Cavendish cut everyone a slice, poured a generous dollop of custard over each one, and the next round of eating resumed. Once again, they were silent except for the murmurs of approval that were pronounced as the spongy, sticky dessert hit the spot. Annabelle could barely stop eating long enough to give Mrs. Cavendish her compliments. It was hardly necessary, however. Mrs. Cavendish watched as they consumed her dish with relish, their concentration and empty plates compliment enough.

Afterward, satisfied, warm, and comfortable, they could do nothing more with themselves but smile. Noticing the glazed look that had crept into Felicity's formerly sparkling eyes, Roger pushed his chair out and stood up slowly, stretching.

"I think it's time I drove you home, Felicity. Why don't you go and get ready?"

"Can I come?" Bonnie said.

"Of course. Go put your coat on too," Roger replied.

When the three of them had left, Mrs. Cavendish cleared the table. Annabelle stood lazily and helped her.

"Shall I put the kettle on?" Mrs. Cavendish asked.

She was a short woman with plump cheeks and glinting green eyes. Her round glasses and bushy, grey hair that was pinned in a tight bun lent her a friendly presence and a sense of practicality and shrewdness, much like a well-loved school librarian. With her long skirts, buttoned-up thickly knitted cardigan, and her functional, yet rather fetching boots, she was the very image of cuddliness and comfort, although when pressed into action, her stout arms and legs possessed the physical strength and toughness typical of women on the islands.

"No, thank you," Annabelle replied, "I'm one deep breath away from exploding!"

Mrs. Cavendish chuckled. "You learn to eat well when it gets as cold as it does up here," she said. "It's certainly good to have you here. Bonnie has been looking forward to your visit for weeks."

"As have I," Annabelle said, as she wet a cloth to wipe the now-bare table. "It's good to see she has such a sweet friend. Felicity seems like a lovely young girl."

"Felicity? Yes, she's almost like part of the family now," Mrs. Cavendish said, turning on the faucet and pushing up her sleeves. "Such a shame."

"A shame?" Annabelle said, as she took a tea cloth and stood ready to dry the dishes.

"Aye. Her parents," the short woman replied, beginning to scrub the casserole dish vigorously.

"What about them?"

"They died in a helicopter crash a couple of years ago."

"Oh dear. I think Roger did mention something about it."

"Bad weather," Mrs. Cavendish said, handing a wet plate to Annabelle, "it happens too often. We get dreadful storms up here. They can keep the flights grounded and the boats moored for weeks at a time. But the worst thing is that they come in quickly and without warning. If you're caught up in one of them while you're in the air, the only thing you can really do is look for a landing spot and pray you get down safely."

"That's dreadful."

"It is," sighed Mrs. Cavendish. "Felicity's life will be very different now." She pursed her lips. "Her mother was incredibly beautiful – Oh, you should have seen her. She could have been one of those models you see in the magazines."

"Felicity is rather pretty herself."

"She's the spitting image of her mother. Her father was wealthy. They owned one of the biggest properties on the island, as well as one in Edinburgh, and one in London. Then all of a sudden, poof, – gone! And nobody but her mother's sister to take care of her in that tiny little house among the crofter's cottages."

The way that Mrs. Cavendish said "crofter's cottages" told

Annabelle that the row of houses near the church was not considered the most desirable part of the island. The neglected appearance of Felicity's home made sense now.

"But what happened to all that wealth? The houses? Surely Felicity should have inherited it?"

"Och," Mrs. Cavendish grunted, "I don't know, dearie. There are rumors and gossip that'll tell you anything you want to know, but I don't believe any of it unless I see it for myself."

"Hmm," Annabelle murmured, as she focused on drying the dishes. She picked up one of the brown bowls and wiped the inside. She remembered Felicity's strange request to speak to her after the service tomorrow, and wondered what on earth it could be about. It was an odd request from a girl so young and delivered so preternaturally. She turned the bowl over and polished the bottom, seeking out a dry corner of her tea towel to do so. Her thoughts turned to the American couple, and their befuddled quest to find their promised land. And then Pip Craven, digging a nondescript piece of ground beside his house for no discernible purpose whatsoever.

Perhaps, Annabelle thought, with growing consternation, life on the island was not as simple and predictable as she had presumed.

CHAPTER NINE
SUNDAY MORNING

AS IF SUCCUMBING to the Reverend's wishes, Sunday morning saw the sun rise in a clear blue sky, banishing the ominous rain clouds of the previous day. The distinctly Scottish northern light poured down like positive wishes upon the unusually rather punctual crowd who attended her service. The sun's rays, however, were not quite strong enough to chase away the extreme chilliness that hung in the air, and it was noted by more than a few of the congregation that the church, crowded and small, was probably one of the warmest places to be on this Sunday morning.

It was standing room only in the church. The small sea of faces gazed intently at Annabelle as she took her place at the front. Many of them were smiling back at her, happy to have the novelty of a different minister grace their Sunday communion. Every pew was full. Bottoms large and small were packed tightly next to each other along the full length of each row. Against the side and back walls and even in the church entrance, between the inner and outer door, stood yet more people, all eager to hear what their visiting clergywoman had to say.

As she began her sermon, Annabelle felt a brief wave of anxiety quickly dissipate as she noticed nods of approval from the audience. Spurred by murmurs of support, Annabelle delivered an address she was rather proud of, and when the time came to sing hymns, the crowd's soaring enthusiasm inside the clifftop church was enough to be heard for miles around. They sang, proud and true, to impress their temporary minister, to celebrate the Lord in his almighty wisdom. And because it would keep them warm.

"In Christ be the glory, Amen." Annabelle concluded.

"Amen," chimed the congregation.

"Thank you all for coming today," Annabelle concluded. "I'm so happy to see so many of you here. Please, enjoy the rest of your Sunday. I'll see some of you at Evensong, no doubt."

At her words Harry Anderson, once more in his Highland dress, suddenly leaped up from his pew at the back, gathered his set of bagpipes, and began blowing a slow, droning melody. Annabelle gazed at the man, then across the faces of the congregation who seemed completely accustomed to the turn of events. Slowly, they began standing to make their way out of the church.

Annabelle walked down the aisle behind the bagpiper. Roger and Bonnie quickly followed, anticipating the crush of locals that were about to descend upon her. After telling Annabelle that lunch was planned for one o'clock, Roger took Bonnie home, accompanied by other locals who were heading in the same direction. To get to Roger's house, it was necessary to pass by the pub, and it was just about opening time. There was quite a crowd joining them on their walk.

As they left the kirk, many of the congregation introduced themselves or refreshed Annabelle's memory about their previous meetings and attendances at her services. Invitations aplenty were proffered for Annabelle to visit and partake in tea and Dundee cake. Everyone took their time, preferring to exchange gossip and chit-chat as they slowly ambled through the large doors of the church into the brisk but bright outdoors.

"Very good, er, what do you want us to call you again?" said an old man who walked with a limp.

"Annabelle, Reverend Annabelle, or just plain old Vicar, please."

"Thank you for doing this, Vicar."

"You're very welcome," Annabelle said, still slightly distracted by the red-haired bagpiper who had now posted himself by the outer door and was serenading the congregation very loudly and squeakily as they left the church.

"I suppose you're not used to that down south," the old man said, noticing the look she shot in the direction of the wailing. "It's an island tradition. Harry always blows the pipes after the service is finished. Wherever he is, he goes to church, and pipes everyone out afterward.

"I see," Annabelle said. "He's certainly got a big personality."

"Oh yes," an elderly woman laughed. She stood next to the old man in a blue silk headscarf. Her thick grey coat looked like it had been made from horsehair. "The only thing bigger than Harry on this island is his reputation!"

"Well, thank you for coming," Annabelle said, shaking their hands sincerely. "I hope to see you again next year."

"At our age, you can't make that kind of promise, Vicar. How about we see you down the pub in a few minutes?"

The bagpiper abruptly stopped his playing and strode over to the Annabelle with a big smile on his face. "Och, that was the best time I've had in this church since there was a wild cat on the loose and everyone stood on the pews screaming their heads off. Wonderful service! Ha!" he said, the bagpipes to his chest once more. He shook Annabelle's hand vigorously.

Annabelle chuckled. "Thank you. I hope it wasn't too cold!"

"Och no!" the man replied. "Do you do those kinds of services down south?"

"Pretty much," she replied, gently trying to pull her hand from the man's grasp.

"Well, come on by the pub sometime, lass. You obviously like a bit of a sing-song so you'll have a great time. Our ditties are a little more near the knuckle than these hymns here, though!"

"Thank you," Annabelle said. "I'll certainly try and pop along sometime if I get the chance."

"Aye," said the man, nodding and smiling as he walked off. "There'll be a free drink waiting for you at the bar when you do, Vicar!" He hefted his bag higher under his arm and pursed his lips to take the chanter in his mouth. He started blaring tunelessly once again. Annabelle watched him go, wondering if the wild cat had taken refuge in his bagpipes until her thoughts were interrupted by a woman behind her.

"Ignore him," she said. She was blonde and middle-aged, and she tightly clutched a large leather purse. "He's as mad as a hatter."

Annabelle laughed once again as she shook the woman's hand.

"It's certainly lively up here!" she said.

"Lively, yes..." the woman sighed, before turning away. "The last thing I want on an island like this. I moved here for the quiet, more fool me!"

The woman moved on and Annabelle turned to face the stragglers coming out of the church behind her.

"Thanks very much."

"Lovely service, Vicar."

"Bit nippy out here, isn't it?"

Another elderly gentleman, white-haired and wearing what looked suspiciously like brown tartan slippers, gave Annabelle a perfunctory handshake but didn't meet her gaze. He walked away, muttering something she couldn't quite make out before stopping abruptly.

"Flowers!" he shouted, punching the air. "Too many flowers!"

"Don't mind him, lassie," a red-cheeked woman who was standing behind him said. She looked like she'd worked outside all her life, judging by the leathery, wrinkled condition of her skin. Her eyes sparkled, however. "That's Mr. Mulherron. He's high church," she added, as if that explained everything.

Many of the conversations went like this, the islanders keen to espouse their long-held views on the church service, the weather, the price of meat, all delivered with a moan, a wry grin, and a glance skyward. Annabelle was held captive until they'd all said their piece. It was a full thirty minutes before the last of the churchgoers said their goodbyes and went about their Sundays. Still, Annabelle was able to build a good rapport with many of them and gain a sense of the collage of personalities and views that made up the population of Blodraigh. She certainly had plenty to recount to Philippa when she returned to Upton St. Mary – and it was still only the second day of her visit.

CHAPTER TEN

ANNABELLE BADE GOODBYE to the last member of the congregation, and still bearing a large smile, eased the door closed and weaved her way between the pews toward the back office. She planned to write a small note of thanks to Father Boyce.

Thinking she was alone, Annabelle put her hand out to catch hold of the office door handle. As she did so, she heard delicate, light footsteps behind her. Annabelle gasped and spun around quickly, half-expecting to find the aforementioned wild cat.

"Felicity!" Annabelle said, as her heart slowed down to its natural rhythm. "You surprised me!"

"Sorry, Vicar," Felicity said in the polite, measured voice she reserved for adults.

Felicity wore a warm, bright red coat and polished shoes. She was clutching something the size of a shoebox, wrapped in thick, worn cloth.

"I'm sorry, I had completely forgotten we had arranged a meeting," Annabelle said. "It's been a rather a hectic morning."

"It was a good service," Felicity replied, smiling.

"Why, thank you, Felicity," Annabelle replied, once again taken aback by the grace and manners of the young girl. Annabelle's eyes flickered over the mysterious package Felicity held in front of her, and she gestured toward the back room. "Shall we go to the office then? You can tell me all about whatever this secret is in there."

Annabelle opened the door to allow Felicity through, took one last look to make sure there were no other people left in the church, and closed the door behind them. Annabelle elected to stand beside the desk, where Felicity had placed her wrapped package.

"Now then," Annabelle said, looking down at Felicity and folding her arms, "what's this all about?"

Felicity breathed deeply, gathering the strength to explain herself. She opened her mouth to say something, but instead looked down at the table top. With her long, slim fingers she carefully pulled aside the cloth to reveal a wooden box with an elegant brass catch and an intricate swirling pattern inlaid in the lid. The wood appeared to be walnut. Annabelle's eyes widened. It looked like a jewelry box, and an antique, expensive one at that. If the box itself were so pretty and aged, Annabelle could only guess at how valuable the contents inside it might be. Felicity turned to her with an uncertain expression as if she half-expected the Reverend to admonish her for revealing something so surprisingly lavish.

"Felicity, what is this?" Annabelle asked tentatively.

"I found it on Thursday when I was playing at the abandoned house," Felicity said, her tone more abashed than Annabelle had ever heard it.

"The abandoned house?" Annabelle asked.

"The one that Bonnie wanted us to show you yesterday. My aunt doesn't allow me to play inside it. I shouldn't have been there."

"Oh?"

"It's supposed to be haunted."

"Ah," Annabelle said. "Tell me what happened then."

Felicity took another deep breath, gazing over Annabelle's left shoulder as she thought back.

"I was with Lynn and Kelly – Bonnie has her piano lessons on Thursday afternoons. We were bored, and we hadn't been to the house in such a long time."

"What's this house like?" Annabelle asked, sitting now. She leaned forward on the desk.

"It's just an empty house. Most of the windows are smashed and the door is just hanging off its hinges. Inside it's not too bad. It's damp and moldy, but there's still a sofa and some tables. There's nothing interesting about it, but we get fed up with playing outside all the time. So we went there to play house."

"I see," Annabelle said.

"Anyway," Felicity continued, "Kelly and Lynn were downstairs in the kitchen. I went to the bedroom. I was just looking around, and I noticed it."

"The box?"

"No, the floor. One of the floorboards looked a bit crooked. I stepped on it, and it moved. I pulled at it, and there it was," Felicity said, nodding toward the box. "In a little hole. Like a secret compartment. I showed the other girls. Of course, they got scared. They thought it was some kind of ghost's treasure, but I convinced them it wasn't. Anyway, we agreed I should hold onto it until we found an adult who could take care of it."

Annabelle pursed her lips. She wasn't sure that Felicity had done the right thing by removing the box, but at the same time, she understood the girl's concern.

"I thought I could trust you, since you're Bonnie's aunt and a minister. She's always saying you're good at solving mysteries and knowing the right thing to do, so I wanted to show this to you and ask you what you think I should do."

Annabelle smiled as she looked at this very serious child. She gently touched Felicity's shoulder.

"Of course," Annabelle said quietly, "Thank you for placing your trust in me."

Felicity eyes glistened, and she put her finger to her lips as she looked down at the box again.

"I think the best thing we can do for now is to store this away in the safe and have a think about it. Would that be a good idea?" Annabelle said.

Felicity nodded.

"But I'm wondering what's inside?"

Without waiting a second, Felicity extended her pale fingers once more and flicked the clasp. When she lifted the lid, it was as if a light had turned on inside the room such was the brilliance of the objects inside.

"Heavens!" Annabelle exclaimed, leaning backward in astonishment.

Inside the box was a myriad of the most exquisite jewelry Annabelle had ever seen. They were all mixed haphazardly together in a mass of glinting jewels and smooth precious metals. It was like looking inside a pirate's treasure chest. The allure of the items was so powerful that for a moment, both forgot themselves and slowly delved their hands into the box to touch its contents.

Felicity pulled out a bracelet of remarkably polished and perfectly round pearls, while Annabelle unhesitatingly went for the diamond necklace that shone the brightest. She was hypnotized for a few moments by the dance of light across its skillfully cut edges as she held it up to the small, barred window in the office.

"These are extraordinary!" Annabelle said in a whisper.

"I know," Felicity echoed, the pearl bracelet loose on her tiny wrist.

Annabelle turned her attention back toward the box, which

though only a handful of inches wide, seemed to contain an ocean of sights. Her eyes scanned an emerald pendant, then a pair of ruby earrings. She noticed an elegant gold chain with tiny, tightly knit links, and then a bracelet with amethyst gems interlaid in gold. Still in a trance-like state, she began taking each item out of the box and laying them carefully on the table. Felicity looked at her, confusion written on her face.

"Um," Annabelle said, "Since we're going to secure these away, perhaps I should take some pictures. We might be able to find out more about them."

Felicity nodded and helped Annabelle as she arranged the objects on the bare table. Annabelle stood to pull out her phone and began taking photos.

"Oh fiddlesticks!" she said, after a dozen attempts. "I've never been good with phones. All these pictures are completely out of focus!"

Felicity craned her neck to see them, before holding out her hand demurely in a gesture of help. Annabelle handed her phone over automatically.

After a few dexterous swipes, Felicity began snapping away, angling the phone with all the composure of a professional. Annabelle leaned over her shoulder to peer at what she was doing.

"Excuse me, Reverend," Felicity said, coolly. "You're in the light."

"Oh yes," Annabelle said, quickly stepping backward. "Please, carry on."

Within a minute, Felicity handed the phone back to Annabelle, who looked at the pictures with an appreciative smile, marveling to herself at what seven year-olds can do these days.

"You're quite the photographer, Felicity!"

The girl shrugged shyly and gazed at her feet. "I enjoy taking pictures," she offered.

"Right," Annabelle said, carefully placing the jewelry back

into the box and snapping it shut, "let's put this away." She wrapped the cloth carefully around the box once again. "These are obviously terribly valuable," Annabelle said, digging around in her cassock for Father Boyce's notebook. "We need to find out who they belong to." After a few more moments rummaging around, Annabelle finally found what she was looking for. After consulting the notebook she had extracted from her cassock's depths, she turned the dial to open the safe.

Felicity frowned as she watched Annabelle secure the jewelry box carefully inside the steel case.

"Do you think I was right to take them?" she asked. "Perhaps I should take them back to the abandoned house. The owner might come for them."

Annabelle locked up the safe, and after hanging her vestments up, dressed for the walk home.

"I don't think so," Annabelle said, tugging on her wooly hat. "You did the right thing, Felicity. There's a story behind that box, and I'm determined to find out what it is."

"What do you mean?" the girl asked.

"Well," Annabelle said, as they left the office, "if you had a box of such pretty jewelry, where would you keep it?"

Felicity answered quickly. "In my dresser."

"Precisely," Annabelle said, as she shut the office door, "I would keep them under my bed. I imagine anyone you asked would answer similarly. The last place anyone would keep them is under the floor of an abandoned house in the middle of nowhere!"

"Yes, you're right," Felicity said. "But then why are they there?"

"The obvious conclusion is that they belonged to whomever lived in that abandoned house. Do you know who that was?"

Felicity shrugged as Annabelle held the church door open for her.

"No. It's been empty for as long as I remember. A long time, I think."

"I see," Annabelle said, stepping outside and pulling out the big, old-fashioned key and putting it in the keyhole. She jiggled it until it connected with the locking mechanism. "So it must have been there quite a long time. There's also another possibility."

"What's that?"

Annabelle turned around and winced slightly as she breathed in the chilly air.

"Somebody who *didn't want to be caught* with them might have hidden them there."

Felicity put a hand to her mouth.

"A thief?" she said, worried.

"Perhaps," Annabelle shrugged. "But that's not for you to worry about anymore. As far as you're concerned, Felicity, that box is now my responsibility. You can forget all about it. Are you ticklish?" Annabelle tickled Felicity in the ribs to bring some levity to a conversation that had turned more serious than she would have liked.

Felicity wriggled and giggled. "No!"

"Are you sure?" Annabelle tickled Felicity some more.

"Ah, no, stop!" Felicity started to run across the tufted, wiry grass outside the church.

"Good!" Annabelle started to chase after her, glad to see the girl behaving more like the youngster she was. After a while, they slowed their pace and began walking down the path, breathing heavily. Annabelle returned to the subject of the box. "Leave the jewelry with me, Felicity. I'm not sure if I'm good at solving mysteries, but I most certainly would like to try!"

"You won't tell anyone where I found the box will you?"

"No, I promise, "Annabelle replied. "Your secret is safe with me."

As they got closer to the cottage where Felicity lived, she started waving.

Annabelle looked over and saw a woman, her dark hair piled up haphazardly and held back by a scarf wrapped around her head. She was standing by the garden gate in a faded red sweatshirt, grey padded waistcoat, and torn jeans.

"Who is that, Felicity?"

"My aunt. She's waiting for me. Thank you Annabelle. I'll go now. Bye."

Annabelle felt she was being dismissed, but nodded and watched the girl run across to the woman. She opened the gate to let Felicity through and they walked into the house together, her arm around Felicity's shoulders.

CHAPTER ELEVEN

ANNABELLE HAD PLENTY to mull over as she walked back to Roger's house. She wasn't quite sure of her bearings, but the wild, unfurling landscape of the island was compelling, and she decided to take a leisurely walk off the main path but in a direction she hoped would eventually lead her to the village. She could then turn right at the crossroads and make her way home.

Her fears of getting lost were quickly dismissed as she saw there were plenty of other people leisurely strolling ahead of her and in the same general direction – many of whom she recognized as having just bidden her farewell at the church doors. She followed the ramblers, careful to pace herself so she didn't catch up with them. She'd had enough small talk for a while and wanted to think in peace. Soon she found herself within sight of the small but charming cluster of buildings and roads that comprised the village center.

As she walked, Annabelle considered how pleasant it was to spend so much time out in the fresh air. In Upton St. Mary, she loved to use her Mini Cooper to get around and though she would not exchange for anything the satisfying experience of revving her little car's motor as she traveled through her parish, she found herself just as invigorated by the process of walking across the wide dales and hills of this Scottish isle.

She allowed herself a small smile at the prospect of returning home with glowing skin and a trim figure. Her smile quickly faded, however, when she realized that her physical accomplishments in Scotland would probably disappear in a matter of moments back in Cornwall after being subjected to Philippa's insistent (and irresistible) pleas to divest her of her warm, fragrant, mouthwatering, freshly baked cakes.

As her thoughts turned to the friends and parishioners she had left behind in Upton St. Mary, Annabelle felt a slight twinge of regret that they were not here. Annabelle pushed the thought from her mind as she reached the outskirts of the village, though a slight pang of homesickness remained somewhere deep inside her chest. She wondered how Inspector Nicholls and his new dog, Molly, were getting on.

The village was busier than it had been on her "tour" with Bonnie and Felicity the previous day. Much like Upton St. Mary on Sundays, the village gatherings didn't end at the church – they continued in the pub. Almost everyone, it seemed, was headed in the direction of the stone-walled Pig and Whistle, their spirits high and their voices loud in anticipation of a good time.

Annabelle followed the crowd into the pub and was met with a dense wall of bodies clad in coats, gloves, and wooly hats. As soon as she entered the musty room, filled already with the smell of beer, she saw that it was even more crowded than the church had been. Cheers, appreciative pats on the back, and raised glasses greeted her arrival, and she found herself shuffled quickly through the bodies toward the bar.

"Tell Father Boyce he can stay on holiday!" someone called out from the crowd, to roars of laughter.

"There's no more room on the boat, Vicar, you'll have to stay with us!" shouted another.

The drinkers parted to reveal a young, pretty, blonde woman waiting for her behind the bar with a big smile on her face.

"Sorry, Vicar," she said, in her light, strong Scottish accent. "It can get a wee bit rowdy on a Sunday lunchtime."

"Oh, it's rather jolly," Annabelle said, exchanging a shaky smile with the grizzled man in a fisherman's sweater and overalls who was drinking a pint of beer next to her and leering.

"I heard you led everyone in a right merry sing-song at the service today," the girl said.

"It was just a few hymns, nothing unusual. 'All Things Bright and Beautiful,' that kind of thing. I think it was the novelty of it all that excited everyone more than anything."

"Aye. That, and the fact that Father Boyce is a rather dour sort. He could make a waltz sound like a funeral march."

Annabelle chuckled along with the girl.

"My name's Mairéad, by the way. I've been on the mainland for a few years, but now I'm the landlady here, sort of – I mean, my dad owns the pub. I look after it when he's on the other island." She offered her hand over the bar.

"Ah yes, Harry. I met him and his bagpipes in church," Annabelle said, shaking the girl's hand.

"I hope he didn't bother you too much," Mairéad replied. She nodded back over her shoulder to point out her father who had dispensed with his bagpipes and was now laughing heartily with regulars at the other end of the bar. "Anyway, what can I get you, Vicar? It's on the house."

"Oh, it's alright. I just popped in for—"

"Ah, come on!" Mairéad insisted. "Just a wee one. A whisky, perhaps?"

Annabelle hesitated for a second, but Mairéad's smile was too sweet and kind to deny. "Oh, alright then!" she said. "But just a small orange juice, please. No ice."

Mairéad nodded and turned around to get Annabelle her drink. Seconds later, the orange juice in her hand, Annabelle took a small sip as she scanned the pub. Compared to the serenity and wide, open spaces of the land outside, the noise and laughter of people crammed shoulder to shoulder inside the fusty bar was a stark contrast.

For a split-second, she thought she noticed the distinctive, mussed-up, thatch-colored hair of the man who had beaten a hasty retreat from the pub the day before, but she lost him in the mass of moving bodies. Just as she was about to make her way through the crowd and mingle some, a voice called her name from across the bar. Carefully easing herself among the tightly knit bodies around her, she saw Harry Anderson, who had made his way to her end of the counter.

"Hello, again," Annabelle smiled, placing her glass down on the wood grain.

"I see you've met my daughter," the man bellowed, and Annabelle suddenly understood why he had developed such a strong, projected voice. It was noisy in the pub. Playing the bagpipes probably helped, too.

"Yes, Mairéad. She seems like a lovely girl."

"That she is. That she is," the man said, nodding wistfully. "More mature than I'll ever be! Ha!"

Annabelle laughed. "You seem to be at the center of everything. Might I ask you something, Harry?"

"Of course! I'd soon go to hell if I didn't let you, wouldn't I!? Ha!"

"Is there anyone on the island who knows about jewelry? Or antiques, perhaps?"

Harry Anderson furrowed his brow and scratched the stubble on his cheek with thick, strong fingers.

"Let's see... Perhaps. What kind of jewelry?"

Annabelle was about to describe the items before quickly remembering that she had photographs on her phone. She fished it from her pocket and pressed and swiped to bring up a picture of the diamond necklace. She turned her phone around to show the pub owner.

"That's a lovely little thing if ever I saw one," Harry mused as he looked over the picture. "Must be worth a pretty penny. Yours?" He scrolled through a few more of the photos.

"Um," Annabelle murmured as she thought of something to say, "Yes. No. Not really."

"There is one guy who might be able to help you. I'll have a word with him and get back to you if you like."

"That would be fabulous, Harry. Thank you ever so much."

Harry smiled and nodded at the throng that filled his pub. "Your service got people in such good spirits, you've probably done more for business than the last pub quiz! Ha! It's the least I can do for you!"

CHAPTER TWELVE

ANNABELLE SIPPED THE last of her orange juice and decided that she should probably start making her way back home. It was nearly one o'clock, and she had built up quite an appetite. Putting the glass down on the bar and giving Mairéad a goodbye wave of thanks, she pushed through the mass of bodies out into the fresh air and left the noisy hubbub behind.

After the stuffy heat of the pub, its air thick with the beer and bitters it served, the fresh air outside seemed wholly purifying. She turned in the direction of home, but when she was mere feet from the pub, a figure silently stepped out from an alleyway to right in front of her. Annabelle looked up and found herself face to face with Pip Craven, his dark, serious eyes holding hers. Up close, she could see that his iconic chiseled visage was a little softer and the skin at his jaw now sagged slightly, but he was still immediately recognizable as the rocker of his youth.

"You're the Vicar, right?" he said, in his broad Birmingham accent.

Annabelle blinked rapidly, finding herself unexpectedly starstruck and a little intimidated. She was standing very close to the man who had provided the musical accompaniment to much of her adolescence. A memory of her father yelling at her to turn down the volume of the Craven Idols' heavy metal music as their long guitar solos and overall emphatic sound crashed loudly from her bedroom popped into her mind. Though Pip was far from the striking, angry young man of his album covers, his eyes, in particular, still carried the brooding magnetism and intense energy that had won him millions of fans the world over.

"Ah... Yes," she said, slowly coming to her senses.

"I heard church was good this morning," he said calmly.

"The congregation seemed to enjoy it," Annabelle said, looking around her before finding her gaze magnetically drawn back to him.

With his eyes still fixed on her, Pip slowly put a piece of gum in his mouth and started chewing it. "Can I ask you a question?" he said.

"Certainly," Annabelle replied. She felt self-conscious but flattered to find herself the object of Pip Craven's curiosity.

"You've seen a lot of deaths, right? I mean, you do a lot of funerals. You know bodies and such. Hear about how people die a lot."

"Well, I—"

"What's the most inexplicable death you've ever come across?" Pip leaned in close to her, his curiosity evident in his tone and those dark, charismatic eyes. "I mean, the strangest one. The one that didn't seem to make sense. Or was just plain *weird*."

"Hmm," Annabelle said, frowning briefly at the macabre question. "I really couldn't say." The question struck her as odd, and an unhealthy interest in death was something she didn't like to encourage.

"What about vampires? Do you know anything about those?"

A slight smile came to his lips. Pip seemed to be amused at the thought. Annabelle felt quite queasy.

"Er, no. But I know quite a lot about—"

"Yes—?" Pip urged, leaning in even further.

"Bats," she said. "We had some in the belfry at one of the churches I interned at as a theology student."

"Did anyone get bitten? Draw blood?" Pip's eyes were wide and his neck fully-extended forward.

"No, no I don't think so. We called in the animal protection people, and they told us not to touch them."

Pip looked disappointed. "What about graves? Ever had any strange goings-on in the cemetery?"

"Well, once somebody thought it was a good idea to leave some dead crows by the church gates." Pip gasped. "We'd clear them away, then more would appear the next night. It went on for a week before we found out they were being electrocuted when they landed on the power line that ran along the street.

"Oooohhhh!" he said, drawing the word out so that it became a moan of satisfaction. "That's good! That's very good!" Slowly, a wide smile spread across Pip's face. Annabelle immediately regretted telling him anything.

"It most certainly is *not* good!" chided Annabelle, her sense of awe at being in the presence of someone famous completely vanishing. "The poor birds were being killed unnecessarily! As Billy Brevil told me after they learned about the food chain at school, crows are important! We had quite a dearth of them for a while, although the farmers were happy enough, I suppose."

This statement only seemed to please Pip even more.

"Thanks, Reverend! I owe you a drink!" he said happily, before turning away.

Annabelle shook her head and took a moment to breathe in deeply as though to cleanse her lungs of the taint left by Pip and his black soul. A slight breeze brushed across her face. She detected the warning signs of an oncoming storm. With the rising wind, Annabelle could almost smell her way to Roger's house. A faint mixture of something sweet and something savory traveled upon it. She quickened her step and arrived just in time to offer a helping hand with the laying of the table, her stomach growling in anticipation of Mrs. Cavendish's Sunday lunch, her queasiness at Pip Craven's inquisition notwithstanding.

CHAPTER THIRTEEN

"I'M AFRAID BONNIE and I will have to miss Evensong," Roger said, once they had all sat back in order to allow their lunch to go down. "Bonnie's yet to do her homework, and I've still got some work to catch up on."

"That's fine," Annabelle said. "Evensong is always a bit of an anticlimax after the Sunday morning service."

Evensong was typically a somber affair, attended by only the most diligent of worshippers. Annabelle had almost forgotten about it. In Upton St. Mary, she only conducted it once a month, yet here on the island, Father Boyce had insisted there would be a demand for it should Annabelle be willing.

With a little time to kill before six o'clock, Annabelle settled herself alongside Bonnie at her desk with the goal of lending a helping hand as the girl completed her homework. Bonnie, however, seemed wholly intent on derailing the endeavor at every turn by discussing all and any topic that wasn't related to the conjugation of the French verbs, *"aller," "jouer,"* and *"faire."*

"Now why don't you use all the tenses of the verb *"to play"* in this sentence about the dog?" Annabelle asked, in her most authoritative voice.

"You've got a dog now, haven't you?" Bonnie asked.

"I do, and I'll tell you all about him once we've finished these exercises," Annabelle said, firmly.

"I wish I had a dog," Bonnie replied, dropping her chin onto her hand. "Daddy says that we can get one when I'm old enough to look after it myself. But I think I am old enough now. We don't need to wait. I mean, what exactly does a dog need but walkies?"

"A dog requires much more than just walkies, Bonnie," Annabelle said. "They need lots of care and attention. And love. Feeding them and walking them and keeping them healthy is only a small part. You have to develop an understanding and—" Annabelle interrupted herself quickly, pursing her lips as she realized how she had been taken in. "Well, never mind. Forget about all that. Come on, let's do these verbs." She pointed at Bonnie's notebook.

"Do you think your dog loves you?"

Annabelle sighed and looked at Bonnie with a mildly disapproving look.

"I think he certainly does a better job of listening to me than you do!"

Bonnie giggled, and finally started following Annabelle's instructions.

Eventually, seeing that it was half-past five and realizing that her presence was proving more of a distraction than a benefit to Bonnie's education, Annabelle kissed the young girl on the forehead and poked her head into Roger's room to announce her departure. She went out into the daylight. It was starting to fade. Making the journey to the church for the second time that day, alone and at dusk, was an entirely different and altogether more intimidating undertaking.

After a few doubtful moments in which she felt she had taken a wrong turn, she eventually determined the faint outline of the kirk's spires against a darkening, clouded sky, and she relaxed a little as she drew close to the plain, unadorned structure.

In the moment between pulling out her key and placing it into the lock, however, Annabelle noticed scratch marks where the two doors joined. There were deep indentations in the wood, next to the large keyhole, as if something massive had attempted to claw itself in between them. They hadn't been there earlier. She reached out with her bare fingers in order to touch the marks.

"Oh!" she gasped suddenly, as the door gave way easily at her gentle touch.

She was certain that she had locked it securely earlier, and a brief glance at the latch confirmed it. The wood of the door had splintered and cracked at the bolt. Someone had forced it open.

Annabelle's heart raced as her focus shifted from the broken door to the empty church. If someone had forced their way in, it was possible that they were still there, hiding between the pews, behind a wall, or in the office. If they possessed something sharp or heavy enough to break the door open, they also had a weapon. Her mind raced through her options. She could hide and wait for the perpetrator to come out – if they were even in there still. Or she could go inside and find out.

Every reasonable, rational bone in her body told her to hide, to call the police, and get herself to a safe place. Yet a more powerful urge compelled her forward. She was deeply offended that someone would break into a church. Her church. The one she was responsible for. She opened the doors and carefully stepped inside.

She listened for a moment but could hear nothing. She switched the lights on and saw no one. The church was small enough that it wasn't really necessary but she wandered around the church interior slowly. After determining that no one was there, she moved over to the office door, the beat of her heart loud in her ears, the prickle of tension making her hair stand on end.

The office door was ajar. Unable to stand the tension, she decided to meet it head on. She barged through, shoulder first, adrenaline running through her veins.

The room was empty. Whoever had broken in wasn't there now. Annabelle's gaze settled on the small safe. The door was hanging open. She had expected it, but still a chill snaked down her spine. The jewelry box was gone.

CHAPTER FOURTEEN
SUNDAY EVENING

A NNABELLE RAN OUTSIDE, anxious and bewildered. Who on earth could have stolen the jewelry box? She had only just secured it away in the safe. No one but Felicity and she even knew it existed! Despite the cool evening, she felt hot with a sense of urgency.

Outside, swirling, thick clouds were outlined by the partly obscured moon's silvery light. She scanned the land around the church, not quite sure what she was looking for but hoping some clue that might help solve the mystery would make itself apparent. From her hilltop vantage point she could see figures – mere specks at quite a distance – ambling toward the church. Parishioners on their way to Evensong.

Annabelle foraged in her pockets for her phone and pulled it out. Shaking and fumbling, she dialed 999 on her third attempt. She paced outside the church as she listened to the ring tone. It seemed to go on forever. Just as she was about to give up, someone answered.

"Hello?" a young woman said, almost shouting to be heard among the background noise of an uproarious crowd.

"Hello!" Annabelle screamed into the handset. "I'd like to report a theft!"

"Vicar?" came the voice over what sounded like laughter.

Annabelle pulled the phone away from her ear to gaze at it in bemusement for a second, before speaking once again.

"Yes! I want to report a theft at the church!"

"Annabelle!" the woman's voice said again, sounding pleased. "You're at the church, you say?"

"Who is this?"

The woman laughed before answering. "It's Mairéad! We spoke at the pub earlier. Harry Anderson's daught—"

"*Mairéad!?* I dialed 999. I need the police!"

"Ah! Well see," Mairéad said, cheerily, "we police ourselves here. There's no station on the island. All 999 calls are directed to the pub."

"But—"

"It's alright, Vicar. I'll send someone along to help you. The church, you said?"

"No, wait—"Annabelle said quickly. She could hear Mairéad calling across the bar. She looked down the hill. A few of the group who were trudging their way up the path waved at her. She frowned and waved back distractedly.

"Okay, someone should drop by shortly," Mairéad resumed.

"I really need to speak to a police officer," Annabelle said. She was growing increasingly frustrated. "This is a serious incident. Are you honestly telling me that there is no police presence on the island whatsoever?"

"I'm afraid so, Vicar," Mairéad said, adding a little laugh.

"Then what do you do if something happens on the island?"

"Well, there's rarely anything more than feral goats to deal with, to be honest with you. Bob McGregor is sort of our unofficial authority in that respect. He's a plumber most of the time, but if you've a problem with a feral goat, he's your man," Mairéad paused for a moment before quickly adding, "This isn't about a feral goat, is it?"

"No! It's nothing to do with a feral goat! I'll need somebody with more than plumbing skills to handle this!"

"Calm down, Vicar, lass! You'd be surprised at what a menace feral goats can be! I tell you, if you can handle one of those tykes, you can handle anything!"

Annabelle closed her eyes and took a deep breath. After a quick glance at the heavens, she calmed herself enough to speak once again.

"I need somebody that can take a report and can conduct a proper investigation. I know this might be rare on the island, but it really is a very serious matter."

"Hmm, well, if it's that bad then I can put you through to the constabulary at Fenbarra – but that's really only for emergencies."

"This *is* an emergency!" Annabelle exclaimed, losing much of her composure again.

"Alright then. I'll put you through. Hold on. Bye Vicar!"

Mairéad's cheerful voice was replaced by a series of clicks, and then another ring tone. Looking up again, Annabelle noticed that there were now around a dozen people walking up the church path. That was quite a lot for Evensong. Four or five was more usual. They were close enough to notice something was awry and were looking at her in bewilderment.

After an excruciatingly long wait, the phone was answered once again, this time by a rather groggy male voice.

"Yes?"

"Hello? Is this the constabulary at Fenbarra?" Annabelle asked pleadingly.

"That it is. Aye," the voice drawled, and it became apparent to Annabelle that whoever was on the other end of the line was chewing something sizable.

"I'd like to report a very serious crime," Annabelle said,

glancing up quickly at the gathering crowd around her, "a theft. At St. Kilda's on Blodraigh."

"Hold on," interrupted the voice, after which Annabelle heard him spit forcefully. "There's a what now?"

Once again Annabelle looked up to the heavens, feeling the first, faint droplets of rain hit her face.

"A *robbery!*" Annabelle said vehemently once again.

"On Blodraigh?"

"Yes!"

"You're not from Blodraigh, are you?"

"No, I'm not. I'm—"

"Aye. Thought so. I could tell by the accent. Where you from then?"

"I'm from England – but what's that got to do with anything!"

"Well ma'am, you see," the man began, his voice drawn-out and casual now, "Blodraigh's a small island. Anything stolen is bound to turn up sooner or later. Try asking the parents of the local kids."

"A box of very expensive jewelry has gone missing." Annabelle stood up straighter. "And your advice is to 'ask the local kids!?'" she said, wondering how she had ended up in this exasperating maze-like conversation.

"Expensive jewelry you say? You won't find much use for them around here. We're all about cèilidhean and barn dances in these parts. Not much call for expensive jewelry at those. Well, you probably just misplaced them. Have a good look around. My wife is always losing her stuff in the car. Did you check your car?"

"Now listen!" Annabelle said, shouting into the handset with a force that made the approaching crowd look up in alarm. "There's been a very serious crime committed here. You will send a police officer – no, a *detective* – to Blodraigh immediately in order to investigate it. If you don't, I will make it my personal mission to see that the shoddy excuse for civilian protection on this island is replaced with something approaching professional!" It was most unlike Annabelle to be issuing threats and flying off the handle like this, but stripped of the kind of support that she was used to back in Upton St. Mary, she felt naked and alone.

"Haud yer wheesht, woman," the man said, with only a little more formality, "calm down, will yer? I can send someone to the island if it's that bad, but there's a storm coming in. All flights and ferries have been stopped. No one will get there until Tuesday at the earliest, maybe later. Shout at me all you want, you'd do better directing it at the clouds."

"Yes, you're quite probably correct!" Annabelle sighed deeply. "Okay," she said, defeated after her outburst.

"What's yer name?"

"Reverend Annabelle Dixon."

"Oh, a minister? Why didn't you say so? Well, as I said, I'll ask someone to come by the island to take a look. But they'll get there when they get there." He burped.

With that farewell, the man hung up. Annabelle dropped her head, a feeling of futility engulfing her. The Evensong worshippers had reached her now and were eyeing her cautiously. She shook her head at the sheer absurdity of the phone call and began to wonder how on earth more robberies didn't occur on the island when there seemed so little precaution against them.

The rain was beginning to gather some momentum now, and the pitter-patter of drops hitting the gravel path was rising in volume. Annabelle looked up to see the group in front of her part in two, and a short man with a red, puffy face rushed past them. She watched him exert himself strenuously for the last few strides, stop, bend over with his hands on his knees, and struggle to gather his breath.

"I've been sent from the pub," the man said, in between gasps for air.

"You're Bob McGregor?" Annabelle said hopefully, stepping forward.

"No," the man said, shaking her hand limply before resuming his bent-over position and taking a few more deep breaths. "Bob had to go off on a call. Rab's toilet got blocked up again. Bob told me to tell you that he understands that this is an emergency, but you see, Rab's toilet gets really bad when it's blocked. You can smell it from the other side of—"

"Yes, yes, okay," Annabelle said, cutting him off.

"Anyway," the man said, "I'm Bruce Fitzpatrick. I'm standing in for Bob."

"And you're the local police?"

"Oh no, I'm a blacksmith. But they thought I was the best one to come because, well, I make candlesticks…"

Annabelle couldn't see the relevance of candlesticks to her predicament at all, but she didn't want to distract the smithy any further from what was already his apparently very tenuous grasp on the gravity of the situation.

"Allow me to explain what happened," Annabelle began. "There was a box containing some very precious valuables that I had put in the church safe. Now—"

Annabelle was interrupted by the sound of a phone. The Evensong crowd and Bruce looked at each other searching for the source of the tone. Their eyes settled on an elderly woman in the group who stared back at them. A second later, the woman started as she realized why they were all looking at her and hastily began rooting around in her bag.

"What?!" she shouted into her phone suddenly. She paused. "Are you sure?!" Her eyes widened at the response on the other end of the line. She quickly looked up at the others around her. "Stop, I'll tell the Vicar to come over. Stay where you are." The woman dropped the phone from her ear, "It's Harry Anderson. He's dead!"

CHAPTER FIFTEEN

"D EAD?"
"*Harry?*"
"He was just in the pub a while ago. I saw him."

The shocked responses came thick and fast. The small crowd of agitated villagers were almost riotous at this surprising turn of events. They were all astonished at how chaotic their usually calm, decorous Evensong was turning out.

As the crowd bombarded the elderly woman with questions that she struggled to relay into her phone, Annabelle turned back to Bruce.

"Shouldn't you be doing something?" she asked.
"About Harry being dead?"
"Yes!"
"But what about the robbery?"
Annabelle shrugged incredulously.
"The robbery can wait!"

Bruce glanced fearfully from Annabelle to the crowd before venturing into action. He stood on the low step to the church. It wasn't much help. It gave him just an inch or so of extra height.

"Everybody, stop yer yabbering! *Now!*"

Bruce's voice got lost in the sound of the rain which was now coming down even faster than ever. A flash of lighting lit up the darkening scene. The clamoring villagers went silent.

"Let's get inside," Annabelle shouted.

The crowd shuffled into the kirk and focused all their attention on Bruce now that they weren't being battered by the elements.

"Good," Bruce said. "Now, Mrs. Blair, who were you talking to on the phone there? And what did they say?"

"It was my son Davy," the woman said. "He's been out on the boat, but they've just finished for the day. He found a body, Harry's body, on his way home when he was walking along the beach!"

"Well, I never!"

"I only saw him at lunchtime!"

The crowd attempted to resume its cacophony of questions and exclamations but was quelled by Bruce.

"Enough! Mrs. Blair, is your wee Davy sure it's Harry Anderson?"

"Aye," the woman said, her voice trembling, "but he's not so wee anymore, Bruce. He knows it's Harry alright. And he said he had his bagpipes with him."

"Everyone listen," Bruce said, growing into his role as leader, "go home. I'll look into this now."

"I'll come with you to the beach," Annabelle said, "perhaps I can help or at the very least offer a prayer."

"Very good," Bruce said. "Come on, then."

Annabelle shooed the crowd outside. They were reluctant to disperse. Bruce began marching away from the church, toward the cliff edge and the ocean. Annabelle quickly followed.

"Vicar," came a call from the crowd behind her, "what about Evensong?"

Annabelle stopped and turned. "I'm afraid Evensong is the

least of my concerns right now. A man is dead, and the church has been robbed. It will surely take more than a few prayers to sleep well tonight."

"But what should we do, Vicar?"

"I suggest whisky!"

As if mirroring the chaos and confusion of her thoughts, the skies began to erupt again with sporadic bolts of lightning. Thunder rumbled seconds after every flash, and the sound rolled around them as Annabelle and Bruce jogged over the soggy grasslands to a point where the route down to the beach wasn't so steep.

Bruce led Annabelle past the ruined castle and Pip Craven's house that sat a little beyond it. Though he was short, Bruce was also a heavy man. He stumbled occasionally as he hurried. As he trotted down a bank, his feet slipped out from under him, and he fell, rolling down the slope and coming to a stop in a heap several yards away among tufts of wiry long grass. Annabelle managed to stay upright and dolly-stepped her way down. She reached out to help Bruce up, her calm, gentle manner a contrast to the turmoil unfurling around them.

They left the ruins and Pip Craven's house behind and shortly reached a craggy outline of rocks beyond which was the beach. As Annabelle got close, she saw there was a steep, pebbly slope before the ground leveled and the sand of the beach and ferociously cold water of the Atlantic Ocean took over. Two male figures stood down below on the wet sand.

"Can you make your way down, Reverend?" Bruce shouted above the lashing rain. "It's slippery on these rocks – especially when it's wet. Be very careful."

Annabelle merely nodded, her sodden hair now pasted to her scalp. She selected a rock to step on. Carefully she followed Bruce, choosing the most stable, even boulders to clamber over. As the larger rocks gave way to the even more treacherous loose pebbles, her feet slipped, sending stones tumbling away from her with each step as she struggled for control. With her arms outstretched and her knees bent for balance, she finally leaped the last few feet onto the sand where the two strangers ran to join her. She looked behind to see Bruce, who she'd overtaken, carefully completing his descent.

"Who are you?" one of the men said, only his sharp cheek bones and thin face visible beneath the hood of his padded jacket, a garment entirely more suitable for the horrendous weather than Annabelle's cassock and coat.

"I'm Annabelle, filling in for Father Boyce," she called out, wincing against the rain lashing her face.

The hooded man looked at his companion, whose beard was so large and hair so thick that only his ears, eyes and nose were clearly visible. He wore no hood or hat, leaving his hair to be tossed about by the wind, but seemed utterly comfortable in the rough conditions. The two men nodded at each other. Bruce joined them, and the bearded man and the hooded man led the other two further down the beach, where a prone figure lay still and vulnerable.

"Oh my!" Annabelle gasped, bringing a hand to her throat.

Although the bagpipes were covering his face, Harry's Highland dress was clearly recognizable. He was lying on his back, his hands up either side of the bag, the drones of the bagpipes splayed out above his head like a grisly headdress. It was a strange, unsettling sight amid the windswept beach, the waves crashing noisily a few yards away.

"We found him like this, didn't we, Fraser?" the reedy voice of the hooded man announced as they circled Harry's body.

"Aye, we sure did. Me and Davy haven't touched a hair on his head."

The wind had picked up and the rain lashed down against the beach in a solid sheet. The three men and Annabelle turned their heads away as they braced themselves against the wind.

"I'll take some pictures," Bruce said, pulling his phone out.

"He looks like he was playing the bagpipes when he died," Fraser, the bearded man, shouted over the chaos.

Annabelle checked that Bruce was done taking pictures, then knelt quickly beside the body. She reached out but stopped when she felt Bruce's hand on her shoulder.

"Should we be moving him? Maybe we need to leave it for the police."

Annabelle glared at him through the sheeting rain.

"You *are* the police, Bruce!" she shouted against the wind, before turning back and reaching out again to pull the bagpipes away from Harry's face. It was a more difficult task than she expected and when she paused, she realized why. The chanter, on which Harry played his squeaking melodies, had been rammed down his throat.

"He's been murdered!" Davy shouted out from underneath his hood. He was barely audible above a loud roll of thunder.

Annabelle bent over further and studied the body intently while the wind and rain battered her face. There was a wound at the front of Harry's head, and blood had run on to the sand. She looked around for some kind of weapon or other clue but found none. She closed her eyes and said a brief, solemn prayer.

"What shall we do?" Bruce asked.

Annabelle gently pulled the chanter from Harry's mouth and stood up, clutching the bagpipes. Something fell from them, and Fraser leaped forward to retrieve it. He held it up and everyone saw that it was a metal rod with a flat tapered end. They all looked at each other. The question of its identity and purpose was written on all their faces, but nobody ventured an answer.

"How far does the tide come up? Can you take the body somewhere safe and dry?" Annabelle shouted at the two men.

Davy and Fraser looked at each other quickly.

"The boat's nearest," the bearded man said, "we could put him in the hold. He'll be safe there until the storm lets up – whenever that may be."

"Do that," Bruce said, and the two men quickly obliged, each one taking an end of the pub landlord and carrying him down the sandy beach. Annabelle turned to Bruce, noticing that the man's attention was now absorbed by the swirling skies.

"We should really get back," he shouted with a concerned look, "the weather's going to get worse very quickly."

"Worse?" Annabelle cried, her hair now strewn across her face, her coat soaked and her cassock clinging to her knees. *How could it get any worse?* But she nodded and let Bruce lead her down the beach a way, the rocky incline now being far too dangerous to navigate. As they set off, she took one last look around and stopped abruptly. In the distance she saw a male figure still and alone on the grassy ground above them, watching silently. Annabelle squinted to see who it was. Spray from the sea mixed with rain from above formed a blanket of grey that made him appear some kind of ghostly apparition, but his outline was unmistakable. The figure, seeing her peer through the murky weather, turned and walked away in the direction of home. *Pip Craven.* She'd know him anywhere.

CHAPTER SIXTEEN

BRUCE AND ANNABELLE trudged up a sandy path that sucked at their feet, eventually returning to the slick, soaked, coarse grass. They sheltered under a wind-affected tree that had grown at a low angle to the ground and away from the beach.

Bruce picked out his phone from his pocket and shouted into it. Annabelle couldn't quite make out what he was saying, and she was far too preoccupied with keeping herself upright to focus on anything else. She held onto the forlorn tree feeling great empathy with it for having to endure such a harsh environment. Eventually Bruce shoved the phone back into his pocket and drew close to Annabelle's ear.

"That was Fenbarra," he shouted inches away from her face, the rain and wind now a loud crescendo, "they've confirmed that all boats and aircraft are stopped. There's no way anyone's getting to the island tonight or tomorrow."

Annabelle nodded. Bruce glanced at the bagpipes she still clutched under her arm, and reached out for them. They walked on for a while, walking inland a little but keeping the coastline in view so as to hold onto their bearings.

"I'll walk you back to Roger's house," Bruce shouted again over the din.

Annabelle shook her head and looked over to the church, which was now in view along with the cottages over to one side.

"No, it's okay" she shouted back, "I'll go visit Felicity. Will you be alright by yourself?"

"Aye, things'll get easier the more inland I go. Nothing I haven't done a hundred times before."

Bruce looked over to the ramshackle cottage, the apple tree beside it swaying threateningly against the onslaught.

"Okay. I'll see you when I see you," he called out, and he began walking back toward the village.

Annabelle hunkered down into her coat and forced herself forward toward the cottage. She slogged up cracked paving stones, in between weeds and straggly bushes, before violently slamming the dirty brass knocker on the front door of the cottage, eager to be heard above the tumult of the weather.

The door was quickly opened by the woman who had stood at the gate earlier. Now up close, Annabelle saw she was rather homely with dark, nervous eyes, her dry hair now tied into a messy braid.

"Yes?" she said, quickly. "Is Felicity with you?" The woman looked around to see if Annabelle was accompanied.

"I'm sorry?" Annabelle said.

"Felicity," the woman repeated. "Do you know where she is?"

"I'm afraid I don't," Annabelle said, alarmed. "Has something happened to her? She's not out in this weather, is she?"

The woman opened her mouth to say something, then stepped back further into the house. "Come in. I can barely hear you out there."

Annabelle hurried inside as the woman closed the door behind her.

"I'm Kirsty Munroe," the other woman said, her arms crossed tightly against her chest. "You must be Bonnie's aunt. Felicity has told me about you."

"But what's happened to her? Where is she? A young girl can't be out in weather like this!"

Kirsty's eyes darkened, and her lips tightened.

"That girl is in a lot of trouble when I finally get my hands on her! I've told her so many times that she wasn't to wander far, and now it's," she glanced at the clock quickly "*seven-thirty*, and she's still gallivanting about the island! I have no idea where she is!" Kirsty's anger made her face go a deep red, and Annabelle could see tears forming. "Och, it'll be no less than she deserves! What on earth was she thinking?!"

"Ms. Munroe, please calm down," Annabelle said, in as soothing a manner as she could. "I'm sure she's safe. She's probably at a friend's house, sheltering from the storm. When did she leave?"

Kirsty struggled to stifle her angry sobs, but eventually looked Annabelle in the eye and answered her question.

"She was supposed to visit her friends who live four doors down, the cottage at the end. She spends most of her time there, getting up to God-knows-what, but I've called on them, and she left there a while back. They thought she'd come back here, but no. Not even a call. That girl has no idea of how much stress she causes me!"

"Listen," Annabelle said, speaking soothingly and placing a sympathetic hand on the distraught woman's shoulder, but inwardly feeling very concerned, "sit tight, and I'll go out to look for her. You stay here, in the event she comes back. Call me on my phone if she does." Annabelle quickly wrote down her number.

Kirsty growled but offered a shrug and a perfunctory nod in reply, overcome with exasperation and worry. Annabelle spun in her dirty, wet heels and left the cottage, out once more into the filthy weather. It had grown even more frightening now. Branches lashed against fences. Doors and windows rattled fiercely in their frames. Annabelle felt the rain change direction as the wind whipped it around as if showing it who was boss. Ahead and slightly to her left, the church stood resolutely against the battering as it had done for nearly two centuries.

She rushed back down the cottage path, looking around her for some clue as to where Felicity might have gone. She called her name. Annabelle looked again over to the church and noticed the doors were firmly closed. She thought back to the lock that had been so decisively broken. On an impulse, she began scrambling up the path toward the church just as a crack of thunder sounded so loudly above that it startled her.

"God, you are angry about something," Annabelle muttered. "I can just, you know, *tell*."

As she reached the doors, she leaned against them. Something was preventing them from opening. A sudden panic overtook her. The events of the evening had already been full of surprises, and enduring the terrible weather had tested both her physical capabilities and her nerves. She had little energy left for further shocks.

She braced her shoulder against the door, dug her boots into the wet gravel, and began pushing with all her might. The door slowly began to move, creating a crack at first, then a gap. Grunting, she leaned in further. Suddenly it broke wide open, the force propelling Annabelle forward through the small entrance hall and depositing her in a heap on the floor of the church aisle.

"Ouch!" she groaned, pushing herself up and clutching her elbow. She winced in pain. A soft pair of small hands pressed gently against her back. She turned. "Felicity! Thank goodness you're alright!" she cried.

The girl's delicate blue eyes were big and full of concern as she looked at Annabelle. "Are you alright? I'm terribly sorry, Reverend. I didn't mean to hurt you."

"I'll be fine. What are you talking about?

"I stopped you from getting in. I pushed the collection table against the door to keep it shut. The lock was broken." Felicity said, suddenly a little coy. "I hope you don't mind. It was heavy, but I managed it eventually. I saw it was you pushing at the door. I moved it so you could get inside. And then... then you ended up on the floor!" Felicity looked down at her lap.

Annabelle got up on her feet, took a few steps over to one of the pews, and flopped down. She held her arm up for Felicity to join her and shuffled over to give her room. The young girl's face was full of remorse.

"Felicity," Annabelle said, putting her arm around the girl's shoulder, "what are you doing in here? Your aunt is going out of her mind with worry. It's dark, and there's a terrible storm outside."

Felicity sighed and looked at the ground again.

"I just felt so awful and guilty. I wanted to hide away. I couldn't bear to face anyone."

Annabelle pulled her closer.

"Come now! What do you have to feel guilty about, eh? What are you going on about?"

Felicity gazed up at Annabelle, her almond-shaped eyes brimming with tears.

"I heard Mrs. Gallacher, she's my neighbor, talking about the church being broken into, and the jewelry being stolen, and about Mr. Anderson being... dead! It was me, wasn't it? It's all my fault!" she gabbled.

"Why ever would you say that, Felicity? How can it be your fault?"

"If I had just left that jewelry box where I'd found it – or just done what I was told, never gone to play in the abandoned house in the first place – none of this would have happened! Mr. Anderson might still be alive! It's *my* fault!"

Annabelle squeezed Felicity against her again.

"Poppycock!" she said. She rubbed Felicity's back. "You did the right thing. If I had found the jewelry box, I would have done the same. The only ones who should be feeling bad are the person who broke into the church, and the person who killed Harry. We—"

"Somebody *killed* Harry?!" Felicity started to gasp and sob.

"Shush, now," Annabelle soothed. "We don't even know if the two are connected. None of it has anything to do with you, Felicity. Do you understand? Shush, shush."

Felicity sobbed a little longer, her head on Annabelle's chest. Annabelle stroked her fine, dark hair until she stopped crying. Eventually, Felicity looked up.

"I suppose," she said seriously.

"Good," Annabelle said. "Now let's get you home to your aunt."

CHAPTER SEVENTEEN

AFTER SPENDING A few minutes to jam the broken lock of the church in such a fashion that it would hold shut, Annabelle took Felicity by the hand back to her aunt's cottage. Kirsty seemed even more angry and disheveled than she had before.

"Where have you been, Felicity? I have been tearing my hair out!" Kirsty's hair looked like she was telling the truth.

"She was sheltering in the church," Annabelle intervened.

"But why didn't you just come home? Why did you go all the way up to the church in this weather?"

Felicity hung her head.

"Och, away wi' ye," the woman said to the girl.

Felicity turned to Annabelle, her earlier distress replaced by stoicism, the kind Annabelle was more accustomed to seeing in the wealthy widows of her parish the day after their unpleasant husbands had died. Felicity said, "I'll be in my room. Please say 'hi' to Bonnie for me, Annabelle. Tell her I'll see her tomorrow at school."

After Felicity had gone to her room, Kirsty grudgingly

allowed Annabelle to wait for Roger to pick her up. Kirsty sat at her kitchen table, furiously working on her laptop while lamenting the loss of her internet connection. Annabelle spent an uncomfortable time waiting in silence.

After fifteen minutes, Roger arrived at the house muttering words she couldn't quite make out about "Southerners" and their "daft ideas." He drove home slowly through the thrashing weather, taking care as he navigated the barely visible, slippery roads while roundly admonishing Annabelle for not wearing a sufficiently thick and robust raincoat.

"Yes, yes, Roger. I get it. In future, I'll wear at least three warm layers and carry a plastic mac with me at all times. Now will you stop your scolding," Annabelle responded irritably.

Her brother looked at her quickly and ceased his chiding. Annabelle stared out at the rain.

Once home, she took a long, hot bath, put on her pajamas, and was given a big mug of hot chocolate by Bonnie, who had only just completed her homework. Annabelle sank into the sofa, her gaze lazily fixed upon the fire that Roger had stoked, her limbs still throbbing from her exertions, her muscles still fatigued. Roger came in the room and shook his head at her fondly, his anger having dissipated.

"Bonnie's all tucked up in bed. You look like you'll need tucking in soon, too. Careful you don't fall asleep there and spill that hot drink all over you."

Annabelle returned his smile.

"It wouldn't be the worst thing that's happened today."

Roger settled into his favored, worn armchair beside the fire, his expression turning serious.

"I did hear something about that. Are you going to tell me about it? You've only been here two days and I'm already asking you for the local news."

Annabelle sipped slowly at the hot, sweet, creamy cocoa.

"Well, first the church was broken into and a jewelry box was stolen."

"A jewelry box? What was Father Boyce doing with a jewelry box? He gets grumpy when he sees a lad with an earring."

"It wasn't his. It was given to me by... someone. To keep safe."

Roger leaned forward.

"Oh? Who?"

"I can't say," replied Annabelle, reaching for her phone and bringing up the photos of the jewelry. She handed the phone to Roger. "The person who gave me the box found it in an abandoned house. Do you recognize these?"

Roger flicked through the pictures before shaking his head.

"Sorry," he said. "They look expensive, though."

"I suspect they are."

"What do you think the story is?"

Annabelle sighed. "I think that once I learn a bit more about those jewelry pieces, I'll learn who stole them."

Roger chuckled. "You sound like a detective on a case."

"Well, it doesn't seem there's anyone else here able to take it on."

"Yes," Roger mused with a wry smile. "Though Bob McGregor does solve a lot of the feral goat problems."

"So I've heard."

"Sad news about Harry," Roger said, getting up to stir the fire a little.

"You heard about that?"

"You can't keep news like that quiet in a place as small as this."

"It looks like he was murdered."

"Wow, no! Really? We have a murderer on the loose? I suppose you're going to try and solve that one as well."

Annabelle shifted in her seat.

"I've got a pretty strong suspicion that the two incidents are connected."

"Oh?" Roger said.

"Yes," Annabelle replied. "A few hours before he was found, I showed Harry one of those pictures. The next thing we know, he's dead."

"Hmm, nasty," Roger commented. "But perhaps it's just a coincidence." He leaned over and poked at the fire. "The island is cut off right now. That means that one of us locals is the murderer. I can't fathom it. I can't think of anyone on the island who would *murder* someone."

"What do you think he was doing at the beach? And with his bagpipes, too? Did you know he was killed with his own bagpipes! Bashed in the head, and a pipe thrust down his throat," Annabelle said.

"Harry always took his bagpipes with him," Roger said, "He liked to play as he walked around the island. Mairéad – his daughter – can't stand the sound of them. You can hear him coming a mile away."

Annabelle grunted. "Well, there you go," she said, raising her mug of hot chocolate, "I didn't know that. I'm already making progress."

CHAPTER EIGHTEEN
MONDAY

ANNABELLE HAULED HERSELF out of bed, dressed, and strolled groggily into the kitchen, feeling fully the effects of braving the storm the night before. She had slept well, drifting off the second her head hit the pillow, but even though the chills and tiredness were gone, they had left behind a series of dull pains and a throbbing headache.

"Just in time," Roger said, as he turned down the radio and rinsed off a few plates in the kitchen sink, "I was about to give up on you totally and put the breakfast things away."

"Where's Bonnie?" Annabelle said, fluffing up her messy hair and yawning.

Roger chuckled. "I took her to school a while ago. It's nearly ten o'clock!"

Annabelle nodded and sidled into a chair, lazily grabbing at the toast and marmalade that had been laid out. Roger poured her some tea.

"People are worried what with having a murderer on the loose and all," Roger said. "I popped into the shop for some milk, and it was all Mr. Glencoe could talk about. He even gave me too much change! That's a first. How are you feeling?" he asked, seeing Annabelle yawn again.

"Fine," Annabelle nodded, "About as good as you would expect after running around in that terrible weather last night." She gazed out of the window as she chewed slowly. "Most of the storm seems to have cleared away, at least."

Roger shrugged. "It's only just stopped raining, and it'll most likely start up again later today. It'll probably rain off and on for a while longer until the storm blows itself out." He looked at Annabelle. "I wouldn't get your hopes up regarding the ferries or the flights just yet. The waves are still too high, and the wind is strong."

Annabelle groaned with disappointment. "We need the police from Fenbarra to get here."

"I suppose you'll be off again today," Roger said, "bothering the locals and playing detective?"

Annabelle shrugged, "Don't know. What are you going to do?"

"Stay at home mostly, but I have to go pick Mrs. Cavendish up. She went to buy some more sugar. She's gone through our entire stock of baking ingredients to satisfy your sweet tooth."

Annabelle smiled at her brother. "I reckon Mrs. Cavendish could make something delicious from a pickle!"

"Well, if you need a lift anywhere, I can take you."

Once Annabelle had eaten, dressed, and tamed her hair, they pulled on their boots and left the house.

"Oh my," Annabelle remarked, as she stepped through thick sludge to get to the car, "it's terribly muddy."

Roger raised an eyebrow as he opened the door. "The storm is the easy part, it's what comes after that's the problem. Mudslides, felled trees, escaped livestock. It's all part and parcel of living up here."

Roger drove slowly along the roads, careful to avoid any particularly threatening puddles or potholes. As they progressed at a snail's pace, Annabelle considered what her next step should be. She pondered the questions that were troubling her as she gazed out of the window at the wide, open fields of grass that were flattened in different directions as the squally gusts of wind ran across them. The Land Rover shuddered, buffeted by the force.

"Well, would you look at that," Roger remarked.

"What?" Annabelle said, spinning around to see Roger pointing out a figure beyond the windshield. She followed his finger and saw a tall, gawky man struggling to pedal a bicycle along the muddy windy road, its wheels sinking a good inch into it. He'd put the bike into too low a gear and was putting in a lot of effort for not much reward.

"Is that Robert Kilbairn?" Annabelle asked.

"Let's see, he's a fair-haired chap who's riding a bike as if his life depended on it. I'd say it was."

Roger rolled down his window as they drew alongside the struggling cyclist. He was pointed in the opposite direction. Annabelle saw that his trousers were almost entirely covered in mud, and specks of it were evident on his jacket and even his face.

"Need a hand there, Robert?" Roger called out.

"No!" Robert Kilbairn replied loudly, shouting above the sound of his own exertions. "Perfectly fine!"

Robert leaped off his bike, grit his teeth, and began pushing it.

"Are you sure, Robert...?"

"Quite sure! Thank you!" Kilbairn stared resolutely ahead and rushed past them.

Roger looked back at Annabelle, and they exchanged amused shrugs before carrying on to the village.

As they approached, Annabelle said, "You can let me out here if you like, Roger. I'm going to go to the pub."

"Bit early for a drink isn't it? They won't be open."

"Oh, I'm not going to be drinking, I want to talk to Mairéad, see how she's coping. A compassionate call from the local clergy. I'm sure that's what Father Boyce would do."

"Whatever you want, Bumble," said Roger, as he slowed the car. Annabelle smiled and opened the door, but before she stepped out, Roger tugged at her sleeve. "Do try and get back home before nightfall this time. I know that once you're set on something, you think of little else, but you did come up here to see us – to see Bonnie – not to fight crime. We'd like to see a bit more of you before you leave."

Annabelle smiled apologetically. "You're right. I'll make sure I'm home in time to do something with Bonnie. I'm sorry. I get carried away sometimes."

"It's fine. That's one thing we love about you," Roger said warmly.

Annabelle waved him goodbye and turned to push her way through the doors of the pub when she heard shouting from down the street. Recognizing Bruce Fitzpatrick, she quickly made her way over to him and his two flustered companions. Annabelle quickly realized they were the American tourists, Mitch and Patti.

"Every time! Every single goddamned time!" Mitch boomed, his voice high with frustration.

"Mitch please, calm down. I hate seeing you like this," Patti soothed.

"Hold on, please," Bruce said, patting the air with his raised palms as he tried to placate the irate American. "I know this is frustrating. I'd really like to help you."

"Everyone," Mitch erupted, raising his voice a few more decibels, "on this island has been nothing, but welcoming, kind, and helpful – except *the one guy* we came to see! Robert goddamned Kilbairn!"

"Mitch, please honey, don't raise your voice," Patti pleaded, before noticing Annabelle walking up to them. "Oh, Annabelle. It's so nice to see you again," she said breaking into a big smile.

"Annabelle!" Bruce said. He clutched her arm and stood beside her. "Maybe you can help these good people."

"What's going on?" Annabelle said, looking at all three of them. "Is Robert Kilbairn still avoiding you? We saw him just now heading up the road. He seemed in a terrible hurry again."

"He always is," Patti said sorrowfully.

"Every single time!" Mitch added, still frustrated, but slightly less loud now in the face of Annabelle's kind, compassionate presence. "We've spent two days chasing him around the island like headless chickens. Whenever we go to the pub, he leaves out the back, or gives us the slip in the crowd. When we saw him riding on the path, he suddenly changed direction and was gone in a flash. He even hid in the bathrooms when we chased him down in a local restaurant. I was banging on the door like a crazy man, but he climbed out the window!"

Patti rubbed her husband's back as he stared at the ground and shook his head to suppress his mounting anger. Annabelle exchanged a pitying look with Bruce.

"Have you tried going to the castle again?" she asked slowly.

Patti sighed deeply. "It's locked every time. It's impossible to get inside, or even see if he's there."

"It's a goddamned castle!" Mitch exploded again. "The wall around it is fifteen feet high and the doors were built to keep the English out! Unless I can buy a one of those giant sling shots..."

"A trebuchet, honey," his wife interjected.

"...Exactly, and, and... a battering ram at the local convenience store, then neither you, me, nor a barbarian horde are getting inside!"

Annabelle held back a small smirk at the man's wit.

"How long are you staying on the island?" she asked.

"We don't know. It was to be two weeks—" Patti said.

"I'll stay as long as it goddamned takes!" Mitch interrupted. "I'm a Lord of the Clannan tribe, and I'll set foot on my land before I leave Scotland. Mark my words."

"Well, there should be some police officers arriving tonight or tomorrow," Annabelle said, "Once they're here, we can let them know about your problem. Hopefully they'll be able to help. At least you know no one's going anywhere."

Mitch and Patti looked at each other, then at Annabelle, a small glint of hope in their eyes once again.

"Thanks, Annabelle. That means so much," said Patti.

"Yeah," Mitch said, the redness of his cheeks already dissipating. "I appreciate it."

Smiling for the first time, the couple wrapped their arms lovingly around each other and set off into the village. Annabelle and Bruce watched them go.

CHAPTER NINETEEN

"THANKS FOR THAT, Vicar," Bruce said, pulling off his flat cap and rubbing a hand through his hair. "I didn't have a clue how to handle that."

"Well, it's not over yet. I just hope the police can help them."

"Aye," Bruce said, putting his hat back on. "Where are you off to?"

"I'm going to visit Mairéad to see how she's doing."

"Ah, I went to tell her the news last night. She was, as you'd expect, quite upset."

Inside the pub, it was gloomy but warm. Shafts of light from the window picked out dust motes floating in the air. Annabelle heard the crash of a door, and Mairéad looking pale and wan came through to the bar from the back. From where Annabelle stood, the young woman appeared to be impassive, but the vicar could sense the overwhelming sadness that resided just beneath the surface of her pale, freckled skin. Mairéad caught sight of Annabelle immediately.

"Oh, good morning, Vicar. I'm afraid we're not open today."

"I've not come for a drink, Mairéad. I've come to express my sincere condolences and to see how you are coping, if you need anything. Such a terrible business!"

"Thank you, Vicar. It was quite a shock."

"Do you have someone with you? Looking after you?" Annabelle looked concernedly at the young woman.

"I have my friend, Anne. She's come over to be with me. I'm alright, thank you." Mairéad gave Annabelle a weak smile. "Look, why don't we sit down? Would you like a drink?"

Mairéad got them both a glass of orange juice, and they sat down at one of the small, round, wooden tables.

"Bruce said Dad's body had been found on the beach. Said he'd been *murdered*. How can that be?" A tear rolled down her cheek, and she pulled a crumpled tissue from her sleeve to dab at it.

"We don't really know, Mairéad. We'll have to wait for the police to arrive to conduct a proper investigation."

"Did he really have his bagpipes rammed down his throat?"

Annabelle nodded.

"I always did hate those things. But now I'm so sad. I'll never hear them again!" Mairéad started to sob in earnest. Annabelle put a hand on her arm. When the younger woman's tears subsided, Annabelle brought out her phone and pulled up the photos of the jewelry.

"Mairéad, do you know anything about these? I showed them to your father in the pub yesterday lunchtime. I'm wondering if they have anything to do with what happened?"

Mairéad peered carefully at the photographs, swiping backward and forward several times.

Finally, she said, "I do remember these. It was a few years ago. I was just a teenager. We have a big ceilidh on Burns Night, and everyone dresses up. Well, as much as anyone dresses up on this island." She looked up at Annabelle with big shining eyes. "There was a woman there. She was wearing this emerald necklace and these ruby earrings," Mairéad pointed at the photos. "I remember because they were beautiful. I'd never seen such magnificent jewelry before. They matched her tartan."

"'Her,' Mairéad?"

"Aye, back then I was just an island girl who'd never been anywhere much. She looked like a vision to me. Beautiful she was, so happy and smiley. The men couldn't take their eyes off her."

"Who was she, this vision in tartan?" Annabelle repeated.

"Oh yes, her name was Moira. Moira Ballantyne. Felicity's mother."

Annabelle stood outside the pub, blinking and considering what to do next.

"Hello again, Vicar! We keep bumping into one another, don't we?" Bruce Fitzpatrick strolled up to her. "How was Mairéad?" he asked quietly as he sidled up.

"As well as can be expected in the circumstances. Poor girl. Such a shock!"

"I've just been to Glencoe's, our local grocery store. I heard a rumor that Harry and Mairéad had an argument before he died." Bruce lowered his voice even more.

"Really?" Annabelle turned and looked back at the pub door.

Bruce looked over Annabelle's shoulder. "Can't be nice having the last words with your father be cross ones. Apparently," he said, warming to his subject, "Harry was seen striding down the southern road by a number of the locals. Mairéad was chasing after him, screaming her head off. She was 'fair reekin' as they say around here. Furious about something or other, she was."

"Do you have any idea what it was about?" Annabelle asked.

"I've no idea, but Harry could be trying at times, very trying. Larger than life he was, but that can get on your nerves after a while, can't it?"

"She didn't say anything about that to me."

"Perhaps it's the shock."

"Hmm," Annabelle said, loathe to believe what Bruce was saying about the bereaved young woman.

"It's a shock for everyone," Bruce continued. "Nothing ever happens on this island. We probably haven't had a murder since the 1300s, and we're a lot more civilized now than we were back then. Where are you off to now?"

"I think I'll go to Kirsty Munroe's. Her house has a perfect view of the church. She may have seen something that could be relevant to the break-in, and if the two of them are connected, Harry's murder." Annabelle decided not to let Bruce in on what Mairéad had just told her about the jewelry.

Bruce nodded. "The locals are all of a tizz this morning. I hope the Fenbarra police get here soon. Joe Conway, he's one of the local farmers, is talking about putting a vigilante group together."

"Pitchforks at the ready, hmm? Well, it is rather alarming. Having a murderer in your midst isn't what anyone wants, especially when they're trapped on the island with you."

"Mind if I join you?" Bruce asked Annabelle.

"Of course not."

The two of them set off. They were becoming rather accustomed to one another's company as they zig-zagged around the island on their various jaunts.

"Did you figure anything out yet?" Bruce asked suddenly. "I mean, about the burglary or the murder."

"Not really, I'm afraid. Did you?"

Bruce sighed. "No. I was up half the night just staring at Harry's bagpipes, trying to put it all together. It's just so...*random*. And I couldn't stop thinking about this, as well." He pulled out the small metal rod from inside his coat. He handed it to Annabelle. She studied it as she walked. "What do you think it is?"

"Looks like it might be something to do with his bagpipes. For cleaning, mebbe?" Bruce suggested.

Annabelle frowned as she turned it over in her hand. Suddenly she stopped walking and ran her finger over the thin, tapered edge at one end, before turning to look at Bruce.

"There were marks on the church doors, as if something had been jammed between them in order to pry the door open. It could very possibly have been this."

Bruce's face lit up. "Aye! Good thinking," he said, taking it from her. "I'll go and check the marks, see if they're a match. If they are, perhaps the murderer used this to break into the kirk. Perhaps he dropped it when he killed Harry. That's the connection!"

They began walking again.

"Perhaps," Annabelle said, looking at the sky absently as she thought it over. "But not necessarily."

"What do you mean?"

"It could have been Harry who broke into the church."

"Harry?" Bruce said, his screwed-up face indicating his disbelief. "I doubt it."

"Ah, we're here." Annabelle said. They were abreast of the cottages.

"I guess I'll leave you here then, Vicar," Bruce said, nodding toward the church on the hill. "I'll let you know what I find."

"Thanks, Bruce."

"No problem," the man said, tipping his hat gently as he turned away.

"Wait," Annabelle said. Bruce raised his eyebrows. "Why are you still doing all of this? I thought you were only filling in for Bob McGregor."

"I still am," Bruce smiled.

"Has he not fixed that clogged toilet yet?"

"Naw. He fixed it alright. But he's always got important work to do after a storm."

"What's more important than a murder investigation?"

"You've been here long enough to know that, Annabelle. The murderers and thieves aren't going anywhere," Bruce said, without an ounce of irony. They stared at each other in silence for a few seconds. "But feral goats, they're everywhere!" Bruce shook his head and carried along the path to the church.

"Of course, feral goats. Why didn't I think of that?" Annabelle murmured.

CHAPTER TWENTY

KIRSTY OPENED THE door moments after Annabelle knocked.

"Vicar."

"Hello, Kirsty. How is everything today?"

"Och, all back to normal," Kirsty replied, dourly.

"May I come in? I have something I want to discuss with you."

Kirsty stood back to let Annabelle through.

"I suppose you're glad I'm not quite as wet as yesterday!" Annabelle joked, chuckling lightly.

"Perhaps," Kirsty replied without humor.

Annabelle followed the small woman, scanning the house briefly as they walked through it. Much as the overgrown yard seemed to indicate, the inside of the house was in dire need of attention. Greying, peeling wallpaper lined the walls, furniture displayed their long and difficult histories by way of chips, scratches, stains and repairs. Even the carpets seemed to have had all the color and life trodden out of them. Worst of all, the fragrance of the house was what Annabelle could best describe as "eau de damp" mixed with a hint of Brussel sprouts. It was a depressing place to live.

"Cup of tea?" Kirsty asked, putting the kettle on.

"That would be lovely, thank you," Annabelle said, as she settled into an uncomfortably hard chair at the two-person table against the wall.

Kirsty relaxed a little as she busied herself making the tea. "Thank you for finding Felicity last night. I don't know what gets into her sometimes," she said gruffly.

"She's a child. Impossible to understand."

"Some children in particular are a mystery," Kirsty said, her back still facing Annabelle as she put hot water into the teapot to warm it. "Is that what you wanted to discuss with me? Felicity?"

"Actually, no."

"Oh?" Kirsty said, glancing at Annabelle over her shoulder.

"There was a burglary at the church yesterday. Between midday and the six o'clock Evensong." Annabelle gestured at the window, which offered a wide view of the path leading up to the church. "I wanted to ask if you'd seen anything. You have a perfect view."

"Naw. I spent most of yesterday staring at a screen, not the window," Kirsty said, pointing out the open laptop on the side of the counter. "Until, of course, that business with Felicity, and by then there wasn't a soul around."

"What do you do, Kirsty?"

"I work as an IT technician. Most of my clients are on the island or nearby, but I do all my work from home. So as I can look after Felicity, you know."

"Doesn't it get boring always being at home?" Annabelle said.

"I go out sometimes. If a local needs their computer fixing, that kind of thing."

Annabelle cleared her throat and hastily pulled out her phone as Kirsty brought a tray of tea to the table and sat herself down.

"Do you recognize any of these pieces of jewelry perhaps?" Annabelle said.

Kirsty looked at the photos carefully, her expression stiff and unyielding. "How did you get these?" Kirsty's eyes darted from the phone to Annabelle. "These belonged to my sister, Moira."

Annabelle put her teacup down and leaned forward. "Are you sure?"

"Without a doubt," Kirsty said, handing the phone back.

"What do you know about them?" Annabelle asked carefully.

"They were stolen about a year before she died. She made a big fuss about it, as anyone would," Kirsty said.

"From the island?"

"No. From her home in Edinburgh."

Annabelle picked up her tea again and sipped as she added this piece of information to the tangled mass of questions in her mind.

"Do you actually have the jewelry?" Kirsty asked, her voice calm and firm.

"They were... hidden on the island. Rather strangely," Annabelle replied, deciding to tread a fine line between truth and untruth.

"And you found them?" Kirsty asked.

"Not exactly, they were given to me for safekeeping," Annabelle replied.

"By whom?"

"I can't say, sorry." Annabelle felt awkward, coming between Felicity and her guardian, but she had given her word to the young girl.

"I see," Kirsty said, taking a small, quick nip at her tea. "And where are they now?"

Annabelle sighed. "They were stolen again. I had secured them in the church for safekeeping. Somebody must have found out, because they broke in shortly afterward."

Kirsty snorted derisively.

"That sounds about right," she said, her voice dripping with bitterness now. "Typical. Anything to do with my sister is cursed."

"What do you mean?"

Kirsty leaned forward, and Annabelle noticed the tight muscles in the woman's face.

"Do you know about my sister?"

"Not really," Annabelle said, leaning back away from Kirsty.

"I'm surprised. There were plenty of rumors."

"What's the truth?" Annabelle asked.

Kirsty snorted again. Her smile was thin and sour.

"The truth is that Moira had everything – and she didn't do anything worth a damn with it. Don't look at me – or this rundown shack of a house – and think she was anything like that. Oh, no. She was cut from a different cloth. Blond, tall, slim, beautiful. She had every boy on the island in the palm of her hand. Of course, she didn't care for that. She wanted more. Got herself to Edinburgh the first chance she got. Snagged herself a husband. All sharp suits and gold watches. Aye. He looked the part, and he played it too, for a while. Coming over to the island in his private helicopter. Throwing money around like he thought he was Saint Nicholas. Pfft! I could tell he was a sham the second I saw him."

Annabelle frowned into her tea. Kirsty's resentment was thick and palpable.

"You don't seem very fond of either of them. What happened?"

"The inevitable," Kirsty snorted. "Eventually, it all went wrong. Ben – Moira's husband – lost everything. Got too big for his boots. I mean, it was all built on sand anyway. 'Investment banker' he called himself. Give me a man who works with his hands any day. You see, you're from down south, you won't understand this, but we Scots like people with their feet on the ground. Shrewd, yes. Hard-working, of course. But we don't go in for all that flash and dazzle. Truth is, they were a pair of idiots, both of them. Even when it was all falling apart, Moira was still spending money on designer clothes, jewelry, and shoes. She couldn't help herself. Tried telling me it was an addiction once – Ha! I wish I could afford an addiction like that, I said."

"And then they died? In the helicopter crash?"

"Aye. Ben was piloting it. Sometimes I wonder if he crashed it deliberately. I wouldn't put it past him. He was a wily eejit."

Annabelle looked down at her tea once again, almost shying away from the angry heat that was emanating from Kirsty.

"And Felicity?"

"What do you think? Moira spent so much money on herself, but she never gave me a penny. Never bought me anything nice. All she did was drop by to tell me how wonderful she had it. And then she went and died. And I'm still here, where I've always been. Where I'll always be. Without two pennies to rub together. Only now I've got her daughter to look after too."

"But what about your job? That must bring in a pretty penny."

"It doesn't make me a lot. I don't have the gift of the gab with the clients like your brother. I only service the locals on the islands. There aren't enough of them to make me much money."

"Didn't her parents leave Felicity anything?" Annabelle asked.

"Ha!" Kirsty grunted, throwing her head back. "No. Felicity's got nothing but me. Nothing but this," Kirsty said, gesturing around her at the dilapidated kitchen. "And the worst thing is, every day she grows more like her mother. She has the dark hair of her father, but the rest of her is Moira. Slim, beautiful, graceful."

Annabelle looked at her, cautiously, turning over the meaning behind what Kirsty was saying in her mind.

"Och, I know what yer thinking. You think it's mean of me to say that about a seven-year-old girl. But I already see it. It's just like when we were kids. Everyone dotes on Felicity. 'She's a princess.' 'She's destined for greatness.' Aye. Well, I'll tell you one thing. If she does ever make something of herself, she'll leave me behind her, just like her mother did. Of that I'm sure."

Annabelle gulped the last of her tea quickly. The conversation had taken a rather more hostile turn than she had expected. Felicity's aunt had plenty of resentment stored up, and Annabelle guessed that Kirsty had few friends to speak about it with. She had obviously touched a nerve.

"You know," Annabelle said, placing her cup of tea in the middle of table, making it clear that she was about to leave, "it's a little unfair to hold Felicity accountable for the hurt her mother might have caused you. She's only a child, and you're the only person she has."

Kirsty stood up.

"Life isn't fair, Reverend. I'm not a monster. I take care of Felicity as best I can. But that doesn't mean I like it. My sister got everything she wanted. I wanted nothing, and I got nothing; except her daughter, that is. I know it's not her fault, but it's not mine either."

Kirsty escorted Annabelle to the cottage entrance and held the door open for her. Annabelle put on her coat, stepped across the threshold and turned back to face the tired-looking, scruffy woman on the doorstep.

"Your sister might have hurt and disappointed you, Kirsty, but Felicity never will. I know I might be too much of an outsider to say that, but sometimes it takes a fresh perspective to see things as they really are. You might never forgive your sister, but please don't punish Felicity for Moira's sins," she said. Annabelle turned around and walked away down the weed-ridden path.

CHAPTER TWENTY-ONE

AS SHE WAS leaving Kirsty's cottage, Bruce called to tell Annabelle that the metal rod they'd found on Harry's body did indeed match up with the marks on the church door. As Annabelle's thoughts turned to Harry's murder, she decided to stretch her legs in the direction of the beach and revisit the site where the body was found.

As she neared the slope that led down to the sand, she pondered the sighting of Pip Craven at the beach the evening before. What had he been doing there? Why had he run off when she saw him? She was about to clamber onto the mound of rocks to make her way down to the beach when suddenly the man himself sprang up, startled from behind a large rock below. Without a word of greeting, Pip scuttled up the wet boulders with the speed and single-minded purpose of a crustacean, and shoved past Annabelle so hard he nearly knocked her off her feet. She stepped back onto the grass just in time.

When he'd taken a few steps past her, Pip stopped. He turned and fixed his eyes dramatically on Annabelle. She took a step back, alarmed by his sudden appearance. "Vicar," was all he said in a low growl, and with that, he spun around and ran off in the direction of his house. Annabelle watched as the long-haired man sprinted off into the misty distance. Seconds later, the two fishermen whom she had met the night before emerged from behind the rocky outcrop.

"Did he go past here?" Fraser, the bearded one asked.

"Pip?" Annabelle responded.

"Forget it," his companion said. Davy Blair's hood was drawn so low this time he could barely see where he was going, "no point in running."

"What's going on?" Annabelle asked, utterly perplexed.

"We just caught that Craven idiot trying to get to Harry's body," Fraser said, puffing.

"No!"

"We were just going down to the fishing boat," Davy explained, "to check the moorings after the storm, and to make sure Harry's body was fine – I mean, as fine as a dead body can be – and we saw Pip trying to climb onto the boat. We shouted out to him, asked him what the hell he was playing at, and all he said was, 'I'm only looking!'"

"Then he ran off," Fraser added.

"Aye. Then he ran off."

"Well, that's incredibly odd!" Annabelle said.

"Not for Pip."

"There's your prime suspect right there, I reckon," Fraser said.

"No," Davy replied, "don't you watch TV? The murderer never returns to the scene of the crime."

"Well, what's he doing then?"

"Pip's just like that," Davy said, "Weirdo. He's into voodoo, witchery, bats. He probably wanted to do some... I dunno... magic with the body. Summon up spirits."

"Maybe he killed Harry as a sacrifice," Fraser said, "and now he's come back to drink his blood."

"Aye. Could be that."

"Stop it!" Annabelle exclaimed. "To hear two grown men talking like this is ridiculous. You can't really believe in that nonsense."

"The question isn't whether *we* believe it," Davy said, "it's whether *Pip* does."

"Pip's all about the devil, magic, that kind of thing. It's all in his music. You should give it a listen sometime. Sounds like a big din to some people, but me and my missus love it." Fraser started playing some heavy air guitar.

"Poppycock!" Annabelle said.

"Have you spoken to him?" Davy asked her.

"Yes, I have, actually," Annabelle said.

"And what did you talk about?"

Annabelle blushed, remembering the strange exchange she had had with Pip outside the alleyway the previous day.

"Well... Nothing really strange..." she muttered. "Just...something about vampires, crows... that sort of thing."

"There you go," Fraser said triumphantly, his silent rendition of a Craven Idols' chart topper over. "Suspect number one."

"Mebbe," Davy replied. "He's made some cracking tunes though."

"Aye, that he has."

"What's the situation regarding the weather?" Annabelle said. "Can the boats come in tonight?"

"No. The storm just hit the inner islands this morning. Waves still choppy. Probably there'll be a thick mist tonight too, so there won't be any planes coming through. Tomorrow morning it should clear, I reckon." Davy looked out over the waves.

"Aye," Fraser agreed.

"Let's hope so," Annabelle replied, nodding at the two men before turning away and walking off. Her head was so full of thoughts that she had completely forgotten why she had gone to the beach in the first place.

CHAPTER TWENTY-TWO

ROGER WAS ENGROSSED in his work and didn't hear Annabelle come in. When she walked into his office and gave a cry of surprise, he almost jumped out of his office chair.

"Oh! Bumble, what are you doing creeping up on me like that? You frightened the life out of me."

"Sorry, Roger," Annabelle chuckled. "I was just a little taken aback. This room has changed so much."

Roger smiled and pulled a chair over for Annabelle to sit beside him. Indeed, the room was quite unlike the rest of the house – and the rest of the island, for that matter. Where all around them could be found rustic charm, weather-beaten rocks, and earthy colors, Roger's workroom was a technological paradise. Against the wall, a long, flat, light wood desk with chrome legs held three large monitors, each displaying complicated swathes of text, graphs, and flashing lights. Beneath them were keyboards, and to the side, speakers. Even one of those furry microphones TV cameramen use hung overhead.

Above the monitors on the wall were shelves of reference

books, and below the desk, several computer towers hummed and whirred. Set at a right angle to the end of the desk, another tabletop housed a printer, multiple gadgets and cables, and a phone. On the walls, Arsenal posters and framed pictures of Bonnie and Roger smiling against the dramatic backdrops of the Scottish island added a sense of color and personality to the gadget geek wonderland, but there could be no mistaking the room as anything other than one entirely dedicated to Roger's work.

"The last time I was here you only had a single laptop," Annabelle said, as she tried, and immediately gave up on understanding the numbers and symbols on the screen nearest her.

"I remember!" Roger said, cheerfully. "That little thing was a real pain to work with – but then again, without it I wouldn't have been able to afford all this."

"What is this thing?" she said, pointing to the furry oblong that sat on a stand above one of the computer screens. "I've seen them on TV when they do outside broadcasts. I've often wondered what they are."

"That's what's fondly known in the industry as a 'dead cat' or a 'wind muff.' It's used when you want to deaden the noise of any wind hitting the microphone. I use it on outside shoots, but I can't be bothered to take it on and off so I just stick it on a stand as it is when I'm indoors."

Annabelle smiled. "It's great to see you doing so well. I have to be honest, I never thought you could make a living programming software and teaching people about it all over the world. Not from here. I don't know how you do it. I can barely use a computer. I have no idea how they work."

Roger laughed and slapped his sister on the shoulder. "Well, the English language is just twenty-six shapes arranged in different ways, but it's done us alright so far! You don't need to understand how computers work, just know that they run the world now. You can do anything with them. Meet people from all around the globe, know whatever's going on the second it happens, read about anything you care to think of, buy things, sell things, learn how to make things. Whatever you want."

Annabelle frowned.

"What?" Roger said.

"Sell things? What about selling jewelry?"

Roger nodded and smiled, seeing his sister's train of logic.

"For something like that," he said, tapping away at the keyboard then clicking a couple of times, "you'd use an online auction site. It's a—"

"I know what they are!" Annabelle said.

"Have you ever used one?" Roger asked.

"No," Annabelle conceded, "but Philippa bought a wonderful plant pot for my garden using one once. She said it was thrilling, placing all those bids and such."

"Yeah, I'll bet. I hope she didn't get carried away. People can end up paying way over the odds in the heat of the moment. Okay," Roger said, turning back to the screen, "let's see."

"We'll never find anything. There must be thousands of jewelry items for sale," Annabelle said.

"Didn't they teach you to have faith in theology school?" Roger quipped. "All we have to do is narrow the parameters. There was a diamond necklace among the jewelry in those pictures you showed me, wasn't there?"

"Among other things."

"Okay... Diamond necklaces... Let's get rid of all the items listed by people in places outside Scotland... Now let's look only at the items listed in the past few days... There. We've got it down to around fifty. Recognize any of them?"

Roger scrolled down the list slowly, turning to look at Annabelle every few seconds.

"That one!" Annabelle cried abruptly, pointing at the screen. "Can you make it bigger?"

"Of course," Roger said, clicking on the image.

"That's it!" Annabelle said, almost breathless with surprise. "The necklace! Someone's trying to sell it!"

"Hold on," Roger said, clicking rapidly. "Let's see what else this person is selling."

"And that's the pearl bracelet!" Annabelle exclaimed, almost jumping out of her seat. "And the earrings! They're all there! Can you find out who's selling them?"

Roger pursed his lips as he clicked the mouse and typed rapidly at the keyboard. Annabelle couldn't follow what he was doing on the screen. She waited in silence for her brother to work his magic, finding herself almost short of breath. Eventually, Roger shook his head.

"Nothing," he said. "Whoever is selling them is covering their tracks well. I can't even get an email address for them."

"Can't we do anything?"

Roger shrugged. "We could report the goods as stolen. This auction site would halt the listing, but that wouldn't help us recover the jewelry or catch the thief."

Annabelle huffed. "What if we arrange to buy them? Could we find out who's selling them that way?"

"Nope. They're using a secure payment system. The most we'd get is an email address – and I would guess they're using a dummy account. Maybe the police could trace the bank account attached, but that takes time. Weeks. Months, if whoever's doing this knows computers – and I suspect they do."

"Okay," Annabelle said, sighing. "Let's report them then."

"As you wish, boss."

Minutes later, Roger had reported all the items, receiving confirmations that the sales had been halted pending further details. He stretched back in his chair.

"Phew, this is way more stressful than work!" he said running his hands through his hair. He looked at his watch. "I should be off to pick Bonnie up from school. Do you want to use the computer? I'm sure your friends back in Upton St. Mary will want to hear what you've been up to – even if they're not entirely surprised."

Annabelle laughed. "I suppose I should. I've not even told them I arrived safely."

Roger patted her on the shoulder again as he left her facing the intimidating sight of three large computer screens.

Annabelle logged onto her email account and ran her eye down the list of new emails that had arrived in her inbox. She went to work deleting, sorting, and filing. Emails pertaining to church business got filed under "Later", and then—

"Oh, what's this?" she said.

To: annabumble7@gmail.com
From: mikenicholls56@yahoo.com
Subject: hello

Annabelle,
I think I told you that I hate computers so I wouldn't be surprised if this didn't work.

I had to visit USM to follow up on a report about Mrs. Guthrie's missing/possibly dead cat (again.) Constable Raven said he could handle it but I wanted to make sure. While I was there, I went to see if you were around. Molly was wagging her tail as soon as she saw the church.

Philippa told me you'd gone to Scotland to visit your brother. (I didn't know you had a brother.) She gave me your email address, and wouldn't stop telling me to message you. Since I had a few moments, I thought it would be a good opportunity to join the 21st century.

Anyway, I wanted to tell you to be careful and stay safe. It gets cold up there, and the sea gets a bit rough. I'm sure Molly would love to see you when you get back, so tell me when you do.

Mike

P.S. Mrs. Guthrie's missing/possibly dead cat turned up on her doorstep after a three-day vacation (again.)

Annabelle smiled as she read the email. She could almost hear the Inspector's commanding voice. She clicked the reply button eagerly.

To: mikenicholls56@yahoo.com
From: annabumble7@gmail.com
Subject: Re: hello

Dear Mike,
    It's a very pleasant surprise to receive your email! I'm wagging my tail at the prospect of seeing Molly again. I'm not so technologically inclined either, but I remind myself it's essentially just like letter-writing, albeit faster and a little more impersonal.

I greatly appreciate your concern, but I'm safe and sound on a rather quaint island called Blodraigh. It's a delightful place with lovely locals, and no crime to speak of.

Having said that, there has been a murder and a burglary at the church while I've been here! There is also no police presence on the island currently due to a rather severe storm we suffered recently.

A box of expensive jewelry was stolen from the church safe. Shortly afterward, the local pub landlord was found dead a few minutes away along the coast. He was hit on the head and had a part of his bagpipes stuffed in his mouth! I'm positive that both incidents are connected.

I'm sure you know me well enough by now to realize that I am determined to discover the truth. Nothing much happens here, but there have been plenty of strange occurrences since I arrived, and the locals are quite lively, so I'm kept busy.

I have often thought of seeking your opinion before realizing that you are actually hundreds of miles away. Nonetheless, if the detective who is to arrive tomorrow (as soon as the weather allows) is half as astute and insightful as you are, I'm sure all these questions will be answered promptly.

Give Molly a big hug from me, and if you should speak to Philippa again, reassure her that Mrs. Cavendish is feeding me beautifully.

Yours sincerely,
 Annabelle

CHAPTER TWENTY-THREE
TUESDAY

FOR THE FIRST time since she had arrived, Annabelle woke up earlier than both Roger and Bonnie. The previous evening's marathon of cartoons, puzzle games, and desserts had tired her hosts out, but had left Annabelle invigorated. It had also provided a welcome respite from thinking about the events on the island. As she made her way into the kitchen in order to prepare breakfast for the three of them, she had a fresh perspective.

"What a nice surprise," Roger said, his eyes fixed hungrily upon the toast and eggs.

"Morning," Annabelle said, before joining him at the table. "My pleasure," she added, before buttering some toast for herself.

They slurped and munched for a while in silence before Annabelle asked, "What was Mairéad's relationship like with her father?"

"Harry?" Roger said, "People thought he was a great guy. He liked everyone, and everyone liked him, but he could be a bit, how shall we say... *overwhelming*. A bit in your face."

"Yes, I would agree there," Annabelle said.

Roger continued, "I thought he was pleasant enough, but he did leave all the running of the pub to Mairéad. He could be rather irresponsible in that respect. Mairéad's a young woman, and I'm sure she would have loved to be out and about. But she was often stuck running the pub all by herself. At times, there was definitely some tension between the two. But she knuckled down as is the way up here."

"She seemed so chirpy when I spoke to her in the bar after the service. But Bruce Fitzpatrick said she was later seen running after Harry, furiously yelling," Annabelle said.

"Wouldn't surprise me. She was probably exhausted. We all have our tipping points," Roger added.

"Did Harry have any enemies?" Annabelle asked.

"Don't think so. Everyone goes to the pub. Besides church, it's the main point of congregation on the island. In a small place like this, it's almost your 'duty' to pop in at least once a week to catch up with everyone. Anyhow, we all knew Harry, and he seemed to get along with everyone, as far as I know." Roger paused for a moment before adding, "Well, except for Kirsty."

"Kirsty?" Annabelle said.

"Yes. Kirsty can be difficult. She had no patience for Harry's antics. What a lot of people would call his 'bonhomie,' she seemed to find contemptuous. But then, Kirsty can be a little dour."

"Hmm, I've noticed." Annabelle said. "Do you think there's anything behind the dislike other than just a clash of personalities?"

"I couldn't tell you for sure. It's just my impression. They are complete opposites."

Bonnie came into the room, yawning. She was dressed, but her hair was all muzzed up at the back. Annabelle gave her a big hug. As they tucked further into their breakfasts, they heard a windy pulsing sound outside. Roger looked at Annabelle with raised eyebrows.

"Looks like it's business as usual up in the air again. The boats will probably be out too."

"Good," Annabelle said.

"I expect the police will be on their way shortly."

"I certainly hope so."

They continued to munch and sip their tea, as the choppy noise grew steadily louder.

Roger frowned. "That's strange."

"What is?"

"The aircraft usually land on the other side of the island. There's a landing strip. We don't usually hear them so loudly over here."

Bonnie dropped her toast onto her plate and ran to the window.

"Wow!" she exclaimed, jumping up and down excitedly, before running to the entrance of the cottage.

Roger and Annabelle exchanged quick, bemused glances.

"Bonnie?" Roger said, following her.

By the time Roger and Annabelle caught up with Bonnie, she was standing on the doorstep, watching a huge helicopter descend onto the land in front of Roger's house. The roar of its engine was deafening. The downwind blew the grass and heathers in Roger's yard around erratically, and forced them to shield their eyes as they squinted to see what was happening.

As their hair blew flat against their heads and their clothes flapped, Roger urged Bonnie and Annabelle forward and closed the door behind them to protect the inside of the house from the draft. The three stood, transfixed, as the bug-like bulk settled itself gracefully on the ground. Roger made a small joke about his colorful heathers, but it was lost amid the noise.

The door of the helicopter opened, and they waited, their mouths gaping. Bonnie was beside herself.

"Who do you think it is, Bumble? Who do you think it is? Could it be...? Could it be...?" She gasped, unable to think who it might be. She was bent over with excitement, hanging onto Annabelle's arm to steady herself.

Eventually, a tall, handsome figure disembarked. He slammed the door behind him and crouched as he jogged away from the helicopter. Once he was past the worst of the down draft, he turned and saluted the pilot. The helicopter rose, spun its nose around, and in a majestic, swift motion, swooped back the way it had come.

Annabelle was flabbergasted. "It can't be."

Seeing his sister shake her head, Roger nodded over to the man and shouted across the noise. "Do you know who that is?"

"Oh, yes." Annabelle said to herself, quietly. She appeared to wilt a little then lifted her chin, cleared her throat, and stepped forward purposefully to meet the visitor as he made his way toward them. She made a valiant attempt to pat down her hair, but it was hopeless.

"Hello, Annabelle," the man said, with a bashful grin.

"Hello, Inspector— I mean, Mike." They stared at each other for a moment. "What on earth are you doing here?"

"Things are quiet at home. I had some days off that I had to take. I thought this was the perfect opportunity to take them."

Annabelle tried to frown at the Inspector but found herself smiling bashfully too. She heard the sound of Roger clearing his throat.

"Oh," she said, turning, "this is my brother, Roger, and my niece, Bonnie."

"Pleased to meet you," Nicholls said, shaking their hands.

"This is Inspector Nicholls. From Truro."

"Ah," was all Roger said. "Can I get you a cup of tea, Inspector? Some breakfast, maybe?"

Nicholls shuffled a little on his feet. "That would be nice, thanks. It's been a long journey."

"I'll say. Come on in then," Roger said cheerily. They all

traipsed inside, Bonnie unable to take her eyes off the Inspector but not saying a word.

Annabelle led their visitor into the kitchen and gestured for him to take a seat while Roger boiled the kettle.

"Thank you," Nicholls said a few moments later, raising the strong tea to his lips and sipping slowly. He let out a deep sigh. "Lovely."

He noticed Bonnie was eyeing him keenly.

"Are you the policeman?" she cooed, inquisitively.

"I am *a* policeman, yes," Nicholls said.

"Are you the detective that's Bumble's boyfriend?" Bonnie fluttered her eyelashes and tipped her head to one side.

"Um—"

"I should really be getting Bonnie to school," Roger said quickly, gathering up his keys. "Annabelle, you know where everything is."

"Daddy said you're the only man who can keep up—"

"Come on, Bon-Bon, let's get going."

"Daddy says Bumble's all goo—"

"Bon-n-i-e," Roger said warningly.

"He says you're her best prospect."

"Bonnie Julia Dixon, car, now!" Roger grabbed her coat from the rack.

"But Daddy—" Bonnie started to object as Roger prodded her out the room. The door slammed shut. Annabelle and Mike sat in awkward silence. Through the window, they could still hear Bonnie objecting as she got in the car.

"But school doesn't start for another two hours."

"I'm sorry about that. She's rather lively, my brother's daughter," Annabelle said apologetically.

"Oh, no," the Inspector said, waving away the notion that he was offended. "It's fine. I should apologize for surprising you all like this."

Annabelle drained the last of her tea. She shot Mike a look.

She was barely dressed and now she was alone with him in the kitchen having been caught unawares by his rather dashing arrival.

"I can't believe you came all the way up here," Annabelle said, "and in such a dramatic fashion, too! It's an incredible surprise." She paused. "I think Bonnie was a bit disappointed at first though," she added gravely. "I think she thought her favorite pop group had come to visit her."

Nicholls chuckled. "Well, she seemed to get over it. To be honest, I was a little worried when I read what you wrote. A murder? No police presence on the island? That doesn't sound good. Add your striking ability to find trouble, and you can see why I'd start to get a little concerned."

"I did call out the police on Fenbarra."

"Yes," Nicholls explained, "and I spoke to them. Their inspector is going to make it over, but he's currently busy. They're close to solving a case they've been working on for a while now, finding the source of a drug route that runs through the islands. He's asked me to take a look at the murder case in the meantime."

"Well, I'm flattered that you're so concerned for my well-being."

"One of us has to be. Philippa sends her regards, by the way," he said.

"She knew you were coming?"

"It was her idea."

Annabelle rolled her eyes.

"How is she?"

"Good," Nicholls replied. "Although she's looking forward to you getting back." Annabelle smiled warmly as he continued, "She can't find anyone as remotely capable as you to eat all the cakes she's been baking.

Annabelle's smile dropped from her face with the suddenness of a fallen rock.

"I see," she said, drolly.

Mike put his mug down. "Now tell me, what's been happening?"

"More than you'd think for an island this size," Annabelle said, standing up from the table. "Tell you what, let me show you around. The quicker you see the island for yourself, the better."

She got up and walked to the front door. "Follow me," Annabelle said, turning to march down the path, "I'll explain on the way."

The Inspector watched her for a few seconds without moving.

"Annabelle!" he called out.

"What?" she called back.

The Inspector gazed at her feet.

Annabelle looked down. Not even on this strange, remote Scottish isle did appropriate walking gear extend to pink pajamas and bunny slippers. Without responding or meeting the Inspector's eye, she spun around and headed back into the cottage.

CHAPTER TWENTY-FOUR

THE INSPECTOR WAITED outside while Annabelle got dressed, and once she was ready, they set off on foot across the island. The sun shone brightly, and the sky was clear but for a few wisps of pale grey-white clouds.

"You're right," the Inspector said as they strolled along, "it is rather nice up here."

"Believe me, it was anything but nice a few days ago. I've never seen such a storm!"

"You look very well for someone who's endured so much strife," Nicholls said.

Annabelle quickened her pace in order to distract from her blushes.

"Thank you. I'm not happy, though. I've got so many questions about what's happened."

"Well, it's good to talk," Nicholls said, his voice softer and friendlier than Annabelle had ever heard it. She looked at him and wondered if all it took to brush away the Inspector's usual stern, direct demeanor was the fresh Scottish air.

As they strolled along, Annabelle told the Inspector everything; from her journey to the island, her time with Roger and Bonnie, her cover for Father Boyce while he was on holiday, to Felicity's discovery of the jewelry box, the burglary at the church, and then Harry's murder. The Inspector listened intently, his face stern and thoughtful, as he considered each piece of the puzzle that Annabelle presented to him. By the time she was finished, they had reached the village. She stopped and looked at him directly, eager for his opinion.

"What do you think?" she asked.

"Hmm," Nicholls murmured, scratching the stubble on his cheek, "do you have any suspects in mind? People acting strangely? Possible motives?"

"Quite a few of those I have met could easily be considered 'strange.' Let's see... There were the two fishermen who found the body and subsequently stored it in their boat. They seemed harmless enough, but I know next to nothing about them. Then there's Robert Kilbairn. He lives at Clannan Castle, to the north of the island, though again, I've not spoken to him. Just seen him whoosh by. A couple of American tourists are after him. He's sold them some sort of lordship, but he seems to be avoiding them. Mairéad, the victim's daughter, was seen having an argument with him in the hours before his body was found."

"Interesting," mused the Inspector.

"And then there's Pip Craven."

The Inspector held his hand up to stop her, his eyes wide.

"Pip Craven? *The* Pip Craven? Of the Craven Idols?"

Annabelle smiled broadly.

"Mike! I didn't know you had such subversive musical tastes!"

"Didn't everyone have that *Sons of Darkness* album at some point? I've still got the vinyl stored in the attic."

"Well, you must let me listen to it some time. It's been a while since I've heard it."

"Definitely."

They gazed at each other for a moment, before suddenly snapping back to concentrate on the matter at hand.

"The very same Pip Craven, yes," Annabelle confirmed, turning to walk again. "Apparently he moved onto the island a while ago in order to 'get away from it all' and clean his life up."

"That makes sense," Nicholls shrugged. "Wild celebrities often do that sort of thing."

"Yes," Annabelle replied, "but that's not the strange part. There are a lot of rumors about Pip's eccentric behavior. About him being up at all hours, interested in the dark arts, and even conducting satanic rituals."

Nicholls huffed. "They've probably just listened to his music and taken it at face value."

"I'm not so sure about that. The first time I spoke to him, he asked me about vampires and strange deaths. I saw him in the distance when we first examined the body, and yesterday the two fishermen had to chase him away from Harry's dead body!"

"Really?"

"It seemed so," Annabelle said, as they approached the village. She saw a long-haired man walking up the road from the church. "Speak of the devil-worshipper."

Pip bowed his head beneath his black locks and crossed the road quickly, utterly failing in his attempt to pretend that he hadn't seen Annabelle.

"Pip!" she called, as the man quickened his pace. "Pip!"

Annabelle quickly crossed the road with a few long strides and stalked the old rocker until he could no longer ignore her.

"Oh, hello," he said meekly, as the Inspector came up and stared at him curiously from behind Annabelle's shoulder. "I didn't see you."

"Tosh! I don't believe that for a second!" Annabelle said. She sounded like a primary school teacher, emboldened now that she had the Inspector with her. "Pip, this is Detective Inspector Nicholls."

"Hello," Pip said, timidly. Mike nodded.

"Now tell me, what on earth were you doing nearby Harry's body yesterday?" Annabelle demanded officiously.

"Nothing," Pip pleaded. "Honestly. I wasn't going to touch anything. I just wanted to look at it. That's all."

"That's a strange thing to do and a weak excuse," Nicholls said, his voice assuming his usual gruffness, "and it'll sound even weaker in a courtroom."

Pip's face contorted in an expression of horror.

"Court?"

"Despite what you see on TV, murderers often return to the site of a killing."

"What? You think I had something to do with Harry's murder?"

"You were watching us on the evening of his murder, you knew where his body was stored, you live closest to the place he was killed, and you were caught trying to get to his body after he died," Annabelle said, copying the Inspector's authoritative tone. "It does sound like you have something to do with it, yes."

"But... no... I..." Pip spluttered and mumbled as he began multiple trains of thought, looking up at the tall figures of Annabelle and the Inspector. Both towered over him. Suddenly he slumped, burying his head in his hands as he shook his head. "I can't tell you. I can't."

"Tell us what, Pip?" Annabelle asked changing her demeanor entirely in the face of his distress and placing her hand on his arm.

"You'll tell someone," Nicholls said gravely. "It's just a matter of who and whether it's now or later."

Pip looked up again. He saw the severity in the Inspector's expression and the sympathy in Annabelle's. He sighed deeply, realizing that he had no option but to come clean.

"I'm writing a book," Pip mumbled. "A crime thriller. It's about a rock band on tour. There's a murder in every town they play. The group has to solve the murders to clear their own names."

Annabelle and Mike looked at each other, baffled.

"I heard from one of the locals that Davy had stored Harry's body on his boat, and... well, I saw pretty much everything you could ever imagine seeing when I was on tour, but not that. I wanted to take a look for myself. I thought it would be good research for my book; that I might learn some things I could use in it."

"Is that why you asked me about strange deaths when you spoke to me?"

Pip nodded.

"And vampires?"

He nodded again.

"And unusual happenings in graveyards?"

"Yes."

"Why were you digging in your garden on Saturday afternoon?"

"I was timing how long it takes to dig a shallow grave."

"Why is that such a big secret? Why couldn't you just tell us that?" Nicholls asked.

Pip sighed once more. "Think about it. I'm the guy who wrote lyrics like *'There are bats above my bed, am I alive or am I dead.'* I mean, it's hardly Shakespeare, is it? Who would read a book by someone who made a career based on shock value and tight trousers? It's not like I had any talent. No. I want this book to be a fresh start. I want to publish the book under a pen name, and have it judged on its own merit. I've been trying to keep the book a secret."

"That's very admirable," Annabelle said.

"And very difficult, apparently," retorted Pip.

"I'm sorry we cornered you so harshly," Annabelle said. "But you have to admit, it did look suspicious."

"I know," Pip said, "I'm sorry. I should have come clean sooner."

The Inspector was less keen to let Pip off the hook quite so quickly. "Hmm well, we'll be keeping an eye on you," he said dubiously. "Don't do anything that might look even the slightest bit suspicious in the future, alright?"

His skepticism was more for show than anything. Even the Inspector had to agree that now Pip's secret was out, the forlorn, bedraggled rocker was hardly the dangerous, menacing presence of his youth. He was rather crestfallen by the fact, actually.

"You can be on your way now. But no going after any more bodies, okay? And no digging up... things."

"No problem, Inspector. All I'd ask is that you keep the boo— my project, a secret."

"Of course," Annabelle said.

Once Pip had gone on his way Annabelle turned to the Inspector. "What do you think?"

"I think you're right. There are some very peculiar characters on this island."

CHAPTER TWENTY-FIVE

"IF I WERE working this case, and I'm not, mind you," Mike added quickly, "I'd have a chat with the victim's daughter."

"Mairéad? Oh, you can't possibly think she had anything to do with it?"

"Maybe not, but she was one of the last people, maybe the last person, to see Harry, if eye witness accounts are correct. And it sounds like she did have a motive."

Annabelle grudgingly conceded that he was right. She just couldn't imagine the young woman had anything to do with her father's death.

They walked over to the pub and pushed through the heavy doors. The pub hadn't been open for business since Harry's murder and the air in the place was even more stale than usual.

"We're not—" a voice called out.

"—Open. Yes I know, Mairéad. We've come to talk to you about your father. We have a few questions," Annabelle called out.

"Oh, hello, Vicar. How can I help you?" Mairéad appeared, wiping her hands on a tea towel. She was still pale. Her fair hair was roughly swept up onto her head and held in place with a clip. Tendrils hung down, and she pushed one of them from her face.

"Please. Sit down. Can I offer you some tea or coffee?" She peered anxiously at them.

"No, no thank you," Annabelle replied. "This is Inspector Nicholls from Truro." Mike nodded silently again.

"We want to ask you about what happened the day Harry died." Mairéad gulped and took a steadying breath but didn't say anything.

Again they were sitting at one of the small, wooden, round tables. Annabelle leaned forward and looked Mairéad directly in the eyes, "Can you tell us if there was anything unusual about the day Harry was murdered?"

"No, no I don't think so. It was a Sunday much as any other. The pub was busy as usual. Dad was here chatting with everyone. You spoke to him, right Annabelle?" Mairéad looked imploringly at the Vicar.

"Would you say you had a good relationship with your father?" Mike intervened.

"Yes, why?" Mairéad turned to the Inspector as if seeing him for the first time.

"How did you get on with him?"

"Well, we had our issues like fathers and their grownup daughters often do, especially living in such close quarters. He was rather... overprotective. But we rubbed along okay, most of the time."

"Did you see your father often, Mairéad?" Annabelle asked.

"He flitted back and forth between here and our pub on Fenbarra, but whenever he was here, which was at least half the time, we lived together above the pub."

"And you didn't argue or get on each other's nerves?" Mike pressed.

"Not usually. My Dad had a big personality, but I am a very patient person. I could put up with him. And he is – was – my

Dad. I loved him." Mairéad's chin began to wobble. Annabelle put her hand on the young woman's forearm.

"The thing is, Mairéad, we have accounts that on the afternoon of your father's murder, you had an argument with him. What can you tell us about that?" she said.

Mairéad sighed. She slumped in her seat. "It's a long story."

"We have time," Annabelle continued gently. Mairéad looked at Annabelle and shifted slightly in her chair to face Annabelle directly. Mike sat back to let the two women talk.

"When I came back from the mainland two years ago," Mairéad began, "I went to work in the pub on Fenbarra. I met a boy who lived there. Alasdair worked with the island's fishing fleet, had his own boat and everything, but Dad didn't think he was good enough for me. Dad would interfere, but he couldn't break us up. I'm a grown woman and entitled to my own life." Mairéad lifted her chin defiantly but almost immediately slumped again. "We planned to get married, but when Dad caught wind of it, he insisted I come here to work."

Annabelle frowned, "But couldn't you have defied your father?" She couldn't help thinking that Harry's action was rather archaic and Mairéad's response rather surprising for someone who'd already branched out on her own and spent time on the mainland.

"Yes, of course, but at first I didn't realize what he was doing. He told me to look after the pub just for a few weeks until he hired someone to manage it."

"And what happened?" Mike asked calmly.

"He basically imprisoned me!" Two spots of color appeared on Mairéad's cheeks. "I was always working, I couldn't get away. He never hired anyone to run the place, and he barely gave me any help! I hardly got any time off to see Alasdair! I was trapped here."

"Did you ever think of just leaving? You're a young woman,

you have your whole life ahead of you," Annabelle was shocked that a father would treat his daughter like that.

"Yes, I thought about it, but he's my Dad, you know? I couldn't just leave him high and dry. I tried to get him to see sense, but all he would do was laugh it off and blow those bloody bagpipes of his!" Mairéad sniffed, and like she had the previous day, pulled a tissue from her sleeve and dabbed at her eyes.

"So what happened on the afternoon of his death, Mairéad? When you were seen arguing?" Mike was cool and casual in his seat. He'd had hundreds of conversations like this.

"Oh, just the same old thing that always happened every Sunday afternoon. The same old argument."

"Tell us about it," Annabelle urged, gently.

"I had plans to meet Alasdair. I was going to catch the afternoon ferry. It leaves at two-thirty, so I have to shut the pub at two o'clock sharp and be on my way. I needed Dad's help to get all the stragglers out of the pub so I could leave on time. But he didn't help, did he?"

"Did you tell your father you were going to meet your boyfriend?"

"Absolutely not, he would have found a way to stop me, but when he didn't help close up the pub on time, I decided to just leave them all to it."

"So what happened?" Mike asked.

"He saw me leaving didn't he? He called me back. Told me the beer barrels needed changing. He must have guessed what I was doing, because the barrels could easily have been changed later. Anyhow, by the time I'd changed them, I was too late. I didn't have time to catch the ferry. I came up from the basement and saw the time and just flew into a fury. Everyone had gone by that time, so I just let rip. I was that mad at him. Told him how he wanted to ruin my life, that he was treating me like a slave."

"That sounds terrible, Mairéad. What did he say?" Annabelle was frowning, her lips pursed.

Mairéad ran her hands over her face, rubbing at her eyes. She looked down at her lap, then back to the two English people sat across from her. "Oh, he denied it as he always did. Said he just wanted someone reliable to run the pub, said he didn't trust anyone else. He said our pubs were his legacy, my inheritance, and that I should be happy to work for the family business. That they would be mine one day and how lucky I was."

"So why were you seen running after him outside, yelling?"

"Because this time, *this* time," Mairéad was angry now, her lips turning white as she grit her teeth, "before he turned away from me to leave, he taunted me. He started playing those bagpipes over my words, smiling. He marched off, leaving me fuming. I couldn't contain myself. I thought I'd catch the next ferry, but then I heard about the storm coming and shutting down all the boats, I realized I'd missed my chance for the day. I was so mad, I took off after him. I was like a fishwife, screaming and yelling after him. It was most unlike me, but I'd had enough."

"What did he do?"

"Nothing. He carried on playing his bagpipes with a smirk on his face, just like always. His bagpipes were like armor, a shield. He just put them between him and me, and it was like he could do anything."

"So how did things end?"

"Well, eventually I blew myself out. Yelled and screamed some, but I knew it was hopeless. Eventually, I turned around and went back to the pub, crying my eyes out. I called Ali, told him what had happened and went upstairs and took a nap."

"Did anyone see you come back here?"

"Possibly, I don't know. It's pretty quiet here on Sunday afternoons."

"What are your plans now, Mairéad?" Annabelle asked gently.

Mairéad straightened, her face brightening a little, a look of resolution settling on her features. "I'm going to run the pub on

Fenbarra. I've persuaded the pub manager there to do a swap with me for a few months. Then when everything's calmed down, Alasdair and I'll decide what and where our long-term future will be. She smiled weakly, "Something good will come out of this, I'm determined about that." Her eyes shone with tears, but her voice was strong.

Annabelle turned to Mike. He gave a tiny nod toward the door, and they took their leave. They walked out into the sunshine, glad to be out of the oppressive atmosphere of the pub and into the fresh air once more.

"What do you think, Annabelle?" Mike asked when they walked a few yards from the pub.

"I think, Mike, that our Harry was a rather unpleasant character."

"Do you believe her?"

"Yes. Do you?"

"Yes, yes I do."

CHAPTER TWENTY-SIX

"Come on," Annabelle said, leading the way, "I'll show you the church."

Nicholls followed, his hands in his pockets. Although this was beginning to feel rather like work for him, he very much intended to enjoy his stroll around the Scottish countryside.

"I'm terribly confused," Annabelle said, exasperation evident in her voice. "It's like a tangled ball of wool that just grows ever more knotted the more I pull at it."

"That's a good analogy," Nicholls smiled.

Annabelle laughed softly. "I like analogies. I use them all the time in my sermons. Helps me communicate what I'm trying to say." They walked on for a bit in silence, each lost in their own thoughts.

They heard a car behind them and turned to see Roger roll up.

"Hello again, Bumble, Mike," he said.

"Get Bonnie off to school, okay?" the Inspector asked.

"Er, yes. What are you two up to?"

"I'm showing Mike around. We've just bumped into Pip Craven. I'll tell you about it later."

"Oh, I'll look forward to that. I'm sure it was an interesting conversation. Would you like a lift to the church? I'm going to Jamie Froggatt's to set up his new router!"

"No, we'll walk, thanks Roger," Annabelle said.

"Righty-ho. I hope we'll see you for dinner later, Mike." Roger drove off, careful to avoid splashing the walkers with mud.

"Why do they call you 'Bumble,' Annabelle?" The Inspector eyed her curiously but with a smile.

"Er, because I'm always busy," she said quickly. "Busy. Bees. Honey. Sweet." She held her breath for a moment.

"Ah." He seemed satisfied with the explanation. Annabelle relaxed. Nicholls said, "Look, you've uncovered a lot of information. There are always some gaps in a case. Whenever I find myself with a mass of details and no bigger picture, I just try to ask myself the right questions – the kinds of questions I already have the answers for in my pile of details but which just need sifting."

"I'm filled with questions, Mike!" Annabelle exclaimed. "That's precisely the problem!"

"Let's try this: I'll ask the questions. You give me the answers," he responded calmly.

"Okay."

"Who knew that you had the jewelry box?"

"Nobody! Well, me and Felicity."

"What about the girls she was playing with when she found it? Did they know?"

"No. She didn't tell them."

"Could someone have seen her bring it to you?"

"She had wrapped it in a cloth. It looked like an old bundle. Nothing more." Annabelle stopped and clapped her hands. She turned to the Inspector, her eyes wide. "Of course! I showed the pictures to Harry before the jewelry was stolen. He knew!" Her eyes gleamed for a moment but then her shoulders dropped and she shook her head. "No. That doesn't make sense. He didn't know that I had stored them at the church."

"Hold on now," Nicholls said. "Show me these pictures."

She pulled out her phone and brought them up. She handed the phone to the Inspector.

He scrolled through the images. "Here, look," he said, giving the phone back to Annabelle and pointing at one in particular.

"Oh! That's just one of the bad pictures I took. You can't see anything, it's all blurry."

"You can see more than you think," Nicholls said. "At the top of the photo there, you can see a window. One with vertical bars on it. And to the side there is part of a closet. You said Harry was at the service, that he had a tradition of playing out the congregation. My guess is that he's also pretty familiar with the office. You never know, perhaps he shared a malt whisky or two with Father Boyce in there. He'd surely know that the window had bars. Anyway, Harry would know enough to recognize where those pictures were taken, I'll bet."

"Yes! You're right!" Annabelle said, in amazement. "You are a marvel, Mike! That must be it!"

Nicholls looked at his feet. "It's nothing. I'm a detective. It's my job," he mumbled.

"So Harry must have realized that I had the jewelry in the church safe and broke in to steal them sometime on Sunday afternoon. That would explain why the tool that was used to wedge the church doors apart was found on his body!"

"Right. Perhaps *he* was the person who had hidden the jewelry box away in the abandoned house in the first place. Or perhaps he was just a common thief and saw an opportunity to make some money."

"Yes," Annabelle said, feeling her thoughts swirling like leaves in a whirlwind, "so Harry broke in to the church, and then sought out a hiding place along the rocky beach. But we still don't know how the jewelry that was apparently stolen from Felicity's mother on the mainland ended up right here on the island. Nor does it bring us any closer to understanding who killed the chap. Or who's trying to sell the jewelry now."

St. Kilda's had come into view, and Nicholls stopped for a moment to look up at the building.

"That's an old church," he said.

"Yes, it is," Annabelle said, her thoughts still swimming. "Nearly two hundred years old. Not as old as St. Mary's, though. That was built in the fifteenth century. The buildings here don't last that long. The climate is too harsh."

Nicholls began walking again. "St. Mary's is more attract—"

He stopped. Annabelle wasn't alongside him. Turning back, he saw her frozen in place, her face blank as she stared somewhere off to the side. He followed the direction of her gaze but saw nothing except an overgrown yard. "Annabelle? Are you okay?"

He walked back to her and noticed the glazed look in her eye.

"Kirsty," she said dreamily, turning to him. "*Kirsty's* the murderer."

CHAPTER TWENTY-SEVEN

"ANNABELLE, WHAT ARE you talking about?" the Inspector said.

"That cottage over there. The one beside the apple tree is Kirsty's. Felicity's aunt's. From the kitchen window you can see the church, and the path leading up to it, as clear as day."

"That's good information, but it's not critical. You can't pin a murder on someone for having a good view of a crime scene."

"It's not just that. She's at the center of everything. The jewelry belonged to her sister, Moira. According to Kirsty, her sister had everything, and Kirsty had nothing. She has little money and is very bitter about how her life has turned out. She also had a cold relationship with Harry whom everyone else seemed to like. She's computer-savvy. She was alone on Sunday. It all fits. Who else could it be?"

Nicholls looked from Annabelle over to the cottage, then back at the determined Vicar. "Coincidences and circumstances can make someone look guilty, but it's never right to condemn someone without evidence."

"Well," Annabelle said, smartly, "there's only one way to get it."

Pushing her shoulders back, she began to stride purposefully toward the cottage. Nicholls watched her for a few moments. He considered that the Scottish air had affected Annabelle's brain. Usually he was the one rushing off to prematurely convict someone.

"I guess this isn't going to be much of a holiday for me after all," he murmured, before dragging himself off in pursuit of a resolute Annabelle.

He caught up to her at the paint-chipped door of the cottage. Annabelle slammed the knocker so loudly the Inspector winced. He half-expected the rickety door to fall apart. Within moments Kirsty opened the door, her scowl revealing that she too had been alarmed at the ferocity of Annabelle's banging.

"Vicar," she said.

"Hello, Kirsty," Annabelle replied.

Kirsty's eyes darted from the Vicar to the tall man beside her. "Who's this?"

"This is Detective Inspector Nicholls," Annabelle said stoutly.

"My name's Mike," Nicholls said, "since I'm off-duty." He gave Annabelle a pointed look.

"We've come to speak to you about something important," Annabelle said, ignoring him. "May we come in?"

Kirsty eyed the duo suspiciously.

"Very well," she said, stepping aside to let them through, "but I've got to pick Felicity up from school shortly. Please make this quick."

She led them to the living room, where the guests settled on an old sofa whose surface was pitted with the indentations of the many bottoms that had sat upon it. Kirsty stood in front of them.

"Would you like something to drink?"

"No, thank you," Nicholls replied.

"So?" Kirsty sat in an armchair, a tartan blanket tossed across its back. She clasped her hands in her lap.

"I believe Harry was the person who broke into the church and stole the jewelry box."

"Oh, do you now?" Kirsty said, unemotionally. "Well, I wouldn't put it past him."

"You don't – didn't – like Harry much, did you?" Annabelle said.

"Must I like everyone on the island? Harry always had a greedy, nasty streak that most people are foolish enough to be blind to."

"But you're not?" Nicholls asked.

Kirsty shifted her narrow eyes to the Inspector.

"Are you implying something?"

"You didn't seem terribly surprised to see those pieces of jewelry when I showed you pictures of them," Annabelle said.

"Why should I have been?"

"Well, the jewelry had been stolen on the mainland several years ago, according to you. It would be quite strange to learn they were back on the island. And coincidental."

"Nothing to do with my sister would surprise me. She could come back from the dead, and I'd believe it."

"Do you think your sister could have lied about the theft on the mainland? Annabelle charged.

Kirsty stiffened.

"Let's suppose your sister was a little economical with the truth," the Inspector said, putting his hand up to placate the two women, "and that the jewelry never left the island. Did she tell you anything about that?"

"Pfft!" Kirsty spluttered, her umbrage at the idea too strong to stay silent. "Fat chance! And you're implying that I covered for her. I most certainly would not do that!"

Annabelle closed her eyes momentarily and took a deep breath.

"Harry, then?"

"Mebbe, if she was stupid enough to be duped by him," Kirsty said. "But the jewelry *was* stolen on the mainland," she added, her eyes darting quickly between her inquisitors.

"Are you sure that's what happened, Kirsty? It's a pretty big coincidence that her jewelry was stolen in Edinburgh and turned up here years later," Mike said.

Kirsty said nothing.

"Could Moira have been in cahoots with Harry over the jewelry?" Mike asked.

Kirsty said, "If that's what happened, if Moira did give the jewelry to Harry, it would make me mad. As mad as hell. But it didn't happen. Not to my knowledge. The jewelry was stolen on the mainland and disappeared. Until you showed me those photos yesterday, that's all I knew."

CHAPTER TWENTY-EIGHT

ANNABELLE AND MIKE stood outside Kirsty's cottage, each silently mulling over their conversation with Kirsty. The sun was still shining brightly, drying the last of the soggy mud on the path. The air seemed clearer and more refreshing after the storm, but their thoughts were distracted and heavy.

"I feel certain she had something to do with Harry's murder, Mike," Annabelle said.

"Maybe, but there's no evidence. Like I've said to you before, we can't accuse someone based on a feeling."

Annabelle sighed. "What shall we do now?" she asked. She was frustrated. She felt sure there was more to find out from Kirsty.

Nicholls pursed his lips. "Tell you what. How about we forget all about this case and go take a walk on the beach? You know, just for fun. Because I'm on leave, holiday, vacation. And so are you."

"Perfect! We can take a look at where the body was found when we get there." She might have been crestfallen after their fruitless interview with Kirsty, but Annabelle was immediately like a bloodhound on the scent again.

Mike sighed but resignedly pushed himself off the stone wall against which he'd been leaning.

His attention was caught by something in his peripheral vision. He flicked his eyes away from Annabelle to a spot behind her, high up on the hill that led to the church. In a flash, his expression changed from one of contemplation to one of horror. He looked back and saw the cottage window wide open.

"Is that...?" Annabelle mumbled, as she squinted to make out the running figure.

"Kirsty? I think it is," the Inspector cried, a second before sprinting up the hill.

Both of them ran with every ounce of strength they could muster. They sliced through the brisk, cold wind with powerful, urgent strides, but the figure of the woman disappeared behind the kirk before they could reach her. They ran up the path that led to the church and then quickly around the side and along the back of it, hands out-stretched to pull on the corners of the building for guidance and leverage. Their feet sent chips of gravel flying.

They ran along the cliff path and could see the coastline for a mile ahead of them. Beyond that they saw the larger islands of Fenbarra, and to the north, Serk. They stopped suddenly.

"Where did she go?" Nicholls asked, panting heavily as he scanned the vast horizon.

"I don't know. I don't see her," Annabelle answered.

"Damnit!" Nicholls shouted, kicking at the ground angrily.

"Why would she run? What is she going to do?"

"Something stupid, no doubt," Nicholls answered, furiously.

"Hold on," Annabelle said, stepping forward, a hand over her eyes to shade them. "I think that's her!"

"Where?" Nicholls said, moving beside her.

Annabelle pointed at a rocky outcrop in the distance, and the realization hit both of them at once, so obvious, and so terrifying that it needed no words. They sprang forward once more, even more determination and speed in their strides now that they recognized what was at stake.

It was mossy underfoot. The springy, gently rolling ground sapped their strength. Nevertheless, with blood thumping loudly in their ears, they persisted, their limbs fueled by the urgency of the situation.

To Mike and Annabelle, the pale-blue sky, the bright green grass lush from all the rain, and the gentle sloshing of the waves in the ocean below now seemed more ominous than tranquil. The wind pressed against their bodies, changing direction frequently as if it were struggling to decide whether to help or hinder them. Annabelle's mouth felt dry from the heavy exertion, and the Inspector's legs began to ache.

Kirsty stood motionless on the very edge of the outcrop, her arms outstretched, apparently oblivious to her pursuers.

As they came within earshot of the woman on the edge, Annabelle screamed her name. It felt, to Annabelle, like she was screaming with the very last breath that remained in her body. "Kirsty!"

The woman spun around quickly, her hair windswept behind her, her face a picture of surprise and exasperation.

"Stop there!" Kirsty cried. "Don't come any closer!"

Mike and Annabelle, skidded to a stop within twelve feet of the cliff's edge.

"What are you doing, Kirsty?" the Inspector shouted fighting to make himself heard against the noise of the wind.

"What do you *think* I'm doing?" snarled the woman in reply, puffing out her chest and raising her chin in defiance. "What I was too stupid to do years ago! What I should have done before any of this happened!"

"What did happen, Kirsty? Tell us what happened?" Annabelle cried.

Kirsty gazed absently across the green expanse behind them. From where she stood she could just see the thick trunk of the apple tree that grew strong and powerful next to her house, even as it rose out from among the creeping weeds.

"Moira. Stupid girl!" Kirsty shouted, the timbre of her voice hard and angry. "All she knew how to do was spend money and have the time of her life. When things started going bad for Ben, he stopped giving her money, asked her to reign her spending in. I thought, 'Good, maybe she'll learn some responsibility.' Hah! More fool me. All the pieces of jewelry were gifts from Ben – he was a good husband to her, she didn't deserve him – but she wanted more money so she could spend it all on other rubbish she didn't need." Kirsty stared mulishly at Annabelle and Mike. Neither moved a muscle.

"So did she sell them?" Annabelle inquired, her face open and her tone even despite her terror.

Kirsty grunted derisively. "That would have been too simple for Moira. She was always trying to be clever. That's what happens when you're very pretty. You never get the blame. You get away with murder, and no one calls you on it. In the end, you think you're untouchable. Moira certainly did." Kirsty's nostrils flared, and she raked at her forearms with her fingernails.

She continued, "No. Harry convinced her that she could make more money by reporting them stolen and claiming the insurance. Harry would take the jewelry and use his connections to sell them abroad, then give Moira a cut of that too, as well as have a tidy little profit for himself. A real pair of underhanded clever-clogs they were."

"How do you know all this?" called Annabelle. "Did Moira tell you?"

"Moira told me everything. Couldn't stop talking about herself, could she? Her wonderful this, her beautiful that. But she didn't tell me about this money scheme of hers. Harry must have got his dirty claws deep into her. I found out later." A gust of wind caught her hair, and she turned her head to allow the strong breeze to clear her face before turning back to look at Annabelle. She continued speaking, but her voice was lower this time. Annabelle and Mike leaned in closer in order to hear her.

"I was at Harry's house, fixing his computer. The thing was a mess, but all it needed was a bit of a clean-up. I was unplugging it, sorting out his cables, and one of them led behind a bookshelf. I moved the bookshelf to get at it – and there it was, the jewelry box. I recognized it straight away," Kirsty sighed. "I'd thought a lot of times about that box of jewelry and had wondered what happened to it. It was just another *thing* to Moira." Her voice rose. "To me, that box of jewelry would have been a life-changing *experience!*" As she spoke, Kirsty's rage boiled over.

Annabelle shot Nicholls a despairing look, but he was focused solely on the sad, angry woman in front of him.

"Okay Kirsty, calm down. We can sort this out. Just come away from the edge, and we can get everything cleared up."

"No! I'm going to tell you everything! I'm tired of bottling it all up! It's now or never!"

"Okay, okay. When did you find the box?"

"About a month ago. I confronted Harry. He told me about his and Moira's little 'arrangement.' About how Moira had died before he could find a buyer. He thought I'd just let it go, the stupid man. I told him the jewelry belonged to me now."

It occurred to Annabelle that the jewelry would have belonged to Felicity, but she didn't think now was the time to point that out.

"Why did he keep the jewelry so long? Why didn't he just get rid of it when Moira died?" Annabelle asked.

Kirsty shrugged, "A dinnae ken. Perhaps he thought he would sell them years down the road when everyone had either forgotten about them or were long gone. Or perhaps *he'd* forgotten about them. That's how he was, careless. He didn't value anything, not even his own daughter.

"Of course, Harry wasn't going to give the jewelry over just like that. In fact, he snatched them off me and laughed in my face. Well, I wasn't having any of it. I threatened to tell the insurance company of his and Moira's little scam."

"So that was why he hid the jewelry box in the abandoned house," Annabelle said. "He was afraid that the insurance company would knock on his door and come looking for it."

"Or the police," Kirsty said. "And with the amount of debt that Moira and Ben left behind, they wouldn't be the only ones after it."

"Kirsty, please," Annabelle implored. She held her arms out. "Come to us. We'll help you."

Kirsty stared intensely at her small audience as she stood precariously on the rocky outcrop buffeted by the strong winds all around her. Annabelle wondered how she managed to stand so still. Kirsty shut her eyes tight and balled her fists before sighing like a punctured balloon.

"I didn't know the jewelry box was in the church. I just saw him marching up to the door. It was odd, because he wasn't playing his bagpipes. He's always playing them like a fool. I watched him go right up to the kirk and break the doors open. Bold as brass! Smashing the doors of a church in clear daylight! That tells you what kind of man Harry was."

"Why didn't you just call the police?" the Inspector asked.

"There *is* no police," Kirsty replied. "We're on our own here."

CHAPTER TWENTY-NINE

"COULD YOU NOT have confided in someone?" the Inspector asked.

Kirsty smiled sadly and turned to Annabelle. "Vicar, you've been on this island for what, two, three days now? You should know the answer to that question already. There isn't a person on this island who would take my word over Harry's. And he knew it. Harry's the center of everything in this town. He knows everyone, knows their secrets, and sees them all the time at the pub. He wouldn't have worried about me seeing him committing a crime. He would have been thrilled knowing that the only person who knew he'd broken into the church was the one person no one would believe."

"What happened after you saw him breaking in?" The Inspector had decided that as pleading with Kirsty to come away from the edge hadn't worked, it was best to keep her talking.

"I watched him come out with something. I wasn't sure what it was, but he was acting furtively so I followed him. It was clear where he was heading."

"The beach," Annabelle said.

Kirsty nodded solemnly. "It's about a mile long, fifteen feet wide. Up here we have this legend that if you hide a love letter under the rocks and someone finds it, they'll end up loving you back. Over the years, most of the kids have left letters – but no one's ever found one. The only way you'd find something there is if you hide it yourself. There are just so many rocks."

"So you knew Harry was going there to hide something?"

"Aye. But I didn't know what. I thought I'd follow him and just see what it was, then maybe come back later and take it for myself – the same way he took from me," Kirsty said, pausing for a second. "Then I saw the jewelry box... The sight of him there... Squirreling away something that belonged to me! The gall of the man! The injustice! And stealing it from a church, too!" Kirsty stopped for a moment to calm herself down, gasping for breath. "I thought, once again, Harry would just get away with everything."

"So you killed him?"

Kirsty raised her eyes to meet Annabelle's. They were wide and vulnerable now, tears emerging at the corners.

"I was up on the large rocks, looking down at him below. It was like I was watching myself, like somebody else was controlling my body. I grabbed the biggest rock I could manage because I thought he might lash out if he saw it was me. I climbed down to him. He was digging and scrabbling around like a fury. I was able to get close to him without him noticing me. But then he turned around, and in my panic I brought the rock down on his head. He went down like a stone." Kirsty's eyes were wild now. She was panting again. "My mind went mad, and I grabbed the bagpipes and shoved the chanter in his mouth and the bag over his face. I thought he might start screaming, but then I just kept it there, holding it down..."

"What happened after that?" Nicholls said, wanting to keep Kirsty focused. Kirsty looked at him as though she hadn't heard what he'd said. "And then what?" he repeated.

"I–I didn't know what to do. I grabbed the jewelry box and

ran home. I hid it where Felicity wouldn't find it. I put the jewelry up for sale online and made sure it couldn't be tracked back to me. I thought I'd sell it, bounce the money around a little, and keep my head down. But then, I don't know how, the listings were stopped. And then you," Kirsty nodded at Annabelle, "came round the next day. You showed me those pictures, asked a load of nosy questions."

"Where's the jewelry now, Kirsty?" Annabelle asked.

"It's on top of the large cabinet in my living room."

Nicholls glanced at Annabelle, then back at Kirsty, still standing bold and resistant on the outcrop. As the wind whipped her dark clothes around her body, and with her fists now clenched tightly by her side, there was a sense of dignified rebellion about her, a sense of immovable pride and fortitude in her small frame, outlined against the crashing waves and endless sky.

"I suppose this is it for me now then," Kirsty said.

"Don't be silly, Kirsty!" Annabelle bellowed against the wind. "You can't do this!"

"Can't I?" Kirsty said, a small smirk appearing on her thin lips. She took a step backward.

"Whoa! Stop!" Nicholls shouted.

"Why? It's my life! Would you take even that freedom away from me?" Kirsty called out. "I know what's going to happen. You'll take Felicity away. And then you'll lock me up for good. Isn't that so?"

Annabelle looked at the Inspector, then back at the woman.

"Aye," Kirsty continued. "Thought so."

"You've got plenty to live for! Think about Felicity! We can work things out," Annabelle cried.

"What? How? Tell me. A bunk bed and prison food? A visit from my sister's child once a month? Forgive me if that's not a deal I wish to accept, Vicar. No," Kirsty said, years of resentment and frustration evident in her tone, "my life's been over for a long time. It was over way before you even stepped foot on this God-forsaken island."

"Kirsty!" Nicholls yelled. "You're not thinking straight! I understand, this happens a lot. You're anxious, afraid, and you don't know what will happen. But you're acting rashly. At least give yourself a chance to think about things. You owe it to yourself and Felicity!"

Kirsty snorted derisively, then let out a full blown laugh, before her wild eyes settled on the Inspector as if he were a child unable to understand something utterly rudimentary.

"You think I'm acting rashly? You think the idea to end it all just popped into my head as soon as you and your girlfriend came along to cause me problems? You don't understand a thing! I've thought about this since I was a young girl. I've had to spend every day in Moira's shadow. I thought about it when she left me alone to rot on Blodraigh while she lived out all of our dreams. I thought about ending it when she died and left me with all her problems to clean up. Don't you dare presume to tell me that I'm acting rashly!"

As if spurred on by the bitterness of Kirsty's words, the wind picked up, lashing Annabelle's hair against her face so roughly that she was forced to turn away. The Inspector shielded his face. Kirsty turned quickly and took a step toward the edge, so close that the toes of her boot hung in thin air, three hundred feet above the violent waves crashing against the ancient cliff face.

"No!" the Inspector cried out. He rushed forward, Annabelle a half-step behind. Kirsty didn't look back. In one second she brought herself up to her full height, looked out at the horizon, and stepped off.

The Inspector lunged, Annabelle screamed, but they were too late and not close enough. Kirsty was gone. They cautiously leaned over the edge of the cliff clinging to a small flicker of hope that she may have survived. Upon seeing the sheer drop and the ravaging force with which the waves threw themselves against it, that flicker was immediately extinguished.

Annabelle closed her eyes in horror and threw herself against the Inspector's chest. He held Annabelle tightly as the utter senselessness of what had just happened passed through them, as mighty and insistent as the waves themselves.

After sobbing gently a few times, Annabelle pulled herself away from the Inspector and looked at him.

"We should call someone," she said, finding some sort of brief solace in pragmatism.

He nodded as he took her hand, "I'll take care of it."

"Let me say a prayer."

Silently, they bowed their heads as Annabelle spoke quietly. When she was done, she looked up to the heavens and crossed herself.

Slowly, still holding hands and with the pace and gait of a funeral march, the two of them began retracing their steps, sharing a silence that was as intimate and somber as the feeling in their hearts.

CHAPTER THIRTY
FRIDAY

THE PUB WAS packed when Annabelle, Mike, and Roger entered it in the late afternoon. They'd decided to go for a few drinks, a final opportunity for them to enjoy each other's company before the two visitors made their way back to the sunny south coast of England.

Mairéad had left Blodraigh for Fenbarra and left the pub in the hands of Bruce Fitzpatrick. As soon as the villagers found out it was reopening, they had descended upon it en masse. It had been an eventful week, and there was plenty for the villagers to discuss.

The three of them found themselves an empty spot in the far corner. They sidled into a comfy booth. Finally they could relax.

When Roger decided to brave the crowds to get the first round in, Annabelle asked Mike, "What do you think will happen to the island and the islanders now?"

The Inspector looked out of the window and scanned the magnificent surroundings; the rolling hills, the spackled light which filtered through the new leaves on the treetops, the wispy clouds that slowly crept across the horizon.

"Life goes on," he said. "The story of what happened here will be passed down from generation to generation but will grow evermore vague until the truth is lost in the vestiges of time. That was Kirsty's problem; she clung to the past. But life always goes on. Whether you want it to or not."

"Yes," Annabelle said, studying the thoughtful expression on the Inspector's face, considering this new, philosophical side of him, a side she hadn't seen before. "It certainly does."

It had been a busy few days for everyone. There had been tears, hugs, late night discussions, and much soul searching. Many cups of tea had been drunk.

After Kirsty's confession and suicide, Roger had picked up Felicity and Bonnie from school and the girls had been enjoying an extended sleepover ever since. While they played and slept, there had been plenty of talk about Felicity's future now that she was entirely without family. These conversations had involved lot of reflection and handwringing, but eventually a decision was made. The authorities were informed, and their approval sought and granted. With Mrs. Cavendish's support, it was decided that Roger would take responsibility for Felicity's future care, and to the girl's delight, they became sisters.

Dinner on Monday night had been a rather emotional affair. Roger had fretted and fought over the prospect of telling Felicity – and indeed, Bonnie – about all that had happened: Kirsty's suicide and her role in Harry's murder; the plotting over the jewelry and Felicity's mother's complicity; and the sudden upheaval that Felicity was about to undergo. Roger had never been adept or comfortable with emotional turbulence. Indeed, a large reason he preferred life on the sleepy island of Blodraigh was his preference for peacefulness and routine.

Thus, it eventually fell to Annabelle to calm him and use her compassionate and sympathetic manner to inform the young girls of what had taken place. Once dinner had concluded, she took them to Bonnie's room and after settling them with cups of hot cocoa, had talked to them about what had come to pass.

To everyone's surprise, the girls showed a remarkable amount of understanding and strength in the face of the revelations; Felicity with her typical maturity, Bonnie with her characteristic positive outlook.

After a long and heavy night's sleep, they all awoke to the sound of birdsong and bright sunshine. Roger took the girls to school while Annabelle and the Inspector spent much of the morning submitting a detailed report to the island's police.

After the Inspector had made some inquiries, three of the local fishermen – including Davy and Fraser – organized a dive crew to conduct a search for Kirsty's body. They conceded even before they began that the chances of finding Kirsty were virtually nil, such was the strength of the tides around the coastline. However, they spent much of the next two days searching the rocky, wave-thrashed seas around the cliffs where she fell. Despite Annabelle's fervent prayers, their prediction had proved to be and was likely to remain, accurate.

With so much going on and so much yet to talk about, Annabelle felt sad that the time of her departure was nearly upon her. She still had much that she wanted to do with Bonnie and felt that her conversations with her brother had been all too brief – though as sincere and as genuine as ever. She would have liked to stay longer, but a sense of routine and stability needed to be restored in Roger's household, and it was better that she take her leave as planned. Besides, the villagers of Upton St. Mary were awaiting her return.

Roger came back to the table, carrying over two pints of bitter for himself and the Inspector, and an orange juice for Annabelle. He set them down and immediately raised his glass, compelling Annabelle and Mike to do the same.

"To a safe journey back to England," he said.

"And to a quiet and safe future for you and Blodraigh," Annabelle added to Roger.

They sat for a few moments in silence, savoring the taste of their drinks and the excitable chatter of the pub.

"So how do you feel about being outnumbered by females now you've had a couple of days to think about it?" Mike asked Roger.

"To be perfectly honest, I think it's a great idea. I was concerned at first, but the more Annabelle talked to me, the more it made sense. Felicity has no one else to take care of her. She spends so much time with Bonnie, she's practically been a part of the family for a while now. My house is big enough, and it won't be any trouble for me financially. Mrs. Cavendish has promised to help, so we should manage. The best thing is that it means neither of them is an only child any longer. I think we will all thrive from the arrangement."

"It must be quite a shock for Felicity," Mike said. "First losing her parents and now Kirsty."

"I don't think Felicity and her aunt had the best of relationships," Annabelle said, frowning a little as she remembered the indignant way Kirsty spoke of her niece. "I didn't get the impression that Felicity was as upset as you might think. And, you have to admit that the idea of getting up to tons of mischief with Bonnie holds a lot of appeal." She smiled.

"True enough." Roger nodded. He glanced up. "The detective from Fenbarra is over there, look."

"He must be wrapping up the investigation. It's an open and shut case after all," Annabelle said.

"Actually, I heard he's been rather busy. One emergency after another cropped up the second he set foot on the island." Roger pointed out a large man in a trench coat. "That's him. Campbell. The one laughing at the corner of the bar."

Annabelle followed the direction of her brother's gaze.

"Oh! He's talking with Mitch and Patti. Coo-ee!"

The tourists noticed Annabelle waving in their direction. Their faces lit up. They quickly made their excuses to the Fenbarra detective, picked up their drinks, and slid through the crowd toward her.

"Hey y'all!" Mitch said warmly.

"Hi, Vicar," Patti added, as Annabelle pressed up against the Inspector to make space for the new arrivals. His thigh was warm. "It's good to see you again."

CHAPTER THIRTY-ONE

AFTER A BRIEF round of introductions, Annabelle turned to the Americans.

"You seem in a far better mood than the last time I saw you. I presume you've finally got to see your castle."

"Did we ever!" Patti said, her bright smile lighting up the table.

"Oh boy," Roger said, smirking mischievously into his drink.

"What happened?" Annabelle asked, curious to see what had caused such a change of heart.

"It's one heck of a story," Patti said, nudging Mitch with her elbow. "Tell them, Mitch."

"You know we were going out of our minds trying to get our hands on this guy, Robert Kilbairn," he said. Annabelle nodded. "Well, yesterday we were walking through the village, and we saw his bike outside the post office."

"We knew that if we bulldozed our way in, he'd just run out the back again," Patti said. "Or hide, or just disappear. Like he'd done a thousand times already."

"Right," Mitch continued. "So I found this stick, and I stuck it between the spokes of one of the wheels on his bike. *Then* we went inside."

"Of course he wasn't there," Patti said.

"He'd seen us. He hid behind the door, and slipped out when we walked in. But as soon as he tried to pedal the bike away, of course, he got a nasty surprise. He was sprawled all over the road."

"Oh my!" Annabelle exclaimed.

"Tell them what you did next, Mitch," said Patti, her voice thick with admiration.

"I ran over to him and said 'Freeze! Or I'll blow your brains out!'"

Annabelle, Mike, and Roger all stiffened in shock, their expressions dropping like stones.

"You had a *gun?!* In Scotland!" Roger cried.

"Of course I didn't!" Mitch chuckled. "But he didn't know that!"

Annabelle spluttered into laughter and was quickly joined by Roger and the Inspector.

"What then?" Roger asked.

"I kept my hand in my pocket," Mitch continued, "you know, to make him think I had the gun in there. Then I made him march us all the way up to the castle. Finally."

"He was babbling like crazy," Patti said, her eyes big and wide at the memory. "Really paranoid and erratic."

"When we got up to the castle and he let us in, we saw exactly why," Mitch said.

"This next part will blow your minds," Patti raised her hands and spread her fingers dramatically.

"Not literally, obviously," Annabelle added, thinking back to the gun.

As Mitch paused for a second before speaking again, his audience leaned in, anticipating a twist in the tale.

"He was growing weed!" he said. " Marijuana! Tons of the

stuff. All over the castle."

Annabelle gasped. Roger shook his head in disbelief. Nicholls laughed, grateful that it wasn't his case to investigate.

"But how?" Roger asked quickly. "Blodraigh is hardly Colombia. I can't even grow basil in this weather."

"Hydroponic lights," the Inspector offered as an explanation. "They let you simulate the right conditions. It's a popular method for growing drugs in colder climates, though it's expensive. You need a lot of space to avoid getting caught, enough that no one can detect the heat or the smell of what you're growing."

"The castle was perfect," Mitch added.

"That's rather clever, actually," Annabelle said. "Totally illegal, but clever. Blodraigh is the last place anyone would suspect such a thing."

"Plus there's no real police presence," Roger said. "There aren't even any officials when you ship stuff back and forth from the mainland."

Everyone took a moment to admire the ingenuity of the paranoid castle recluse who had conducted such an operation.

"But what about your lairdship?" Annabelle asked.

"That turned out to be a little scam Robert was running on the side," Patti said. She gave a little sigh.

"But we got something better," Mitch said his eyes glinting. "Once we found out about the castle, we told Mrs. Beattie. She's the lady who runs our B&B. She told us a detective had just arrived on the island. And when we got hold of him, he rushed right over. Apparently they've been investigating this case for a long time, but they hadn't been able to figure it out. There was a big reward for any information about it." Mitch exchanged a quick smile with his wife. "And we got the lot!"

Annabelle chuckled as she raised her glass.

"Well, here's to you leaving Scotland with much more than you came with!"

Mitch licked his lips and said, "Oh no, we're not going back to

America!"

"We're buying the castle!" Patti cried giddily, waving her hands with excitement.

"That's right," Mitch said. "You know, we came here for that castle, but we just ended up falling in love with the whole island, and everyone on it. With the reward money, and Kilbairn off to jail, the castle will go up for auction soon."

"It's not in great condition," Patti said, "but Mitch is very good with his hands."

"And since a lot of people get scared off buying a place that was the site of a major crime, we'll get a great price. Inspector Campbell assured us we'll get us first refusal."

"That's wonderful!" Annabelle said.

"I suppose we'll be neighbors now then," Roger said, with a little laugh.

"Yes, I suppose we will, buddy!" Mitch said, clinking his glass against Roger's and taking a sip.

"Come on, Mitch," Patti said, taking her glass and standing up. "Let's leave them to chat among themselves. We've got to get to know our new neighbors."

"Sure, honey. Have a safe trip back, you two. The next time you come up, I expect you to stay with us for a bit – we've got plenty of room!"

The couple linked arms and rejoined the crowd around the bar, leaving the three of them to exchange expressions of amazement.

"I've lived here for a decade," Roger said, shaking his head, "and I think more has happened in the past week than in that entire time."

The Inspector chuckled as he sipped from his glass. "I think you can blame Annabelle for that. She has a talent for stirring things up wherever she goes. Or simply when she stays at home."

Annabelle gently elbowed the Inspector. "That's not true!"

"It most certainly is!" Nicholls said, winking at Roger.

Suddenly a distinctly long-haired figure shuffled out from the crowd and loped toward them.

"Vicar! I thought you'd left already."

It was Pip, and he seemed in a good mood.

"We're leaving today. We're just having a little drink before we do," Annabelle said, as Pip sat in the warm spot Mitch had just left.

"Have you heard the news?"

"Which news?" Roger asked. "The massive drug bust, or the revelation that Kirsty Munroe murdered Harry Anderson?"

"The drugs, of course! Incredible. I come all the way up here to get away from them only to find masses of the stuff on my doorstep!" Pip shook his head, as if still unable to believe it. "Hey, Inspector. You got any good stories about murders and the like? I'll bet you get a lot of gruesome stuff happening down south."

"Oh, Pip!" Annabelle moaned. "Not that again!"

"Call it research, Vicar. Hey," Pip leaned on the table, "by the way, thanks for that story about the crows. Gave me inspiration for a neat little subplot. So what do you say, Inspector, got anything for me?"

"Actually, I wouldn't mind hearing some of *your* stories. You know, from when you were on the road with your band," Nicholls said. "Did you really burn your guitar on stage?"

Pip chuckled. "It just caught fire, I've still no idea how! Unfortunate that I was playing it at the time!"

Nicholls laughed. "I'll tell you what. How about I give you my new email address, and we can exchange some stories."

"That'd be great!" Pip said, immediately fishing around in his denim jacket for a pen.

Once the Inspector had written down his email address, Pip shook hands with everybody at the table. He let them know how much he would like to see them should they visit Blodraigh again and took his leave, though not before the Inspector could wish him good luck with his 'project.'

"You know, I never actually found out how you two met," Roger said to Mike and Annabelle. They were still sitting pressed up against each other on the bench opposite him. They hadn't moved since they made space for Patti to sit down even though there was now plenty of room to spread out.

Annabelle and Mike looked at each other briefly.

"We both work in the community, so our work inevitably causes us to cross paths," Annabelle said, looking at Roger carefully.

"I see," Roger said, a twinkle in his eye "You certainly seem to have struck up a good relationship."

"A very fruitful one, wouldn't you say, Annabelle?" Nicholls smiled, looking at her warmly. He put his arm around her shoulder and gave her a brief squeeze.

Annabelle blushed slightly and hid herself behind her glass as she took a long sip.

"It would be nice for both of you to come up next time. Perhaps there'll be more fun, and less chasing murderers, illegal drug growers, and the like," Roger joked.

Annabelle flashed her eyes in admonishment at her brother, recognizing exactly what he was implying.

"That sounds like a great idea," Mike said. He checked his watch quickly. "Well, we should get going."

Roger checked his watch too.

"Mrs. Cavendish should be here with the girls any minute."

They gulped down the last of their drinks, and stood to leave. Annabelle stopped at the door and turned back toward the crowd.

"Bye everyone!" she called out. "Take care of yourselves!"

Every single face turned in the direction of Annabelle and the Inspector.

"Come back soon, Vicar!"

"We'll miss you!"

"You're always welcome in Blodraigh! The pair of you!"

CHAPTER THIRTY-TWO

AMID SHOUTS AND laughter, the three of them left the pub, and took a few steps down the road.

"So you're making the journey back together?" Roger said, the mischievous tone in his voice still present. He couldn't resist teasing his sister.

"I guess we are," Annabelle replied evenly, as they ambled around the corner of the pub. "It should make the long ferry and train journeys pass a little faster."

"Who said anything about ferries?" Mike said, a wry smile playing on his face.

"What do you mean?"

Before the Inspector could answer, the distant, rhythmic sound of propellers reached them. Annabelle's eyes widened.

"You didn't?!" she cried, as the sound of the helicopter grew louder.

"I most certainly did," the Inspector replied.

"How?" Roger asked, impressed once again.

"Steve, the pilot, and I did our basic police training together. He flies the police helicopters and life flights in the North of

England. He's used to flying in rough weather, so I asked him to fly me up here as a favor. Now, he's going to fly us home."

They watched as the helicopter landed amid the roar of blades and the thrashing of grass in front of the pub. Roger and Nicholls exchanged a solid, respectful handshake, and the Inspector walked to the helicopter.

Annabelle and Roger looked at each other lovingly, and hugged.

"He's a good man," Roger said, just loud enough to be heard above the helicopter's noise.

"He is," Annabelle nodded.

"You could do a lot worse."

"Roger..." chided Annabelle. "It's not like that. We're just friends."

Roger glanced behind Annabelle at the helicopter. "Not many friends would travel all this way to make sure you're safe."

Annabelle smiled, and a second later, young, high voices caught her ear.

"Bumble! Don't leave!"

"Annabelle!"

Skipping up the path from the village, satchels and ponytails tossing behind them like sails, Bonnie and Felicity were approaching with big smiles across their faces. Mrs. Cavendish followed a few feet behind, crying out for the girls to slow down as she struggled to keep up with them in her long skirt and heeled boots.

Annabelle braced for impact. The girls slammed into her, and she hugged them tightly, feeling more than a little sentimental that it would be the last time she saw their happy, innocent, faces for a while. When they pulled apart, the girls were ready to bombard the departing vicar with questions.

"Is that your helicopter?"

"Is the Inspector your boyfriend now?"

"Will you be getting married?"

"Can we be bridesmaids?"

"Would you prefer a girl or a boy?"

"Girls!" Mrs. Cavendish reprimanded as she finally caught up with them. "That's enough! The poor vicar!"

Annabelle chuckled good-naturedly.

"It's alright, Mrs. Cavendish," she said with a smile. "In answer to your questions, girls: No, that is not my helicopter. We're just borrowing it for the trip home. I will do my best to come back later in the year, and I have no intention of marrying anyone in the immediate future – though if I do, you can be sure that you will not only both be bridesmaids, but you will be some of the first to know."

The girls smiled gleefully, swapping glances giddily and clapping their hands.

"And Mrs. Cavendish," Annabelle said, "I am eternally grateful for your hospitality and care and especially the numerous culinary delights you've introduced me to in my short time here."

They embraced briefly, and Mrs. Cavendish grinned broadly.

"Please take this," she said, pulling a small, tatty notebook from her coat pocket.

"What is it?" Annabelle asked, taking it slowly and carefully thumbing it through.

"A book of recipes my mother gave me a long time ago, and to which I've added in recent years."

"Oh, Mrs. C.!" Annabelle exclaimed, handing the book back. "I can't take this, I'm sorry. That's far too precious a gift. I wouldn't be able to do it justice."

"It's not for *you*, Vicar! It's for Philippa!"

"Oh!" Annabelle said.

"You've spoken about her at length to me, and it's patently obvious that we are kindred spirits. Philippa sounds like one who understands the art, the love, and the power of a perfectly prepared dish. Tough old birds like us may be a dying breed, but we still recognize a kindred soul when we hear of one. Philippa will know what to do."

"But—"

"Don't you worry, I've got them all memorized. And anyway, I could write a book twice that size now."

Annabelle grinned at the strange sense of sisterhood Mrs. Cavendish felt for Philippa, despite having never met her.

"I am sure she will be sincerely touched by the gift," Annabelle said, pocketing the book.

"I'm not worried about sentiment, Vicar. I just want my Scottish pancake recipe to spread its wings beyond the limited borders of this little island."

"Well," Roger said, as he placed his hands tenderly upon the heads of the two girls stood either side of him, "I suppose this is it."

Annabelle gazed at the beautiful faces of the people she loved.

"For now, Roger. Just for now," she smiled, before turning away from her brother and walking up to the helicopter. The Inspector held the door open for her and took Annabelle's hand to help her up into her seat. The crowd on the ground had swelled as the locals, drawn by the sound of the helicopter, had come to see what all the fuss was about. Annabelle and Mike waved one last time as the helicopter took off.

The chopper's tail lifted and the nose dropped, causing Annabelle to yelp as it swept over the countryside, which rose and fell like grassy waves beneath them. They both gawped in wonderment as the church spire came into view, high atop one of the tallest points on the island, the cross at its head glorious against the orange light of the falling sun.

"Isn't it magnificent?" Annabelle cooed, looking at the Inspector.

"It most certainly is," he replied.

"The island is so beautiful from up here."

Nicholls shifted his gaze from the island's alluring landscape and settled upon Annabelle.

"There's beauty all around us, if you take the time to look."

Annabelle turned to face him and saw a softness in his eyes.

Suddenly the helicopter jerked backward. Annabelle and Mike jumped in their seats. Their hands shot out to steady each other.

"Sorry!" the pilot called back through the noise of the blades. "My fault."

Their fingers now intertwined in the middle of the seat, Annabelle and Mike made no move to disentangle them. Instead they smiled bashfully as the helicopter ploughed on across the darkening sky. They sat back and relaxed as they peered out the windows at the lights down below as their thoughts turned to home. Philippa, Molly, the villagers, and Upton St. Mary would all soon rise up to meet them, but for now they were alone, basking in the simple pleasure of one another's company.

REVERENTIAL RECIPES

CONTINUE ON TO CHECK OUT THE RECIPES FOR GOODIES FEATURED IN THIS BOOK...

WONDERFUL WHISKY MARMALADE PUDDING

Butter for greasing
8 tablespoons marmalade
4 oz. butter, softened
4 oz. sugar
2 tablespoons Drambuie (optional)
Grated rind of 1 orange
2 eggs, beaten
6 oz. flour, sifted
1 ¼ teaspoons of baking powder
Pinch of salt
Milk

Grease a 2 lb. pudding basin, and spoon 4 tablespoons of the marmalade into the bottom.

Cream together the butter and sugar until pale and fluffy. Beat in the remaining marmalade, Drambuie, and orange rind.

Add the eggs a little at a time, beating after each addition. Fold in half the sifted flour, then fold in the rest with the baking powder and salt. Add a little milk to give a soft-dropping consistency.

Pour the mixture into the basin, cover with buttered greaseproof paper or foil, and secure with string. Allow some room for the pudding to rise. Place in the steamer or a boiling pan of water and steam for 1 hour. Don't let the pan run dry or the marmalade will burn.

Invert the pudding on to a serving plate. Serve with lots of custard or cream and a bit of extra warmed marmalade. **Serves 4.**

Note:

You can also cook this in the oven in a *bain marie*.

SACRED SCOTTISH PANCAKES

4 oz. flour
½ teaspoon bicarbonate of soda
1 teaspoon cream of tartar
1 tablespoon sugar
2 teaspoons cooking oil
1 egg, beaten
Approximately ¼ pint milk

Sift the flour with the bicarbonate of soda and cream of tartar into a mixing bowl. Stir in the sugar and oil, then beat in the egg and milk gradually until a thick batter is formed.

Heat a griddle until hot. Wrap a small piece of fat in a piece of kitchen paper and use to grease the pan between frying each batch of pancakes.

Drop batter onto the hot griddle, a spoonful at a time, leaving room for the batter to run. Cook until golden-brown on the underside and bubbles rise on the surface. Turn over and cook the other side.

Keep the pancakes hot in a warm tea-towel while cooking the

remaining batter. Serve with maple or golden syrup and fresh cream. **Makes approximately 16.**

Notes:
These are sometimes called drop scones. They are traditionally cooked on a griddle. If a griddle is not available, a heavy-based frying pan can be used, or the pancakes can be cooked directly on the hot plate of an electric cooker.

DEVILISHLY DELICIOUS DUNDEE CAKE

8 oz. flour
Pinch of salt
8 oz. butter
8 oz. sugar
4 large eggs
12 oz. golden raisins/sultanas
12 oz. raisins
6 oz. candied mixed peel
4 oz. candied cherries
Grated rind of half lemon
3 – 4 oz. whole almonds, blanched

Pre-heat the oven to 300°F/150°C.

Grease an 8-inch round cake tin and line with double greaseproof or parchment paper. Tie a band of brown paper round the outside of the tin and let it extend about two inches above the rim. Set the tin on a double piece of brown paper on a baking tray.

Sift together the flour and salt. Beat the butter until soft. Add the sugar and cream until light and fluffy. Beat the eggs into the mixture, a little at a time. Fold in the flour, and when evenly combined, fold in the golden raisins, raisins, mixed peel, cherries, and lemon rind. Chop 1 oz. of the almonds; add to the cake mixture. Spoon into the tin.

Arrange the rest of the almonds over the leveled cake surface. Bake just below the center of the oven for 3½ hours. If the cake shows signs of browning too quickly, cover the top with a sheet of damp greaseproof or parchment paper and reduce the heat to 275°F/135°C for the last hour. Remove the cake from the oven when a skewer comes away clean from the cake.

Cool in the tin for 30 minutes, then turn out and cool on a wire rack. Wrap the cake in foil, with the greaseproof or parchment paper still in place. The cake is best kept for at least one week and up to one month to bring out the full flavor. **Makes a 4 lb. cake.**

OMNIPOTENT OATCAKES

8 oz. oats
2 oz. whole wheat flour
½ teaspoon bicarbonate of soda
½ teaspoon sugar
2 oz. butter
1 teaspoon salt
Hot water

Pre-heat the oven to 375°F/190°C.

Pulse the oats in a food processor to make an oat flour. For a coarser texture, you can leave the oats as is. Mix together the oat flour, whole wheat flour, salt, sugar and bicarbonate of soda.

Add the butter and rub together using fingers until the mixture has the consistency of breadcrumbs.

Add the water a little at a time, and combine until you have a thick dough. The amount of water needed will vary depending on the oats. Use your hands to form a ball.

Dust flour on a work surface and roll out the dough to

approximately ¼-inch thick. Use a cookie cutter to cut out 2-inch rounds.

Place the oatcakes on a baking tray and bake for approx. 20-30 minutes or until slightly golden brown at the edges. **Makes 16.**

All ingredients are available from your local store or online retailer.

You can find printable versions of these recipes and links to the ingredients used in them at https://www.alisongolden.com/horror-in-the-highlands-recipes/

USA TODAY BESTSELLING AUTHOR

A Reverend Annabelle Dixon Mystery

KILLER AT THE CULT

Alison Golden

Jamie Vougeot

KILLER AT THE CULT

BOOK SIX

The characters and events portrayed in this book are fictitious. Any similarity to real persons, living or dead is coincidental and not intended by the author.
Text copyright © 2019 Alison Golden
All rights reserved.

No part of this book may be reproduced, stored in a retrieval system, or transmitted in any form or by any means, electronic, mechanical, photocopying, recording, or otherwise, without express written permission of the publisher.

Cover Illustration: Rosalie Yachi Clarita

Published by Mesa Verde Publishing
P.O. Box 1002
San Carlos, CA 94070

ISBN-13: 978-0-9887955-1-8

Edited by
Marjorie Kramer

CHAPTER ONE

Annabelle smelled the sticky, sugary scent as it wafted over her. She shifted uncomfortably in her seat.

To her left, slices of chocolate caramel shortcake lay piled in a mound the shape of a pyramid. Cherry Bakewells, their soft, white icing topped by a single, red glacé dot, stared back at her. A light brown, coffee sponge, its ganache filling oozing at the edges, stood smartly at attention, powdered sugar and walnuts elegantly sprinkled across its surface. Round lemon tarts lay like replica suns on a vintage blue and white plate, accented by dotted orange slices and bright green leaves, while the moistness of the neighboring sunken apple cake in which she could *see* the sugar crystals was apparent as it glinted in the sun.

Annabelle had snagged a table at Flynn's tea shop next to the window display, a decision she now realized hadn't been her best.

The sweets were imprisoned beneath clear glass domes, but when her nostrils weren't being assailed, her eyes watered with the temptation she was desperately trying to hold at bay.

She looked outside as she waited for the sweet aroma to pass. It was Saturday, and the tearoom was busy. She pressed her lips together and fingered a teaspoon as she waited for her tea to brew.

After a minute, Annabelle lifted the Union Jack cozy covering her teapot and, placing a forefinger on the lid, poured tea delicately into her china cup. She blew across the surface of the hot, almost orange liquid, making ripples in the surface. The warm, damp, steamy response made her nose tickle. She sighed and looked out of the window again, propping her elbows on the table and ignoring her mother's admonishments that were bouncing around her head. Her hands cradled the elegant, eggshell blue cup decorated with yellow and red flowers. She took a sip. The taste made her smile as she thought of her father, a London cabbie, who after taking his first drink of tea after a hard night's work on the streets of the city, would smack his lips and say, "Good cup of tea, that. Put hairs on yer chest."

It was a beautiful day. The sun shone. The villagers wore shorts and t-shirts. They were out in force, making the most of the gorgeous mid-June weather. It was market day, and the stalls were set up in the village square. Ernie Plumber, the greengrocer, was barking out prices. Colorful fruit and vegetables were laid out on his produce stall as they had been for decades. Veg lay to the right, fruit to the left; apples and cauliflowers at the back, strawberries, peas, and broad beans at the front. Annabelle doubted Mr. Plumber had changed the configuration of his stall in the twenty-five years he'd been working the market. And good for him, she thought, his customers knew just what to expect. Routine and stability were what the locals liked about their village.

The Upton St. Mary Chapter of the Women's Institute was an exception to that rule. Right next to the greengrocer's stall, the WI had set out their homemade cakes and jars of honey and jam. They lay on a linen-covered table with pamphlets about the chapter's speakers' schedule splayed out in a neat fan next to them. Annabelle made a mental note to talk about that to the ladies manning the table. Given the precise arrangement of the leaflets, she knew from experience that no one would dare pick any of them up. No one would learn that Mr. Nancarrow from the undertakers would give a talk next month on how burial ashes could be transformed into jewelry or of the repeat outing planned for August to a pole dancing class in Plymouth.

The earlier trip to the Twisted Butterfly had caused quite a stir among some in the village. A few of the women, headed by Philippa, her church secretary and housekeeper, had come to Annabelle to urge her to *do something*. They were a small yet vocal bunch, but they had left Annabelle's cottage dissatisfied, her advice to think of it as an "extreme yoga class" buzzing in their ears.

Veteran WI members, Mrs. Gates and Mrs. Polwerrin sat on stools behind their table nattering, interrupting their conversation only when elderly Mrs. Freneweth paused to show interest in their cakes. The WI ladies welcomed her, beaming at their prospective customer. They were proud of their wares and loved to show them off. Annabelle was confident that pleasantries would be exchanged, compliments about the cakes would be paid, surprise would be expressed over their relative inexpensiveness, money would be exchanged, and the customer would eventually shuffle off, marveling at the bargain they'd just scored, and happily anticipating a lovely sit-down later with a slice of newly purchased cake and their beverage of choice.

As she watched the scene playing out just as she had anticipated, the cake in question being a pale yellow Victoria sandwich, Annabelle's mind wandered to Inspector Nicholls. Mike. He liked a jam-and-buttercream filling too.

Annabelle's table jolted forcefully, sloshing the tea in her cup. She quickly lifted her elbows from the table to steady her hands as china on the table tinkled.

"Billy, watch what you're doing! You nearly spilled the Vicar's tea!" Mrs. Breville let out an exasperated sigh. "Sorry,

Reverend," she said, shaking her head and rolling her eyes simultaneously.

Annabelle straightened the linen tablecloth. "It's perfectly fine, Mrs. Breville. No harm done."

Annabelle regarded the cause of Jeannette Breville's frustration carefully. "But what have you been doing with yourself, Billy?" The ten-year-old boy had a purple and black shiner, and a graze above his eyebrow. Both arms were in slings.

"Ah, it's nothing, Annabelle."

His mother nudged him. "It's "Reverend" to you, Billy."

"Ah, Reverend, sorry. Took a tumble. From Big Boy."

"Who?"

"Big Boy, the new pony at Tinsley's." Tinsley's was the local riding school.

"Gracious me, looks like it was a little more than a tumble, Billy."

"Nah, was my own fault. Didn't grip with my knees hard enough." Billy lifted one arm to scratch his face and Annabelle saw the plaster cast wrapped around his hand and wrist. "Fair bounced, I did. Dad always did say horses were dangerous."

"Really?"

"Have a mind of their own, see? He'd prefer I take up motorbikes, when I'm older of course," he added, "but that always makes Mum cry."

Annabelle stared at him nonplussed. She had a tendency to agree with Billy's dad up to the part about the motorcycle. "Well, please be careful, Billy. We need you in one piece for the show, don't forget, and your mum and dad need you for a lot longer than that!"

She gave the boy a quick rub on his head, the only part of him she could find uninjured. Billy was to play the part of Pharaoh in the village's performance of the story of Joseph and his coat of many colors. Annabelle was directing.

When Billy and his mother moved off, she returned her

attention to the scene outside her window. The villagers who were milling around the market stalls had been joined by some strangers, two women Annabelle hadn't seen before. They were handing out flowers, or trying to, anyway. The locals seemed to be employing various tactics to avoid the women. Eyes were downcast, backs were turned, mothers put protective hands on their children's shoulders to guide them away even as the youngsters stopped to stare. One villager even spoke to the two women angrily when they tried to press a flower on him, lifting his hand as though he had a flea in his ear.

Annabelle frowned. The women didn't seem unpleasant. Their faces were open and friendly. One of them wore a long, print skirt almost to the floor, a crinkled loose cotton top and flat, strappy sandals. The other was dressed in working clothes, a pair of sturdy cotton trousers and a plaid flannel shirt, warm for such a midsummer day. She topped it with a canvas jacket and a gardening belt full of pouches and pockets lay around her waist.

Katie Flynn, the teashop's owner, walked up to Annabelle's table.

"Is there anything else I can get you, Reverend? Any cake today?"

Annabelle could still smell the sugar emanating from the display of cakes in the window to her left, but she tamped down the urge to indulge.

"No, thank you, Katie," she said patting her stomach. "I'm trying to be good."

Katie laughed. "You're a vicar, Reverend. You can't not be good."

"Oh, I don't know about that. I can be tempted by a good slice of Devil's Food Cake as easily as anyone, as you well know. Katie, do you know who those people are? The ones with the flowers?" She pointed to the two women who were now talking to the ladies from the Women's Institute, who for their part, were engaged in the very English dance of trying extremely hard not to be rude while obviously wishing they were a thousand miles away.

"Oh, they're the people from the big house outside the village. The one at the end of Lolly Lane, past Oakcombe Cottage and the Hamiltons.'"

"What're they doing? They seem to be handing out flowers and talking to people."

"Yeah, they do that. Or try to. They ask for money. Sometimes they set up a table to sell stuff. They put one up outside the newsagents last week, until Frank Hammett shooed them off. And they have some kind of paper they try to sell, too. I'm not sure they're very successful. People around here aren't into what they're into."

Annabelle swiveled in her chair, her eyes wide. "And what's that?"

Katie shrugged. "Not too sure, meself. They've never come in here. I'd send them away if they did. I'm not having them bothering my customers. I just know they come in on market days and hang around."

"Hmm. Interesting." Annabelle looked again at the WI women. The two strangers were still engaging them, but Mrs. Gates was standing now, pointing across the street. Mrs. Polwerrin was hard at work rearranging pamphlets that didn't need rearranging.

"What do I owe you?" Annabelle smiled at Katie and fished about in her cassock folds for some money.

"It's on the house, Vicar. Don't trouble yourself, it was just a cup of tea. Come back and see us later in the week. You're always welcome."

Katie cleared Annabelle's table and disappeared into the kitchen at the back of the teashop. By this time, Annabelle's fishing had transformed into a deep dive. Finally she wrestled a few coins onto the table. She left them as a tip. She brushed aside the hair that had fallen into her eyes and stood to walk out, bidding her fellow tea drinkers goodbye as she weaved her way carefully through tables laden with porcelain and hot, brown liquid. In her flowing cassock skirts, a busy tearoom was a potential disaster zone.

When she reached the street, mercifully without incident, Annabelle looked around. It was close to midday, and the market was quieting down after the mid-morning rush. She caught sight of the two women, now talking to two men who were easily distinguishable from the villagers by their embroidered smocked shirts, knickerbockers, and scraped-back, tiny braided ponytails. No self-respecting Upton St. Mary villager would be seen in garb like that unless they were Morris Men.

Annabelle pondered the idea that they might, indeed, be local folk dancers in traditional costume, but she couldn't see any wooden sticks or bells, or an accordion for that matter. *Pity*, she thought. She enjoyed a good jig as much as the next person, although when they cracked their wooden batons together, it made her wince. One slip and someone could get a nasty bruise. She momentarily thought back to Billy Breville.

As she regarded the group, something about the woman with the working clothes caught Annabelle's eye. She squinted to peer closer. The woman was carrying a gray, white, and brown rabbit in one of her pockets. Annabelle recognized the breed. It was a small, lop-eared rabbit. She had had one as a pet when she was a girl. Its small head with its big, black eyes poked out of its canvas home, its nose bobbing up and down, its oversized bunny ears splayed out. Shrewdly or not, Annabelle couldn't decide which, the rabbit sat at eye level with the children that passed and they noticed it immediately. Annabelle watched as a villager and her young daughter walked past the group and over to the teashop.

"Mummy!"

"Hmm?"

"There was a rabbit in that lady's pocket."

"Of course there was, Summer."

"No, there was, Mummy. I want to go and look."

"We don't have time."

"But M-u-m-m-y!"

Flustered, the woman took the girl's hand and pulled her along as her daughter continued to glance back the way she had come, unable to take her eye off the sight of the cute, winsome bunny. Annabelle's heart hurt a little as she watched. She felt for both mother and daughter, their relationship disrupted by their competing urges.

The church bells rang out, and Annabelle gathered herself. Bell-ringing practice. She needed to get home. She'd ask Philippa about these newcomers who were inspiring so much gossip, and perhaps, trouble. She was quite certain her church secretary would know all about them, probably too much. And Philippa would be only too pleased to share her opinion on the subject.

CHAPTER TWO

Annabelle shut the door to her cottage with a bang.

"Philippa! Philippa!" she called. "Are you here?" The heavenly smell of freshly baked cupcakes drifting toward her from the kitchen announced the fact that Philippa was indeed there.

The older woman's face popped out from behind the back door. "Cooee, Reverend. Just doing some sweeping. Gardener man has been here doing the grass, and there's cuttings all over the steps."

"Oh, well, never mind that. Finish what you're doing, and I'll put the kettle on. I want to chat to you about something." Annabelle bustled about, putting the kettle on to boil and warming the teapot. She set a tray with cups and saucers, milk but no sugar because neither she nor Philippa took it in their tea any longer. They were both being "good." The smell of the cupcakes, though, was a distraction. She opened the cupboard to get out some plates but closed it again and resolved to sit outside where the temptation would be less. More tea would help.

"You're tormenting me, Philippa," she said as she took the tea tray outside to her garden. Two young dogs, Molly and Magic, ran up to her, their brown tails wagging at one end, their pink tongues hanging out at the other.

"Whoa, doggies, you'll make me spill my tea." Annabelle set the tray down on the bench and made a fuss of the two dogs, who, once they realized she had nothing for them, returned to playing with one another in a shady corner populated by purple foxgloves, pink hydrangea, and two crabapple trees.

"What's that?" Philippa said, as she moved some planters back into position. She walked over to where Annabelle was now sitting.

"The cupcakes you've made. The ones currently sitting in the oven. You know I'm trying to be good."

"You're always good, Reverend, you're a vicar," Philippa laughed. "Anyhow, those aren't for you. They're a rehearsal snack for the children. We need to keep their strength up. You're putting them through their paces with all that singing. Audrey Beamish says her daughter sings from the moment she gets up to the moment she goes to bed at night. That takes a lot of energy, that does."

"And demands a lot of patience from the rest of her family, I shouldn't wonder," Annabelle replied.

"There are some very high notes, to be sure. I can hear her from two streets away."

Annabelle's idea to stage the story of Joseph and his fabulous coat had initially been a modest one. She'd envisaged a few songs and an equal number of children, but with the unbridled enthusiasm and imagination of the villagers, the project had developed into a major production. It now encompassed the entire songbook, virtually the whole village population of under-fifteens, and an army of parents who were managing everything from building sets to making costumes, from printing programs to plastering on makeup. Everyone was talking about it, and their expectations were causing Annabelle, who'd taken on the role of producer, director, and occasional cast member, a myriad of sleepless nights. She was taking to her knees a lot.

"I must say that the last time I dropped by, it looked like primary school playtime with all that running and shouting, but I'm sure you know what you're doing. Organized chaos, wouldn't you say?" Philippa said, optimistically.

In Annabelle's experience, rehearsals erred far more on the side of chaos than organized. She had had to break up a fight during the last one. The thought of adding Philippa's sugary treats to the mix was one that didn't bear thinking about. The children didn't need *more* energy. However, Annabelle decided to keep her own counsel for the moment.

"Listen Philippa, I saw some people today, in the market square. Two women. They were handing out flowers to passersby. Do you know anything about them?"

Philippa sniffed.

"Would these be the people hanging around bothering folk? Enticing them with flowers and animals, using the children to trick the parents into conversation about their blasphemous views?"

"Well, yes. Although—"

"The men who wear funny trousers?"

"Um, yes, but—"

"No one wearing trousers like that can be up to any good, Vicar. And who knows what those women hide up in those flowing skirts."

"Well, no perhaps not, Philippa. But what do you know about them?"

"They're heathens, Reverend. They have strange ways. They live at the big house at the end of Lolly Lane. I've heard all kinds of stories of funny goings on. Mr. and Mrs. Cuddy who live at the end of the lane say they've heard yelling and hollering at all times of the day and night. And the food they eat! All plants, you know?"

"I see, well—"

"Vegans, I think they call themselves. But it can't be good for you, can it? We're not cows, are we?"

"That's certainly unusual, however—"

"But see, they're clever. They worm their way under people's skin. Start out all nice, chatty, and that, and before you know it, you're imprisoned by some kind of cult you can't escape from!"

"I'm sure it's not as bad as that, Philippa. You're exaggerating, surely?"

"I don't think so, Vicar. Charlie Bishop went to the house for a cup of tea and barely came away with his life! They wanted him to stay for dinner, but you know how he likes his meat."

Annabelle fought back painful memories of the hot dog eating competition they'd held at the last church fête at which Charlie had been the undisputed winner and also the first in line at the doctor's surgery the next morning.

"I'd stay well away, if I were you," Philippa finished.

"Hmm, it all seems rather mysterious, certainly."

"Cooee!" Barbara Simpson from the Dog and Duck clicked the gate shut and waved as she tottered up the garden path in her leopard print stilettos.

"Hello Barbara. How are you?" Annabelle said.

"Fine, Vicar, fine. Just popped by with some of my old makeup. I thought you might be needing it for the show." She handed Annabelle a large bag of cosmetics. Pallettes of eye shadows and tubes of lipsticks with evocative names such as Blastin' Blue and Opulent Orange assailed her eyeballs. Glitter and shimmer featured strongly among the selection.

"Thank you, Barbara, that's very generous of you." Annabelle looked down at the bag again. "The false eyelashes in particular will come in very handy."

"We were just talking about the cult people from the house at the end of Lolly Lane," Philippa said.

"Ooh yes, Vicar. They're a bad lot, they are. Been coming

into my pub, handing out their flowers, they have. I shoo them out sharpish."

Philippa sat up straighter and wagged her forefinger at Annabelle, invigorated now she had an ally. "I think they've brought bad blood into the village. Ever since they arrived, bad things have been happening."

"Like what, Philippa? Come on, tell me. I'm sure it's not as bad as all that," Annabelle said.

"Well, there was that business between Demelza Trevern and her cousin, Angie," Philippa said.

"That was a fight waiting to happen."

"And then Billy Breville got thrown from his horse."

"Ah yes, I saw Billy earlier."

"And we had a man in the pub the other day picking fights with some of my locals. I had to throw him out on to the street and hose him down to cool off!" Barbara added.

Annabelle looked doubtfully at the two women. She was extremely reluctant to pay attention to their gossip, but she had to admit she was intrigued by the group of strangers.

"Hmm, well, I'm sure it's all just a coincidence."

"There's no such thing as coincidences, Reverend. No such thing. It's all God's work." Philippa clasped her hands around her knee and leaned back, pursing her lips.

"Speaking of God's work, are you seeing the Inspector this week, Reverend?" Barbara asked, her eyes wide, her eyebrows high.

Annabelle wasn't sure what God had to do with the relationship between her and the Inspector, but she knew the villagers' curiosity in it was intense. Since their return from Scotland some weeks earlier, they had taken to regularly walking their dogs together. They had been seen crisscrossing the fields surrounding Upton St. Mary in all weathers. The newsagent was keeping a running tab of their sightings. The barman at the Fox and Duck was taking bets on an engagement. Meanwhile, a group of twelve year olds had lain in wait one Sunday afternoon, vowing to follow the pair throughout their ramble. Possibly because the Inspector had been onto them before they'd even left the village, they had been left for dust at the one mile mark and gone home to report to their parents who pretended to tell them off while hanging on to every word. Annabelle knew all this because she would overhear snippets of gossip and find conversations swiftly concluded when she walked in a room. However, no one, not even Philippa, had dared breathe a word to her directly.

Annabelle took it all in good humor, although she had developed an enormous sympathy for high profile celebrity couples who had the populations of entire countries hanging on their relationship's every development. The truth in her case was, however, far more mundane.

Although Mike came to the village with Molly every weekend, and their rambles across the countryside were the highlight of Annabelle's week, even more so than Sunday communion, their relationship hadn't progressed beyond the occasional hand holding. She was in quite a tizzy about it and desperately wanted things to move on, but the Inspector appeared to be taking his time. She didn't know what to make of it and was determined to keep everyone in the dark until she did.

She knew her being a vicar may be part of the slow moving nature of their relationship, and if it were, it wasn't the first time Annabelle's clerical collar had stood in the way of her love life. She had long ago reconciled herself to the fact that her cassock wasn't exactly an aphrodisiac, and this was in large part why her long country walks with Inspector Mike Nicholls and their passionate, far-reaching discussions about the state of the world, religion, and the goodness and badness of people from their different perspectives had warmed her heart toward him.

She was sure he enjoyed their time together as much as she did, but she also knew, of course, that in many people's eyes being a vicar put her in a class of women quite different from the norm.

What many overlooked, however, was that underneath her clerical robes she was just like any other. She was a girl who wanted love, companionship, and someone she could rely on.

"No, he's gone to a conference," she replied to Barbara, ignoring the older woman's rapt expression. "'Innovation and Learning in 21st century policing.' He couldn't wait." Annabelle rolled her eyes. Mike hadn't been exactly enthusiastic. She remembered the words "poncy" and "pointless" being used in relation to it. "But I am looking after Molly while he's away."

Despite herself, Annabelle let out a small sigh, and Barbara leaned over to pat her hand. "Don't worry, the time will fly by, dear," she said, her eyes conveying the fact that she knew full well that it wouldn't.

Annabelle sat up straight on the bench. "Oh! It's nothing. I have much too much to be doing. There's a show to put on for starters and many children to corral."

In an instant, she made a resolution. She would find out more about the strange group living in the house at the end of Lolly Lane. It would distract her from the Inspector's absence. She drained her cup. She would keep her plans to herself for the time being. "I'd better get going. We have a rehearsal at two, and those children won't direct themselves. Thank you for the cupcakes, Philippa." Annabelle leaned over, "And the makeup, Barbara."

CHAPTER THREE

After a busy week, the Saturday morning market was once more in full swing. Annabelle wandered from stall to stall, greeting market sellers and customers alike. It made her heart sing to see this centuries-old tradition still running. For many of the locals, their Saturday morning visits to the market were an important part of their week, the trips carefully planned and keenly anticipated by the villagers. The goals to buy fresh produce and meet up with friends were an indelible mark in their weekly routine and forced them to rise early rather than idle their time away with a lie-in.

It was barely ten o'clock, but it was already sweltering. The weather had been unseasonably warm over the past few days, and as much as they longed for sunshine when they didn't have it, the villagers were ready for this hot, humid heatwave to be over.

"I'll be in church tomorrow, Reverend. It'll be the coolest place in town," a stout woman of around fifty said to Annabelle, holding out the neck of her low cut shirt and flapping it vigorously back and forth.

"It's always the coolest place in town, Mrs. Beamish," Annabelle smiled.

She waved to the ladies on the WI stall, but skirted it, mindful of the danger it posed to her waistline. She'd been "good" all week, and she didn't want to mess things up now.

Today she'd eschewed her cassock and was wearing a loose cotton shirt and pants along with her dog collar. While her working robes were inordinately forgiving, Annabelle's "civvies" had been getting tighter in recent months. Now though, she could tell her hard work was paying off. Her clothes were feeling a little looser. She reminded herself of the promise she'd made. A shop in London sold "clergy couture," and she'd vowed to treat herself when she'd lost a few pounds.

"Whoops! Sorry!" Annabelle yelped as she stepped back into the path of old Mrs. Penhaligon.

Mrs. Penhaligon was an elderly lady of, rumor had it, around 95. She was a little stooped as she pushed along her wheeled shopping basket, a prized possession that had been donated to her by the church. Annabelle, keen to help keep the elderly independent and connected to the life of the village, had instigated a fundraising drive to deliver these rolling carts to every villager over the age of seventy. The parish council, urged on by her, had organized bake sales and bingo nights to pay for the carts that were made in Mr. Carrick's workshop on Poldark Street. Mr. Carrick, an enthusiastic, amateur metalworker had volunteered to build the carts. He was a perfectionist, and it hadn't been an easy or inexpensive job, the aging population of the village being the size it was. However, the carts had proven to be indestructible. Annabelle was confident they would easily outlive their owners and secretly, she hoped they would be passed down from generation to generation, making them bargains at their price.

"That's okay, dear. No harm done."

Annabelle waited as Cynthia Turnbull gave her daughter an arithmetic lesson at Mr. Plumber's stall. "The strawberries are

"Julia, stop it. Your plans were so grand."

"It was just a simple donkey sanctuary! A few donkeys! And maybe some moor ponies. Do you know how terrible their life is? There isn't enough food for them in the wild. Some of them are starving to death!" Julia protested. "But of course, Theo could see no use for them and thought they would be a liability and a waste of time."

There was the sound of boots bounding up the steps outside. The door opened with a bang.

"Evening, ladies."

Annabelle turned to see a young, lithe man cross the threshold. He shared the same coloring as Suki, and there was a distinct family resemblance, but where Suki had a world-weary insouciance, her brother had an easy smile and lively, twinkling eyes. He was dressed casually in a button-down shirt, sleeves rolled up to his elbows and faded jeans. He had scuffed cowboy boots on his feet.

Sally beamed when she saw him. She bounded over. "*This* is Theo!" She put her arm around his shoulders. The young man looked at Annabelle and swung his arm proprietorially around Sally's waist. "Hello."

"Theo, this is Reverend Annabelle Dixon from Upton St. Mary, the village down the road. She's come to meet us."

Annabelle stood. His eyes widened, and he held her gaze. He took her hand and bent over, raising her fingers to his lips.

"Charmed, Reverend," he murmured, capturing her again with a direct look as he stood upright.

"Oh, um, nice to meet you, Theo. I thought I'd pay you a visit and welcome you to the area, introduce myself." Theo was certainly dashing, and Annabelle felt herself becoming self-conscious under his gaze. Her face flushed a little.

"You've certainly chosen a wild night to visit us."

"Have I?"

"Haven't the girls told you? Tonight is the night we celebrate the legend of St. Petrie and Lord Darthamort."

"Ah yes, they did mention it. Perhaps you could tell me more about this St. Petrie. I can't say I've heard of him."

"You haven't heard of the legend of St. Petrie and Lord Darthamort?" Theo let go of Sally and pulled out a chair. Annabelle shifted slightly away from him, expecting him to sit next to her, but he put his foot on the seat and leaned on his knee, supporting himself on his forearm. His hand dangled level with her chin, and Annabelle noticed a small, faded tattoo in the crease between his thumb and forefinger.

It was a swastika.

Theo looked down at her. "Legend has it that St. Petrie and his companion, Lord Darthamort, work together to reward the good and punish the bad. Darthamort is a half-goat, half-demon figure that punishes criminals and other unpleasant people, while St. Petrie, a benevolent soul manifested in human form, rewards the good with gold. It's a legend that originated in Bavaria circa 1534. A movement grew up in the early part of the twentieth century that advocated vigilante justice in areas where the local law enforcement was considered inadequate or non-existent. The movement adopted the legend as their rallying point, their message as a manifesto, and the Darthamort and St. Petrie characters as mascots. The movement gained momentum in Europe but faded away as Hitler came to power."

"Oh my, that sounds rather sinister." Annabelle was taken aback.

"Oh, not at all. Today, nothing like a movement exists, of course, but still in Northern Europe, the legend is celebrated with parades and the Darthamortlauf."

"The what?"

"It means the Darthamort run. Young men dressed as Lord Darthamort run through crowds with tiki torches, cracking whips, and scaring small children. It takes place mostly in towns in Germany, Austria, and Switzerland. It's all a bit of fun, really."

"It doesn't sound like it."

"Oh, the crowds only pretend to be scared. They love it, really."

"But how does this relate to you here? We have no such traditions." *Thank goodness.* "Why do you celebrate the legend?"

"The idea of rewarding good while punishing evil is universal, I think we can all agree on that. We don't go in for all that vigilante nonsense, but here at the Brotherhood, we like to perform good deeds and hope to spread good cheer. We stand up against evil when we encounter it. Twice a year we have our own version of the Lord Darthamort run. We'll be doing it tonight, in fact, after dinner. Are you staying to dinner?"

"Oh, I don't know." Annabelle looked about her, flustered.

"Please do, Reverend, we'd love to have you," Sally said.

"Certainly we would. The more the merrier, especially this evening," Theo added. "Have you been given the grand tour yet?"

"No, no, I haven't."

Theo looked at Julia and Sally. "Well, let's leave the girls to work." Julia let out a low growl. "And allow me the honor of showing you around the old house. Dinner should be ready in…?" Theo looked quizzically at Sally.

"About an hour or so."

"Perfect." Theo held out his arm for Annabelle to take and despite her reservations, she found herself swept away by this charming, handsome, charismatic man.

CHAPTER SIX

They were sitting in a cluttered room in the main part of the house. The huge, arched, ornate window at one end framed the early evening summer sun that streamed into the room, exaggerating the caked-on dirt and dust, and bathing them in a warm, hazy glow.

Around the table sat Annabelle and the group members she had met earlier, Sally, Julia, Suki, and Theo. Two other members of the Brotherhood had joined them and were introduced to Annabelle as Thomas and Scott. Margaret was missing. No one mentioned her.

Theo sat at the end of the large oval table in front of the window. He was cast in shadow, the sun behind him creating a golden aura around his silhouette like an enormous halo. Suki and Sally sat on either side of him. Scott and Thomas, who Annabelle recognized as the men she had seen at the market, still had their tiny plaited ponytails, but their knickerbockers had been replaced by regular work pants. Annabelle sat between them.

Theo raised his arms to say grace. As she observed the scene, it struck Annabelle that it looked like a cross between the Last Supper and the Resurrection. The group held hands and closed their eyes, but Annabelle kept hers wide open. Suki caught her eye and winked.

"Let's praise St. Petrie for blessing us with this food."

It was a grace unlike any Annabelle had ever heard.

"Thank you for meeting our physical needs of hunger and thirst. We praise you for the bounty that you provide. Bless this food as we fuel our bodies and our souls so that we may work for the glory of your name. Bless us and the family and friends beside us and the love we share," Theo opened his eyes. "Amen. Let us eat."

"It may look like the River Thames after a bad storm, but it's actually a vegan soup," Suki reassured Annabelle as she passed her a bowl of thick, gray slurry. "It's full of goodness. And quite tasty if you're hungry." She leaned in to whisper, "Best of all, it has virtually no calories."

A salad of rocket leaves and kale topped with orange, red, and green heritage tomatoes lay in a wooden bowl on the table alongside a tray of dense, rustic bread.

"All the results of our own efforts. The hot weather ripened the tomatoes really early this year," Julia told Annabelle, her eyes sparkling.

The soup was surprisingly good and extremely filling. Annabelle chatted to Thomas and Scott on either side of her.

"And what do you do, Thomas?"

"Er, I–I'm a photographer."

Thomas sat silently, his chair set back from the table a little, one pudgy hand placed on his knee as he supported himself, the sleeves of his button-down shirt rolled up to his elbows. There was a slight sheen on his forehead, and he repeatedly pushed his round, rimless glasses higher on his nose while avoiding virtually all eye contact with those around him. His wispy, pale hair was damp from the warm summer evening. He ran a fingertip across his brow.

"What kind of photography do you do?"

"Ohh, m–mostly nature photography. I enjoy roaming the countryside and taking pictures of the animals, the landscape, drops of dew on a leaf, that k-kind of thing." He paused and shot a quick look at Annabelle before continuing, "but I do take typical C-Cornish shots, like the fishing boats and c–cream teas." He paused again, "They're especially popular with the tourists. I sell a lot of postcards of s–scones, j–jam, and," Thomas gathered himself to put extra effort into his final words, "clotted cream."

"And how long have you been with the Brotherhood? I hear you moved down from the north a short while ago."

"A couple of years." Thomas' confidence increased as he spoke, Annabelle's interested expression never straying from his face. He sat up straighter, taking his eyes off his soup to flick glances at her as he spoke. "Ever since my mother went into a h–home." Thomas finished his sentence on a whisper. "She's in her eighties," he said apologetically, trailing off.

"I hope she's happy there."

"I lived with her until I could n–no longer care for her." Thomas looked down at his lap, but sensing that he had a sympathetic listener, lifted his gaze quickly, "We had to sell her house to pay for the home. I was living hand to mouth for a while. Then I bumped into Theo one day while I was out taking pictures, and he offered me a place to stay. He was very kind."

Thomas pulled a photograph from his pocket. It was of a falcon launching off the water with another, smaller bird caught between its claws. "S–sorry for the s–strong subject matter, V-vicar. It was such a s–stunning s–sight. The falcon just s–swooped down and s–scooped the other bird up."

"It is remarkable isn't it? Nature can be brutal, I see it all the time." Annabelle thought back to the children at the most recent rehearsal. "All part of God's holy plan, I suppose. But I have to say, I much prefer pictures of scones and jam and clotted cream. Much more my kind of thing." She smiled at Thomas, who nodded vigorously and once more pushed his glasses up higher on his nose. He took a sip of his soup and the lenses clouded over on the lower rim. He looked at her over the fog.

"I like to do things the old fashioned way. T–trays of developing fluid, stop baths, drying lines, that k–kind of thing. I develop my p–pictures in a room in the east wing. It's very kind of Theo to allow me the space to do that."

"But you contribute to the income of the group, do you not?"

"Well, yes, my p–postcards and greeting c–cards bring in a bit at the local markets, and I occasionally sell large, f–framed p–prints of my wildlife pictures for a decent price."

"Well then, you deserve your space."

Thomas considered Annabelle's point seemingly for the first time. He tucked in his chin. "Perhaps I do," he said, putting a hunk of bread into his mouth and tearing off a big bite.

"And what about you, Scott? What's your story? Where do you come from?" Annabelle turned to the big man on the other side of her. Between his eyes were frown lines that gave him a dark, surly expression, and as he sat hunched over the table, a thick, hairy arm stabbed at his food like he was murdering it. Annabelle thought his behavior unnecessarily violent considering that the meal consisted entirely of plants.

Scott was a blacksmith, and as Annabelle watched him forcefully skewer a misshapen slice of tomato, she questioned the wisdom of his choice of vocation. He didn't seem the sort of person with whom one would want to hang around too often especially if he was wielding a red hot poker in one hand and a hammer in the other.

Before Scott answered her, he picked up his soup bowl with huge, red, scarred hands and drank directly from it. Annabelle waited good-naturedly as he drained his bowl and put it down with a bang, smacking his lips together and wiping his mouth with the back of his hand. Out of the corner of her eye, Annabelle saw Suki looking over at Scott with appreciation at what was obviously, to her, clear evidence of testosterone-fuelled masculinity.

"Not much to tell, Vicar. I'm a traveller by heritage, but my parents tired of the life before I was born. I grew up on a rough estate in East Anglia. I think it's in the bones though, travelling, not wanting to stay in one place. I was in regular work, but Theo came up to me one day at a market in Suffolk and asked if I'd like to join the Brotherhood. I took a bit of persuading but eventually, it seemed like a good idea. I thought that perhaps it'd be a way to see a bit of the country. I've been with them ever since."

"Do you all get along? I mean, with each other?"

"We can get on each other's nerves at times, but we rub along pretty well."

Suki was still staring at Scott. He caught her eye and barely suppressing an eye roll, he turned his head to Annabelle and pointed to her clerical collar.

"Never been much of a churchgoer meself. What are you doing here?"

"Oh, I'm just here to check you out," Annabelle said, widening her eyes. She waggled her head, a smirk flitting across her lips. "Make sure you're on the up and up. Just kidding," she added quickly when she saw Scott's coarse, meaty hands clench and his expression darken. She wondered if there were a bit more than family history behind Scott's decision to take to the road. "I saw Julia and Sally at the market and thought I'd introduce myself. They invited me here to meet you all. Make sure you're not up to no good." She trilled nervously and thumped her fist on her thigh. Scott regarded her curiously, his frown lines deepening.

"I think you'll find us all just yer ordinary folk, keeping themselves to themselves, if you know what I mean."

"Ah, I know exactly what you mean, Scott," Annabelle agreed. "More salad?"

"Yes, please!" Scott said, his eyes lighting up. "I love a good salad."

"I thought you'd be more of a meat man."

"I was until I got here." Scott was tipping up the bowl to scoop the last of the salad onto his plate. "Totally changed what I eat. My diet used to be all meat, preferably wrapped in pastry and washed down with beer. And now here we are in Cornwall, home of the famous Cornish pastie, and I wouldn't touch one of 'em with a barge pole. I love my veg. If she could see me now, my old Ma would be proud as punch and totally confused, 'cuz I couldn't stand them when I was a nipper. I wouldn't mind the odd bit of cheese now and again, though."

Scott didn't say any more, and Annabelle watched him as she ate Julia's tasty coconut curry. She marveled at the odd sight of this beefy, hirsute man shoveling lettuce and tomatoes into his mouth, chomping away with his eyes closed in delirium, until the clanging of a spoon against a mug interrupted her. Theo stood and waited until he had everyone's attention.

"Peace everyone," he addressed the group, as Sally handed out glasses filled with light gold wine. He cast his eyes around. "As you all know, tonight is the celebration of the legend of our saviors, St. Petrie and Lord Darthamort. I hope you are ready for a fabulous evening. The celebration will commence at 9 PM sharp down by the bonfire." Theo looked ahead to Annabelle, "I do hope you will join us, Reverend."

Annabelle raised her eyebrows, surprised by this invitation. She looked around the table and saw that all eyes were on her awaiting her answer.

CHAPTER SEVEN

The others began to bang on the table in a rhythmic, steady beat. Thomas was slapping his knee, Scott was making the plates bounce on the table, Suki picked up her fork and tapped it against her mug. Even Julia drummed her fingertips on the tabletop.

Annabelle put her hands to her ears as the beat got faster and faster until there was a cacophony of thumps and bangs as her fellow diners abandoned their rhythm and pounded randomly with their implements.

Theo stood like a conductor in front of them, his hands aloft, his eyes closed. Drawing his hands together and then quickly apart with a flourish, he gave the command to end the display and immediately, everyone went quiet.

Annabelle let out a huge sigh of relief. The others at the table looked past her, and she turned to see Sally walk in with the biggest crumble she'd ever seen. It dwarfed her rhubarb flan. She leaned over to Thomas and whispered, "What's going on?"

"Th-Theo's just psyching us up for the celebration. He likes them loud. N-None of us are really loud people, if you know what I mean, so he revs us up a bit. Gives us some alcohol to help things along, which of course, because we're usually teetotal, has an immediate effect."

"But what's going to happen?"

"After we've had crumble, we're going to rumble, as we say. We'll go back to our rooms to prepare and then meet outside by the bonfire. Theo will have his "come to Jesus" moment, and then we'll make some noise and dance around a bit. We watch the fire burn out and go to bed around midnight. It's just a bit of harmless fun."

Annabelle looked at the other six people around the table. Sally was dishing out the crumble, and they were passing around the bowls. She noticed Julia reach out and spoon cream on to her pudding.

"What's that?" she asked Thomas.

"Pureed tofu. It's not that bad. Go on, have some. It tastes like sour cream."

"Don't you want your crumble, Vicar?" Scott asked her, eyeing her bowl greedily.

"No, no, thank you. I'm being…good," she replied, not looking at him.

"Mind if I have it?" he asked.

"No, go ahead."

Scott pushed his bowl out of the way and slid Annabelle's over to him. He fell upon it greedily.

Annabelle barely noticed. She was more concerned with the febrile atmosphere that now pervaded the room and everyone around the table. Gone was the quiet murmur of gentle chitchat, and in its place was now laughter, shouts, and the odd backslap. Suki and Sally were arm wrestling. Julia was smiling and jiggling her knees up and down. Thomas was attacking his dessert and letting out loud murmurs of appreciation. Scott finished Annabelle's dessert and began singing to himself while performing a strange dance that looked like a mashup of the

Funky Chicken and the Macarena. They all appeared giddy with anticipation. Annabelle would have thought them roaring drunk except that they'd only had one glass of wine each. There was an air of mania present. Cutting through it all, Theo sat watching her serenely. *What had she got herself into?*

There was a bang from the hallway outside.

"Hey! *Hey!* Where is she? Sally!" yelled a man from the hallway.

The raucous scene quieted immediately. Sally went pale and stood up. As she did so, the door burst open and in came a man, red-faced, unshaven, and rough. He was panting and sweating, wearing an old t-shirt and worn jeans. There were dark shadows under his eyes.

"Sally!"

"Dad, what are you doing here?"

"I've come to get you."

"What? No..."

"You're coming home. With me."

"Dad, I—"

The man strode quickly across the room toward his daughter, his jaw and fists clenched tightly. Theo stood gracefully and put himself between the man and Sally, his hands raised.

"Look, Richard—"

"Get out of my way, you." Richard put his hands on Theo's arm to push him. Theo stood firm.

"You need to listen to your daughter, Richard."

Richard thrust his red, lined face into Theo's smooth, handsome one. "I've *been* listening. I've listened and listened. And the time for that is now over. *You,*" he poked Theo in the chest with his forefinger, "are a menace. A snake. You charm young women, vulnerable women, separating them from their families, stealing their money."

"I haven't stolen anyone's money, sir."

"Not yet you haven't, but you will, given time. That's what

you're all about, you sorts. Breaking up families, gaining the trust of poor saps, leaving nothing but misery and broken relationships behind you." He looked over Theo's shoulder at his daughter as he spoke.

Theo said, "I can assure you that's not what I want nor intend. Sally is free to leave us at any time. It is her right to do as she pleases."

"You've addled her mind!"

"She is an adult, and she has chosen to remain here, sir."

"Only because you've brainwashed her. It's now time for her to come home. She needs to be where her mother and me can d– deprogram her or whatever it is, you've done to her."

"Dad, it's not like that." Sally was pleading.

"We don't brainwash anyone, Richard. Everyone operates from free will here. We come and go as we please. We encourage each other to do so. We are the very opposite of brainwashed." Theo was preternaturally calm, his expression and voice cool and relaxed in the face of the seething, older man. Richard's lips were pulled back as he bared his teeth like a hostile dog.

Scott stood to intervene. He was much larger and threatening than Sally's father, but what Richard lacked in presence, he made up with fury and a father's protective instinct.

"Sit down!" he shouted at Scott. Scott glanced over to Theo. Theo gave a slight nod, and Scott slowly sank back into his chair.

"Richard, we don't want any trouble, but you can't just come in here and kidnap your own daughter."

"Why not? You did!"

"Come on, man, now you're being ridiculous. Calm down, and break some bread with us."

"I'm here to take my daughter home."

"Dad, please. You're embarrassing me."

"Come with me, Sally. Now!"

"It's your choice," Theo said to Sally. "You can stay or go. We will bless you whatever you choose."

No one spoke. The shocked audience watched the drama unfolding in silence.

Sally looked wildly about her. She was blushing furiously, clenching and unclenching her fists. Her gaze flickered between the two men as she considered her choice.

"No, Dad. As I've said before, I'm staying here. You can't make me. I'm not a little girl anymore."

Richard growled and took a step closer. Theo put his hand on the man's chest. Richard slapped it away. Scott stood then and walked over. He grabbed Richard's arm, his bulk and menace acting as a brake to prevent a fight breaking out.

"You heard what she said. I think it better that you leave." Scott's voice rumbled low and quietly in his East Anglian burr.

Richard glared at Scott. He looked back at Sally, who had turned her back on her father and was being comforted by Julia.

Richard turned to Theo, "You, you are a coward and a psychopath! I will get you for this, taking my daughter away from me, upsetting her mother!" He spun on his heels to leave, but quickly swirled back, and taking Theo and Scott by surprise, managed to land a left hook that knocked Theo to the ground.

Scott grabbed Richard by the arms and bundled him backwards, pinning him against the wall, the two men's faces just inches apart. Theo struggled to his feet, gingerly feeling his jaw. "Leave him. Just be on your way, Richard. You've no business here."

Richard shrugged himself out of Scott's grasp. "I'm going, I'm going. But I *will* get you." Richard furiously pointed his finger at Theo before stumbling out of the room, closely followed by Scott. A moment later, they heard the entrance door clang shut, and the atmosphere in the room relaxed, but only slightly.

Sally ran from the room, sobbing. Suki followed her. Theo let out a sigh. "Perhaps we should move again," he said, sitting down slowly.

"We can't do that!" It was Thomas. Theo looked at him in

surprise. "I—I like it here," Thomas added quietly, looking down at the table.

Theo shrugged, "We may have to if he keeps on pestering us." Thomas, his eyes downcast, quietly picked up his spoon and resumed eating his dessert.

Julia reached into her pocket and pulled out Barnaby. She put him on the table. Even the little rabbit seemed wary, not straying far from his owner, despite the remnants of salad that were left at the other end of the table.

CHAPTER EIGHT

Annabelle sat on Sally's bed in her messy room. Fallen plaster had left holes in the walls and the air smelled of damp. The tremendously high ceilings were draped with cobwebs. Despite this, Sally had made it as "girly" and presentable as she could. Nets covered the heavy faded curtains, and old Christmas tree lights had been hung across the pelmet and around the room. On her bed, Sally had laid a quilt made of bright, randomly colored, eight-inch squares. There were also a myriad of pillows and cushions at its head. It was a dark room, but the evening summer sunlight streamed through the window, dust motes bouncing along on invisible currents of air, birds chirruping outside as they prepared for dusk to fall. It was hot, and the atmosphere in the shabby room was stifling.

Sally leaned forward on a rickety wooden chair in front of a mirror, distorted, and spotted with age. She was putting on theatrical makeup, painting black swooping eyebrows that extended way beyond her natural ones. A mask stretched across her eyes and nose. It was white, and she had painted on it silver, purple, and black tiny furls that curled and uncurled in intricate patterns across it. The design extended to her eyebrows and temples. She had painted directly onto her skin with tiny brushes so that the line between mask and skin was barely discernable. Annabelle marveled at her patience. The odd slick of lipstick was about all she could manage and even then it was rather a hit and miss affair.

"Does everyone go to this trouble?"

"Oh no, Julia will wear her mask plain. Suki might show up and ask me to paint her, it depends."

"What about the others? The men? What do they do?" After the scene in the dining room, Annabelle had felt obliged to stay. She had comforted Sally and watched her as her emotions stilled, her art calming her. Now her hands were steady, her eyes clear, and her brush strokes firm and confident.

"The men will wear different masks. The women represent St. Petrie, goodness, peace, happiness. They are the light. The men dress up as Lord Darthamort. They represent justice, the punishment of all that is dark and evil."

"Two sides of the same coin."

"Exactly. Because Lord Darthamort is half-goat, half-man, the masks are more like headdresses. They are furry, bear-like. They cover their heads entirely, and they have real fur, feathers, horns, and teeth! The boys make them themselves from roadkill and the dead animals we find."

"That's quite something," Annabelle said. Sally looked in her mirror at Annabelle's reflection. "For vegans, I mean. Don't they object to putting something like that on their heads?"

"They don't. The masks are quite scary, and I think the boys enjoy the opportunity to let loose. They really get into character. Well, Thomas doesn't, but Theo and Scott do. You'll see."

"I'm not sure I want to find out."

"Oh, it's fine. It's just a bit of fun! Just a group of grown-up kids, yelpin' and a-hollerin' around a bonfire."

There was a knock on the door, and Suki floated in. Her feet were bare. Pinned into her hair were small, white, star-shaped flowers.

"Your hair looks lovely," Sally said.

"Thank you. Jasmine smells so divine, I thought I'd carry it around with me. My hair seemed the perfect place for it." Suki brushed a tendril of her fine, pale hair from her face. "Would you do my makeup, darling?"

Sally got up from her chair. She turned it to the window, gesturing for Suki to sit down. With the tip of her finger, she tilted Suki's chin upward. On the table next to her was an array of make-up, brushes, and applicators. Sally dropped a fine brush into a tumbler of water, and then she dipped it into a tiny glass jar before leaning in and getting to work.

With her jaw set in concentration, she painted in silence with the exception of gentle murmured instructions to Suki to look down or tilt her head to one side or the other. Suki, mindful that even the tiniest movement could spell disaster, did exactly as she was told and remained silent.

When Sally finally stepped back, Annabelle was amazed at the result. Unlike Sally, Suki wasn't wearing a mask at all. Sally had painted directly onto her face.

She had enveloped Suki's eyes in silver paint. It reached across her upper and lower lids, winging out to her temples, into the corners of her eye sockets, and down her nose ending in sharp points. In the middle of her forehead, she had painted a shining blue orb. Directly above Suki's eyebrows and at the outer edges of her eyelids, were blue and purple flowers. They added color and a sense of glamor. All these elements were joined by sweeping black lines that swooped and swirled in complex lattice patterns around Suki's eyes, showing off her clear, sky-blue irises. The black swirls continued across her nose, forehead, and down to the apples of her cheeks. Glitter and tiny sparkling jewel-colored rhinestones finished off the effect. It was masterful, mysterious, and Annabelle had to admit, rather alluring.

"Golly, that's incredible!" she exclaimed.

"Would you like me to do you?" Sally asked.

"Oh, um, well, um..."

"It washes straight off."

Annabelle looked at the two brightly colored, glamorous women and then at her plain, unadorned reflection in the black spotted mirror.

"Oh, go on then. It can't hurt, just this once," she said, shutting out the negative voice in her head that sounded suspiciously like Philippa's.

Thirty minutes later, Annabelle had her own mask. Hers was lighter, brighter, and more colorful than Suki's. In addition to black swooping lines, Sally had blended yellow powder across Annabelle's nose and cheeks. Red, purple, and blue shades curved in a "C" shape from the ends of her eyebrows to the middle of her cheekbones. Light blue had been stroked across her brow bones along with lilac and pink. Sally had traced the black lines with gold dots which gave the decoration a three dimensional effect. In the middle of Annabelle's forehead was a silver rhinestone surrounded by six smaller ones. Sally had finished her eyes off with smoky gray and brown eye shadow, eyeliner, and lashings of mascara, tilting Annabelle's chin to the light so she could apply it accurately.

Sally stood back, and Annabelle blinked rapidly several times in succession. She wasn't used to wearing eye makeup. She looked in the mirror at her reflection.

"Ohhhhhh," Annabelle could hardly believe who was looking back at her. "Ohhhhhh," she repeated, stunned. "It looks absolutely beautiful. Thank you." She turned her head to the right and left, examining Sally's work. "Gosh, is that really me?" She leaned in closer to examine the fine detail of Sally's work. The black, gold, pinks, yellow, and blues made her eyes sparkle and pop, while her long, black eyelashes framed them so they looked bigger and appealing.

"Let's take a selfie!" Suki said.

Before Annabelle could grasp what was happening, Suki and Sally had crowded around her. Suki held out her phone and took one photo after another, adjusting the angles, as she pouted and posed like an experienced model.

"Here, let's take Annabelle on her own. It's not every day a vicar gets to look like this. There has to be evidence!"

Suki and Sally moved away from Annabelle as quickly as they'd moved in, and Suki took more pictures, pressing the button on her phone repeatedly.

"Smile, Annabelle, smile!"

Annabelle smiled shyly. She felt a little awkward. "Throw your hair back, girlfriend! Flick it! Go on!"

"Well, I, er, don't norm— Oh, what the heck," Annabelle tossed her head and twisted her shoulders sideways to the camera in poses she'd seen the other two women hold.

"That's it!" Suki called out, snapping away. "You can even pout, you know, push those lips out. Show us what you've got."

"Thank you," Annabelle said, standing up. "But I think that's enough, now."

"We've got to go, Sukes. It's nearly time," Sally said. "Is your mother joining us?" Sally tossed a white shift over her head and stepped into a pair of white slip-ons.

"Good grief, no. You know what she's like. Wouldn't be seen dead at such a thing. Give me your phone number, Annabelle. I'll text these to you."

The voice that sounded suspiciously like Philippa's was starting to gain momentum in Annabelle's head. She was feeling a little uncomfortable about what had just happened, but she gave Suki her number. Her phone pinged as the photos arrived.

"You go ahead, I'll catch up," Annabelle said. The two women hurried out of the door.

She sat down and opened up Suki's text. She had sent

Annabelle five photos, two of the three of them, three of Annabelle on her own.

Annabelle scrolled back and forth between them, admiring Sally's work, and marveling at the glamor it bestowed upon all the women, but unsure it was entirely fitting for a woman of the cloth. There was one photo that caught her eye in particular. It was one of her by herself, a close-up, spontaneous. Her hair was back off her face, she must have just "flicked it." She was looking at a point beyond the camera from one side, her mouth curved in just a hint of a smile. The light of the room had combined with the colorful makeup to enhance the natural bright blue of her eyes and the pleasing contours of her face. Even Annabelle could see she looked quite lovely, radiant. A well of pride grew in her chest.

"Roger. I'll send it to Roger, he lives far enough away." Her brother lived on a remote Scottish island with his daughter. "Bonnie will find it fun, too."

CHAPTER NINE

The bonfire raged in the middle of a clearing in the woods, far away from the house. Yellow flames licked and wrapped their way around the logs, branches, leaves, and twigs that the members of the Petrie Brotherhood had collected from the estate in the days prior. Sparks shot into the air, glowing brightly against the black and blue sky as they rose, burning themselves out of existence on their downward arc. Lanterns hung from the trees, and lines of sparkling lights were strewn between them.

The group held hands in a line by the fire. The heat warmed their faces, the smell of smoke filled their nostrils, and in Thomas' case, made him sneeze. The group swayed from side to side in unison, their eyes closed. They were humming quietly.

Annabelle felt her skin prickle. The huge bonfire continued to crackle and pop. She worried the fire might spread. Everything was so dry that it wouldn't take much more than a single spark. The oppressive atmosphere of earlier had lifted, but the heat of the day hadn't dissipated. In the distance, she heard a low rumble of thunder.

She sat on the stump of a tree some yards away. She had declined to take part in the ceremony, choosing to take the role of observer. Sally, Suki, and Julia were all dressed in white, their masks partially obscuring their faces, while Thomas and Scott wore fearsome headgear made from a patchwork of matted, dark gray and brown fur. Large, hooked plastic noses protruded from below the eyes that were small and beady on one mask, glowing and green on the other. Real, crusty horns curled outward while wide, grinning mouths revealed many tiny, sharp teeth. Human eyes could be seen peering from behind them. Pheasant feathers fanned around the necks and flared out across the shoulders, the rich, speckled shades of brown and rust adding some beauty, but not enough to offset the hideousness.

The bodies of the two men were clothed in brown fur. At their feet were wooden clubs and long leather whips. They looked fiendish, grotesque, devastating.

The group in front of the fire was getting louder now, swaying more wildly, their eyes closed. They dropped hands and moved apart. Scott picked up a drum made from animal skin stretched across a wooden barrel. He began to thump it slowly, creating a low, steady, beat. Suki banged a stick against a huge metal triangle. Julia strummed a tiny banjo. It was a cacophony of tuneless, random sounds.

Barnaby poked out from Julia's pocket, his little head popping up shyly before bobbing out of sight again. Sally and Thomas continued to sway to the music, Thomas moving self-consciously. Even though the men were clad head to foot in costume, their movements gave them away. Scott, for all his bulk had rhythm, while Thomas had none at all.

Deep in the trees, a man's voice boomed. It was Theo. He was suspended high up in a tree, standing on a platform. He still had on the shirt and jeans he had been wearing earlier. By his feet was a Darthamort mask.

At the sound of his voice, the others stopped their noise.

They stood still, waiting as Theo, his feet apart, held a large, smoked glass bowl high in front of him, chanting something Annabelle couldn't quite hear. In his hand, he held a suede baton. A deep, booming note resounded from the bowl as he hit it gently. It vibrated in the air, the sound getting louder as the seconds passed before the note eventually faded away.

Theo set aside the bowl and cupped his hands around his mouth to shout over the noise of the crackling fire.

"Dear followers, we gather here to celebrate St. Petrie and his brother, Lord Darthamort. We honor their blessings and worship their souls. We praise them, praise all living things who show us what it is to be sentient beings, of what is good and right." Theo dropped his hands and looked down. He caught sight of Annabelle and smiled. He raised one hand to his mouth again and gestured to her with his other.

"We are further blessed this evening by the presence of the mighty Reverend Annabelle Dixon."

Annabelle shifted awkwardly on the tree trunk, uncomfortable at being incorporated into this strange ritual and unsure where it was leading.

"Her presence is a sign that further demonstrates we are on the right path."

Annabelle sat bolt upright. She started to object, raising her arm, pointing a finger skyward. "Hey, I say, that's—"

But Theo carried on.

He raised his face to the now dark, starless sky, his arms outstretched, his eyes closed.

"Join us, join us, Lord Darthamort, St. Petrie. Guide us, your faithful servants to your glory. Praise be, praise the Lord, Lord Darthamort. Amen."

Annabelle jumped up indignantly and stood on the tree stump. "Stop! Stop!" she shouted, but her voice was drowned out by a bone-shaking roll of thunder. The sky lit up as a streak of lightning tore across it.

The group around the bonfire yelled in unison, "Praise be! Praise the Lord! Lord Darthamort! Amen!" They each reached down and threw something into the fire. In the darkness, Annabelle couldn't see clearly, but she caught sight of a shadowy shape projected against the backlight of the flames. Horseshoes. They were throwing horseshoes. As they released them into the fire, the group ran, scattering into the trees, whooping, screaming, and yelling. Annabelle watched them wide-eyed, her fists clenched. She was left alone by the bonfire. Another flash of lightning split the sky.

There was a roar at her shoulder, and she screamed. She leapt off the tree stump and stepped back. Bright green eyes shone back at her, white teeth standing out in the gloom. There was a cackle, a voice she recognized as Scott's before he ran away, roaring back into the trees.

Annabelle, unwilling to be caught off-guard again, looked quickly in all directions. A woman's shriek pierced the air followed by a laugh. Annabelle wondered if she were being silly. Perhaps she needed to lighten up. She started to walk into the woods.

Every few yards, young, spindly saplings were interspersed with older trees, their large brown trunks providing good coverage and hiding places. Annabelle weaved in and out, catching sight of flashes of white while hearing footsteps and rustling, roars and squeals, as the shadowy hunters and their pale prey ran between trees and behind bushes. The sounds of leather slapped against trees snapped through the air. Annabelle lurched toward the sounds, rebounding through the trees like a pinball in a game that was permanently in play. Disoriented, she stumbled as flashes of lightning and rumbles of thunder continued to clash violently overhead.

A Darthamort figure ran up to her, roaring feet from her face, whipping his leather rope on the ground and slicing fallen leaves in two. This time, Annabelle didn't balk at this attempt at intimidation. She smartly stepped aside behind a tree trunk putting distance between them, hiding her fear beneath an upturned chin and quick footwork. Her assailant cracked his whip and roared once more before running off.

She'd had just about enough of this. Philippa was right. This was a silly, mischievous joke at best, an evil, manipulative stunt dressed up as an honorable, fervent ritual at worst. She thought back to the scene with furious Richard Venables. Perhaps Theo was the kind of person to prey on souls who were looking for redemption. Perhaps Theo targeted them and led them astray.

Annabelle stalked through the woods toward Lolly Lane. The ground underfoot was bumpy and covered with low brush. More than once, her feet were ambushed and ensnared by tough, wiry vines like animals in a trap. Driven by her desire to get home to safety, warmth, and comfort, she blindly pressed on. Branches brushed her face, startling her. She pushed them aside.

Finally, when she could no longer hear the roars and screams through the trees, she saw the lights of the Hamilton's and Cuddy's homes. Thank goodness, not too much longer now. Ooof!

Annabelle flew through the air. She landed on her front with a thud. She closed her mouth too late and gasping, spitting leaves and dirt, she pushed herself to her hands and knees to see what had caused her to fall.

She could see a shadowy outline behind her and gingerly put out her hand to pat the lump. It was soft but inert. She felt fur, rough, wiry, sharp even. She felt tiny, hard, jagged teeth. Her eyes widened in the dark as she attempted to see what she was feeling and frantically moved her hands around, patting the features she could feel under her fingertips. When she felt the bony curves of two horns, she jumped to her feet with a yelp.

Above her, there was another flash of lightning, illuminating the sight in front of her before it all went black again. Annabelle sat down on the ground. She could no longer see what faced her, but she knew what was there. For in the second of light that the storm had provided, she had clearly seen what had brought her down. She now sat next to a gruesome sight, a man's body lying on the forest floor, his arms outstretched. Before the darkness prevailed again, she had noticed a small, black mark in the center of his chest.

Annabelle leaned over to wrestle off his headgear as another streak of lightning lit her up from above. Large, fat raindrops plopped down onto the man's face. He didn't flinch. His face had settled into a different kind of mask. As the light disappeared again, Annabelle peered around, looking for help, a clue, anything. She listened, hoping to hear noises above the sounds of the thunder, but she heard nothing. Even the squeals and the cracks of whips had ceased.

She sat back on her haunches, covering the man's wound with her hands, willing for there to be movement beneath them.

But in the woods, among the trees and the animals, under the black, oppressive sky, Theo Westmoreland lay quite dead, as though in sacrifice to the saviors he worshiped.

For there could be no doubt, the placement of his wound was too precise.

Theo had been brutally murdered.

CHAPTER TEN

Annabelle dropped her head to pray, but behind her bushes rustled. Her heart jumped. She turned toward the sound to see Thomas, a camera on a strap around his neck. He was no longer in costume, and as he raised his camera to his face, light from his flash lit up the scene before him.

"Reverend—" he stopped abruptly. "What's going on?" His voice rose to a falsetto on the last syllable.

"Theo has come a cropper," Annabelle said, her voice shaking.

Thomas crouched. "Is he d–dead?" his hand hovering over Theo's body.

"Looks to me like he was shot, once through the chest. Probably killed him instantly." Annabelle looked at Thomas carefully.

Thomas' hand continued to hover above Theo's body. His breathing was heavy.

"Who c–could have done this?" he said.

"We must call the police. And gather up the others."

"Listen, it's q–quiet now. The rain m–must have sent them indoors. They'll be sheltering inside."

Annabelle punched 999 into her phone. "Police, please." She was put through. "I'd like to report a suspicious death." She gave the details to the operator and hung up.

"What should we do n–now?" Thomas asked her.

"Well, I need to stay with the body until the police arrive. You could go up to the house."

"If I do that, I'll h–have to tell them what happened. I don't think I could do that, Vicar."

"Fair enough. Let's put that off until we have to."

They moved over to a fallen tree and sat next to one another to wait. The tops of the trees above them were providing good cover against the rain, but slowly and steadily their clothes became plastered to their bodies and their hair.

"You're wearing regular clothes," Annabelle said. "What happened to your costume?"

"What? Oh, I took my c–costume off as soon as we ran into the trees. I always do that. I've no interest in running around roaring, chasing people, scaring them. Not my th–thing at all."

"So what have you been doing?"

"What I always do, Reverend." He grasped his camera. "P–pictures. I got some great night shots, especially of the s–storm."

They heard a shout and the sounds of people walking through brush. Leaves parted, and Sally and Scott appeared a few yards away, beams of light from flashlights illuminating their path. Sally had removed her mask, Scott had dispensed with his headdress but not his costume. Annabelle jumped up, putting her hands to her face to protect her eyes as the light from Scott's torch immediately found her.

"Have you seen Theo?" Sally asked. "He hasn't turned up at the house." It must have been raining hard beyond the trees, because both Scott and Sally were drenched. Strings of hair framed Sally's face and her white skirt clung.

"Yes, um…"

Sally took a step toward Annabelle.

"Don't come any further, Sally!"

"What is it? What have you got there?" Sally peered around Annabelle at the figure on the floor.

"Is that—? Is that— Theo! Oh, my gosh! Theo!"

She lurched forward, but Scott grabbed her. Sally struggled against him, but he held her firmly around her waist.

"I'm very sorry," Annabelle's voice was gentle.

"Is he dead, Vicar?" Scott's voice was gruff.

"I'm afraid he is."

The sound of Sally's wail rose as she sagged against Scott, who struggled to hold her upright.

"We're waiting for the police. They'll be here soon."

"Who found him, Reverend?" Scott asked, his voice still low and hoarse.

"I did. I tripped over him on my way back to my car."

Sally let out another wail.

"Calm down, Sally lass," Scott urged her. Sally pulled herself furiously out of Scott's grasp and sat cross-legged on the ground among the leaves. She put her head in her hands like a petulant child before exclaiming, "Oh, but what about Suki? And Margaret? They need to know. We must tell them! Oh poor, poor Theo!" Sally looked at Scott frantically.

"They mustn't come down here. It's a potential crime scene," Annabelle said.

"A crime scene?"

"He may have been killed deliberately. Shot," Thomas said, provoking another wail from Sally.

Scott put his hands on his head. "No, no, no."

"You must keep the others away, Scott," Annabelle reiterated.

He nodded. "I'll make sure they stay up at the house."

"I'll come with you," Thomas said. He helped Sally up, took her other side, and the three of them stumbled their way back through the trees, leaving Annabelle alone in the woods with the body once more.

She shivered and looked around. She scrubbed at her face with a mixture of leaves and grass, hoping to remove the makeup, which now seemed wholly inappropriate, from her face. Her phone pinged. She looked down. It was a text from Mike. He'd sent her a photo of the dogs lying by the fire in her cottage. He'd taken it the day before he left for his conference. She smiled.

What are you doing?

She looked over at Theo's body.

Sitting in the woods with a dead body for company.

She pressed the back button repeatedly before retyping her message.

Just sitting around. You?

Finished my homework. Ready for tomorrow's session on The Role of Counter-Drones in Rural and Community Policing. Bound to be riveting. Now to bed. Early start.

Good night, Mike. Sleep tight.

You too, Annabelle. Don't do anything I wouldn't do.

Annabelle pursed her lips in a rueful smile.

I'll try not to.

She put the phone down and waited. She could hear the wail of sirens in the far distance.

CHAPTER ELEVEN

The police detective striding toward Annabelle wasn't Mike. That was for sure. He was older, sturdier, and he wore a trilby hat.

He did wear the same trench coat, however. Annabelle wondered if the dark gray raincoat came with the job as part of the uniform. She watched the policeman nervously. She felt a little shaken and mistrustful and disoriented, unable to discern who was friend and who was foe. However, she was glad the loneliness of waiting had been replaced by the bustle of a murder investigation in full swing.

The detective stood in front of her, his feet apart, his arms folded. "So, you're the local vicar? The one who found the body?" His voice was gravelly, his eyes unfriendly. He looked her up and down, and Annabelle wondered if her attempts at removing her makeup had been successful.

"Yes, that's right, Inspector...?"

"Chief Inspector. Ainslie, Brian Ainslie."

"We normally get Inspector Nicholls."

"Get a lot of murders around here do you?" Ainslie squinted

at Annabelle. "Nicholls is away, so you've got me for your troubles. Now tell me, Vicar, what do you know?"

The Chief Inspector got out a notebook and pencil, an increasingly rare sight. Even Mike had upgraded to a tablet after Annabelle pointed out he'd spend less time behind a desk if he did. "You don't use a tablet, Chief Inspector?"

"Nope. When I was in the field, back in the day, paper and pen did me alright. And they'll do me fine once again."

Annabelle waited as he licked the end of his pencil and readied himself to write down her words.

"Now, how did you come to find the body?"

"I tripped over it as I was making my way back to my car. It was, is, parked in Lolly Lane. I couldn't see well in the dark, and oof, there he was."

"Hmph. You seem very calm about it."

"When you're in my line of work, Chief Inspector, you see all sorts. This isn't, unfortunately, my first murder investigation."

Ainslie stared at her, narrowing his eyes. "Seems a strange place for a vicar to be at this time of an evening. What were you doing here? Were you part of...with these...*people*?" He waved in the direction of the big house behind him. In the distance, she could see the remains of the bonfire that earlier had been fierce, flaming. Only glowing embers remained.

"The group, the Brotherhood, invited me to their celebration."

"The who? The what?"

"The Brotherhood of St. Petrie. That's what they call themselves. The people who live in the big house."

"The Brotherhood of...? What on earth's that when it's at home?"

"That's what I was here to find out, Chief Inspector. It seems they live here in a sort of commune under the auspices of doing good in their local community. I came to find out more about them. They've been wandering through the village and putting the wind up the locals a little."

"Is that so? In what way exactly?"

"Oh, they just chat, give out flowers, sell a few things. Nothing harmful. They're strangers though, and the villagers are always suspicious of strangers, especially when they act and dress so differently. You know how it is in small communities."

"More of a city man, meself."

Annabelle relayed to the Chief Inspector everything she'd learned about the group including a description of the ceremony they had performed earlier.

"A bunch of weirdos, then."

"Well, I wouldn't—"

"And this chap," the detective thumbed in the direction of Theo's body. It had been covered with a white tent. "What do you know about him?"

"Nothing really. He seemed charming, a little fervent perhaps, a little manipulative, but relatively harmless."

"Any enemies?"

"Really, I have no idea, Chief Inspector. I only met him a few hours ago."

The detective wrote her words down, ending his writing with a decisive flourish and looked up.

"Hmph, right Vicar. That will be all for now. You may go up to the house and wait there until my sergeant has taken your statement. It seems clear to me that the murderer must be one of the people out here at the time, and seeing as you were one of them, you can't be discounted."

"Excuse me, Chief Inspector! Are you saying that I am a suspect?"

"Can't rule you out, Vicar. You have no alibi, so you will just have to wait it out in the house until we're through. I'm sure it's nothing, but for now, please humor me."

The flaps on the white tent parted, and out stepped the local pathologist, Harper Jones. She spoke to a constable standing guard who pointed over to Annabelle and the detective. She acknowledged them with a tip of her chin and walked over.

"Good evening, Chief Inspector, Reverend," she said looking at them both before addressing Ainslie. "Harper Jones, I'm the local bones." They shook hands. "Reverend?"

"I found the body," Annabelle said simply.

"What can you tell us, Dr. Jones?" Ainslie interjected.

Harper swung her gaze from Annabelle to Ainslie and gave her summary report without pausing for breath.

"He was shot through the chest from close range. Death would have been instantaneous. The wound is unusual, though. Not the typical shotgun wound that you'd expect in these parts."

"Time of death? He was seen around 10 PM, and then this vicar lady here found him shortly afterward."

"That sounds about right. I'll have more for you in the morning. We'll remove the body now. We're done here."

Harper gave Annabelle a warning look, "Take care of yourself, Reverend," before walking away, peeling off her paper coverall as she walked to her car.

Annabelle hesitated, but seeing the Chief Inspector looking at her squarely made her realize she had no option but to follow Harper away from the crime scene and carry on up to the house.

CHAPTER TWELVE

Margaret Westmoreland was sitting in the same deckchair on the steps outside the kitchen much as Annabelle had found her earlier except that now her hair was rumpled and she looked as though she had aged ten years. It was dark, the only light being the red glow from the end of a cigarette as Margaret pulled on it, her hands shaking. The rain had stopped. Theo's mother clutched a coat around her. On the ground next to her sat Suki wearing an oversized cardigan, the long sleeves of which she used to wipe her face as tears streamed down it silently. Her head was in her mother's lap. Margaret stroked her daughter's hair and stared blankly ahead.

"I'm so terribly sorry for your loss, Margaret," Annabelle said. Margaret didn't look at her but waved her cigarette around, causing flakes of smoldering ash to fly into the air.

Suki lifted her head. "Who could have done this, Annabelle?" she cried. "Th–Theo was a friend to everyone."

Sally's father wasn't too keen on him.

Margaret dragged on her cigarette. She had an empty tumbler in her hand. On the floor next to her was a bottle of gin.

It was almost empty. Margaret picked it up by the neck and unsteadily sloshed what was left into her glass.

"Get me some ice, would you?" She waved the tumbler at Annabelle. Annabelle ignored Margaret's impertinence and took it from her, went into the kitchen and over to the fridge. She opened the icebox and picked out the ice cube tray, holding it over the glass as she popped out a couple of cubes into it.

"What did you tell the police?" Margaret asked when Annabelle came outside again. It was cooler now that the storm had moved on but still warm enough to sit outside comfortably despite it being nearly midnight.

"I told them what I saw, that I was observing the ritual, and that everyone disappeared into the woods. I didn't hear anything except people yelling and screaming. And I didn't see anything that would pertain to...to Theo's death."

"That stupid legend." Margaret jabbed her cigarette into the ashtray perched on the stone balustrade next to her and lit another. "Someone was always going to get hurt. All that heightened emotion, running around, and screaming, and those ridiculous masks offering anonymity. It was asking for trouble."

"But Mama, the others said that Theo had been shot!" Suki looked wildly at Annabelle. "Shot! We don't have any guns. How could it have happened?" Suki stopped. "Perhaps it was a poacher? Someone shooting rabbits. That could be it. It could, couldn't it, Annabelle?"

Annabelle seriously doubted it, but the alternative was to point out that Theo had been murdered and probably by one of the people he lived among.

"The police will find out who did it, Suki. I'm quite sure of that."

"Hmph," Margaret squinted as she pulled again on her cigarette but made no other comment.

Annabelle decided to leave them with their grief and ventured into the house to find the others. She could hear the sounds of Sally still wailing. She found a bathroom and splashed water on her face, washing off the remnants of makeup still left there. Her earlier antics seemed foolish now.

The police had commandeered the former drawing room as their interview suite. Two police constables that Annabelle didn't recognize stood at the doorway. Inside, she found Sally being comforted by Scott who still had his arm around her shoulders. Sally was leaning with her elbows on her knees, her hands covering her face as she sobbed into them. Thomas came up to Annabelle as she walked in the room.

"She's very upset."

"Yes, I can see. Perhaps I can help."

Thomas stepped aside, and Annabelle crouched down next to Sally. "I'm so sorry, Sally. This is terribly difficult. I know you held Theo in very high regard."

"I *loved* him!" Sally raised her head from her hands. "Oh, he didn't love me, but that doesn't matter now. I *adored* him."

Scott started, but he didn't take his eyes off her, merely clasping one of her hands that were now in her lap scrunching a crumpled tissue.

"Who could have done this? Who?" Sally repeated. "He was one of the nicest, most charming, most compassionate men you could ever meet. He couldn't have been kinder to me when I first arrived. He was always willing to help out in the kitchen, and he was so clever. He did all the accounts!"

Annabelle kept her expression neutral. "It *is* truly devastating, Sally. I'm sure the police will do all they can to find out who did this."

Sally looked into Annabelle's eyes. "Do you think, oh my gosh, do you think it was my *dad*?" Both Thomas and Scott looked away, but Annabelle held Sally's gaze. "I don't know. I'm sure the police will question him and get to the truth." She turned to Scott. "Do you know where Richard went, Scott? After you led him out?"

Keeping one arm around Sally, Scott spread his other hand wide. "No idea. I watched him stumble down the driveway and into the woods." Sally gave a little squeal and hid her face in her hands once again. "After he disappeared, I came back inside."

"D–Do you know...Was he really shot?" Sally said.

"It looks like he was, yes."

Relief flooded Sally's face, her shoulders relaxed. "Well, there you are then. It couldn't have been Dad. He doesn't know how to use a gun. I doubt he's ever even held one." She stopped squeezing her tissue for a moment. "But if it wasn't Dad, then who was it?" She started working the tissue again. "I mean, if it wasn't him, it could have been one of us?" Sally looked at the two men in turn. Scott was still sitting next to her, but now he was leaning forward, his feet apart, his elbows on his thighs. Thomas stood a few feet away, leaning against the large stone fireplace, his hands in his pockets.

Sally jumped up, a look of fear and disgust on her face. "I'm not sitting here. I'm leaving. Who knows what kind of monster I'm sharing this house with?"

"You'll do no such thing, ma'am," a commanding female voice boomed. A tall, slim woman with cropped blond hair walked into the room. She was wearing a gray, short-sleeved t-shirt over a white long-sleeved one, and black cargo pants. She looked fit, sharp, and trim. Annabelle's first thought was to wonder how she could wear cargo pants and still look stylish. She had tried on a pair once and her image in the changing room mirror had come back to her via her nightmares. Accompanying the policewoman were Julia, Suki, and Margaret.

"You're all to stay here. This is a crime scene, and until we find out who committed this heinous act, Chief Inspector Ainslie has instructed that you are to stay on the estate," the woman said in a South London accent.

"What? Even me?" The words were out before Annabelle registered she was saying them.

The woman eyed Annabelle. "Yes, even you."

"But this is The Reverend Annabelle Dixon from St. Mary's in the village," Suki said. "Surely, you can't think..."

The woman looked Annabelle up and down. Annabelle felt the color rise in her cheeks. The woman's face remained implacable, however, and it was clear Suki's entreaty would have no effect.

"Look, my name is Scarlett Lawrence. I'm the sergeant running this case with Chief Inspector Ainslie, and if he says you're all to stay here, then you're all to stay here, got it?"

Everyone except Margaret nodded.

"Now, I'm going to call you over and take your statements one by one. When I've done you, you're free to leave the room, but you have to stay in the house, alright?"

"But what should we do, Sergeant?" Suki lamented. She sighed, standing on one foot, wrapping the other around her ankle. She tilted her head.

The woman rolled her eyes. "It's late. Go to bed. That's what I would do. Now, hand me your phones. You'll get them back when the Chief says so."

Amid much muttering and sighing, the seven of them handed their phones over. Sergeant Lawrence dragged an old chair over to a table in the corner of the room. As they waited to be called, they sat in silence some yards away on faded, dusty couches, except for Thomas, who stood looking out of the window over the lawn and the woods beyond.

Margaret sat stoic and upright on a *chaise longue*, the fabric of which depicted, if one looked closely, scenes of the hunt; a fox chased by hounds and red-coated men on horseback. Next to her, Suki, still dressed in diaphanous white, held her hand. Across from them on an equally faded, pale green couch sat Sally. She looked exhausted and desolate. Next to her was Scott. He looked down at his lap, his lips pursed, his arms folded. Julia perched stiffly on the edge of the couch next to him.

Annabelle stood next to the fireplace looking at the forlorn group around her, her arms behind her back. It was not a happy scene.

One by one, Sergeant Lawrence called them over and took down their statements. After they had read and signed them, each person filed out of the room without speaking or looking back.

Only Annabelle stayed. Despite her efforts, she fell into a doze on the couch. She awoke sometime later when there was a bang and a clang, as a door was pushed open and left to close under its own weight. Chief Inspector Ainslie stormed in, his bulk creating its own updraft.

"Okay, give the Vicar her phone back, and she can go," he said to his sergeant. He thumbed at Annabelle. "I spoke to Nicholls. He vouched for her."

With her back to them, Annabelle's eyes widened at the sound of Mike's name. Her heart swelled a little. Ainslie walked around to her. "You can go home, Vicar. But make sure you check in with us tomorrow, okay? We're close to arresting someone, and you're not out of the woods yet." He chuckled at his little joke.

"Arresting someone? Already?"

"Yeah, open-and-shut case, no doubt about it. You were here. There was an altercation tonight, wasn't there? Between the father of one of the women who lives here and the victim. A Richard Venables. We had more than one statement that described how he threatened the deceased. We've not picked him up yet, but we will. We have officers combing the woods and the local area for him, so it won't be long."

"I see, Chief Inspector. Well, if I can be of any help, please let me know."

"A quick word with the big man up top wouldn't go amiss, Vicar, but we practically have it in the bag." Ainslie was loquacious now that he had a strong lead, and he clapped Annabelle on the shoulder as he pushed her out of the door into the night.

"Can one of my chaps help you to your car?"

"That would be very kind, Chief Inspector."

"Raven!" he yelled at Constable Jim Raven, one of the local bobbies, who was standing by a patrol car on the gravel driveway. "Take the kind Vicar here back to her car, would you?"

"Of course, Chief Inspector."

"Thanks, Jim. It's next to the Cuddy's in Lolly Lane. Seems an awfully long time ago that I left it there."

"It's been quite a night, hasn't it Reverend?"

"It certainly has, Jim. It certainly has."

CHAPTER THIRTEEN

Annabelle opened her eyes and stared at the ceiling. The events of the previous night slowly began to seep into her mind like the spread of a puddle below a dripping pipe. When she'd arrived home, she had turned on her phone to confront a stream of texts from Mike that variously communicated his horror at her situation, concern for her well-being, and frustration at her ability to get herself into all kinds of trouble. She'd replied calmly to reassure him that she was alright and to thank him for his help. Because of him, she'd been able to sleep in her own bed, something for which she was incredibly grateful.

Biscuit pushed open her bedroom door and padded into the room. She jumped onto the bed, and Annabelle's early morning reverie was broken as the cat nonchalantly walked across her stomach. "Oof. Don't mind me, Biscuit."

The ginger tabby blissfully squeezed her eyes tight shut as Annabelle rubbed her finger down her nose, before Biscuit folded her front paws and pinned Annabelle to the bed by settling on her chest.

"Maybe I'm finally getting somewhere with you, pussycat," Annabelle said.

With Biscuit's face not far from her own, Annabelle thought about Theo, his charm, his attractiveness, his magnetism. From what she'd seen at the house the evening before, while strange and a little disconcerting, the members of the Brotherhood didn't appear to be harmful. A bunch of people acting a little strangely, that was all. But none of them had alibis. Any one of them in the woods would have been free to murder Theo, hiding behind trees or hidden by masks as they were.

Margaret, meanwhile, had been alone at the house. She had been cool about her son's death, but Annabelle knew from extensive experience that people grieved in various ways, and she wasn't inclined to put too much store by Margaret's reaction. However, her indifference when Annabelle had first arrived marked her out as a complicated woman. Still, it was hard to believe that she would kill her own son.

And who could blame Richard Venables for holding a grudge against Theo? His daughter was a grown woman and entitled to make her own decisions, but Annabelle could conceive of how her moving away, living an unconventional life, distancing herself from her family, and possibly giving away her money might make a father feel. Annabelle had to admit that Venables' outburst and the threat he'd leveled at Theo the previous evening made him the prime suspect, but there was something about the Chief Inspector's insistence that he must be the murderer that unsettled her.

Annabelle sighed and gave Biscuit one last apologetic scrub between her ears.

"Sorry, kitty, time for me to get up."

Annabelle had a rehearsal for the show later that day. Corralling the children into some form of coherent musical arrangement would require all her energy. She would need to put

Theo's murder out of her mind. Her phone pinged. It was a text from Mike.

Let the police do their jobs, Annabelle. Stay out of it.

She smiled. She knew that he knew her well. Now, though, he was reading her mind.

Annabelle hurried down her garden path and opened the gate. She didn't want to be late for rehearsal. The last time that had happened, she'd arrived at the village hall to find Johnny Curnoweth shinning up the drainpipe to join three of his friends on the roof. Inside the hall, things had been no better, and it had taken her half an hour to bring the rowdy youngsters under control.

As she banged the gate shut and turned to hurry the short distance to the hall, she pulled herself up abruptly to avoid bumping into the man coming along the pavement.

"Chief Inspector Ainslie! What are you doing here?"

"I was just coming to tell you, Vicar. We apprehended Richard Venables last night. We've got our man."

"Is that so? Please walk with me. I'm on my way to rehearsal, and the children will literally be climbing the walls if I'm late. Tell me what happened."

The Chief Inspector fell into step beside her.

"We found him hiding in the woods. Not far from the house. He'd parked his car on a path that runs through the trees. He was fast asleep! Put up no resistance at all when we arrested him. As I said last night, open-and-shut case. Threatening the victim, proximity to where the victim was found. We have him banged to rights."

"Well, you certainly seem to have motive and opportunity, Chief Inspector. But what about the murder weapon? Any sign of that?"

"Bones, Dr. Jones that is, said he was killed with some kind of bolt through the heart. We haven't found it yet, but we're on it. Anyhow, Reverend, the killer has been taken into custody, and your villagers can sleep safely in their beds. Tell them, Vicar. Tell them the good news!" The Chief Inspector raised his hand and waved as he peeled away to his car leaving her to shake her head as she continued to walk down the street.

The rehearsal was bedlam. Even the oldest children, Trevor Bligh and Caroline Lowen, were disruptive when they got into an argument on whether the part of Joseph could be played by a female.

"Cross-gender acting is perfectly acceptable, Trevor! The Greeks did it, Shakespeare did it. Pantomime dames are played by men all the time!"

Trevor rolled his eyes. "Yeah, and they're ridiculous! We're meant to laugh at them. This is the *Bible*. You can't have a man played by a *girl*."

At the other end of the hall, Billy Breville charged around, his arms, having escaped from their slings, outspread. He was making loud airplane noises and inciting several other boys to do the same. One of them was Nicholas Pettit. His four-year-old sister, Maisie, was playing the part of "Sheep." A lively girl, she was not to be outdone by her brother. Her attempts at keeping up were having disastrous consequences as three boys in battle formation turned to go back the way they had come, oblivious to the little girl coming up behind them. Faced with three ten-year-old boys coming at her fast, Maisie put her fists up to fight. A sheep, little Maisie was not.

Annabelle clapped her hands. "Children! Children!" The kids ignored her, continuing to careen around the room and make a lot of noise. She started a rhythmic clap she'd been taught by

Mrs. Bellon, the primary school teacher. It had been a lifesaver. In a few seconds, all the children were standing still, or at least, as in Maisie's case, had slowed down. They mirrored the clap back, slapping their hands together in unison until they had all calmed down.

"Now then, children! Gather together. You know what to do."

The children all moved to the center of the room and shuffled around until they were lined up in rows. The sopranos were on the right, the altos on the left. Smaller ones at the front, taller ones at the back. The very little ones, of which there were eight, roamed around in no particular order at the front. Annabelle's only expectations of them were that they look adorable and not disrupt the proceedings too much.

Annabelle tapped her music stand with her baton. When she'd come up with the idea for the show, she had hoped Mr. Fenwick, her choirmaster, would take on the task of directing the children's singing, but he'd gone so pale when she mentioned it, she thought he might have a stroke. She was beginning to understand why.

Annabelle surveyed the children. "Goodness me! We have been in the wars."

Sitting on a chair against the wall was eleven-year-old Tabitha Brunswick. She had a bandage wrapped around her head, and there were crutches propped against the wall next to her. Her mother was hovering, anxious to leave, but worried that another calamity might befall her child if she did so.

In the middle row, Billy Breville's black eye was now golden and black, but he still had casts around both wrists, now adorned with what looked like graffiti but which was, in fact, the early efforts of multiple ten year olds at producing a signature.

Chloe Simmons had a nasty bruise on her elbow and two bandaged fingers, George Cracker had his arm in a sling, Nancy Rinker was wearing orthopedic boots on *both* feet, and Timmy

Trebuthwick had nasty grazes on his right shin and forearm as though he'd been dragged.

"Let's go over the colors again."

Annabelle walked to a large metal cupboard that had once housed stock items for the local shop, but which now lay home to the Sunday school paraphernalia. On the front of it, on a large piece of butcher's paper, she had written in big, red letters, the words to one of the songs they had been struggling with. It was a long list of colors. She'd hoped to get away without using such prompts in the final performance, but when she'd tried to get the children to sing the list by heart, the results had been farcical and no amount of practice had improved the situation. Many of the children could only remember up to the fourth color and simply mumbled to the halfway point before giving up entirely after that, leaving only one child, Hermione Plaistell, a pious, overconfident, thirteen-year-old, to sing through to the end. Unfortunately, Hermione more often than not finished on an off-key high note that simply wasn't possible to ignore.

"Remember, breathe at the end of the rows, kiddos. Here, here, and here." She tapped her baton on the paper.

"Deep breath, now." Annabelle breathed in through her nose and the children did likewise. She'd been teaching them to breathe deeply and let the air out slowly as they recited the list. Even that hadn't gone smoothly. Jud Whitworth had held his breath for so long he'd gone bright red and then blue before fainting dead away onto the wooden parquet flooring.

"And! Red and yellow and pink..."

The assembled children, grim determination fixed on many of their faces, began to sing the colors of Joseph's multicolored dream coat, taking deep, noisy breaths at the end of every other row, their energy tightly wound as they focused upon getting through the song without collapsing.

CHAPTER FOURTEEN

Eventually the rehearsal was over. The children went home, leaving Annabelle to potter about the hall, stacking chairs and picking up litter in restorative silence. As she peeled off a green boiled sweet stuck to the wall, she heard footsteps behind her. She turned to see Constable Raven. He was chewing his lip.

"Constable? Jim? Are you alright?"

Raven had taken off his police cap and was turning it in his hands. He frowned and pursed his lips.

"Yes, I'm alright, Vicar. We got that guy, you know. Venables."

"Yes, the Chief Inspector told me earlier. He seemed quite certain that Mr. Venables is the murderer."

"He is that, for sure." Raven twisted the cap in his hand with some violence now, turning each hand in opposite directions. "Certain, I mean."

"But...? You're not?" She nodded at the cap in Jim's hands. "You're going to ruin the structure of that hat, if you're not careful. It will never be the same." Jim immediately stopped his fidgeting.

"Oh, I don't know, Vicar. Everyone's cock-a-hoop down at the station. And he does have motive."

"And opportunity."

"Yeah, that too. But, oh, I don't know..." Annabelle waited as Raven paused. He looked at the ceiling and then down at his feet. "There's something funny. At the house. Nobody's paying it any attention, but I think it's important. They're overlooking something."

"Oh?"

"Look, if I show you, will you promise not to tell anyone?"

"You know I can't do that, not if it's something relevant to the investigation. And if it is relevant, shouldn't you be telling the Chief Inspector? Or at least, his sergeant?"

"I have told them. They know about it. But they're not interested in following up. It may not be anything, but I'm concerned we have the wrong man. We don't have the murder weapon yet and so far no concrete evidence to connect Venables to the killing."

Annabelle took a half-eaten sandwich left on the keys of the piano between two fingers. She dropped it in the bin.

"It may well have been him, but there's another line of inquiry I think we should pursue," Raven persisted.

Annabelle straightened up and looked directly at him. He looked tired and strained, not the jovial, community-oriented copper who loved kicking a ball around with the local lads and delighting the six-year-olds at the village school by bringing Cleopatra, the police dog, into class.

She picked up the final chair. It had been tipped over on its back.

"Here, let me do that for you, Vicar." Raven took the chair from her and stacked it on top of the pile next to the piano.

"Alright, Jim, let's do it," Annabelle said, coming to a decision. "Let's go up to the house, and you can show me whatever it is. But I'm not promising to keep it a secret. Not if I think it important."

"Thanks, Vicar. I appreciate it. I've brought the car with me. We can go up there now, if you like."

Raven drove the sole police car assigned to the village force slowly through the streets and out into the countryside beyond. The sun shone brightly, and the sky was a clear, crystal blue. The rolling fields on either side were a mixture of crops and pasture, broken up by the hedgerows and trees that stretched outward to the horizon. Annabelle thought that from where God sat, the countryside must look like a huge, irregularly patched, green blanket, all sewn together with brown thread.

"Did you hear anything about the type of weapon used?"

"Dr. Jones called in her report this morning. His heart stopped obviously, but the thing that stopped it was some kind of bolt."

"Yes, Chief Inspector Ainslie told me."

"The thing is, the victim could have been stabbed or shot, it isn't clear. I know they use bolt guns with animals to stun or kill them so the farming community might have some ideas. Ainslie put some guys onto it this morning."

"It would have taken a lot of force to stab him with a bolt."

"I would think so. We haven't found it yet, so we can't narrow things down."

They turned off the country road and into the overgrown driveway that led up to the big house. There was a policeman standing at the front door, but apart from that there was nothing to suggest anything untoward had happened.

Annabelle didn't get out of the car immediately.

"Jim, what do you know about Sergeant Lawrence?"

"Don't know much about her at all, to be honest. Decent officer. I mostly only hear the gossip from the Truro station. I get the impression she likes Inspector Nicholls. Not sure about his thoughts exactly, though she's more his type than Shenae in the canteen who *definitely* likes him. Why do you ask?" Jim wasn't always the height of tact, or maybe the gossip about Annabelle and the Inspector hadn't reached him.

"Oh nothing, nothing at all." Annabelle waved away further discussion. "Let's get this done, shall we?"

Raven got out of the car and nodded to the policeman standing at the entrance to the house. "The Reverend's just coming to pick something up that she left here last night," he rumbled in a low voice. Annabelle looked around her, surveying the horizon, unwilling to catch the policeman's eye in the midst of being party to an untruth. The police officer scrutinized Annabelle's clerical collar and waved them through. There was no sign of anyone inside.

"Follow me, Vicar."

Raven walked up the enormous stone stairway that led away from the entry hall. They turned left when they reached the landing, and in silence, the pair walked down corridor after corridor until they reached a room that stood at the furthest point from the front door. Yellow police tape crisscrossed the entrance to the room. Raven held his finger to his lips as he reached for the doorknob. "This is the victim's bedroom," he whispered. He lifted the tape for Annabelle to duck under. "Be prepared."

The room was dark. The old, dusty, navy-blue curtains that covered the tall floor-to-ceiling windows and were thread through with silver were closed. Only a sliver of light escaped between the two drapes and illuminated the room, providing a spotlight glare for the dust floating through the thick air. There was just enough light to see what was in the room, and it sent a chill through Annabelle as she looked around.

"Whoa," Annabelle exclaimed in a whisper the moment she stepped inside. Raven tried the light switch. It didn't work.

Like Sally's room, this one was large, with high ceilings and a picture rail that ran all around the walls. But where the ceiling of Sally's room was covered with ornamental plaster, here the ceiling was adorned with a fresco of chubby angel babies and their voluptuous mothers. Earthy colors combined with pale pink and blue to depict a soft, pleasing, visual feast. Mothers and cherubs relaxed and played alongside one another atop clouds set against a sky as blue as Annabelle's eyes. While the fresco was faded, there was no doubting the skill of the artist, the faces of the figures being exquisitely drawn.

But it was the rest of the room that caused Annabelle alarm. The heavenly scene began and ended above her, the delightful overhead backdrop only serving to throw into stark relief the decoration all around the space. Annabelle stood still, her eyes roaming about as she sought to determine what it could possibly mean.

Against the center of one wall, there lay a rumpled bed covered by a bright red flag. A black swastika inside a white circle lay at its center. The flag was dirty and streaked with mud. A pair of battered lace-up boots lay on the floor.

Above the bed, two crossed scythes, dusty and tarnished but threatening nonetheless, were held up by nails driven directly into the ancient plaster. On either side, Nazi memorabilia lay in shadow boxes hung from the picture rail. Annabelle looked closely and saw medals, pins, and uniform insignia pinned to the backing like grotesque insects that no one except the collector is interested in viewing. Above the scythes, three dusty pistols were displayed, one above the other. Another antique gun lay on an old, upturned leather chest.

Around the room were posters featuring Hitler Youth, while another Nazi flag was draped over a leather armchair. Raven picked up a large book and flicked through it.

"What is it?" Annabelle asked.

"Looks like a book of German Third Reich stamps."

"Not your regular collector, then?"

The room appeared to have been ransacked. Drawers had been emptied, clothing strewn across the floor. A chest had been upturned and a photograph lay on the ground, the glass frame smashed. The picture was an old black and white, a photo of a man Annabelle didn't recognize. He had a sharp, oiled, short back and sides haircut and a stern, thin-lipped expression.

"We should get out of here," Raven said. Annabelle continued to stare.

"This is all very strange," she said eventually. "I can't quite reconcile this scene with the person I met."

"Seems like he had a secret life, doesn't it?"

"It does look that way, Jim." She fingered the Nazi flag laying on the chair. It was flimsy, thin, and threadbare in places. "Indeed it does."

"I thought that we should follow this angle up, but the Chief discounted it. 'Bit of a hobby' was how Ainslie put it." Jim sniffed and pursed his lips. "I tried to get Sergeant Lawrence interested, but she too wasn't concerned. What do you think, Reverend?"

Annabelle continued to look around the room. On a dresser stood a mirror alongside a small box marked with Nazi symbols. Inside were seven ivory-handled razors all engraved for a day of the week. She took one out and opened it. She held it up to the light. It was shiny, bright, and sharp. The sunlight piercing the room from between the gap in the curtains caught the edge of the blade, blinding her momentarily. She shuddered and gently closed it before placing it back in the box and closing the lid.

She turned to face Jim, finally giving him all her attention.

"I think, Constable Raven, that I am very thirsty and that I should go and seek a cup of hot tea. I will go downstairs to the kitchen to see if I can find someone who will join me and over our tea, we can have a nice little chat about...*things*, if you get my drift."

"Yes, ma'am, I mean, Reverend," Jim said puffing out his chest. He almost saluted, delighted to have his concerns validated. "But now we should leave, Reverend. It's more than my job's worth for you to be found here. Allow me." He raised the caution tape again. Annabelle slipped back under and with a quick look around, Constable Raven did likewise and secured the room.

CHAPTER FIFTEEN

Annabelle looked up as she rose from bobbing under the caution tape, her eyes shifting to the end of the landing. She got the distinct impression that someone was there, ducking out of sight. She ran to the corner but saw nothing down the long corridor that led away from her.

"Are you alright, Vicar? Would you like me to wait for you?" Jim Raven asked her, running up.

"No Jim, you be on your way. I'll get a lift into the village from someone or I'll walk. I've no idea how long this will take. No need to make you wait. And it'll be better if I'm on my own. I'll be less conspicuous."

Jim looked at Annabelle, several inches taller than he, with her flowing cassock and clerical collar, her brown, chin-length hair and bright, blue eyes that sparkled with intelligence. "I don't think you could be inconspicuous if you tried, Reverend. Are you sure? If we're right and there's more to this murder than meets the eye, you could be sharing your tea with a killer!" He whispered his last few words.

Annabelle waved his concerns away. "Nonsense, I'll be fine. I can't be putting people at ease with a uniformed bodyguard at my shoulder, can I? I'll call you if I get stuck."

"Well, if you're sure," Jim said, concern flooding his face.

"I'm sure, off you go." Annabelle made her way back through the house into the courtyard. It was early afternoon, and the sun was just past its peak. She could feel the heat on her back as she walked over to the doors that led into the kitchen. Before she opened them, she peered through.

Barnaby was hopping around the table, and behind him, Julia was at the sink filling the kettle. Annabelle knocked on the windowpane. Julia turned and waved her in. She seemed quite cheery.

"Hello, Vicar. Would you like a cup of tea? I was just going to make one."

"I'd love one, Julia. Thank you. How are things with you? Have you recovered from last night?"

"I was sorry to hear about Theo even though I wasn't his biggest fan. The idea that he was murdered is terrible. I spent the morning sitting with the others. Suki and Sally are in a dreadful state. I sent them outside to pick berries to distract them, keep them busy. Sally's father is in custody down at the police station, did you hear?"

"I did. Seems plausible, but very sad for Sally. What do you think? Do you think it was he who was responsible? That he was the murderer?"

"I don't know, but he had good reason to be angry with Theo."

"How so?"

Julia came over and put two mugs and a teapot on the table. She poured the tea. "We don't drink cow's milk here. But we have some oat milk, would you like that in your tea?"

"Um, yes. Why not?"

"Do you take sugar?"

"No, thank you."

Julia passed a mug over to Annabelle and took a sip of the scalding liquid in her own. Annabelle sipped her tea. She tried not to wince.

"Sally was in love with Theo," Julia said.

"Yes, she told me last night."

"She never said as much, not to us anyway, but you could tell from the way she looked at him. I'm pretty sure he played on it too. He didn't reciprocate, but he led her on. Let her believe there might be a chance. Theo wasn't a very nice person at times."

"And you think her father knew this? That Theo was leading her on?"

"I suspect so. He was young once, wasn't he? He probably recognized the signs. Sally's infatuation made her vulnerable, and I think her father's fears were very real and justified. Sally would have done whatever Theo wanted. She, of course, can't see any of this. I tried to tell her, but you saw how she was with him. Completely infatuated, I tell you."

"Having your father show up unannounced and demand you return home with him is hardly the way to win the heart and mind of a grown woman. She was in a no-win situation."

Julia acknowledged Annabelle's point over the rim of her mug. They heard the sounds of female voices float down the hall outside the kitchen. Suki and Sally talked in low voices before appearing at the door, both of them carrying a basket of fruit. Suki had strawberries, Sally a basket of gooseberries.

"Hi Vicar," Suki said, softly pressing her lips together.

"Hello," Annabelle said. "How are you today?" Both women looked exhausted, their youth and beauty hidden behind clouds of grief. Purple half-moons lay beneath their eyes, and their hair was disheveled. Sally's eyes were red and swollen. Her nose, too.

"Would you like some tea?" Julia asked them. "I can make you chamomile or peppermint. They will help."

Suki's reply was negative, but Sally responded, "Mint would be lovely. Thanks, Julia."

Sally slumped in a chair at the table and put her hands to her face, sitting silently as Julia bustled around filling the kettle again and taking a teabag from a tin in a cupboard. Suki took the berries to the sink and started to wash them under a running tap. A heavy, brooding, sorrowful atmosphere emanated from them and hung over the room like a toxic mushroom cloud.

Annabelle leaned over and rubbed Sally's back, and beneath her hands, Sally's face crumpled as she started to sob silently.

"There, there," Annabelle cooed. Julia brought over the tea and returned to the sink where Suki had abandoned the berries to go sit on the steps outside in the sun.

"How am I going to go on without him?" Sally moaned.

"You'll find a way," Annabelle said. "One always does, in time."

Sally reached over and pulled a tissue out of a box. She wiped her face and blew her nose.

"He didn't love me, you know. Theo. He said so. He was beautiful and charming and kind and loving. But he could be very cruel. He treated me as though I was some kind of irritant after I told him my feelings for him. Once, he…he actually pushed me! I couldn't understand it. He was so nice at first. I thought there was the possibility of a future between us. But he just turned cold. Then, that scene with my dad." Sally rolled her eyes and looked up at the ceiling. "Dad always was a hothead. He loves me but just doesn't know when to stop. He's always interfered in my life, telling me what to do, who to hang with. I have never seemed to be able to cut the ties completely. One of the reasons I joined the Brotherhood was to get away from his overbearing ways. But he just followed me, didn't he?"

Annabelle patted her arm. "Fathers sometimes take a long time to accept that their little girls are all grown up."

"It was certainly a struggle for my dad. And now look where that's got him."

"Had he turned up here before?"

"Last night was the first time, but he's been harassing me and others in the group for a few months now with letters and phone calls. He started soon after I joined. I hoped after we moved from up north, he'd leave me alone." She looked wildly at Annabelle, fear in her eyes. "I should have done something! Stopped him somehow. Perhaps Theo would still be alive if I had. Oh, it's all my fault!" She started to cry again.

"Shush, shush, now," Annabelle said. "Theo and your father were on a collision course, and nothing you did or said would have changed the outcome."

Sally sobbed a little longer, finally wiping her eyes as she took big, shuddering breaths. Julia handed her tea over, and she sipped loudly.

"Why don't you go to bed for a nap?" Julia said. "You look beside yourself."

"That's a good idea," Annabelle said. "You look all in. I think even if you go now, you'll sleep all the way until morning."

Sally put the warm mug to her forehead and closed her eyes. "It does sound like a good idea." Annabelle helped Sally up.

When they got to her bedroom, Sally detached herself from Annabelle and walked over to run water into the sink in the corner of her room. She stared at herself in the mirror until steam began to rise. After soaking a washcloth, she held the hot towel to her red, puffy face, pressing it gently into her eye sockets.

"Sally, did you ever go in Theo's room?" Annabelle was sitting on Sally's bed.

Sally dragged the cloth down her face, wiping her cheeks as she looked at Annabelle's reflection in the mirror above the sink. "No, he didn't allow anyone in there. Not even Suki. He got sick once, and she tried to take him some soup. He screamed and yelled at her to get out. I think he threw something at her."

"You're sure no one went in there?"

"Hmm, I don't think so... Perhaps his mother? I'm sure no one else." She finished wiping her face and dried her hands.

She sat on the bed next to Annabelle and bent to take off her shoes. When she straightened, she said, "You know, now I come to think about it, Theo could be a bully. He had some strange ways. Secretive."

"How so?"

"He would go off for hours on end. He never told us where he went and would refuse to answer if we asked. And he really didn't pull his weight in the Brotherhood."

"And you didn't complain? There were no arguments?"

"I think some were a little resentful."

"Who, Sally? Who was resentful?"

"Well," Sally hesitated. "Julia and Scott. They used to moan about him a bit, but I suppose after a while we just got used to it, to him." She let out a long sigh. "I'm exhausted."

Annabelle helped Sally into bed and drew the curtains. "Sleep tight. Don't let the bedbugs bite."

"Don't joke, Reverend. There's a very real possibility of bedbugs in a place like this."

CHAPTER SIXTEEN

Annabelle made her way back to the kitchen. As she walked down the hallway to the former servants' quarters, she met Thomas going in the opposite direction. He stopped by the door. He was carrying a tripod and had a camera slung over his shoulder.

"Hello, Thomas, how are you today? Headed out?"

"H-hello Vicar. Yes, thought I'd get away for a b-bit. It's like a graveyard in here. The policeman said we could go outside if we stay inside the grounds."

"Well, it's a lovely day for it. Have you seen Margaret at all? I'm wondering how she's doing?"

"I h–haven't seen her today, but then I rarely see her, to be honest. She stays in her room most of the time. I wouldn't expect t–today to be any different."

"She must have been close to Theo. Not every mother and adult son could live together like this."

"P–possibly, but they didn't seem so particularly. I mean, she isn't exactly the w–warm and fuzzy type, is she?"

"But still, she has to be devastated. Her only son dead."

Thomas shifted, anxious to be away, but his face softened. "P–perhaps she's holding it all in, Vicar?"

"Perhaps. Well, have a good time on your shoot, Thomas."

"B-bye, Vicar." Thomas pulled the round, black door knob toward him and went outside, strolling across the courtyard, gripping his tripod easily in one hand and holding his camera in the other.

Annabelle followed the windowless passageway to the kitchen and found Julia still pottering about. She was rolling out pastry, her strong, veined arms working the dough with a heavy marble rolling pin.

"How's she doing?" Julia asked.

"I think she'll be better after a good sleep. What are you making?

"Pie, chickpeas and veggies. I'm just going to freeze it though, no one feels much like eating. Would you like some tofu ice cream? I made some earlier. Should be just about ready."

Annabelle was pretty sure her efforts at being "good" were going to be secure for the length of time she stayed at this particular house. "Were you vegan before you came here?"

"Oh yes! I became a vegetarian when I was a girl after I learned that my Sunday roast was formerly one of the gorgeous cows that lived in the field behind our house. I haven't eaten meat since. I stopped eating anything that came from an animal when I was at uni, so it has been years now." Julia gave Annabelle the determined look of one who has had to defend her choices many times. "I've seen how people treat animals. It is disgusting."

Julia carefully picked up the round of pastry with her rolling pin and draped it over the pie dish. She gently pushed the dough into the corners with her fingertips and then reached into a drawer to fish out a fork, pricking the pie base to prevent it from rising in the oven. "When I moved in with the Brotherhood, they still ate meat. I was horrified and made a commitment to veganism a condition of my joining them. Theo was game, and I soon converted the others. It helped that I did all the cooking."

"Who was in the Brotherhood when you joined?" Annabelle had reclaimed her mug of now-cold tea and cradled it between her hands as she sat at the table across from Julia.

"Theo and a couple of blokes who have since left. It was just the two of us for a while."

"Did you get to know him well?"

Julia paused pricking out her pastry crust and looked up. "Oh no. I know he was abroad for a bit. Asia, Australia, I think. And he went to university somewhere, but on the whole, he didn't talk about himself much. After a few weeks of just me and him, Thomas arrived, then Sally, and finally, Scott. Of course, Suki and Margaret came along for the ride once we moved in here."

"So you're the longest serving member now?"

"I suppose I am." Julia bent over to place the pie in the oven. In its day, the large kitchen would have contained a big iron range, but now there was only a small white freestanding stove that wobbled when Julia opened the door.

She stood up, pink from the rush of heat that had escaped from the oven, and she wiped her hands on her apron. "Not that it means anything. We are a fluid community. People will come, people will go."

"What do you think will happen to the group now?"

"I really couldn't say. Theo was the key to having this house to live in, but I don't know who owns it. An uncle, I think. Without Theo here to fight for us, we may be cast out on our ear."

"It isn't Margaret's house then?"

"No. After her husband lost everything in the crash, I believe they went from being very well off to almost destitute. Serves them right, those sort. Then he died, and she really was up a creek without a paddle. There's some rumors floating around that she has a wealthy brother, but he refused to help her, and she had to throw herself on Theo's mercy. She was here as Theo's guest.

He extended the invitation for her to live here as a courtesy. What exactly Theo's arrangement was with the owner, I can't imagine."

"So what will you do? If you can't stay here, I mean."

"Roll on, I guess. Something will work out. I don't need very much, just somewhere to lay my head, a small job, and Barnaby, of course. I can't forget him. He goes everywhere with me." Annabelle looked at the rabbit who had fetched up next to the warm teapot on the table and was dozing. Julia wiped her hands on a tea towel featuring the faded faces of a royal wedding couple. "Cooking in a vegan café might be fun. More tea, Vicar?"

"No, thank you. I should be going. I'm glad to see you're doing so well, and I hope Sally feels better after her sleep. I'll come back in a couple of days and see how you're all doing." Annabelle opened the doors to the courtyard and squeezed past Suki who was still sitting on the steps.

"Are you off, Reverend?"

"Yes, I'm going to walk back to the village. It's a lovely day, and it shouldn't take me too long if I cut through Lolly Lane."

"I'll walk with you a way. I could do with the exercise. It's no fun being cooped up in the house, especially under the circumstances," Suki pushed herself up, wearily.

"Of course. How is your mother holding up?" They started to walk across the courtyard and out beyond an archway into the grounds.

"I haven't seen her today. She didn't answer when I knocked on her door, but that isn't unusual. She's a funny old bird, my mother."

"She seemed shocked last night, understandably. She was very composed, but stunned, I thought."

"I think you're being kind. She was distant and aloof. Worse. She's jaded and cynical. She's been like that since Dad died. Actually, she's always been like it but more so since he passed away."

"Does she have any support? Any family to help her? Besides you?"

"Nope. It's just Mother and me now. All my grandparents are dead. Mum has a brother, but they don't speak. There's been lots of trouble in her family."

"Will you stay here, do you think?"

"I don't know. My uncle inherited all my grandparents' money *and* cut Mum out of his will, making Theo his beneficiary. He has no children of his own and is in a care home. This is his house. Theo persuaded him to let us use it. I've never met him, but Theo knew him well. Goodness knows what will happen now."

"So who will benefit from your uncle's will now that Theo is gone?"

"I don't know. Me, perhaps? But I have no contact with my uncle. He could have left his estate to a bunch of cats, for all I know."

They walked in silence until they reached the outer trees of the woods.

"Look, I'm going to leave you here," Suki said. She looked back in the direction of the house. "I don't really want to go back there so soon."

"Of course. I understand."

Suki hesitated. The two women stood awkwardly, each waiting for the other to make a move.

"If I can help with anything…?" Annabelle said. She raised her eyebrows expectantly.

Suki gave her a strained smile. "No, there's nothing, Reverend. Thank you for coming by."

"Well, I'll be seeing you then," Annabelle turned to walk away.

"Actually, there is something, Annabelle, Reverend. Look, it's probably nothing," Suki paused. Annabelle waited.

Suki sighed. "It's just…well, Theo and Scott had a blazing

row a couple of days ago. I went over to the forge to see Scott, hang out with him for a bit, and there they were, going at it hammer and tongs." After her initial hesitation, Suki's words had come out in a rush, like water after a dam had broken. "It was over money. Scott was accusing Theo of stealing funds from the group, that he wasn't distributing it fairly and not keeping proper records so we couldn't trace what happened to it. Theo was furious. I've never seen him so angry. At one point, Scott grabbed him. Scott's a good earner for the group, and I think he feels underappreciated."

Suki's shoulders sagged, and she looked down at the ground. She gently kicked a stone with her foot. "I can't believe he's a murderer, though. I didn't tell the police because I didn't want to get him into trouble. But perhaps you could talk to him? He seemed to like you when you were at dinner the other night. Scott can be a little uncommunicative at times. Surly. He doesn't like everyone. And perhaps he knows something. He's at the smithy if you want to go see him."

"Thanks, Suki. You go back to the house and see how your mother is. I'm sure she could do with some company however she may appear."

The two women went their separate ways. Suki went back up to the house while Annabelle, after initially pressing on through the trees, changed her mind and walked out of them again. She decided to take a route that skirted the outside of the wood. It would take her much longer to get home, but it offered open skies, a clear view, and didn't entertain the darker corners of her imagination.

CHAPTER SEVENTEEN

Annabelle decided to leave talking to Scott for another day. She was eager to be home. At the junction with the main road, she eschewed the path tracked into the grass next to the hedgerow, and noticing the green public footpath sign that pointed across the fields, crossed the road to climb over the stile. Navigating it in her cassock wasn't easy, but after several attempts and much gathering of skirts, she managed it without snagging anything.

As she walked down the gentle slope into the village, her mind once again turned to Mike. They'd walked this grassy path just a couple of weekends ago. It had been a hot, sunny day like this one, and the dogs had gamboled up ahead; not far, but far enough for them to have a good stretch. They'd brought a picnic and walked down to the river, spreading their rug in the shade under the trees that overhung the water.

It was a romantic spot, and Annabelle thought, hoped, that Mike might take their relationship to the next level with a kiss. Even some kind of declaration of intention would have been progress. But while there'd been lots of direct eye contact and the occasional touching of fingertips, it had been incidental and accidental and hadn't led to anything. She felt clouds of hopelessness descend, and she uncharacteristically felt sorry for herself.

She looked about her at the glorious countryside and sighed as she pressed on, telling herself she had much to be grateful for and that "God works in mysterious ways," a truism she usually avoided in her work because she felt it hackneyed, supercilious, and unhelpful. She stopped to pick up a long, unusually straight brown stick. It would be perfect for staking the sunflower she had grown outside her kitchen window, but which was so bent over on itself that the yellow petals almost touched the ground. Annabelle put the stick in her belt and tightened the knot in front of her. "Come on, Bumble," she whispered to herself, using the nickname her brother had coined for her. "Pull yourself together. Stiff upper lip and all that."

"There are three things to remember, Bumble," her mother had told her late one afternoon after a hard day's cleaning other people's houses. "When times are tough, 'pull yourself together,' 'least said, soonest mended' and 'mustn't grumble,' are the best pieces of advice. Don't forget them, and you won't go far wrong."

Annabelle smiled at the memory. Annabelle's parents were solid East London folk whose pride in their daughter's acceptance to Cambridge University was matched only by her graduation three years later. Annabelle's success had been extraordinary among her peers, and she knew that she lived her dream of being a countryside rector largely because of her parent's sacrifices and the beliefs they had instilled in her, attitudes that still formed the basic fabric of traditional British life.

Annabelle looked ahead of her at the jumble of dwellings that rose up in the middle of the rolling green and yellow fields that spread outward as far as her eye could see. Upton St. Mary had been relatively untouched by modern development, and the view had remained virtually the same for centuries.

She studied the roofs of the family homes and small businesses. Gray slate and tile covered the medium-sized and larger buildings, while thatch protected the smaller cottages, the care of which generated a thriving business for Johnny Morton. Johnny was the local thatcher who traveled the county fixing and replacing the thatch in a craft that had been handed down in his family for generations. Inside every house, whether large and lavish or humble and homely, she knew good people lived there, genuine people, all in need of respect, support, and an opportunity to thrive. She considered it her job to minister and take care of those people. She lifted her face to the sky. It was just that sometimes, it would be nice if someone could take care of *her*.

In the center of the huddle of buildings, also reaching up to the sky was the soaring, majestic stone spire of St. Mary's. Annabelle was particularly fond of the effect of the yellow lichen that grew on the steeple's sides. It made the five-centuries-old spire appear to glow when the sun shone in the late afternoon, a sight she could see now as she made her way there. Annabelle always fancied that the spire acted as an alternative compass needle for villagers and travelers, directing them to a place of care and comfort when they were away from home. She distracted herself from her thoughts of Mike, their stalled relationship, and the group in the big house by focusing on her church and the comfort and sense of belonging it gave her. She quickened her pace, suddenly wanting to be home already.

As she walked the last few yards to her whitewashed cottage, her pace slowed, however. She spied Constable Jim Raven and Philippa standing outside her garden gate. Raven's hands were in his pockets. Philippa's arms were folded. A police car stood at the curb.

"Here she is," Raven said. He looked fresh-faced, ruddy, much more cheerful than he had earlier.

"Finally. Annabelle, we've been looking for you *everywhere*." Philippa was flustered. Pink spots flushed her cheeks. She was wearing a brightly colored apron imprinted with yellow dahlias.

The fact that she was wearing it in public alarmed Annabelle. Philippa was meticulous about not wearing housekeeping garments when out of the house. 'Pinnies' were for indoors only.

"Is something wrong?"

Philippa took her by the arm and quickly guided her up the garden path. "I was doing the church accounts, and there was a knock at the door. You've got a visitor. That's why Constable Raven is here. He's *security*." Philippa raised her chin and straightened her back.

Annabelle stopped abruptly and took her arm from Philippa's grip.

"What do you mean, he's *security*?" Annabelle looked over her shoulder at Raven who shrugged and raised his hands, palms up.

Philippa nodded briskly toward the front door. "In the kitchen," she said, her eyebrows raised.

Leaving Philippa behind, Annabelle pushed open the front door and marched down the hall to her rustic, cozy kitchen. It was her favorite room in the house. It had exposed beams running across the ceiling and down the walls. It was a place of calm, communion, and cupboards full of cake.

She pushed open the natural wood door to see a woman sitting at the table, a teapot, two cups and saucers, a milk jug, and sugar bowl in front of her. At the sound of the opening door, Margaret Westmoreland slowly turned to her and looked her up and down.

After a day of corralling forty schoolchildren, a prowl through a dusty bedroom, a ramble among woodland, and an hour's hike through the hilly countryside, Annabelle was not looking her best. Her hair was fluffy and mussed, the hem of her cassock was dusty, and her face was flushed from sun and exercise.

Margaret, in contrast, wore a black and white dress with a blue leaf and pink flower print. The sleeves were sheer, and around her neck she wore a single string of pearls. There was a matching bracelet around her wrist. Her hair was freshly styled and she wore a full face of makeup, her lipstick matching the pink of her dress exactly. She was enveloped in a haze of floral scent.

"Margaret! So good to see you!" Annabelle's arms swung back and forth, and she was immediately conscious of behaving inappropriately, like an awkward schoolgirl. She clamped her mouth shut, cupping her elbow in her hand, her other hand covering her chin and mouth. She looked steadily at Margaret before pulling out a chair to sit down.

"Oof." Annabelle doubled over, as the stick in her belt jabbed her in the ribs. "Sorry, sorry. Forgot it was there." She stood to open the back door, and pulling the stick out like a sword, threw it outside without taking her eyes off her visitor. With her foot, she kicked the door shut and plopped down on her chair, lifting the teapot and immediately pouring herself a cup. "Now, where were we?"

Margaret stared at her.

"I hope I haven't made a mistake," she said. "It took quite some convincing to get permission from that ghastly police sergeant to come here."

"Ah, that's why you've got *security*?"

"What?"

"Constable Raven. He's here to escort you."

"I told them as the mother of the murder victim, I needed some spiritual support."

"Ah, I see." Annabelle put her cup down and dipped her chin, focusing her gaze on Margaret as she looked at her from under her eyelashes.

"Except that's not why I'm here, at all."

CHAPTER EIGHTEEN

"I heard you were at the house earlier, talking with the others. I saw you coming out of Theo's room. I wanted to…to explain." For the first time, Margaret Westmoreland looked vulnerable. She blinked rapidly. Her eyes were moist.

Annabelle's heartbeat slowed, her shoulders relaxed. "Please, Margaret, go ahead. Take all the time you need." She reached over and placed a box of tissues within Margaret's reach.

The older woman took one and blew on it delicately. "You see, Reverend, I loved my son, very much. He was charming and kind. He was smart and such a cheeky little chap when he was young." She smiled at her memories, focusing on a point behind Annabelle's head. She gave a little sniff and dabbed her upper lip. "But he could also be cruel and selfish. There's a strong streak of spitefulness and malice in my family, and Theo didn't escape its curse."

Margaret had been looking out of the window directly ahead of her, but now she focused her gaze on Annabelle. "Reverend, it pains me to say this, but I was ashamed of my son. I know that sounds terrible, but I was, I am. Oh, I know I might come across as one of those frightful women who care only about appearances, but I'm not, in fact, one of them. I have wondered over and over if I had anything to do with Theo's...problems, or if I could have done anything about them had I known earlier."

"What problems were they, Margaret?" Annabelle asked gently. She handed the older woman another tissue. Margaret wiped her eyes, her tea long forgotten.

"I have an uncle, you see. We haven't spoken in years. He has no family, and as his closest relative, I was his heir before he disinherited me."

"Over what?"

"I can't even remember now, any number of things. It doesn't matter. He was an all-round nasty piece of work." Margaret once again looked over Annabelle's shoulder, lost in thought before remembering herself. She shook her head briskly. "My uncle is Lord Drummond." She paused, but seeing no recognition in Annabelle's face, she continued, "He was a friend to the stars, politicians, aristos, in his prime. He was named in a political scandal in 1982 that brought down half the Cabinet. But he started out as simple Alexander Drumrof, a poor German refugee who made his way to England as a teenager along with the rest of my family just before the breakout of World War II. After they anglicized their name to Drummond, Alexander made a pile of money in arms dealing. Later, he received a title for *services* to the country and dished out favors to the rich and famous. He did it for years and profited handsomely. He lived in splendor in Kensington, only moving down here a decade or so ago. After my husband died and we lost everything, I appealed to Alexander for help. I begged, Reverend. Can you imagine how humiliating that was for me?" Margaret's voice was thick. Annabelle leaned over to hold her hand.

"He refused to help us, so I begged a little more. The more he refused, the more I begged. In the end, we came to...a deal." She gulped. "He offered to educate Theo at a private boarding school.

He'd settle a small trust on him for day-to-day expenses and make him his heir." Margaret took her hand from Annabelle's and rubbed her brow. She stared down at the table.

"That doesn't seem so bad. What was the problem?"

"It was what he wanted in return. He wanted Theo to live with him during the school holidays. We weren't to see him on a regular basis, just the occasional weekend. I would oversee his trust fund until he was eighteen, which meant that if I were careful, I could use it to live on. But Alexander became Theo's de facto parent."

"I see. That is very cruel." Annabelle's eyes were full of pity for the woman, although she couldn't help wondering why, in order to support herself and keep custody of her son, she hadn't simply gone out to work. The price of charity seemed terribly high.

"But that wasn't all."

"Oh?"

"If I'd thought Alex would have been a good influence on Theo, I wouldn't have been too concerned. I realize that must sound terribly callous of me, but people of my class are different to yours, Reverend." Annabelle drew herself up, preparing for an insult that Margaret's condescension implied would be forthcoming.

"People like me regularly give our children away to those who we believe will develop them, give them character, prepare them for the destiny we believe is theirs. Cozy family mealtimes and mother and son outings are secondary to other priorities. No, it wasn't that Theo would be going away. It was what he was going away to do."

"And what was that, Margaret?" Annabelle was utterly befuddled at this point from all the twists this story was taking.

"Alexander was going to brainwash him," Margaret said baldly.

Annabelle stared at her. "Really? How?"

"He was planning to indoctrinate him in his political beliefs. My uncle, for all that he owed England, for all that he paid homage to the freedoms and privileges he had benefitted from since his settlement here, was a Nazi sympathizer. He has been his entire life. He's 93 now.

"All this Lord Darthamort nonsense was Alexander's doing. It was he who taught Theo about exploiting people. Alexander told him that most people are sheep crying out to be shepherded, that Theo would be doing them a favor if he became their leader. Clearly Alexander was right, at least in part, because Theo had no trouble getting people to believe in him. It was Alexander who created this whole charade about Petrie and Darthamort. Theo simply lived it out and got others to live it out too.

"Reverend, my son came to believe that kindness, decency, and honor were akin to weakness. He despised other people. He saw them as tools with which to exact a better situation for himself, and moreover, he took pleasure in using them. I heard that Richard Venables called Theo a psychopath. I would agree with him."

Annabelle took a sip of her tea. It was cold, but she hardly noticed. "You heard about that?"

Margaret turned down the corners of her mouth. "Suki told me. Alexander wanted to mold Theo into his own likeness. I don't know exactly how he did it, but Theo, on the occasions when we would see him, changed from the boy we knew. He was darker, more brooding. His personality changed completely. He would take long walks alone in the countryside. He started hunting, something in which he'd shown no interest before. He would lambast us with far-right, Aryan-state, anti-semitic, nationalist politics. We didn't know what to do. Eventually, Theo turned eighteen and decided to go to university abroad. We supported that, in the hopes that if he was away from the toxic environment created by Alexander, he might come around. But when he finally came home after graduating and spending some years flitting about the world, it seemed that he hadn't changed one bit."

"That's a shame."

"But he had learned to hide his nature better. In some ways that was worse. Now he appeared to be the Theo we had known as a young boy, but there was a hateful personality lurking just under the surface."

"Did you know about his room?"

"Yes, he didn't hide it from me. I was beholden to him, dependent. I was probably the only person he was truthful with, and I kept his secrets, to my shame."

There was silence for a moment. Annabelle considered the question she felt compelled to ask, "Were you ashamed enough to kill him?"

"My own son? Don't be ridiculous. Why would I do that?"

"For shame."

"I wouldn't kill him. I may be pathetic, but I'm not depraved, even if he was. Besides, he was my meal ticket."

"How did you support yourself once Theo was eighteen?"

"During the years I was in control of his trust fund, I'd invested a little. We lived off that. It was hardly anything, but the markets were slowly recovering. It wasn't enough in the end though, and we ended up here." Margaret breathed out through her nose and drummed her fingertips on the table. "Look, I'm not proud of my circumstances, Reverend. I know who, and what I am. I was born into money, gained more of it through marriage, and lost it all. In the process, I ruined relationships, never worked, and drank too much. I am totally useless and ill-suited to poverty. My son is, was, more pragmatic, less burdened, and could bend with the wind. He was clever. He could make honey from milk. I needed him.

"Other people adored him. He could wind them around his little finger. Women were always falling in love with him. Sally is only the latest in a very long string of girls. But he never cared for any of them. He was only in love with himself. My sticking with him might not have been honorable, but it was expedient. And it kept me in gin."

"Do you not have any other family you could turn to? Besides Suki?"

"No. Suki is as useless as I am at the practical things in life, but at least she has a sunnier disposition. She's young and beautiful. Someone will marry her, and she'll be alright. She'll probably inherit my brother's estate now that Theo is gone, although I suspect that she'll burn her way through it in unfortunate haste."

"So Suki has a motive for killing her brother. Could she have killed him?"

"Good grief, no. Suki couldn't roast a chicken let alone shoot a person, especially her own brother. What kind of people do you take us for?"

"Then what about a spurned lover, one of those girls you mention?"

"It's possible, but I doubt it. They always tended to be easily impressionable, vulnerable girls. Ones who would fall for his tales."

"And so what was your exact purpose for coming here today? To tell me all this, if it weren't to expunge your soul?"

"That definitely wasn't it. I'm way beyond redemption, Reverend. I know that. If I'd had more courage or been a better mother, none of this would have happened. The reason I'm talking to you is to tell you about Thomas. The police seem pretty stuck on this Richard Venables, but I've seen you snooping around, and I think you should look at Thomas."

"Thomas? What about him?" Annabelle was surprised. After Margaret's tale of depravity and hate, talk of mild, gentle Thomas was startling.

"Thomas is a Jew. His mother, the one he thinks no one knows about, survived the concentration camps. She was just nine when she was liberated, an orphan. I went to visit

Alexander one day; his care home is just a few miles away. I hoped I could get him to change his mind about his estate and leave me at least a little in his will when he died."

"And did he?"

"Did he what?"

"Change his mind and leave you something?"

"No, I left it too late to ask. He was beyond reason. But I did see a name on a bedroom door that intrigued me. *Eta Reisman.* When I got back, I asked Thomas about her because they shared such an unusual last name. He confirmed that she was his mother. He told me not to tell the others. I looked her up in the Holocaust database. She was her family's sole survivor. They were members of the Resistance in Belgium. Her father forged papers. Eventually, though, they were shipped off to Buchenwald. It's true," she said, interpreting Annabelle's look for one of skepticism. "Look her up."

"And you think Thomas may have known about Theo's Nazi sympathies and harbored a grudge?"

"Well, wouldn't you?"

CHAPTER NINETEEN

Philippa was fuming.
She was vacuuming the living room carpet, her mouth pressed into a tight moue. Yesterday she'd discreetly applied herself to some gardening while Margaret Westmoreland had been talking to Annabelle, but now she'd returned to her chores in the house. The church accounts lay forgotten across the dining table, files and loose papers piled meticulously in accordance with a system known only to Philippa, while around the table, she pushed the vacuum with such vehemence that it was a testimony to her skill with one that she didn't destroy any furniture.

Annabelle viewed the ferocity with which her housekeeper and church secretary was flying around the room and silently wondered if the vacuum was Philippa's version of a broomstick, before chastising herself for such an uncharitable thought. Annabelle was the reason for Philippa's bad mood. When Margaret Westmoreland had left the cottage, accompanied by PC Raven, Philippa had knocked on the back door. Annabelle was sitting at the kitchen table, papers in front of her, a pen in her hand.

"Coo-ee Annabelle! Is it alright if I come in?"

"Yes, yes, the coast is clear."

"I was getting on with the accounts when that woman arrived, but shall I put the kettle on?"

"Gosh, I'm fine, Philippa. Really. I've had so much tea today, I'm going to drown if I have any more."

"What about a scone, then? I've made some fresh."

"No thanks. You know I'm trying to be good."

"What are you doing?" Philippa was hovering.

"I'm setting out the program for the show. Working on the cast list. Woe betide me if I leave anyone out. Parents will have my guts for garters." Annabelle didn't lift her eyes from the list that she was working on.

Philippa slapped her thighs with her hands and looked about her. She opened a cupboard and brought out a cylindrical tub. She took off the lid and waved it under Annabelle's nose.

"Chocolate Hobnob?"

Annabelle recoiled. "No, Philippa. I told you, I'm trying to be good. Anyone would think you didn't want me to lose a bit of weight. Wasn't it you telling me a while back that I should?"

Philippa ignored Annabelle's question because it was true. She rapped the tube of Hobnobs on the table's wooden surface, roughly pulling out a chair and sitting down with a plop. She stared at Annabelle.

Annabelle sighed and put her pen down wearily. "What is it Philippa?"

"Oh, nothing." Philippa picked up a napkin from a pile that lay on the tabletop. She started rolling it up from one corner.

"Philippa? This wouldn't have anything to do with the visitor I just had, would it? The one who brought her own *security*?"

"Well, I was wondering what business she had here. She lives up with that cult. She could, for all we know, be a murderer. And she is, after all, a *vegan*." Philippa didn't look up from her rolling. The freshly ironed and starched napkin now curled up at the corners.

"I'm not at liberty to divulge our conversation, Philippa, I'm sorry."

"But Reverend, there's a murderer on the loose."

"The police have someone in custody. And besides, if I have information relevant to the inquiry, the place to share it is with the appropriate authorities." Annabelle was being officious on purpose. She knew Philippa was simply fishing for gossip.

"Well, I think you should share it with us, Annabelle. The villagers could be in danger!"

"I really don't think that's the case, Philippa. Now, if you don't mind, I need to get on with this list. I'm missing two names." Annabelle dropped her head and started examining the paper in front of her.

"Right. Well. I'll be off home then. I'll see you in the morning."

Philippa stood up abruptly and with an injured air swept out of the room, leaving the tube of Hobnobs on the table. Annabelle looked up and with a roll of her eyes, pushed them out of arms reach.

Now, as she stood at the doorway to the living room, Annabelle considered that perhaps she should share Margaret's information, at least with the police. Her conversation with Theo's mother had weighed on her overnight. She felt she was breaking a confidence. She wrestled with the idea of betraying Thomas, but Margaret's news was pertinent, and Annabelle felt she had a duty to tell the police what she knew.

"I'm going down the station, Philippa." Philippa gave no reply. Annabelle really was in the doghouse. There was a rap at the door. Annabelle answered it.

"Oh, hello Vicar!" It was Barbara. She was wearing a violet and gold dress with matching eye makeup.

"Hello, Barbara, what can I do for you?"

"Well, um, I need to speak to Philippa. I heard her vacuuming so thought I'd drop by."

"Come on in. I'm just on my way out."

"Oh good, um, going anywhere nice?"

"Just the police station. See you later." Annabelle stood back to let Barbara by, the pub owner's strong perfume tickling her nose as Barbara wafted past. Halfway down the garden path, she patted her pockets, and then rummaged in her bag. She'd left her phone inside the house. Turning, she made her way back up the path. As she opened the front door, she heard Barbara and Philippa talking in the living room.

"We can Google him, Barbara."

"Google? That can't be right, Philippa. You're thinking of goggle box, surely?"

"I'm not, Barbara. Google, as in googly eyes. Like the Reverend when the Inspector is around. Googly."

Annabelle closed her eyes. She picked her phone off the hall table and shut the front door quietly.

"Good morning, Mr. Penrose!" she called out as the elderly man walked his gray Pitbull, Kylie, on the other side of the lane just as he had every morning for years, long before Annabelle arrived in the village.

Mr. Penrose raised his walking stick in salute. "Lovely morning for it, Vicar." Annabelle sneezed, Barbara's perfume having finally overwhelmed her.

A few minutes later, Annabelle pulled her Mini Cooper into a parking space outside the police station. She quickly ran up the steps into the old building. Behind reception stood a familiar face, Constable McAllister, Upton St. Mary's only female police officer.

"Hello Reverend. We don't see you in here very often."

"No, thank goodness," Annabelle smiled. She'd always liked Jenny McAllister. The woman was friendly and efficient, and Annabelle suspected the station wouldn't operate nearly as well without her. "I wonder if Chief Inspector Ainslie is in."

"He's not, I'm afraid. But Sergeant Lawrence is here. Would you like to see her?"

"Oh, um," Annabelle didn't want to see the slim, spiky sergeant with the sharp haircut, but couldn't put her finger on exactly why. "Yes, that would be lovely, thank you."

PC McAllister disappeared and shortly returned. "She'll be with you momentarily."

"Thanks, Jenny." The desk phone rang, and the constable reached for the receiver.

"Upton St. Mary Police."

The police station reception was small and Annabelle, not expecting to wait long and not wishing to intrude, turned to examine the police noticeboard with unswerving dedication.

After seven minutes, she sat down. After another seven, she started to read a recent police report about the capture of a swan found wandering along the M5 near Exeter. Five minutes after that, she got out her phone and started scrolling aimlessly.

Eventually, Sergeant Lawrence appeared. She opened the door to the back office of the station with force. "Morning," she barked. "Sorry to keep you waiting." Annabelle didn't get the impression that the sergeant was sorry at all, but she stood to follow the woman who was dressed as before in black combat pants, a black t-shirt, and this time, a vest more suited to the streets of New York than Upton St. Mary.

"Gosh, a bullet-proof vest in our little village," Annabelle said, laughing a little longer than was appropriate.

Lawrence looked down at what she was wearing. "Not bullet-proof, stab-proof," she said.

"Oh, right."

"So, what can I do you for? Is it about the murder investigation?" Sergeant Lawrence sat back in her chair. She didn't look at Annabelle, but at her computer screen, her arms stretched out, fingers poised over the keyboard.

"Yes, I received some information yesterday. From Margaret Westmoreland. I thought you should hear it." Annabelle spent the next few minutes relaying to the sergeant what Margaret had told her about her family history, Theo's fascination with Nazi history, the Lord Darthamort connection, Thomas' mother being a Holocaust survivor, and Margaret's opinion that her own son was a nasty piece of work. She carefully omitted her own visit to Theo's room courtesy of PC Raven.

Sergeant Lawrence typed all of this into her computer.

"Why are you telling me this?"

Annabelle was taken by surprise. "Because I thought it relevant to the investigation, Sergeant. There are several lines of inquiry I thought you might be interested in following up."

Sergeant Lawrence typed furiously ending with a final thump as she finished her sentence before flicking a switch. Her screen went dark. She swiveled in her chair and leaned her forearm on her desk, looking at Annabelle intently.

"Thank you for coming in today to tell us this. We will review your information and take action if we think it necessary." The sergeant reached for her phone, effectively dismissing Annabelle.

"Necessary? But of course it's necessary. At the very least, you should speak to Thomas about his mother."

Lawrence didn't look up from her phone. "We have someone in custody. We're just waiting for forensics before we file charges. We are quite sure we have our man."

"But, but...There hasn't been a thorough investigation. You're making your facts fit your theory."

The woman looked up. "Is that so? Learned police investigative procedure from Inspector Nicholls, did you?"

Annabelle went pink. "I –I don't see how that's relevant."

"He talks about you, down at the station in Truro. Seems to think a lot of you." Sergeant Lawrence muttered something under her breath that Annabelle didn't quite catch. There was a bang as a door was roughly pushed open. The bulk of Chief Inspector Ainslie appeared in the doorframe, blocking out the light that would otherwise have streamed in from the brightly lit reception.

"What's going on, Scar— Ah, Vicar. What are you doing here?"

"Miss Dixon came to give us some information about the murder investigation, sir," Sergeant Lawrence said. "I've logged it all. She was just leaving."

"I see. Well, thank you for coming in." Ainslie said. "We'll be in touch if we need to speak to you again." Lawrence looked sharply at Annabelle. Annabelle stood, but hesitated. "You can run along home now," Ainslie's gaze hardened, and he leaned in. "Let us professionals handle this investigation. We know what we're doing."

Annabelle's eyes half closed and the pink spots on her cheeks got pinker. "Well then, I shall leave you to it." She walked, her chin high, to the door before turning. "And by the way," Lawrence and Ainslie looked at her in surprise, "it's *Reverend* Dixon." She spun on her heel and left the station, almost forgetting to acknowledge Jenny as she passed. She climbed in her car, strapped herself in, and started the engine, blowing out her cheeks. A small smile crossed her face. *He talks about you, down at the station.*

As she looked over her shoulder to reverse her Mini out of her parking space, she noticed a familiar figure push against the doors of the station. The man squinted. It was the first time in nearly two days that Richard Venables had seen daylight. He looked disheveled, unshaven, and there were bags under his eyes. Deep lines on his face made him look older than he had just a couple of days earlier. He shrugged on a bomber jacket and quickly tripped down the steps. He turned in the direction of the High Street, passing villagers walking in the opposite direction. No one except Annabelle paid him any heed.

CHAPTER TWENTY

Annabelle was having a hard time concentrating. She was writing her notes for Sunday's sermon. A few words would come, but then her eyes would stray to the garden outside. For a while, she sat mesmerized by the sight of her bees methodically flying back and forth into and out of their two hives. If only life were so orderly. She got up and poured a glass of water, drinking it over the kitchen sink, as she waved to Mr. Penrose who was now taking Kylie for her afternoon walkies.

She turned and sighed, flopping back down on her seat at the table. She picked up her pen and bent over, ready to start writing again, only to be interrupted by Biscuit jumping onto her lap, an action so rare that Annabelle put down her pen to stroke the cat's cheeks and look deep into her eyes, "You're not sickening for something are you, Biscuit?"

Biscuit purred and forcefully pushed her head under Annabelle's hand. With her paw, she prodded the pen out of Annabelle's reach. "Okay, okay." With one hand, Annabelle scratched Biscuit's ears, with the other she began tapping out a text.

Venables was released. What do you think that means? Annabelle waited to see if she would get a response, rubbing Biscuit's ears between her thumb and forefinger as she waited. There was a ping, and she picked up her phone eagerly.

They can't have enough evidence, and they've run out of time. They have to let him go.

Do you think I should speak to him?

To Venables? Leave it to Ainslie. There's obviously a maniac out there, and until he's caught, you could be in danger.

But I might be able to find something out they can't.

Seriously, Annabelle, leave it to the police. They're the professionals.

A little stung by Mike's last text, Annabelle didn't reply. She buried her nose in Biscuit's fur and then lay her cheek on her silky, soft coat, reveling in the feel of it against her skin.

There was a rustle, and Philippa, once more wearing the dahlia-patterned pinny, starched to a standard that would make a sergeant major smile, appeared in the doorway, duster in hand.

"Venables has been released," Annabelle said simply. Philippa gasped with horror.

"No! A murderer is on the loose! I told you!"

"Calm down, Philippa. Mike says they wouldn't have let him go if they had evidence."

"But still, either way, there's a murderer on the loose." Philippa started to pace the kitchen floor, wringing her hands. "I must tell people, warn the village!"

"Mike says I should stay out of it."

"And he's right! You could be in danger if you go blundering in!"

Annabelle blinked at Philippa's retort. Respect for her detecting skills clearly wasn't in evidence among those who knew her best.

She heard a clacking on the path and looked out to see Barbara hastening through her gate and up the garden path. There was a smart tap at the door.

"Back again, Barbara?"

"That man, the one I barred, the one they arrested for the murder up at the big house, he's out, Reverend. I saw him at lunchtime as he left the newsagents," Barbara said, before she'd even set foot over the threshold. "Want me to speak to him? Get him to talk to you?"

"Don't encourage her, Barbara!" Philippa said marching over to Annabelle's side.

"Oh yes!" Annabelle replied, her eyes bright. Seeing Philippa's fuming expression, she quickly changed it to, "Hmm, that might be helpful," in a low voice. Philippa huffed and looked mutinously at Barbara.

"I'll get him in the pub, Reverend. I'll text you," Barbara said, ignoring Philippa.

"I thought he was barred from your pub," Philippa said.

"If he's going to be in one of the pubs, and he surely will be, it might as well be mine. That way, I can keep an eye on him."

Annabelle smiled. Barbara was a matriarchal figure like no other, and the village would be much the worse without her.

"Right you are, Barbara!" Annabelle was suddenly full of energy and enthusiasm. "Synchronize watches! I'll wait for your say-so."

Annabelle tottered around the potholes on Lolly Lane, doing a little dance as she first avoided one, then another. Despite the heavy rain of two nights ago, they still resembled moon craters rather than ponds, and they still presented a significant threat to her ankles. Annabelle had decided to make another pastoral visit to the Brotherhood. She wanted to talk to Thomas about his mother and check on Sally. If she had time, she'd speak to Scott about his argument with Theo. She couldn't help but feel that Ainslie and Lawrence were overlooking something important.

As she approached the gate at the end of the lane, the prospect of walking through the trees, past the site where she'd found Theo's body, began to trouble her. She started to mutter quietly to herself and jammed her hands in her cassock's pockets as she watched where she put her feet.

"Reverend!" Rebecca Hamilton was in her neat, orderly garden. She was hanging out washing. "I'm glad I caught you. Will you have a cup of tea?"

Rebecca was in her thirties, her slim figure not filling out her clothes that hung from her, wrinkled and shapeless, her auburn hair pulled up in a messy ponytail and secured with a scrunchy.

"Why not?" Annabelle replied, thirsty from her pothole dancing and keen to dispel her heavy feelings by spending some time with this busy, cheery woman.

They went inside to the Hamilton's messy and well-loved kitchen. Rebecca pulled out a chair for Annabelle only to find a pile of clean laundry piled on the seat.

"Oh!"

In one swift, seamless movement, Rebecca turned a basket full of dirty laundry onto the kitchen floor and swept the clothes on the chair into it, tossing the basket into the corner and triumphantly presenting Annabelle with the empty seat.

"I'm guessing that's not the first time you've done that, eh Rebecca?"

"Story of my life," she said laughing. Rebecca put the kettle on. "What is going on? The police have been coming and going for days. One said there had been a murder! Is it true?" Rebecca was a very competent mother of five. Nothing much fazed her. She seemed positively energized by this latest piece of news.

"Unfortunately, yes. Monday evening."

"Golly." Rebecca sat down and pulled the lid off a tin. "Chocolate finger?"

"Oh, no thanks, I'm trying to be good. But don't mind me." Rebecca didn't, and she grabbed a couple of custard creams before putting the lid back on and placing the tin on a top shelf away, presumably, from her three sons and two daughters.

"It wasn't anyone we know, was it?"

"Theo Westmoreland. Did you know him?"

"Theo. Was he the good-looking, charming one?"

"Yes."

"Oh dear, that is a shame."

"Did you know him well?"

"Oh no, but he seemed such a nice man. He had an easy smile. He always waved to the children when he went by. Such a difference from that other chap who lives there."

"Which other chap, Rebecca?"

"The dark, swarthy one, the one who works at the smithy down the lane and around the corner. He were having a right go at that Theo the other morning when I went past. Monday, I think it was. Pointing his finger, waving his arms. I couldn't hear what he was saying, mind, but they weren't having a friendly chat."

"Have you told the police this, Rebecca?"

Rebecca folded her arms. "Well, no. They haven't asked."

"Hmm, well, if they do come around, be sure to tell them, won't you?"

"Okay, Vicar, I will. I hope they get whoever did this and fast. I don't like to think of something like that happening so close. I'll have to keep the kids in after school. Don't want them roaming around with a killer on the loose."

Annabelle drained her cup. "Well, I must be getting on. Thank you for the tea. Much appreciated."

"Least I can do. You've got your hands full with that show you're putting on, but I will say the children are enjoying themselves. They're singing at the top of their lungs all the time. The only reason they're not here now is because they went to the Palmer's house to practice some more. Eleanor is singing in her sleep!"

"I'm glad they're enjoying it so much. I think it's going to be quite a performance, one way or another."

"I bet it will be, Reverend. Well, I won't hold you responsible. I know what it's like." Rebecca burst out laughing and patted Annabelle on the back. She followed her to the door.

"Bye, Rebecca. Thanks again for the tea."

Annabelle hurried off. She looked at her watch. Scott might still be at the forge. Perhaps she'd skip the big house, make her way to the smithy instead.

The gate at the end of the lane creaked ominously as she swung it open, and when it clanged shut, her brooding mood returned. As she got closer to the site where she had tripped over Theo's body, her heart beat faster. The summer late-afternoon sun was low, but there were a few hours of daylight left. She could see clearly, but the shade of the trees and the swaying of the leaves brushed by the light breeze were unnerving. The memories of last Monday night plagued her, even as she tried to stamp them away with her feet. She rounded a tree.

"Hello again, Vicar!"

"Oh!"

CHAPTER TWENTY-ONE

Thomas held his camera to his face. There was a whirring sound, and he lowered it. "S–sorry, did I surprise you?"

"Yes, you did, Thomas. Do you always go around taking pictures like that, jumping out and scaring people?" Annabelle steadied herself as she leaned on a tree trunk to catch her breath.

"S–sorry," Thomas tried again. "Are you alright?"

"Yes, yes, thank you." Annabelle pushed herself off the tree and started walking again. Thomas fell in beside her. Up ahead on the path, she could see the white tent that had covered Theo's body two nights ago. Yellow police tape wrapped around trees delineated the crime scene area.

"Are you going to have another l–look, Vicar?" Thomas nodded toward the tent.

"What? Good grief, no. I'm walking to the forge," Annabelle said. "What have you been doing out here?"

"Just looking for a f–few good shots. B–birds, deer, voles, anything. I don't discriminate. Any living creature will do. It's a bit quiet though, today. Perhaps all the activity out here has made the animals go f–further afield."

"Hmm, well I hope you don't jump out on them like you did me," Annabelle frowned.

"Sorry, Vicar. I can be a bit awkward s–sometimes." Thomas sighed and pushed his glasses up on his nose as he stared at the ground. "I know the others get a bit f–fed up with me at times. They think I have my head in the clouds, that I go out with my c–camera and lose track of the time, returning back at all hours, forgetting to show up for m–meals and m–meetings. And that does happen sometimes, not as often as they think, but it makes me unreliable in their eyes." He sighed and Annabelle looked at him sympathetically. Loneliness was most stark when it occurred among a crowd.

"When did you start to get interested in photography, Thomas?"

"I picked it up when I was about f–fourteen. My nan gave me a camera for my b–birthday. I love being outside, just me and Doris – that's what I call my camera, after my nan."

Annabelle didn't blink. Fred Caravaggio at the coffee shop called his espresso machine "Caesar," and no one seemed to pay him much mind.

"...I love the countryside and the animals, l–love being by myself. No one takes much notice of the p–person behind the lens, and that suits me just fine."

Thomas stopped and peered at Annabelle through his rimless glasses. After continuing for four more steps, Annabelle stopped too. She looked back at Thomas, who shied away from her gaze, and it occurred to her just how little Thomas wanted people to notice him.

"Is there something else, Thomas? Something you're not telling me?"

Thomas looked all around him. He fingered a leaf on the shrub next to him, avoiding Annabelle's eyes.

She walked up to him and took his hand. He let the leaf drop and looked into Annabelle's open, earnest face.

"It's what Theo said the other night and what might still happen now he's g–gone." Thomas waited for Annabelle to respond. When she remained silent, he continued. "It's my mother, you see." He sighed and paused. He took a deep breath before continuing. "I told you that I used to live with her, that she got too f–frail for me to care for her any longer, that I put her in a home. I had to sell the house to pay for her c–care." His voice cracked and he looked down at the ground. There were more deep breaths as he released his hand from Annabelle's and rubbed his palms on his thighs. Annabelle waited patiently as he calmed himself. "That's why I joined the B–brotherhood. It's virtually free to live here. I can do my photography and contribute to the group while being able to c–come and go as I please. I visit my mother at least three times a week. She's in Exeter. I c–catch the b–bus to go see her. We used to live much further from here, and I didn't get to see her very often then. It was like Christmas when we moved so close. I couldn't believe my l–luck. If we have to move away again, well, it would be very hard." Annabelle's eyes flickered. "I don't talk to the others about Mum. I like to keep myself to myself. She's happy, and that m–makes me happy. As long as she remains so, and I can go visit her and do my photography, it'll work out."

"Why don't you tell the others your concerns? They might be able to help."

"I don't want them to make f–fun of me. They think I'm out shooting pictures when I go to see her. If they find out I've been deceiving them, they m–might not like it."

"Why do you think that?"

"I don't know. I just do. The most important lesson I learned at school was that it's best to keep my own counsel. Safer that way."

Annabelle reached out and took his hand again. "Least said, soonest mended, eh?"

"Look, I've said too much. They're nice people here, good people. I'm the one that's a little...off. I know that. F–forget I said anything." Thomas withdrew his hand and clasped his camera. He played with the strap.

"Is there anything else, Thomas, that you want to tell me?"

Thomas looked down. He let out a big sigh. "I have a confession to make. I know you're not C–catholic, nor am I, but I think it would be for the best if I tell you what's on my m–mind."

"Okay," Annabelle said. "What is it you want to tell me?"

"After Theo died, I did something I shouldn't have. I–I went in his room. I–I got mad about what I saw in there, and I kicked a few things about." Beads of sweat were appearing on Thomas' brow. "I know I shouldn't have, but I was so angry."

"What made you angry, Thomas?"

"Theo was always so m–mysterious. He had a tiny swastika t–tattoo on his hand, did you know that? He n–never let anyone in his room, and I was curious so I slipped in Tuesday after the p–police had gone. He had all this Nazi stuff in there! My m–mother is a Holocaust survivor. The rest of her family died in the camps. The idea that Theo was a Nazi s–sympathizer made me so mad. I know I shouldn't have, but I was taken by a fury. I c–couldn't stop myself. My mother, my dear sweet mother had been t–traumatized, nearly killed, lost all her family because of people like him. I threw a f–few things around. I'm sorry. I sh–shouldn't have." He breathed heavily. "Look, I must go b–back. I'm hoping the police will let me out of here tomorrow. I normally see M–mum on a Th-thursday. She'll be confused if I don't turn up." Thomas made to move off.

"Goodbye, Thomas."

He started to trudge toward the house.

"I hope you get to see your mother again soon!" she called to him before the trees swallowed him up.

Annabelle watched him go, mulling over what he had just told her and what relevance it might have to Theo's murder. She turned to face the white tent once more and squared her shoulders. She would have to leave the path and cut through the trees to go around it. She gritted her teeth, and humming loudly to herself, continued to stomp her way into the brush and back onto the path beyond.

CHAPTER TWENTY-TWO

The pony coming toward her was agitated.

As Annabelle opened the metal gate into the cobblestone yard, the animal side-eyed her. And perhaps unnerved by her flowing, black cassock, it trotted nervously sideways, the whites of its eyes showing as it threw its head. The pony's owner held on firmly to the horse's bridle, and to Annabelle's relief, brooked no nonsense. The baseball-capped woman clicked her tongue and urged the pony to "walk on" as she heaved her body into its flanks.

Annabelle flattened herself against the gate. It was at times like these that her city upbringing and lack of experience in certain country ways were underscored. Grateful that she had avoided a nasty bite or painful, trodden-on toes, Annabelle exhaled when the pony passed her only to be immediately flayed about the face by the swishing of a coarse, hairy tail.

"Oh, oh, dear me," she said, brushing her face and picking horsehair off her robes. Checking carefully to make sure there were no other large animals that might assail her, she walked up to the smithy's open door where the air temperature immediately rose by a significant degree. A red-hot coal fire roared in the furnace. Scott was bent over it, his eyes covered with clear plastic goggles, his workman's shirt and jeans protected by a filthy, heavy apron. His hands were bare, and now Annabelle could see clearly why they were so red, scarred, and rough. He turned and on seeing Annabelle, called in a deep, loud voice, "Out the way, Vicar."

Annabelle leapt back as he carried a glowing chunk of iron from the fire. He threw it on his anvil and started attacking the metal. Using the tongs, he quickly turned the burning lump over, hitting it repeatedly with the hammer, intent on working it into shape before it went cold and rigid. When the metal cooled, he briskly plunged it back into the furnace to warm it up some more.

Annabelle flinched and blinked every time the hammer came down. Scott's muscular, hairy arms sent droplets of sweat into the air. He was concentrating hard, seeming to have forgotten Annabelle was there, and she heard a few choice words muttered as he shaped the glob on the end of his tongs to his liking.

Annabelle waited quietly until he finished pounding the metal and had cast it aside to cool. He stood staring into the burning embers of his furnace, wiping his hands. She coughed.

Scott ripped off his safety goggles and regarded her.

"Oh hello, Vicar. I'd forgotten you were there. Um, sorry about my language."

Annabelle waved away his apology. "Mind if I have a look around? I've never been to a forge before," she smiled.

Scott swung his palms forward. "No, go ahead. Take your time. Just be careful you don't trip. Smithies aren't the tidiest of places, and you could fall on something nasty." Scott wiped his hands on his apron and walked over to an outside tap. He washed his grimy hands in the cold stream that gushed from it, a juddering noise pulsating the pipework as it ran.

"Fancy a cup of tea, Vicar?"

"That would be lovely, thank you."

Scott picked up a blackened kettle, shook it, and satisfied there was sufficient water in it, put the kettle inside the forge on top of the glowing coals. He picked up a pair of bellows and puffed some air into the cinders, making them glow a deep red, giving them life.

Annabelle was walking slowly around the room. It was dark, the only light coming from the furnace and the daylight that came in through the door. The air was surprisingly smokeless, but it was dry and heavy. It made her eyes itch.

In addition to Scott's forge and anvil, there was an old, well-worn wooden workbench. Marks, cuts, and gouges all spoke to the fact that the bench had been used over many years. On top of the workbench, there was a huge vise, its handle laying in the two o'clock position over the edge of the bench. Strewn on the surface, around it, and on the wall were a myriad of tools, all of them made from cast iron and wood, some greatly weathered. Annabelle couldn't see a modern, mass manufactured tool among them.

"How did you come by all these old tools? I feel I've stepped back in time, like I'm on one of those living history programs."

"Some I brought with me, but most were already here. It was like time had stood still when I arrived. I walked into a smithy fully equipped with tools that probably hadn't been used since the early 1900s. I couldn't believe it when I showed up. They might look old and worn, but you won't find anything near as good at any of those DIY shops in town. It's a privilege to work with tools made to this level of craftsmanship."

"What are you making now?"

"Ah, this? It's a fireside set. Shovel, poker, and tongs. They sell well around these parts."

"What else do you make?"

"I shoe horses, and the farmers will often bring me their tools for mending. A lot of them have their favorites, often from way back. Even though they have all these newfangled machines, they like their old faithfuls the best."

"What are these?" On a table in the corner, there was a basket of thin iron rods, each about four inches long.

"Oh that's a custom order. For Brian Dawson."

"He makes doors doesn't he?"

"Yeah, he uses these in his hinges."

Annabelle continued to walk around the workshop, looking high and low at the workman's treasures that filled the room. There were shelves crammed with jam jars full of screws, screwdrivers, hammers, planes, saws, drills and their bits, files, borers, calipers, scrapers, wrenches, pliers, and punches. There must have been hundreds and hundreds of tools. Different lengths of wood were propped around the walls, cobwebs strung between them. She counted four ladders. Five chains of different weights hung from the ceiling, and various contraptions made from pipes and sheet metal bolted or welded together graced other parts of the floor.

"How long have you been doing this work, Scott?"

"All my life. My grandfather taught me. Being a smithy was his life's work, but my dad wanted no part of it. Pops was delighted I showed an interest. He taught me everything he knew. It's all I've ever done."

"Tell me again, how did you end up in the Brotherhood?"

Scott took the kettle off the coals with a hooked metal stick and set it on the workbench. With his apron protecting his hands, he poured the water into two tin mugs, dropped in a couple of teabags, and stirred with a battered metal spoon.

"Sugar?"

"No, thank you."

He fetched some milk from a thermos.

"Don't tell Julia," he said, his voice low, even though Julia was hardly likely to hear him.

After fishing the teabags out, he handed one of the mugs to

Annabelle. He walked over to where blocks of tree trunk were piled up ready for chopping into firewood. He pulled two out for them to sit on.

"Please, sit down, Vicar."

She took the mug he offered her. Despite his best efforts, he had managed to transfer a spread of sooty fingerprints onto the mug. Annabelle blew across the steaming surface before taking a sip.

"Theo recruited me."

Theo. Always Theo.

"I was living mostly off my farrier work, shoeing horses, but that's not really enough to live on, not even in Suffolk." Annabelle raised her eyebrows. "Newmarket, the racehorses, you know?" Annabelle nodded. She wasn't a fan, but she knew about Newmarket, the British epicenter of horseracing. She blew on her tea again. "Anyway, I'd make a few things and sell them at the local markets. That's where I met Theo. I wasn't interested at first, but he kept coming around and talking to me. Said I could do so much better if I lived with the Brotherhood and that he could help me get more work and bigger projects like fencing and gates and railings for the big houses in these parts. It still wasn't what I really wanted to do, but you know, needs must, and this seemed an opportunity to get out of a rut."

"What did you really want to do?"

"I'd like to work in films."

"Seriously?"

"Oh yeah, there's lots of money for metalworkers in the movies. Especially with all those historical and fantasy films they put on now. They all need weapons and helmets and armor. You can make a good living doing that if you know the right people."

"So why are you here in deepest Cornwall? We're almost off the end of the country. Surely the film industry is based in London?"

"Yeah well, it were Sally who persuaded me. Theo gave up, at least he stopped coming round, and Sally started showing up at my stall instead." Scott's eyes softened. "She seemed so nice. I thought it couldn't hurt to join them, just for a bit. To see how they were. How they lived."

"And how long ago was that, Scott?" Annabelle looked down at the dregs of her tea. There were tiny flat black bits at the bottom, ash probably or perhaps tiny splinters of metal. Annabelle suppressed a shudder. "Roughage," her mum would have called it.

"Aw, see. Must be a year or so ago now."

"And you're still here."

"Yeah, still here, toddling along. Not going anywhere though really, am I?" Scott breathed in deeply and let out a long exhale.

"That's a big sigh."

Scott looked at her. He was leaning with his elbows on his knees, his mug of tea between them. "Yeah, I suppose," he said looking ahead again. He swirled the tea in his mug and took a swig.

"What will you do now?"

"Now?"

"Now that Theo is dead?"

"I don't know. Hadn't really thought about it. Think I'm going to stop being a farrier, though. It's becoming too dangerous. I had a skittish pony in here yesterday. Wouldn't stand still for nothing. Kicked out a bunch of times right at my head, and we had a hard time getting even two new shoes on. Had to abandon the job partway through, and the owner took him away. Said she hadn't had him long. She'd bought the pony for her daughter, but the girl hadn't been able to handle him. She said if he didn't settle soon, they'd have to sell him on. She'll have trouble selling one like that, though."

"Hmm, that's unusual. People around here know their horses. They don't normally overreach. Do you know who the owner was?"

"No, but she did say she came over from Folly's Bottom. Brought him over in a trailer because he was too difficult to ride. I haven't had one that obstreperous in a long time, and I've shod some of the most purebred horses on earth. I've never known horses as badly behaved as the ones I've had here recently. The pony yesterday was just mean. The one I had in just before you came was no walk in the park, neither."

He gave his tea another swirl and threw the dregs on to the cobblestones outside. "Anyhow, Vicar, if you don't mind, I must get on."

Annabelle jumped up. "Yes, of course."

Scott put out his hand to take her mug. "Maybe now he's gone, it'll be better without him."

"How do you mean, Scott?" She looked at him, but he averted his eyes.

"Just that Theo could be a little...divisive. He liked to pit people against each other. Good people. Kind people. People who otherwise got along. He liked fooling them. It was like a game to him. He'd make them think he was all charm and good looks, then once they'd fallen for his game, he'd laugh at them behind their backs."

"You didn't like him much, then?"

"Hah! I didn't like him at all. Not that I'd kill him, mind," he added quickly. "He knew he couldn't pull the wool over my eyes. I could see him for what he really were. Mostly, he stayed away from me."

"Scott," Annabelle said, walking up closer to him, "I heard that you had an argument with Theo a few days ago."

Scott stood and started cleaning up. He began to rub down his anvil with a rag. "Did you?"

"I heard from two people that it was a furious row and that you grabbed him at one point."

Scott stopped his cleaning. He threw the dirty cloth onto the anvil and stood looking down at it with his hands on his hips.

"Well, maybe I did, Vicar. But so what?" He looked at her evenly. He shrugged. "My work brings in the most money for the group, not that you'd know it. All the money we make goes into one pot. There's a budget for our food and stuff, and we share what's left over equally. That's what we agree to when we join.

"Theo managed the money, but he didn't keep records so we never really knew how much we made or spent or shared. And I think he used to take more for himself. Keep money back. I challenged him, and we got into a bit of a barney. He denied it all, of course, and the others think the sun shines out of his you-know-where so they're blind to his game. He just used to slip and slide around, cheating us all, making us mad with one another, and he'd get away with it!" Scott's voice got thicker as he spoke, and he splayed his hands. "Finally, it all got to me, and when he came here on Monday, I lost my temper. Yes, I got angry with him, and yes, I grabbed him. But nothing more!"

"So if you didn't like one another, and you weren't doing the kind of work you really wanted, why did you stay?"

"Because I'm a fool."

"You don't seem like much of a fool to me."

"Maybe not, but we can all be made fools of by other people, the right people. No one is immune." Scott stared off into space, before snapping back to the present, his attention caught by someone outside. Before she could turn to see who it was, Annabelle heard Sally's voice.

"Come to bring you some tea, Scott." Sally appeared at the doorway and smiled sadly. The gruff, grizzly man melted. His shoulders dropped, and he smiled shyly. His face was red from the heat of the forge but Annabelle could have sworn he was blushing.

"Oh, thanks Sally, love. That's too kind."

Annabelle took a moment to wonder why Sally would bring tea from the house when Scott had his own tea-making facilities at the forge. Her tea was bound to be stone cold.

"How are you feeling now, Sally? Do you feel better?"

"Oh, yes, Reverend. I'm much better, thank you. I needed some fresh air, so I thought I'd wander down here to see Scott."

Scott ducked his head and brushed at his face. He turned his back on the two women and busied himself at his workbench. Sally walked up to him and put a hand on his shoulder. She spoke quietly to him, and he took the mug from her. He held it in two hands and they chatted quietly. Sally laughed gently at something he said. Annabelle couldn't hear what they were saying but one thing was obvious.

It hadn't been Theo who'd been making a fool of Scott. It was Sally.

CHAPTER TWENTY-THREE

Thomas dropped the paper into the developing fluid. He watched it sink to the bottom of the tray, swimming from side to side like a stingray. He looked up at the pictures he'd taken. They were drying on the lines that zig-zagged across the room. He peered closely at them.

Like many of the rooms in the big, old house, the window went from floor to ceiling, making it problematic as a darkroom. When he'd moved in, he'd taped black paper, several layers, to the cracking, peeling, metal window frame, sealing the edges with extra tape to prevent chinks of light seeping in. He'd stacked a jumble of old clothes by the door, and every time he closeted himself inside the room, he stuffed the clothes into the gap between the bottom of the door and the floor. To complete the conversion of the former bedroom to a darkroom, he'd tacked a rubber strip around the entire doorframe and rigged a developer's lamp to the existing light fitting. The lamp gave him a muted glow to work from, and he never switched on the regular light.

Thomas was never happier than when he was in his darkroom. He'd often wondered if he'd been a small, earth-living creature in a previous life, some kind of scurrying or burrowing animal. He loved being solitary, observing the daily interactions of everyday living. He enjoyed being unremarkable and going about his business undisturbed. It was what made him a good photographer. He was unobtrusive and able to catch life on film in its most natural state.

Thomas was old-school. Not for him the intangible indiscrimination of digital photography, the manic clicking that resulted from the sense that there was no downside or waste to taking twenty shots where one would have sufficed. He composed his frames carefully, and every time he set his camera into motion, there was purpose and meaning behind his shot. Where other photographers clicked away at all and anything, Thomas' eyes darted around constantly searching for a composition that supplied enough substance for him to release his camera's shutter. He even enjoyed the cumbersome process of developing prints, the smell of the chemicals involved, and the way the photographic paper slowly gave up its secrets. The old photographic ways suited Thomas' personality: unhurried, restrained, methodical, and consequential.

He looked across his lines of prints, examining each one in turn. One was of Sally, hiding behind a tree. Her back leaned against the trunk, her palms flat against it. Her eyes were closed behind her elaborately painted mask, her dramatic black eyebrows testimony to her artistic ability and steady hand. There was a shot of Theo, running, his ugly mask incongruous against the rest of his attire, his jeans and shirt. Thomas had slowed the shutter speed on his camera so there was motion blur. It trailed behind his subject giving it an eerie glow. It was almost certainly the last image of Theo alive. Shots of Suki and Scott in mock combat were next. Suki was laughing. Scott's mood was less easy to discern underneath his mask, but the exaggerated way he stood in apparent threat implied that Suki had no reason to fear him.

The final shots were not of people, but of woodland nightlife.

That Thomas had been able to shoot any at all was surprising considering the amount of shrieking and activity taking place. It would have been understandable if the shy, quiet, nocturnal animals that lived underground or in trees or who cloistered themselves away in the camouflage of the bush had stayed hidden until the drama was over, but Thomas' quick eye and low-key presence had rendered some nightlife nature portraits that were truly striking.

He'd caught a hedgehog, its spines various shades of brown and gray, strolling through the undergrowth, hidden mostly from view by a layer of last year's leaves. Its snout was lifted to the camera, its black eyes, inquisitive and alert, giving Thomas the perfect view of its dainty face peering out. In another image, a barn owl sat proud and serene on a branch, its white and gold colors blending into its surroundings, apparently impervious to the undignified revelries going on beneath him.

Thomas continued to scan the lines of drying images, silently selecting his keepers. He looked down at one print that he'd just submerged. The picture was appearing before his eyes. As it manifested, he leaned forward. He lifted his glasses to peer even closer, his face inches from the fluid's surface. He picked up a pair of tweezers and lifted the print to the nylon wire above. He suspended it with a peg. He stared at the photograph again, then at the others on the line, flicking back and forth between them, his heartbeat quickening. He heard a noise and turned toward the door, his eyes wide. He dropped his glasses to his nose, a slick of sweat appearing on his brow.

The door opened slowly. Thomas didn't move even though light streamed in from the hallway outside. A dark figure silhouetted against the light moved into the room and shut the door.

"You. It was you," Thomas heard himself say.

CHAPTER TWENTY-FOUR

Annabelle pushed open the door to the Dog and Duck. Barbara was behind the bar. She tipped her head toward a solitary figure sitting by the unlit fireplace.

Annabelle could see Richard Venables' slight, wiry body was wound taut. He was leaning on his elbow staring into a pint, cupping his cheek in his hand. With the other, he methodically turned over a fifty pence piece on the wooden tabletop, heptagonal side by heptagonal side.

"Good evening, Richard. How are you doing?"

Venables looked up, "Who are you?"

"Annabelle Dixon, Reverend of St. Mary's." She stuck out her hand. "I was at dinner the other evening, just before Theo Westmoreland was killed."

Venables took her hand, but there was no enthusiasm in the shake he gave it. He returned to staring into his pint and turning the coin. "I don't remember, sorry."

Annabelle sat down. She could see Barbara in the background miming. She shook her head. No drink for her. She refocused her attention on Venables. "I've been talking to Sally."

Richard stopped his fidgeting and looked up.

"How is she?"

"She's very upset. Her friend is dead, and her father was arrested for the murder."

Venables sighed and returned to fidgeting with the coin. "I didn't do it. They let me go." His voice was flat.

"You were involved in an argument with Theo. You threatened to kill him."

"Yeah, and? I didn't kill him," he repeated, looking up at Annabelle, his chin still supported on his hand. "I wouldn't! After they threw me out of the house that night, I simply wandered around, furious. I thought I'd keep walking until I'd calmed down. After a bit, there was all this noise, people running around. I could see they were doing funny stuff in masks and such, so I walked away from it all. I didn't want them to see me and for there to be another scene."

"So what did you do between the time you left the house and the time the police picked you up?"

"I just walked and walked. Those woods are big. I went back to my car and was dossing there for the night when the police found me. But I had nothing to do with killing that guy. Nothing at all!"

He pursed his lips. Annabelle looked at him steadily. Her hands were clasped in her lap.

"Do you know what a bolt gun is?"

"Uh, sure I do. I work in a slaughterhouse. We stun the cattle with them. Used one for years. Look, I've been all through this with the coppers."

Venables sat up, and tossed the coin onto the table. Annabelle gave a slight start. Venables lowered his shoulders, and pushed out his chin, before closing his eyes for a second. Life seemed to drain out of him.

"Look, I've got previous. From when I was young. Since then,

I've made it my business to get clean. Settled family life, steady job."

He leaned forward. Annabelle leaned back, slightly alarmed. The way Venables thrust out his chin unnerved her.

"I wouldn't wreck everything I've worked for, not after twenty years, because of that twit."

He leaned back and Annabelle relaxed. "But what about Sally?"

"Sally is my only child and that...that man stole her from me! Any father would do the same thing. He turned her head, distanced her from her family. I was worried he'd take her money, but I was much more worried that he'd take her from us, and we'd never see her again. You hear such stories.

"She would've come to her senses eventually. I just wanted it to happen sooner rather than later, and I didn't want to see her be made a fool of. Her mam and me have given her everything. She is our precious doll, and it hurt her mam so much when she went off like that, without a word, and well, you saw me. I lost my rag, didn't I?" He clenched his fists. "But I didn't kill anyone."

Richard put both elbows on the table and hid his face in his hands, rubbing his eyes. A moment later, he sat back, blinking, his face red. He let out a sigh. His shoulders heaved and returned to rest. He regarded Annabelle with sorrowful eyes.

"Can you help me, Reverend? I've really messed things up, haven't I? I don't know what to do. I want to take Sally home with me, especially now, but I daren't show up at the house, and I'm not sure she'd speak to me if I did. What do you think I should do?"

"Perhaps you could give her some space, Richard. Allow her to come around in her own time. Let her know that home with you and your wife is a safe place for her. Encourage her with honey, not vinegar."

"Could you talk to her, Reverend? You seem to understand."

"I think she needs to hear directly from you, Richard. Quietly, no drama, no shouting."

Venables nodded. He looked down at his pint. "I could drink less, too."

Annabelle stood. "That would be a step in the right direction, yes. Good night, Richard."

"'Night, Vicar."

CHAPTER TWENTY-FIVE

"Thomas! Thomas!" Sally was walking around the house. Thomas hadn't shown up for breakfast. That wasn't so unusual, but when he didn't turn up for lunch either, she had started to worry.

Everyone in the house was on edge. Now that Sally's father had been released, there was some small amount of relief for her, but the others weren't entirely convinced of his innocence. And even if Richard wasn't the murderer, the specter that someone else, someone still on the run, possibly even one of their own, had killed Theo was making them nervous and suspicious of one another. The night before, Sally had been forced to intervene in an argument between Scott and Margaret over her smoking in the house. Scott said he got enough smoke during the day, he didn't want it at night as well. Margaret had insolently ignored his grumbling. The atmosphere had caused Julia to take to her room with Barnaby while Suki had been squabbling with everyone.

Sally was devastated not just by Theo's death, but also by the rancor in the house and the thought that her father might be the killer. She found it hard to believe he was guilty, but things didn't look good for him. In the past couple of days, she'd confided in Thomas when she'd felt particularly troubled. Having gone for hours without seeing him, she missed Thomas' undemanding, comforting presence.

"He's probably in his darkroom," Suki had said to her. "Isn't that where he goes to be alone?"

"Yes, but he wouldn't have been in there for twenty-four hours straight, surely? He has to eat! Oh, I don't know. Perhaps I shouldn't bother him if he's in there. He doesn't like people disturbing him. The light ruins his photos."

"But still, if you're worried about him. You could just knock. If he replies, all's well."

"I don't know what you're so concerned about? Antisocial misfit," Margaret said nastily. "Maybe he was Theo's killer? Perhaps he's done a runner!"

"Don't be silly, Margaret. Thomas? No, never. He's much too sweet, much too docile," Sally said.

"Well, it had to be someone. Who do you think it was, if it wasn't your father?"

"I don't know. I don't know! I can't imagine any of us here killing anyone, least of all Theo." Sally looked at the two women, anguish written across her face. They looked back at her, skeptically.

Sally pushed aside the curtain Thomas had rigged outside the door to his darkroom. She knocked quietly on the door three times. Thomas was a quiet, observant man. It wasn't necessary to make a lot of noise to get his attention.

There was no response. She knocked again and called his name quietly. When no one came to the door, she turned the handle slowly.

"Thomas? Thomas? Are you in there?" She cracked open the door gingerly, unsure whether to go in. She put her eye to the crack and swiveled it around taking in as much of the room as she could. She couldn't see much, except...There! There was a puddle on the floor, the surface rippling every time a drop fell from the table above. Sally opened the door sharply and slipped in, shutting the door quickly. She turned to see what was causing the fluid to seep onto the floor.

Downstairs, Margaret had stirred herself enough to help Suki in the kitchen with the dinner.

They heard a noise. Both paused in their preparations.

"What was that?" Suki asked.

"I'm not sure," Margaret said uncertainly. They heard the noise again.

"Someone's screaming," Margaret said.

"It's Sally. Something's happened to Sally!" Suki replied.

Suki pushed away from the kitchen table and began to run. Margaret waited for a moment before pulling off her apron and throwing it on the table. She chased after her daughter, the sounds of Sally's screams echoing down the hallway, getting louder with every stride.

CHAPTER TWENTY-SIX

The emergency call came through to the Upton St. Mary police station just fifteen minutes before the end of Constable Raven's shift. Under normal circumstances this would have been cause for a stream of uncharitable verbiage from the constable but deaths, certainly possible murders, were serious enough for him to put the inconvenience aside. He dialed Ainslie's number.

"Ah, Chief Inspector?"

"What is it, Raven? I'm just about to turn into my driveway."

"Um, sir, there's been another suspicious death. At the big house in Upton St. Mary."

Raven held the phone away from his ear when Ainslie realized he would need to turn right around and get back to the village without so much as a cup of tea.

"Yes, sir, I'll get there right away. See you shortly."

Raven rammed on his cap and jogged to the police car. As he reversed out of the car park, he plugged another number into his phone and put it on speaker.

Annabelle was pruning her roses when the call from Raven came through.

"Constable, what can I do you for?"

"Reverend, there's been another death at the big house."

Annabelle chopped the head off a perfectly beautiful red rose. She cringed. "Fiddlesticks!"

"I know, it's a terrible thing," Raven said. "Ainslie won't be there for another forty-five minutes. Shall I pick you up on the way?"

"Thank you, Jim, but it'll be quicker if I make my own way there. See you in a bit."

Annabelle pulled off her gardening gloves and ran inside. She poured some water into a glass and popped the rose into it. She stared at the bloom for a moment, sighing, before shaking herself. She trotted upstairs to change out of her gardening clothes but stopped halfway. She wanted to get to the house before Chief Inspector Ainslie. No doubt he would throw her out as soon as he saw her. Gardening clothes would have to do.

Annabelle's royal blue Mini Cooper sped along the road out of the village and along the lane to the big house. She spun the wheel to turn right up the pitted gravel driveway, her back wheels spinning out and kicking up dust in her haste. Righting the car, she kept her foot down on the accelerator, bumping along the track and skidding to a halt outside the door.

Her arrival coincided with that of Constable Raven who had motored there at a much more leisurely pace.

"What do you know, Constable?" she whispered as they walked in together. She was relieved to see there was no policeman on duty at the door this time.

"Not much, body's a male, that's about it. Woman was a bit, er, hysterical."

"Then it can be one of only two people."

"Oh?"

"There's only two men left here. Scott and Thomas."

Annabelle showed Constable Raven to the kitchen. They looked through the glass door to where four women were assembled. Sally was sitting at the table, a crumpled tissue once again at her mouth. Julia sat next to her, holding her hand. Suki stood behind, patting Sally's shoulder. Margaret stood aloof from the crowd. She leaned back against the sink, a glass of clear liquid cradled against her chest. She looked pale.

"Did you know they call themselves the 'Brotherhood of St. Petrie?'" Raven looked at the four women dubiously. "They don't look very brotherly," he whispered.

Annabelle shook her head, "It's just a name. It means they're a group, they're all in this together."

"They're in what together, Reverend?"

"You know, life."

Annabelle pushed the door to the kitchen open.

"Hello Annabelle," Suki said. There was a tremor in her voice.

"I'm sorry—" Annabelle began. There were heavy footsteps outside and the kitchen door opened with a bang. Scott's large form entered the room.

"What's going on? There's a police car in the driveway and more in the distance. They're coming this way."

"It's Thomas," Margaret said. "He's dead."

Scott looked around the room at everyone. "What? How?"

"Sally found him."

"He was in his darkroom. Drowned," Julia said.

Scott looked at her darkly. "No way." He stomped out of the kitchen and down the hallway to the flight of stairs that led to the upper rooms.

"Stop, sir," Raven called after him. "You can't go in there. I have to seal the crime scene." Raven chased after Scott who was running now. Annabelle followed. Scott was fast, and Raven lumbered in his wake, but Annabelle had several inches on the constable and soon left him behind. Scott conveniently led them to Thomas' room, running down corridors, and skidding around corners. Just before he reached the room, Annabelle caught up to him and rather bravely put herself between the larger man and the doorway, their faces inches apart.

"Best if you join the ladies in the kitchen, sir," Raven called out, panting from behind and leaning on a bannister rail. Scott glared at Annabelle mutinously. "It's for the best. There's nothing you can do for the victim," the policeman added.

"For Thomas," Annabelle said gently.

Scott, on hearing Thomas' name, relaxed his features in defeat. He quietly acquiesced and moved away from Annabelle. He went back the way he had come, flicking one last mulish look at Raven as he passed.

Raven walked up to Annabelle. "Quick, the others will be here soon. Don't touch anything and take as few steps as possible, okay?"

Annabelle nodded. Her heart was beating hard in her chest, and her fingertips tingled.

"So it's Thomas?" Raven asked.

"Yes, it's Thomas. Thomas Reisman. He's been a member of the Brotherhood for a couple of years."

Raven took a handkerchief and turned the doorknob carefully. Immediately, they smelled the metallic, acrid fumes of the darkroom chemicals. Raven reached for the light switch but Annabelle held out her hand. She pointed to the safelight and to the pictures hanging from pegs on the lines strung across the room. They peered through the gloom. A creak made Annabelle start, and she felt a cold sensation curl around her toes. She looked down. Fluid had seeped through the weakened seam of her old gardening shoes. Next to her foot was an upturned tray. Photographs were strewn on the floor. Lying face down was

Thomas, his cheek lying on one of the prints. His glasses were on the floor next to him, smashed. His face was white, his lips were blue.

Sighing, Annabelle crouched down, placing her hand on Thomas' shoulder. She closed her eyes and said a silent prayer. She looked at the prints upon which Thomas lay. The bonfire, sparks fizzing into the smoke, flames curling around wood featured in one. Another was of the stormy sky, two crows flying across it. But it was the one by Thomas' shoulder that interested Annabelle the most. Thomas had taken a wide angle photo of a barn owl in a tree next to a clearing, a fallen tree trunk to one side of it. The bird appeared to be looking at something, but before she could take a closer look, "What have we got, Raven?" Chief Inspector Brian Ainslie appeared in the doorway. "What are you doing here?" He glared at Annabelle.

"Man, about thirty, sir. He's been identified as Thomas Reisman. Been a member of the Brotherhood for about two years. This was his darkroom. Looks like he was drowned." Raven spoke in a rush. Annabelle sidled past Ainslie and onto the landing. "Chief Inspector," she mumbled as she passed him. He paid her no attention although she thought she heard a tutting sound. She hurried along down the staircase and back to the kitchen where the four women and Scott still congregated.

Annabelle sat down at the table a little out of breath. "What happened?"

Sally stuttered in between her tears.

"I found him. He hadn't come down to breakfast or been seen all day so I went looking for him. Oh, Annabelle, it was awful. Poor Thomas, he didn't deserve that. He wouldn't hurt a fly."

"And do you think it was definitely murder?"

"How could it not be? You can't drown yourself in an inch of liquid, surely," Margaret intoned.

"Where were you these past twenty-four hours?"

"We were all here, except for Scott."

"I was at the forge."

"You mean, do you mean, could it be..." Suki stammered, "...one of *us*?"

They all looked at one another. There was a bump and a shout from upstairs. They looked up at the ceiling.

Margaret, who'd moved closer to the table, moved back to the sink again. Julia let go of Sally's hand and folded her arms. The atmosphere in the room got a little cooler.

"But surely not. It couldn't be any of us. I mean, why would we?" Suki said.

"Why would anyone? I mean, Thomas?" Sally said.

"Wait a minute. Your father's out of police custody. It could have been him. He could have come back to finish the job he started," Margaret said. Julia nodded.

Sally looked affronted, but she said nothing.

"Perhaps it's a random person from outside coming in," Suki offered. "It wouldn't be hard in this rambling old place. Especially at night."

"But why?" Julia interjected. "A serial killer picking off his victims at random? In Upton St. Mary? Really?"

Annabelle opened her mouth to speak but closed it again. The idea seemed utterly implausible, but after the strange goings-on she'd encountered since she'd lived in the village, nothing would surprise her.

CHAPTER TWENTY-SEVEN

Annabelle banged the garden gate shut and walked up the path as she shrugged off her jacket. "Philippa! Are you here?"

She sat on the back doorstep and leaned over to unlace her gardening shoes before she went inside. When she'd first moved to Upton St. Mary, she hadn't fussed too much about wearing footwear in the house, but a few of Philippa's disapproving looks and barely disguised tutting had cured her of the habit. She tossed the shoes to the side where they would lie protected from the elements by the porch overhang until the next time she pottered in the garden.

"Philippa!" She opened the back door. "Oh!"

Sitting at the kitchen table, nursing a mug of tea, was Mike.

"Hello, Annabelle," he smiled.

"Mike!" Annabelle beamed. "You're back! I wasn't expecting you until next weekend."

"I'm taking a break. Tomorrow's session's on 'Social media and the police: Tweeting best practices,' whatever that means.

They're expecting me back in the evening. I thought I'd stop by and see the dogs. And you, of course."

Annabelle was still grinning. Mike was in his civvies, jeans and a light jumper, his brown hair tousled in what Annabelle thought was a rather attractive manner. He scratched his light stubble. "I thought we could take the dogs for a walk."

"Yes! I think that's a splendid idea! I've got tons to tell you," Annabelle said. "Let me go and change."

"You're fine as you are."

"I'm in my gardening clothes." She looked down at herself. She was wearing a pair of old dungarees that were muddy and ripped over a shapeless t-shirt that had once been emblazoned with the words, "More Tea, Vicar?" but which were now so faded they were barely noticeable. Her socks had a hole in them. Catching sight of herself in the mirror, she saw that her hair needed a good brush after a day of weeding and crime scene investigation.

"And you look fine in your gardening clothes. Come on, the dogs are bursting, and they don't care what you're wearing."

Molly had gone to the coat rack in the hall where the leads were kept as soon as Annabelle had arrived home. She was now patiently sitting by Mike's feet, the leash in her mouth, her brown eyes looking at him in appeal. Magic, like his mistress, wasn't quite so disciplined and was running around the kitchen, his tail banging against the kitchen cupboards, giving the occasional bark and odd little jump.

"Oh, alright." Annabelle was secretly delighted to go as she was. She would have wasted ten precious minutes deciding what to wear and dressing to suit the occasion was all so much *effort*. Magic followed her into the hallway where she took his lead off the peg it was hanging on before tying herself into her hiking boots.

Mike joined her. "Let's go to the moor. We haven't been there for a long time. We can all have a good stretch. Lord knows I need it after being cooped up for days on end. It'll be light until nine. We could stop off and have a drink at the pub before going home."

"Sounds good to me," Annabelle agreed.

"I've got a map in the car."

"Oh, er, can't we use the GPS?"

"Nah, let's do it the old-fashioned way. There's nothing like using a proper Ordnance Survey map to navigate your way around a Cornish moor."

"Well, if you're sure..." Annabelle, for whom all the squiggles and symbols on a paper map were guaranteed to amount to a lost couple of hours, surreptitiously checked the amount of battery on her phone and slipped it into her back pocket. She hadn't forgotten the time she went on an orienteering field trip with her high school class. As leader of her group, she had managed to get them lost on a cliff's edge. All six teens had to be rescued by the local air/sea rescue. She hadn't trusted maps since.

She got into the passenger seat of the car, and off they set. They were headed for the rugged expanse of granite and grass moorland that stretched for miles, famous for the wild ponies that grazed there and its collection of stone formations dating back to the Bronze Age. The dogs whined in the back, their tongues hanging. They were looking forward to a long workout.

"Shouldn't we follow the public footpath?" Annabelle said sometime later as she pointed at the green sign to their left.

"No, I'm sure the map says this way. And the worn track, it goes this way too." Mike was holding out his map, peering at it and then at the landscape around him, squinting.

"Alright," Annabelle said. "If you're sure."

Mike wasn't sure, but he wasn't about to say so. They'd been walking for two hours and the car was nowhere in sight.

They walked on. The dogs were slower now. Having bounded and frolicked for a good while at first, they were tired but good-naturedly pressed on alongside their owners. All around them was gently undulating moss and heather punctuated by the occasional bush, tree, and rocky outcrop. Large granite stones piled on top of one another in gravity-defying configurations cast long shadows and appeared ominous in the fading sunlight. Above, the sky was turning dark blue, the clouds long and wispy as though God himself had breathed them into being.

They hiked for another hour during which their stroll became a trudge, their conversation intermittent.

"Look, there's some trees over there. We parked by some trees." Mike was going by sight, his confidence in his map-reading skills undermined, and his sense of direction guided by hope more than evidence or even intuition. They changed direction once more and headed for the trees, hoping that this time they were *the* trees. They plunged into the woodland, the treetops casting low shadows on the ground making it difficult for them to see their way.

Annabelle looked up. The moon was full, the stars were out.

"Isn't this romantic?" she sighed.

"Romantic? We're lost in the middle of a bloody moor. At night. How can it possibly be romantic?" Mike shook out his map roughly. "Shine the light, would you? I'll try once more to get our bearings." Annabelle sighed and stomped over to him through the rough wild grasses at her feet. She shone her phone's light at the map, the beam bouncing off it so brightly that she had to squint.

"We wouldn't make very good spies, would we?

Mike looked at her. "Spies?"

"Anyone looking for us would find us in no time at all with a light this bright."

"Well, let's hope they do, because we are well and truly lost," he mumbled as he looked at the map. He lifted his head as he tried to fix on a landmark, before peering down at the map again, seemingly none the wiser. "Anyway, we're not spies, and spies don't use maps. They have gadgets and tech, and oh I get it, this is because I wouldn't bring the GPS, is it?"

"No, no." Annabelle pursed her lips and looked skywards.

"Well, you were right. About the GPS, I mean. I shouldn't have been so pig-headed."

"We'll get out of here, even if we have to walk all night. If worst comes to worst, Philippa's sure to send out a search party in the morning. Say, I'm sure I've seen this tree before."

"We should be getting to a crossroads soo— Arrgh!!" Mike leapt three inches into the air. There was a rustle in the trees next to them, followed by the sound of munching. Mike backed up, pushing Annabelle behind him until they reached a tree trunk some yards away. As they rounded it, Annabelle gasped and jumped as she bumped into a soft, velvety, hairy snout. A pair of big dark brown eyes, framed by long, black eyelashes, and covered in part by straggly pale brown hair regarded Mike and Annabelle mournfully. The sound of chewing continued, before the eyes closed and dipped to the ground once more. It was a chestnut brown pony, unconcerned by its company. Even the dogs were too tired to offer more than a quick sniff.

The pony's fair, long mane lay over its eyes and hung down low over the sides of its neck, its frame stout and sturdy. The pony stood alone, but Annabelle noticed two more through the trees, one a piebald, the other a gray. They all had shaggy long manes and rough coats.

"Wild ponies!" Annabelle whispered to Mike.

"Great, just what we need to add to our evening. Wild animals." Mike looked back at the pony warily. "Are they really wild? Like they could attack us?" The pony lowered its head to the floor to pull up more grass. It didn't look very wild.

"We'll be fine. Let's just not startle it."

Annabelle made to step out from behind the tree. "Stop!" Mike looked in the distance. Through the trees they could see two beams of light bobbing up and down. "Someone's coming!"

CHAPTER TWENTY-EIGHT

"But that's good, isn't it?" Annabelle said. "They can rescue us."

"No one coming out to these parts of the moor this late at night is up to any good, Annabelle. Trust me on that."

A car pulled up and the engine turned off. The lights stayed on. A door opened and another, smaller, beam of light appeared. They heard swishing noises as someone moved through the bracken, the light swaying from side to side. Mike, with Annabelle still behind him, retreated as the light came toward them. The ponies were alert now and had lifted their heads, watching. A woman emerged into the clearing. The piebald pony steadied itself and the woman walked toward it, talking softly, one hand out, the other behind her back. The pony allowed her to get close, and she quickly slipped a halter over its neck, rubbing it between the ears and feeding it from her hand. When she turned and walked away, a length of rope in her clenched fist, the pony obediently followed.

"But I thought they were wild!" Mike whispered to Annabelle. She shrugged.

"Let's follow them," she whispered.

They tracked the woman at a distance to a path that crisscrossed the moor. Parked next to a signpost was a battered Land Rover, a horse trailer coupled to it. The interior light came on to reveal another woman. Together the pair coaxed the pony into the horse trailer, all the while talking in a foreign language, their voices low.

"They're stealing the pony!" Annabelle exclaimed, her whisper feverish. She got out her phone. "I'll write down the number plate."

"K-B-D-1-2-Y" Mike relayed to her. The two women clambered into the front seats, and the interior light flashed on once more. The women were young, slim, and in their early twenties. They both had long hair, one was blond, the other brunette. They were focused and grim-faced as they sat looking out through the windscreen, before the driver turned to look behind her. The car swayed as it reversed away down the bumpy track.

Mike and Annabelle moved out from behind the trees.

"What do you think they are playing at?" Annabelle asked.

"I don't know, but text me that number, and I'll forward it to the guys at the station."

"Let's get back to the car. It's over here," Annabelle said looking at her phone.

Mike looked at her, astonished. "The car's over there?" He narrowed his eyes.

"Modern technology isn't such a bad thing, you know."

"Well, why didn't you say something?"

"Because you were so determined to do it your way. And I was quite enjoying myself. And now it looks like we may be on the hunt of some pony rustlers, so it's all good. Come on. You promised me a drink. If we leave now, we'll get one in just before closing time."

When they got to the Dog and Duck, a barman Annabelle hadn't seen before served them; a pint of real ale for Mike, an orange juice for Annabelle.

"Here you are, Vicar. I'm just leavin'," said Miles Chadwick who was vacating the table by the fireplace. It was the one that Annabelle had sat at when she'd spoken to Richard Venables. Mike and Annabelle sat down, the dogs curling up under the table by their feet. They continued the conversation they'd had in the car on the way back from the moor. Annabelle had brought Mike up to speed on the two murders and the characters who lived in the big house, as well as the angry confrontation between Theo and Venables and the fact that Venables had been released from custody just prior to Thomas being killed.

"So who has a motive?" Mike asked.

Annabelle threw up her hands and rolled her eyes. "They all do!" She leaned over the table and spoke so quietly, that Mike had to do the same. "Suki is in line to inherit her uncle's estate, Margaret was ashamed of her son," Mike raised his eyebrow skeptically. "He was a Nazi sympathizer and all round bad egg. It's not out of the question she might have murdered him, if unlikely."

"Okay, who else is in the frame?"

"Thomas' mother was a Holocaust survivor. He said he didn't find out about Theo's Nazi beliefs until after his death, but Thomas knew about the swastika tattoo Theo had on his hand, so he could have been lying. He might have murdered him in a fit of rage or due to some misplaced justice. He admitted to roughing up his room."

"But then he was murdered."

"Yes."

"Okay, who else?"

"There's Sally."

"She's the daughter of the guy arrested, is that right?"

"Yes, Sally was in love with Theo, but it wasn't requited."

Mike pushed his glass around and smiled at Annabelle's use of the old-fashioned term.

"It could have been a crime of passion, Mike!"

"Okay, okay," Mike put up his palms. "It's possible."

"Scott is in love with Sally, so Theo was his love rival. Perhaps he bumped Theo off to get him out of the way. They'd also had a falling out about money. Richard Venables, Sally's father, hated Theo for luring her to the Brotherhood. Julia hated him because he turned down her idea of setting up an animal sanctuary. I bet even Barnaby the rabbit wasn't too keen on him. Perhaps Theo threw his carrot tops away or something."

"Alibis?"

"None of them have one. They were all either in costume, hiding from one another in the woods, or in Margaret's case, alone in the house."

"And what about the weapon?"

"So that's the other curious thing. Theo was killed with a bolt through the heart. They use bolt guns in slaughterhouses to stun the cattle. Venables admitted to me he had worked in one."

"Well, there you are then."

"But why would he admit it so freely if he had something to hide?

"Annabelle, criminals aren't the sharpest knives in the drawer. You wouldn't believe what I've heard in an interview room. One told me he didn't have a mother once. He had 'M-U-M' tattooed across his knuckles!"

"But you see, Scott also makes bolts at his forge. They are on the table in the corner. Anyone could have taken one." Annabelle was still leaning forward, pressing her forefinger repeatedly into the small oak table.

"And Thomas' death? What's your theory?"

Annabelle threw herself back in her chair. She raised her hands, her palms upward. "He drowned in a inch or so of liquid, some kind of chemical used in the process of developing photographs."

"That would have taken a man, surely."

"Maybe, but with the element of surprise, I reckon a woman could have done it."

"Hmm. Well, I'd follow the money. Seems like Theo had a lot of enemies. Greed is nearly always behind a case like this. Jealousy and hate tend to be secondary motivators. Very possible, but not as likely. As for Thomas' death, it might be related, or it could have to do with something completely different. Perhaps Thomas killed Theo, and someone else killed Thomas for revenge?"

"I can't imagine Thomas killing anyone. He was a loving, sensitive soul. He loved nature, wildlife."

"Perhaps Venables killed them both. Ainslie obviously thinks so."

"Why would Venables kill Thomas? Why would anyone kill Thomas?"

"Perhaps Thomas knew something. Something we don't know about. Annabelle, look, I know you want to help, but you don't have to go around solving all the world's problems, you know. Ainslie's on it. It is his job."

"Do you know his sergeant?" Annabelle asked, pushing her brown hair behind her ear.

"Scarlett? Yeah, she's alright, good at her job." Annabelle held her breath. "A bit prickly, though. And she's always asking me for coffee. I have to keep turning her down, or I'd never get any work done."

"Really?" Annabelle lifted her glass of orange juice to hide the smirk that crept across her lips.

They heard a shout for last orders.

"Would you like another drink?" Mike asked.

Annabelle hesitated, "No, thank you. Best be getting home. I've got a busy day tomorrow, and you've got to trek back to Truro yet."

Mike picked up their empty glasses and deposited them on the bar.

"Thanks, Barbara," he said. Barbara was polishing glasses behind the counter.

"Oh, hello Inspector, didn't see you there." Barbara fluttered her false eyelashes in mock astonishment. She would have to have been blind not to see the couple sitting at the fireplace.

"'Night, Barbara," Annabelle said.

"'Night, you two," Barbara winked at her. Annabelle pretended not to notice.

Five minutes later, they rolled up to Annabelle's cottage. Mike kept the car engine running,

"By the way," he said gently. "I forgot to mention, I liked that picture of you in the mask."

"Oh!" Annabelle's eyes widened. "Oh!" She blushed, grateful for the low light.

"I thought you looked very mysterious and exotic. Rather beautiful, in fact."

"Did you?" Annabelle's blush was furious now. She'd wondered why she hadn't heard back from her brother. She looked out of the window and took a strand of hair, twirling it around her finger. She looked down at her lap.

Mike draped an arm over his steering wheel and looked at her. The light from the street lamp highlighted his profile. Silence filled the car like a heavy blanket, pinning them to their seats, freezing them in the moment. Neither of them moved nor spoke until Magic yawned and whined in the back.

"Well, I—I must be going," Annabelle said. Her hand darted around looking for the door handle.

"Will I see you tomorrow? Before I go back to the conference?"

"Yes, no, maybe, I don't know." Annabelle was now in full panic mode. She was yanking on the door handle. "Like I said, I have a busy day."

Seeing her struggle, Mike reached across her slowly and carefully pulled the lever. He pushed the door open for her. "I'll get the dogs," he said.

"No, it's alright, I can do it."

"Okay, good night then, Annabelle. Sorry about getting us lost." he said.

"Er, um, good night, Mike." Annabelle stumbled out of the car. As she straightened up, she paused. "Actually—"

"Yes?"

She turned around and bent over looking at Mike across the passenger seat. "Tomorrow. Yes."

"Ten thirty? Coffee, perhaps?"

"Yes, um, see you then. Goodnight." Annabelle opened the back door of the car and the dogs jumped out. She hurried up to her front door as gracefully as she could, knowing that Mike was watching her. He waited until she was safely in the cottage, and with a flick of his eyebrows, he drove off.

CHAPTER TWENTY-NINE

Annabelle opened her eyes. She immediately remembered what today was.

She clenched her fists and opened them again. She shut her eyes tight and held her breath. She exhaled slowly. Today was the day. The day she dreaded all year. The one that when it was all over, she would treat herself to a long soak in the bath and a big piece of cake, maybe two. Except this year, she was going to skip the cake.

It was the day for Biscuit's annual check-up. And that meant wrangling her into her cat carrier. Annabelle supposed these trips to the vet were the cause more than any other for Biscuit's mostly indifferent relationship with her owner. She knew it couldn't be fun being trapped in one of those carriers, but she had hoped that Biscuit would get used to it in time. Yet, despite many experiments, Annabelle had not found a set of conditions that placated her ginger tabby. Instead, she had reconciled herself to the fact that it would be necessary to walk down the Upton St. Mary high street with a cat that was intent on the feline equivalent of screaming bloody murder at least once a year.

Annabelle got up and went to her wardrobe. First, she donned a pair of heavy jeans and a t-shirt. Next, she put on a sweatshirt, a pair of thick gardening gloves, a pair of rubber boots, and finally a mask that she'd borrowed from Andy Kedgewick. Andy was a champion scuba diver who spent most of his time in exotic parts of the world swimming with wildly colorful fish. Andy was a popular speaker at the Women's Institute although Annabelle wasn't sure if his annual invitation was down to the entertainment the women derived from his slideshow of unusually shaped coral reef or the visual of the tanned, muscular diver himself.

There was nothing exotic about the task Annabelle had in mind, however. She knew from bitter experience that getting Biscuit to the veterinary clinic required meticulous planning and stealth worthy of a military operation. She said a little prayer.

Annabelle reached into the bottom of the wardrobe where she'd hidden the cat carrier the night before, and opening its door in readiness and hiding it behind her back, crept out of her bedroom in search of Biscuit.

She found her cat sleeping by the radiator in the living room. Annabelle nonchalantly walked up to her, looking up at the ceiling, muttering to herself, as if Biscuit was the last creature on her mind. As she got close, Biscuit lifted her head sleepily and regarded Annabelle with disinterest. For once, Annabelle appreciated her indifference and walked past her before circling back. Quick as a flash, she reached out with her gloved hand to grab Biscuit by the scruff of her neck and whisk her into the cat carrier. By the time Biscuit realized what was happening, it was too late, and Annabelle, in a well-executed move, dropped the lid down, fastening it securely before sitting on it to make absolutely sure Biscuit couldn't get out.

"Phew," Annabelle said brushing her hair from her mask. A feeling of exhilaration hit her. She raised her arms in the air, her fists clenched. "I did it! And no war wounds. No scratches or bites!" Biscuit was mewling loudly. "Sorry Biscuit, it won't be for long. We've got to go see Dr. Whitefield. For shots and things. You'll be fine. You'll see." She kneeled down and poked her finger through the wire before pulling it back quickly. She'd come this far without injury, best not to spoil things now.

She heard the back door open and close.

"Yoo-hoo, it's only me!" Philippa called out.

"I did it, Philippa! I did it!" Annabelle held up the cat carrier gleefully. She felt as proud as a toddler showing the postman her belly button. Biscuit was still howling inside.

"Well, that's a relief. Last time, I wasn't sure you'd get out of here alive," Phillipa said.

"Oh, my gosh, wasn't that terrible?" answered Annabelle. "I had scratches everywhere. And I had no idea how to get her down from that overhead beam. She stayed up there for two days, you know."

"I do know, Vicar. I was the one who climbed up and got her down.

"Oh yes, that's right. You were very brave, Philippa."

"Hmm, I don't know about that. More like exasperated. The standoff couldn't continue. Anyway, that's all in the past now. Where were you last night? How's the investigation coming along?"

"I was stumbling around the moors with Mike. We got lost."

"I'll bet you did, Reverend." Phillipa turned away, a small smile playing on her lips.

"No, we did, Philippa. And we came across two women taking a wild pony. We think they were rustling. It was very strange."

"Hmm, that is odd. You're not going to investigate that too, are you?"

Annabelle pursed her lips, turning down the corners of her mouth and waggling her head from side to side. She raised her eyebrows and looked at the ceiling.

"Annabelle," Philippa chided. "You won't have time for your congregation at this rate!" Philippa pulled out the flour from the cupboard, followed by a packet of sugar. She opened the fridge and set some butter on the counter. She busied herself lining a cake pan until she could hold herself in no longer.

"And how is the Inspector?"

"What? Oh, he's alright." Annabelle flopped in a chair at the kitchen table, her scuba diving mask pushed up onto her forehead. She took a breather, basking in the euphoria of knowing her day's toughest task was behind her, and it wasn't even 9 AM. "He's going back to the conference tonight."

"Will you see him again? Before he goes back, I mean."

"I don't know, Philippa." Annabelle was a little tetchy. A vague sense of loss and sadness crept over her, like she had made a mistake or missed an opportunity, perhaps made a fool of herself the previous evening.

Philippa changed the subject. 'I'm glad they have that man in custody again. That girl's father. From the big house. The one Barbara was talking about."

"They have? No one said so in the pub last night." Annabelle thought back and realized that Mike and she hadn't exactly invited social conversation as they had hugged their table in front of the fireplace. An icy wave ran through her as she suppressed a shudder of embarrassment. Biscuit was letting out a constant stream of yowls and now that the euphoria from her capture had waned, Annabelle was feeling the beginnings of a headache.

"They hauled him back in after the second murder almost immediately. The Chief Inspector's convinced it's him, so they say. What do you think?"

"Oh, I don't know. Venables was very angry that evening, that's for sure, and he'd clearly been drinking. And he threatened Theo. But why would he kill Thomas? Thomas was a sweetheart who just wanted what was best for his mother. Why would *anyone* want to kill him?" Annabelle sighed. "Anyway, it's nearly time for Biscuit's appointment. I'd best get going." She quickly ran upstairs to change before returning to the kitchen wearing her cassock and clerical collar.

Annabelle stood in front of the cat carrier and gave a short, sharp exhale, her hands out in front of her as if she were preparing for a bout of karate. With a sudden thrust, she picked up the carrier, prompting Biscuit to let out a particularly aggrieved growl. "Come on Biscuit, it isn't that bad. Anyone would think I was torturing you."

CHAPTER THIRTY

On the way to the vets, Annabelle passed Penelope Paynter on her chestnut mare, Equinox. She gave them a wide berth and Penelope raised her hand in thanks as she passed. Annabelle thought back to the pony rustling and the injured children at the rehearsal. She decided to make some phone calls.

"Pat? It's Annabelle. No, no, everything is fine. Tell me, I saw Tabitha was on crutches at rehearsal the other day." There was a pause as Annabelle listened to Tabitha's mother's reply. "Really? That's terrible." Another pause. "I know, but still. Give her our love, won't you? Tell her I hope she's is able to cast those crutches off very soon."

After the call ended, Annabelle phoned the Simmonds family, followed by the Crackers, the Rinkers, and the Trebuthwicks. Chloe had shown up to rehearsal with broken fingers, George with his arm in a sling, Nancy had injured both her feet, while Timmy was covered in nasty grazes. They all had a similar story. All had been injured in falls. From horses.

Annabelle nipped into a parking space a few doors down

from the veterinary surgery along the pretty high street that ran through the village. The cobbled street had low pavements that rose barely two inches either side of the road and was lined with stone mews cottages, some of them whitewashed, their square frontages unchanged in centuries thanks to their listed building status. The restrictions on development that preserved the heritage of the village gave it a timelessness rare in today's fast-paced modern world. Aside from the street lamps, cars, and fashions, one might think Upton St. Mary locals still lived in the 18th century.

Annabelle texted the information about the children's injuries to Mike before hurrying around to the passenger door. She reached in to grab the cat carrier. She wanted this visit to the vet to be over with as soon as possible. Biscuit was still mewling bitterly. Annabelle swung the carrier around and with her foot, closed the car door, only to nearly overbalance onto the pavement.

"Careful, Vicar!"

Sally bobbed and stretched out her arm to steady Annabelle, who was taller than she by some inches. With Sally was Julia. Barnaby was with them, poking out of Julia's jacket pocket as usual, his ears askew, one down, one up, propped there by the fabric of her jacket.

"Oof, thank you, I'm fine. Just taking Biscuit to the vet. She's not a fan."

"I can tell."

Julia bent down and made little clicking noises with her tongue. Biscuit immediately stopped her noise and leaned forward to investigate Julia's face. She sniffed the fingertip Julia laid on the carrier grille.

"What? How do you do that? She's been making a racket for the past thirty minutes!"

Julia smiled. "You just have to have the knack, Reverend. Not everyone has it."

"Well, I wish you could teach me. How are things up at the house?"

"Oh, you know, a little somber. We wanted to get out for some fresh air, so we thought we'd take a walk into town. They arrested my father again, did you know?" Sally said.

"Yes, I did hear something about that."

"I simply can't believe it. I know my father can be a hothead, and I know he's got form, but that was decades ago. He would never kill anyone, let alone two people and certainly not someone like Thomas." Sally wrung her hands and looked like she was about to cry again.

"At least we're getting on a little better. Now that Sally's father has been arrested again, we can stop suspecting one another," Julia said.

Sally glared at her. "How nice for you."

"How are the others doing?" Annabelle asked.

"Margaret stays in her room, mostly. I took her some supper last night. We hadn't seen her all day. She looked pale and tired, but she was alive," Julia said matter-of-factly. "Suki, is well, Suki. Dippy. The selfies continue unabated." Julia, sensing Biscuit was getting restless, leaned down to click her tongue at her again.

"And what about Scott? He seemed very perturbed the other night."

"Scott's still very upset about Theo. Thomas' death has just made it all the harder. He feels so bad that some of his last words with Theo were spoken in anger," Sally said.

"Were they? I didn't know that." Julia was surprised.

"They were arguing about money, Julia," Annabelle explained.

"They also discussed your idea for a donkey sanctuary," Sally added. Her voice had a hard edge to it.

"What about it?" Julia was suddenly a lot more alert.

"Said we couldn't afford it. He told me yesterday when I went to see him at the forge. Theo and Scott did argue about money, but they agreed on the subject of your donkey sanctuary. Neither of them wanted it."

"Scott never told *me*."

"No well, he, um..." Sally started to falter, "...also thought that you weren't, um, up for the responsibility. Said if you were so emotionally attached to animals that you needed to carry a rabbit around with you all the time, you wouldn't be able to manage, and the rest of us would have to help out. He didn't want to get lumbered with the work of it if you couldn't cope."

Julia took a long breath in through her nose and drew herself up to her full height.

"Is that so? Well, it's nice to know who your friends are, isn't it?" Julia jammed her hands in her pockets, causing Barnaby to shift over. He seemed unperturbed. Julia stared at the ground, tapping her foot.

"I'm sorry, Julia. But perhaps he's right. You are a bit... well, fragile at times. I know you love your animals, but..." Sally trailed off as Julia looked up angrily.

"I shall have something to say to Scott when I get back." Julia strode off.

"Oh dear, I've made things worse, Reverend." Sally looked imploringly at Annabelle. "Things aren't good at the house. We're all nervous, all on edge. Everyone wants the culprit to be my dad, and I feel stuck in the middle. I can't mention my doubts because if it wasn't him, it must have been one of us! I don't know what to think. It's an awful situation to be in."

Annabelle put Biscuit's carrier down on the ground and ignored the yowling that had started up again now that Julia had moved away. She took Sally in an embrace.

"I do hope things get cleared up for you soon. Perhaps you should go home, spend some time with your mother. I'm sure she needs you, what with your father in custody."

Sally pulled away from Annabelle and sniffed.

"Yes, perhaps you're right. Perhaps I'll get away. I don't know how the Brotherhood can possibly stay together after this." She pressed her lips together sadly, tears welling in the corners of her eyes. "I should catch up with Julia. I said too much. I'll talk to her some more. Calm her down. Goodbye, Vicar. I'll see you soon."

"Goodbye, Sally. Take care now," Annabelle watched as Sally walked quickly down the street, past the newsagents, the estate agents and new curry house, before acceding to Biscuit's demands. She sighed, bent down to pick up the carrier and pushed open the white wooden door beneath a bright green awning that announced "Veterinary Surgery."

Inside, the reception area was brightly lit with fluorescent lights. The walls, like the outside, were painted brilliant white and were bare except for the noticeboard that announced the date of the next cat adoption fair, the details of a number of lost pets, and the availability of local animal bereavement services. The tiled floor was white too, although not quite so brilliant as the walls. The floor wasn't even, and cracks had appeared in the tiles.

Annabelle didn't recognize the young woman behind the reception desk, her face so smooth it was shiny, but as so often happened, the receptionist recognized her.

"Good morning, Reverend. Who do you have with you today?"

"Biscuit Dixon, annual checkup." Annabelle lowered her voice. "Vaccinations," she whispered, pointing down at the carrier and shaking her head.

"Ah yes, here you are," the woman looked up from her computer. "Someone will be out to see you in a minute. Please take a seat."

Annabelle walked over to one of the chairs and sat down, placing the carrier on her lap. Biscuit looked around at her fellow patients, and letting out another yowl, promptly backed up as far as her carrier would allow. Annabelle looked around too, assessing the terrain. Veterinary surgery waiting rooms were often fraught, unpredictable places.

She caught the eye of Justin Case, an unfortunately named teenage boy who she knew had an equally unfortunate habit of occupying the only cell at the police station on a semi-regular basis. Justin was partial to petty pilfering, a tendency he appeared unable, or indeed, unwilling to curb. Faced with the recurring news that her son had stolen seemingly random items of zero value, items such as odd ends of rope, empty bottles, packaging peanuts and the like, his exasperated mother would cry, "What for, Justin? What for?" "Just in case," he assured his mother, when she bailed him out of a morning following the previous night's transgression, "It's my name, innit?" In this case, Justin held a cage containing a bearded dragon whose only moving body part appeared to be his eyelids.

Across from him sat Mr. Penrose, but today he didn't have his Pitbull, Kylie, with him. Instead, a miniature English Bulldog sat in his lap, its nose flattened like a boxer's, its pink tongue hanging out as it panted.

"New puppy, Mr. Penrose?"

"Yes, isn't she gorgeous? I'm thinking of calling her Clarissa."

Clarissa had a white snout, forehead, and neck, but the rest of her was brown. Her loose, wrinkled skin looked like an expensive camel-colored overcoat, the type of which is generally worn by managers of Premier League football teams on winter match days. However, in Clarissa's case, it was three sizes too big for her.

Clarissa slowly looked around at Annabelle before her eyes dropped to Biscuit and indifferently roved away again.

"She's lovely," Annabelle said optimistically.

"Biscuit!"

Annabelle stood up, pleased to be away from the staring reptile and the breathless Clarissa.

"That's us!"

"Come with me." Biscuit started to yowl again and the veterinary assistant took the cat carrier from Annabelle. Silence immediately descended.

"How do you do that?"

"What?"

"Get her to cooperate. She fights with me constantly."

"Oh, you just have to have the knack. If you don't have it, you don't stick with this type of job for very long. Animals always know, you know." The veterinary assistant left the small consulting room leaving Annabelle wondering what exactly it was that animals knew, when they knew it, why she didn't know it, and what it all meant.

A few minutes later, the door swung open and Dr. Whitefield, the vet, came in. Annabelle always thought Dr. Whitefield resembled a cow. He was huge, with floppy jowls and big, fat hands. All he had to do was take a black marker pen to his white coat and the transformation would be complete.

"Good morning, Reverend. How are you?"

"Very well, Dr. Whitefield."

"Who have you brought in to see me today?"

Annabelle went through the same routine she had at the reception desk.

The vet opened up the cat carrier and lifted Biscuit out. Annabelle stepped back in alarm, her arms in front of her face ready to defend herself, but Biscuit was as floppy and compliant as a sleeping baby.

"How do you *do* that?"

"You have to have—"

"I know, I know, the knack." They both finished together and laughed.

The vet examined Biscuit, took her temperature and gave her the necessary shots, all without drama or injury.

"I don't know how you animal people do it, I really don't. The fuss she makes on the way here is beyond comprehension," Annabelle marveled.

"How are things in God's world?"

"Oh, you know, heavenly as always," she replied.

"I hear you've been up at the big house, getting involved in that murder investigation."

"Just helping out where I can. Part of my chaplaincy, really."

"Isn't that where Julia Snow lives? Small lady, strong, loves her animals. She's part of that cult, isn't she?"

"It's not technically a cult, but yes, she lives there. Do you know her?"

"We vets all know one another in these parts."

"She's a vet?"

"Oh yes. It was a few years ago now. She had to stop practicing, she went off the rails, you know. It was a terrible shame."

"Oh?"

"There was this horrendous equine neglect case. Julia worked for an animal charity. She had to shoot over a dozen horses. Went off her rocker and had to retire. Disappeared completely until she resurfaced in Upton St. Mary in that cult. I was so surprised to see her in the market square the other d— Wait! Reverend!"

The door swung closed.

The vet peered out into the hall.

"But Reverend, what about your cat?" he called after her.

"Philippa! Call Philippa! She'll know what to do!"

CHAPTER THIRTY-ONE

"Annabelle! Philippa told me I'd find y—. Hey, are you alright?"

Mike had been coming through the door of the veterinary surgery just as Annabelle was leaving it. She'd hit her nose on his chin. Deep, bone crushing pain was spreading like treacle through her head. Her eyes closed, but she nodded as she covered her face with her hand and lumbered over in the direction of her car.

"B—big house. N—now," she mumbled.

"But Annabelle, wait. Slow down," Mike said.

"N—no time." She reached her car and pulled open the driver's door.

"F—Follow m—me." She got in, and shaking her head very carefully in order to clear it, started the engine.

"Oh, alright." Mike ran over to his car parked a few spaces away and set off a few yards behind her.

As she raced around blind, hairpin bends and shot straight across crossroads, Mike stayed close to Annabelle's bumper wondering where on earth they were going.

"Crazy woman," he muttered, before pulling on his handbrake in order to effect the sharp right hand turn Annabelle had made at the last moment.

They were on a gravel and sand path now, and Annabelle's tires were raising dust as she bumped and banged her way along. The trees that formed the forest tunnel they were driving through opened up to reveal the frontage of a house that had once been magnificent, but which was now in a state of decrepitude.

Up ahead, Annabelle got out of the car.

"Sally, Sally!" She banged on the door and tried the handle. When it didn't open, she ran around the side of the house and under an archway. Ahead of her, Sally came out from the kitchen.

"What is it, Annabelle?"

"Julia! Where's Julia?"

Mike ran up. "Annabelle, what's going on?"

Annabelle was panting, her head was hurting, and where her nose was, it felt like there was a pancake on her face. "Julia. Julia's the murderer." She gasped, and leaned over. Mike took her hand and put an arm around her.

"But Annabelle, how do you know that?" Mike asked.

"There's no time to explain. We need to find her fast!"

"She's down at the smithy with Sc—" Sally stopped and put her hand to her mouth. She caught Annabelle's eye.

"Oh!" Annabelle turned to Mike who was looking between the two women frantically, desperately hoping one of them would explain what was going on.

"We have to get to the forge and stop her, Mike!"

"Okay, which way?"

"This way," Annabelle made to retrace their steps back to the car when Sally stopped them.

"Scott has his smithy over near the old stables down by the main road," Sally explained to Mike. "But the quickest way to get there is that way." She pointed across the lawn. The ground fell away in a gentle slope. There was no way to see the smithy, only the general direction in which it lay.

Mike took off across the grass. "Are you coming?" he yelled looking back at Annabelle. She wasn't following him. She had run out of the courtyard but gone in a different direction.

"This way, it's quicker!" she shouted.

Bemused, Mike skidded as he spun around on the grass to follow Annabelle. They were running away from the smithy. *How could it be quicker?*

Annabelle rounded a corner of the house and ran over to another building set apart by a gravel driveway full of weeds. There, parked up against the brick wall of the garage were two quad bikes. Theo had shown them to her the night he had given her a tour of the house and grounds.

"Surely not, Annabelle?" Mike said. Annabelle looked at him, her eyes ablaze now, all fogginess gone. "Silly question?"

"Yes, very," Annabelle replied.

"Do they work?"

Annabelle hoisted up her cassock's skirts and climbed on. She turned the key in the ignition and the engine revved. A pleasant whiff of gasoline settled around her, not that she could smell it. "Yep!" She set her shoulders, "Let's go!"

Mike jumped on the second quad bike and off they went, the big fat wheels flattening the grass as they bounced and bumped their way across the lawn.

"Stand up in your seat!" Mike cried out over the noise of the engines.

"What?"

"Stand up in your seat as you go over the bumps! Makes for an easier ride! Oh, and lean to the opposite side when making a turn!"

Annabelle was soon handling her bike like a pro, hanging off the side as she navigated corners and adjusting her speed to keep her wheels on the ground. But then Mike overtook her with a smart shortcut around a tree.

"Nooooooo!" Annabelle shouted and increased her speed, regaining the lead as she jumped a bump and gracefully moved with the bike's momentum as it flew through the air and hit the ground.

Mike continued to snap at her wheels, but Annabelle held him off with some fancy feinting and devilish daring, pulling off some impressive moves that made him wonder whether there was something she wasn't telling him about her youth.

As they went over the summit of the gentle hill in front of the forge, the building came into view. As the bike's engines slowed to a puttering, the forge appeared deserted. They clambered off their bikes and ran inside. What greeted them caused them to pull up short.

Up against a wall was Scott, his eyes wide. In front of him, pressing a captive bolt gun to his chest, was Julia. The room was cool, the coals in the furnace black and lifeless. On the floor was a hunk of metal, hard and misshapen. Tongs lay nearby.

Julia kept her eyes on Scott, her jaw clenched.

"Julia. Steady now—" Annabelle's voice was soothing.

"I knew you'd find me eventually."

"We can work this out."

"No, we can't, Reverend. What's done is done. And I don't regret it. Theo was an evil man. Evil! He refused to let me have the animals. He refused! After he'd promised!"

"Julia, please. It's okay. Put the gun down." Annabelle walked slowly up to her, stopping a few feet away.

"You don't understand! I love animals. I always have. When I was a child, I had more pets than friends. It didn't matter what they were – fish, rats, guinea pigs, birds, cats, dogs. I loved them all."

Annabelle nodded, "They are all God's creatures."

"All I ever wanted to do was work with them. I never considered anything else. And I did! For twenty years. Then... then..." Scott made a movement. Julia pressed the bolt gun into his chest harder and growled.

"Okay, okay," Scott said, his voice trembling, his hands up by his ears. He stopped moving.

"Tell me, Julia," Annabelle said.

"There was an animal welfare call." Julia's shoulders slumped, but she held the gun firmly. "I was called out to a farm where a horse dealer had neglected his animals. It was horrendous. We were able to rehabilitate and rehome many of the horses, but fifteen of them were too far gone." Julia's eyes were streaming with tears. She took one hand off the gun and roughly wiped at her face. "Barnaby is my therapy animal. I've had him since that day." She looked down at the lop-eared rabbit in her pocket, his droopy ears clearly reflecting his owner's downcast mood.

"I had to shoot them all. It devastated me. I had a breakdown and couldn't work anymore. That's how I came to join the group. I met Theo when I was hiking one day. We got talking, he was a good listener, and I told him my troubles. He enticed me into," Scott moved again, and Julia pressed down harder with the gun, clenching her teeth as she spoke, "the *group* with promises that I could work with animals again. I grew the vegetables and fruit and such, but I really wanted to help animals. I'm good at it, and *so* many need my help.

"So what happened?" Annabelle asked gently.

"Before I joined the Brotherhood, Theo promised me that if I pulled my weight and showed my commitment to the group, I could set up an animal sanctuary for injured, neglected, and old animals, ones that couldn't find a home. So at every place we stayed, I devoted myself to the group, went out and made friends with the locals, soliciting donations, selling our produce. I did everything asked of me, and we were very successful, but my dream was to start a donkey sanctuary. They often have nowhere to go when their working lives end and live in terrible conditions, sick, and neglected. But every time I talked to Theo about it, he kept making excuses that we hadn't enough room, or we hadn't enough money, or we were moving too often.

"When we moved here, with all this space, I could see my dream turning into reality. I had more than contributed to the Brotherhood, so I drew up a business plan. I envisaged the donkeys being shipped here from the continent or Ireland or other places around the country and cared for until the end of their natural lives, safely and peacefully. We could offer open days, an adopt-a-donkey scheme, and school trips. I did so much work to prepare, to get him to agree, and he'd *promised* me! And finally, he said no. Wouldn't even consider it. He laughed. Every time he passed me he would make *donkey sounds*. I just flipped. I had had it." She pushed the bolt gun harder into Scott's chest as though he were Theo. "Theo was a nasty, mean cad who cared about no one but himself. The legend of St. Petrie and Lord Darthamort? Pah! He couldn't care less about being a good person. He was just out for himself."

"So you killed him?"

"It was easy. The hardest part of the plan was to make myself a Darthamort costume. It made me sick to do it, all that fur and teeth, but I did it for the donkeys. Once the fireside ceremony was done, I changed into it so I could move around without being noticed. With us all running everywhere, you couldn't tell there was an extra Darthamort. Besides, no one paid any attention to me. They were all busy chasing or escaping."

"Theo was too lazy to wear the full costume. He was easy to spot. I'd saved my bolt gun from my days as a vet. It was the one I used on the horses, but this time I used it on Theo. Seemed fitting, justice. Very Lord Darthamort-like, punishing evil."

"And Thomas? What about him? What had he done to hurt you?" asked Annabelle softly.

Julia closed her eyes. She rocked back on her heels. Her head dropped. Slowly she released her pressure on Scott's chest and her hand fell. She staggered over to a chair by the cold forge and sat down. Scott sank to the ground. They all watched as Julia dropped the gun to the floor and put her head in her hands.

Annabelle leaned over and quietly picked up the weapon. Mike relaxed and stifled a yawn in the background. Annabelle had the situation in hand. He knew all he had to do was wait. He was only needed for the arrest.

"Thomas. Poor, stupid, silly Thomas. He got caught up in this by accident. I didn't want to kill him, but I had no choice. He caught me on film. I couldn't see well with my Darthamort head on. I had to take it off to deliver the kill. After Theo was dead, I saw Thomas snapping away and suspected that he'd got a shot of me. He didn't realize at first, but later when he was inspecting his photos, he saw he'd captured me in the background of one of them. I went to his darkroom, and he told me he knew what I had done. I destroyed the photo after Thomas was dead. He didn't even put up a fight.

"I thought that would be it, but then I found out about this piece of—" Julia stomped furiously over to Scott who put his hands over his head, cowering. "You betrayed me too!"

That was Mike's cue. He quickly slipped over and took Julia's wrists.

"Julia Snow, I am arresting you for the murders of Theodore Westmoreland and Thomas Reisman. You do not have to say anything, but it may harm your defense if you do not mention when questioned, something which you later rely on in court. Anything you do say may be given in evidence."

Julia nodded sadly, all her fight gone now. "Aren't you going to cuff me?"

"I don't think there's any need for that. I don't think you're going anywhere."

Julia looked up at Annabelle. "But how did you know it was me?"

"I learned from Dr. Whitefield that you had been a vet and had had a breakdown, and that you knew how to use a bolt gun. Obviously, you had had a disagreement with Theo. I realized that you must have disguised yourself in a Lord Darthamort costume to shoot him. But what really clued me in was a photo I saw in Thomas' darkroom. There was a picture of an owl stalking a rabbit. But it was no ordinary field rabbit. It was Barnaby. I could tell by his ears. You couldn't carry Barnaby while wearing the Darthmort costume, so I figured you must have left him on the ground while you killed Theo and gone back for your rabbit later."

Julia nodded. "Clever. I could tell you were smart. You care about animals, in your own way. What will happen to me now?"

"You will be held until your trial and then jailed for the duration of your sentence. In time and with luck, you will go to an open prison where you'll be able to work outside. You might even be able to work with animals. That's probably the best you can hope for," Mike said.

Fifteen minutes later, a police car arrived, and Julia was dispatched to the station in Truro. There was an argument when the accompanying police officer refused to take Barnaby into custody along with Julia. After a standoff, Scott offered to take care of him, and Julia acquiesced.

"Aren't you going too?" Annabelle asked Mike.

"In a bit. But first we have something to do."

"What?"

"We have to return the quad bikes!"

"Oh yes!" Annabelle's eyes widened. She started to run. "Race you!"

Mike clambered on to his bike and roared off, closely followed by Annabelle.

Scott came out of his smithy, cradling Barnaby and watched

the scene, the two of them on their bikes, retreating in the distance, their hands wide as they gripped the handlebars, their bodies hunched over, and Annabelle's cassock flowing out behind her.

"How about that? A vicar on a quad bike. That's not a sight you see every day is it, Barnaby?"

EPILOGUE

"Annabelle!"

Annabelle was dashing down the corridor in the village hall. There was just half an hour to go to the performance. The children's excitement had been building all day and was only topped by the near hysteria felt by Annabelle and the legion of parents who had volunteered to help.

In the toilets that were tonight acting as the boys' and girls' dressing rooms, girls were giggling and twirling in their costumes while boys were good-naturedly tolerating the ministrations of their mothers who were scrubbing stage makeup onto their faces. The makeup team was led by Barbara, who had taken on the leadership role with relish and who had needed absolutely no training whatsoever in the application of thick, bright, overstated cosmetics.

In the kitchen, Joan Pettigrew, the pianist was warming up by fingering her scales on the window ledge, while the boys on electric guitar and drums, Nathan Mead and Sammy Burke, were tuning and loosening up. The low sounds of a bass guitar and the occasional crash of cymbals rose above the cacophony of sound that resulted from forty children who were about to deliver the results of two months hard work and sing at the top of their voices and from the bottom of their hearts.

Annabelle turned to see Mike coming toward her. He smiled.

"You're back! You're here!"

"Of course."

"You've come to see the performance?"

"Wouldn't miss it for the world. I know how hard you've worked on it. I can't wait. I'm sure it's going to be magnificent and heartwarming and that everyone in the audience will absolutely love it."

"I do hope so."

"I also wanted to tell you about the pony rustling, but perhaps now isn't a good time?"

"I'd love to hear it, but later. I can't think about anything but the show right now."

"I brought you these. A sort of good luck gift." Mike reached into his pocket and pulled out a small box.

Annabelle's eyes widened, and she took the box from him. Haltingly, she opened it. Inside was a tiny pair of rose gold cross earrings embellished with shimmering blue diamonds.

"Ohhhhh, you bought these for me? They're beautiful! Thank you." She kissed him on the cheek. He smelled of pine. "I shall put them on right away and wear them for the performance. My lucky charm," she beamed. They stood there staring at one another, their eyes shining.

"Well, good luck then." Mike swung his arms, not sure quite what to do with them. "Break a leg." He took a couple of steps backward and gave a small fist pump before turning and walking into the performance hall. Annabelle, clutching the small box, watched him walk away, an idea forming as she wondered whether she had the time, or the nerve, to pull it off.

The children filed into the room, their faces solemn but twitching with nervous grins as they worked to remember Annabelle's instructions.

"Smile, sing your hearts out, and most of all, have fun," she had told them at the pre-performance pep talk.

Camera flashes popped, and Kevin Poulter, dad to Sharon and the videographer for the night, started filming. Parents, siblings, grandparents, uncles, and aunties had come from miles around to see the performance and the atmosphere in the room was hot with anticipation. It was standing room only, and as the children took their places, they searched for their families in the crowd.

Spontaneous applause broke out at the sight of the children and continued as the musicians filed into the room. Annabelle brought up the rear and entered carrying her conductor's baton, acknowledging the audience and walking up to the music stand to take her place in front of the children. The clapping died down and a murmur rippled through the room. The packed audience of proud parents, family members, other locals, and visiting clergy looked at one another in surprise. For Annabelle was wearing a dress.

The lightweight shift in dusky pink skimmed her body. It reached to just below her knees. Tulip-shaped, three-quarter length sleeves ended at her elbows. A small band of white in the upstanding collar was just enough to mark her as clergy, while on her feet were a pair of pointy, slingback pumps in a matching shade of pink. The outfit was modest and pretty and feminine. The solid shade accented her blue eyes perfectly.

The crowd was momentarily dumbstruck, but as Annabelle raised her arms to begin the first song, the clapping started back up and got louder and louder, punctuated by the odd cheer as the crowd communicated their approval of this new vision of their beloved Reverend.

Annabelle had caught sight of Mike sitting in the front row.

Now the lights dimmed, and she smiled at the children, as she waited for the applause to die down. She flicked back her hair and drew everyone's attention, her new earrings glittering in the half-light.

They made it! All the way through the list of colors. Granted they'd been carried along by the fourteen year olds, Trevor and Abigail, but they were all making noise on the long last note, nearly all of them tuneful.

Annabelle had told the children to "la" or hum if they forgot the words, and bob their heads in time. Taking her words to heart, four-year-old Maisie bobbed her head like she was at a Led Zeppelin concert. She was in the front row wearing her sheep's costume made from many cotton wool balls glued to a vest.

Things had been chaos in Maisie's household earlier. Just before they left the house, she had become unhappy with her sheep costume. She'd wanted to be an angel instead, so her harried mother had compromised, and Maisie had gone on stage as a sheep angel. She was now, in addition to her sheep costume, wearing a pair of wings and the biggest, longest, emerald green clip-on earrings Barbara's jewelry collection could bring forth.

After the concert was over, in appreciation for the childfree hours that rehearsals had provided and the amount of effort the concert had demanded of Annabelle, she was presented with a huge bunch of flowers and two bottles of hard liquor. Many of the grateful parents and enthusiastic locals crowded around Annabelle to personally offer their thanks and congratulations.

Sally walked up pushing an elderly woman in a wheelchair.

"Sally, how are you?" Annabelle held out her hands. Sally took them briefly.

"I'm well, thank you, Reverend."

"Where are you living now? I heard you all moved out and went your separate ways."

"Yes, that's right. Scott went up to London to search for streets paved with gold. Margaret and Suki found a cousin of her late husband to go live with. We keep in touch, well, me and Scott do."

"And you? What are you doing?"

"I'm working at the care home in Mevagissey. I live-in. I'm really enjoying it. Elderly folks are so much fun. This is Eta Reisman, Thomas' mother." Sally indicated the woman in the wheelchair. The senior looked up with rheumy eyes.

Annabelle bent down and placed a gentle hand on her knee. "So pleased to meet you."

"Eta can't hear you. She's deaf and nearly blind, but she has a lovely soul. Guess who lives at the care home with her?"

Annabelle raised her eyebrows.

"Alexander Drummond! They sit and have tea together most days. He's a bit too far gone to know what's happening, but Eta is as sharp as a tack and knows exactly what's what. She teaches me every day how to be a better person."

"And how are things with your father?"

"Improving. I'll go home eventually but not just yet."

"I'm glad things are working out for you. I wish you well, Sally."

"You too, Reverend. Fabulous performance!"

When the crowd thinned, Mike, who had been standing back giving her the space to chat with her parishioners, came over. "Great job, Annabelle. I told you it would be fantastic."

"Your lucky charm earrings made all the difference."

"I'm sure that was it."

They both smiled and gave each other a hug. Over his shoulder, Annabelle's eyes widened as she saw Chief Inspector Ainslie coming toward them.

Ainslie was as big and burly as always, his trench coat flapping as he marched toward her, except this time he was wearing a huge grin. He was carrying Maisie, who had dispensed with her sheep costume and whose angel wings were now askew. In her hand was a bouquet of gladioli that she was swishing through the air like a light saber.

"Hello, Chief Inspector, I didn't realize you would be here tonight."

"Couldn't miss my granddaughter's star performance now could I?"

Annabelle looked at Maisie who was now bashing the Chief Inspector over the head with her flowers.

"Maisie's your granddaughter? I had no idea."

"Wasn't she fantastic? When she let out that "moo," right on time, I couldn't have been prouder."

As he spoke, Ainslie seemed oblivious to the fact that Maisie was attaching her earrings to his large earlobes and stroking his bald head. Mike, in particular, tried to focus on what the Chief Inspector was saying, but the sight of his boss wearing huge, dangling costume jewelry while his granddaughter lovingly pet his head as if it were a small animal, made it difficult.

"Anyhow, Nicholls, well done on the cases. Both the cult thing, and the pony thing. Glad to see you so committed. We weren't sure about you, but you put your back into those cases and got results."

"The murder case had nothing to do with me, sir. I was merely the arresting officer. It was all the Reverend here. She made the deductions, worked out who the killer was, and got them to confess. She should be recommended for a community award."

"Yes, you're right, I suppose." Ainslie coughed. "Well, congratulations for apprehending the murderer with the help of your lady friend here." He nodded at Annabelle. "She might not be one of us, but I can see that the two of you are a team, so I'll see what I can do. I shall be recommending you for a promotion when I get back in on Monday. See that you don't mess up, alright, or get distracted with, er, God and such."

Annabelle squeezed Mike's hand. He squeezed it back.

When everyone had gone, Annabelle flopped down on a chair and fanned herself with a program. Mike sat down more carefully beside her.

"So what did happen about the 'pony thing?'"

"We tracked down the person who was helping the rustlers," he said.

"Who was it?"

"It was a vet in Liskeard who'd developed a taste for the good life. The women would steal the ponies from the moor and in return for a cut of the profits, the vet would drug the ponies so they were docile. The women would clip their coats so they lost their rugged, wild look, then they sold them off as children's pets. Of course, after a time, the drugs wore off and the ponies reverted back to their natural wild selves. Nasty. Someone could have been killed. We've apprehended all three, and they'll face trial later in the year."

"How awful. What will happen to the ponies they stole?"

"Three of them are staying with their owners and will be subject to welfare checks for the next three years. Two of them have gone to a horse and pony sanctuary near Tintagel. When they are ready, new homes will be found for them."

"Thank goodness. All's well that ends well, then. That's a big relief. And perhaps the number of walking wounded in the village will go down."

"Look, why don't we go back to your place? Celebrate your success. I've got some champagne in the car."

"Do you ordinarily go around with bottles of champagne in your car?"

"No, of course not. I brought it specially." Mike looked at her oddly.

"Come on, then. Let's go." Annabelle linked her arm in

Mike's and off they set, Annabelle's heart full of triumph and anticipation.

At the cottage, Annabelle grabbed two glasses from the cupboard and joined Mike on the red sofa in her cozy living room.

"I've got something else for you. I popped in to see my sister on my way home from the conference, and she gave me this," Mike said.

"You told your sister about me?"

"Of course! Your brother's *met* me." Mike placed a white cardboard box on her lap. Around it was wrapped a pink ribbon with a large gold and pink bow on top.

"It isn't a cake is it? I'm trying to be good."

"Good? You can't not be good. You're a vicar."

"No, I mean with my eating. I'm trying to eat fewer sweets. Slim down a bit."

"Well, that's a shame, because my sister's a Master Baker. She works for one of the top London restaurants as their patisserie chef. She'll have you knee deep in cake before you know it, if you let her."

Annabelle rolled her eyes. "Good Lord, I am done for."

Mike lifted the lid on the box. "I think it's time you were just a little bit bad, don't you?"

Annabelle leaned over to look in the box. What she saw nearly caused her to fall face first into it.

The heart-shaped cake was covered in cream. Around the edges were piped red roses and across the face of the cake were sprinkled tiny red hearts. A few more lay scattered on the cake tray. A chocolate arrow speared the cake and the word "Love" had been written in chocolate and placed at an angle, supported by more roses, on the surface. It was simple, tasteful, and elegant. And it shocked Annabelle to her core.

"It's made with buttercream because I know that's your favorite."

"Oh, Mike. You are full of surprises. Thank you."

"Shall I get a knife so you can have a slice?"

"You want me to eat it?" She looked at him in horror. "I'm not going to eat it. I'm going to frame it!"

Mike raised his eyebrows.

"Oh, alright, but not just yet. I want to look at it some more. And when I do take a bite, just a little. Then you must take it away or I'll scoff the whole lot."

"Okay, deal. I'll take it down the station. They will inhale it."

"I'll save the decoration. You'll never hear the last of it otherwise."

They sat quietly for a while. "I wouldn't worry about being good, if I were you." Mike said. "I think you're quite good enough as you are."

Annabelle turned to look at him. Mike leaned toward her, and when their lips touched, she felt she was melting and on fire at the same time. Their kiss lasted a full ten seconds.

"What took you so long?" she murmured when they broke apart.

"You could have made the first move. Haven't you heard? Kissing is an equal opportunity sport."

Annabelle shuddered. "No siree."

"No, well, maybe not. But you know, you're quite intimidating."

"Me? Intimidating?"

"You're so *good*. And holy. And everyone loves you. And well, you're a vicar. I'm a divorced detective."

Silence descended once more.

"You look lovely in your dress," Mike said eventually, quietly.

"Thank you. It's a bit more feminine than my cassock, isn't it?"

"Well, I don't mind what you wear, but I will say that cassock is a little off-putting."

"In what way?"

"Well, um, there's rather a lot of *cloth*."

Annabelle smiled.

"Look, it's not every day one falls for a female vicar. I've certainly never fallen for one before. It's different. I wasn't quite sure of the rules."

"The villagers haven't helped. They've been placing bets, you know, and I think Philippa and Barbara have been trying to track you down. I overheard them discussing how to do it. They were googling you."

"I think they wanted to give me a talking-to. There's a pile of messages from them back at the station."

"And then there's your other female admirers."

"My what? Who?"

"You said yourself Sergeant Lawrence keeps inviting you for coffee."

"Yeah, but that's profession— Really? You think? No!"

It was Annabelle's turn to raise her eyebrows.

"And, according to Jim Raven, there's Shenae in the canteen."

"The one with the piercings?" Mike dropped his head back onto the back of the sofa. "Gosh." He started to laugh. Annabelle joined in, and soon they were laughing uproariously, Mike's arm around Annabelle, her giggling into his shoulder.

When they stopped laughing, Annabelle propped herself up on one elbow and brushed the hair away from her face. She looked down at him. "Seriously though, I may be a vicar, I may have a flock and God at my side, but I also want a partner, a living, breathing person. At the end of the day, I'm just a girl who wants to be loved and cherished. I want someone supporting me, lifting me up, and helping me with the everyday stuff of life. And I will do the same in return."

"I would like to be that person for you, Annabelle."

"I would like to be that person for you, Mike."

They watched the last minutes of the sunset, the bright white light of the sun fading and turning the sky around it gray and pink before the glow disappeared completely. The dogs now lay in front of the fireplace, the occasional sound of their tails making a dull thump against the fireside rug. Even Biscuit jumped on Mike's lap and settled herself down.

Annabelle reached to turn on a low light. Mike put his arm around her shoulder, and she kissed him gently before laying her head on his shoulder. She scratched Biscuit at the base of her ears. Biscuit purred. The dogs yawned and closed their eyes. All was still and dark and silent. Life didn't get any better than this, Annabelle was certain. Life, love, God, and dogs.

And cats. Don't forget the cats.

REVERENTIAL RECIPES

CONTINUE ON TO CHECK OUT THE RECIPES FOR GOODIES FEATURED IN THIS BOOK...

LOVELY LEMON TART

For the base:
6 oz. digestive biscuits or graham crackers, crushed
3 oz. butter, melted
1 oz. brown sugar

For the filling:
3 tablespoons corn flour/starch
⅓ pint water
Finely grated rind of 2 lemons
Scant ¼ pint lemon juice
3 oz. sugar
2 egg yolks

Pre-heat the oven to 140°C/275°F. Place the digestive/graham cracker crumbs in a bowl and work in the melted butter and brown sugar.

Use this mixture to line the base of an 8-inch flan ring. Place in the fridge to set firm while making the filling.

To prepare the filling, mix the corn flour/starch and water

together in a saucepan. Add the lemon rind and juice and bring slowly to the boil, stirring constantly with a wooden spoon. Simmer gently until the mixture thickens, then remove from the heat and stir in the sugar.

Leave to cool slightly, then beat in the egg yolks. Pour this mixture into the chilled crumb base.

Bake in a very cool oven for 30 minutes.

PIOUS PLUM & ALMOND CRUMBLE

2 oz. butter
4 oz. soft white breadcrumbs
2 oz. soft brown sugar
2 oz. flaked almonds
½ teaspoon ground cinnamon
1 lb. plums, stoned and lightly poached
Heavy whipping or double cream, whipped to serve

Preheat the oven to 180°C/350 °F.

Melt the butter in a pan. Stir in the breadcrumbs, sugar, almonds and cinnamon.

Put the plums in a pie dish, then sprinkle the breadcrumb mixture over the top. Bake in a preheated oven for 30-35 minutes.

Serve cold with the cream. **Serves 4.**

Note:

This is a very versatile recipe with many variations. The

plums can be substituted with lightly poached apples or rhubarb and instead of flaked almonds, try using chipped walnuts or Brazil nuts.

REFORMED RHUBARB FLAN

6 oz. general purpose/plain flour, sifted
3 oz. white cooking fat or lard
2-3 tablespoons water
1 lb. rhubarb, cut into 1-inch lengths
1 egg
6 oz. sugar
1 oz. cornflour/starch
1 oz. butter
Grated rind of 1 lemon
Juice of 1 lemon made up to ¼ pint with water

Preheat the oven to 180°C, 350°F, Gas mark 4.

Put the flour into a bowl and rub in the fat until the mixture resembles breadcrumbs. Add the water and mix to a soft dough. Chill for 30 minutes.

Roll out the pastry and line a 10-inch flan tin.

Arrange the rhubarb in circles in the flan tin.

Put the egg, sugar, cornflour/starch, butter, lemon rind,

lemon juice, and water in a pan. Bring to the boil slowly, stirring all the time.

Spread the lemon mixture over the rhubarb. Place in the preheated oven for 30 minutes, then increase the heat to 200°C, 400°F, Gas mark 5 for a further 15 minutes. Serve warm.

Variation:

This flan can be made with orange instead of lemon. Follow the recipe but reduce the amount of sugar to 4 oz. and add ½ teaspoon ground ginger, if preferred.

SOULFUL SCONES

6 oz. general purpose/plain flour
½ teaspoon salt
4 teaspoons baking powder
2 teaspoons ground almonds
2 oz. butter, cut into chunks
2 oz. golden raisins/sultanas
¼ pint milk
A few drops of almond extract/essence
Milk, to glaze

These scones are delicious to eat just simply buttered, or you can make a real Cornish cream tea out of them by spreading with butter, then strawberry jam, and topping with clotted or lightly whipped double cream.

Preheat the oven to 200°C, 400°F, Gas Mark 6. Sift flour, salt and baking powder together in a bowl, then stir in the ground almonds.

Add the butter, and rub it in until the mixture resembles fine breadcrumbs then add the golden raisins/sultanas.

Make a well in the centre of the mixture, and pour in the milk and almond extract/essence. Mix lightly with a wooden spoon or fork until a soft dough is formed.

Turn the dough on to a floured board and knead gently until smooth. Roll out the dough to ½-inch thick and cut into rounds with a 2 ½-inch cutter.

Place the scones on a lightly greased baking sheet, and brush the tops gently with milk.

Bake in the oven for 7-10 minutes, or until the scones are well risen and golden brown. Remove from the oven and cool on a wire tray. **Makes 10.**

All ingredients are available from your local store or online retailer.

You can find printable versions of these recipes and links to the ingredients used in them at https://www.alisongolden.com/killer-at-the-cult-recipes/

USA TODAY BESTSELLING AUTHOR

A Reverend Annabelle Dixon Mystery

FIREWORKS IN FRANCE

Alison Golden
Jamie Vougeot

FIREWORKS IN FRANCE

BOOK SEVEN

The characters and events portrayed in this book are fictitious. Any similarity to real persons, living or dead is coincidental and not intended by the author.
Text copyright © 2021 Alison Golden
All rights reserved.

No part of this book may be reproduced, stored in a retrieval system, or transmitted in any form or by any means, electronic, mechanical, photocopying, recording, or otherwise, without express written permission of the publisher.

Cover Illustration: Rosalie Yachi Clarita

Published by Mesa Verde Publishing
P.O. Box 1002
San Carlos, CA 94070

ISBN-13: 9798716429833

Edited by
Marjorie Kramer

NOTE

Barnet, short for "Barnet Fair," cockney rhyming slang for "hair."

CHAPTER ONE

AWAY FROM THE main routes that connected cities such as Paris, Reims, and Calais, nestled in a valley of rolling hills, and small enough to be largely obscured from view by a cluster of oaks, it was mostly bad directions or lazy driving that caused visitors to discover the subtle charms of Ville d'Eauloise. Should a traveler ignore the many signs directing them toward the glamor and bustle of the far larger metro areas and decide to veer off the highway onto a narrow, rutted trail instead, they would soon find themselves descending an incline, gentle in places, steep in others, their route shrouded by ancient trees, and on sunny days, dappled with light that made its way through the canopy above.

And if they continued on, the travelers would, after a time, emerge from the woods to find a small village. From a distance, it looked like a higgledy-piggledy collection of buildings, but up close it was something quite different. Monstrous, stone villas loomed tall, separated by lanes and alleyways that weaved their way like a warren through the village. They cast shadows at all times of day. The buildings, some with turrets and crenellations, were dotted with windows, graced on either side with painted shutters and the occasional colorful window box, but which couldn't hide their age or in some cases their decrepitude.

The village existed in a state of almost perfect preservation from centuries before. It was a study in history. The narrow, steeped cobblestone roads provided shortcuts and hideaways and surprise destinations that to a local were practical, sensible, and of little note, but which were to a visitor, unfathomable, mysterious, and exciting. The village was so discreet and unspoiled that it appeared at first glance to be so untouched by modern life that it was as if even time itself couldn't find it.

On arrival, the visitor would almost certainly be drawn to *l'Église de Saint-Mathieu*, the oversized church that sat in the center. The church overlooked the village like a mother hen, dwarfing the much smaller civic buildings, homes, and businesses around it, and acted as a focal point for any gathering that took place. Every small alleyway and lane led directly to the plaza that lay in front of the church's gigantic steps and its enormous oak entrance, while local cafés, a restaurant, and stores faced the church on all sides as if in supplication to God for bestowing prosperity upon them.

However, travelers rarely ignored the draw of the cities and only occasionally made the rickety journey off the main highway. For the most part, life in the village followed patterns and rhythms that were set in place long ago, and which were performed with the consistency of a grandfather clock. Today was no different.

Inside the somber, cavernous interior of the church, one so big that it dwarfed the congregation even when the entire population of the village attended as most did every Sunday, the stained glass windows amplified the light that streamed through them. The bright, mid-morning sun disseminated jewel-toned light so that it alighted on pews, on chipped stone walls carved with grotesque faces, and on shiny memorial plaques commemorating local lives lost in gold leaf. To churchgoers, it was like being inside a vast, complex kaleidoscope.

Today, however, the aged, medieval building had been decorated further. Broad white ribbons had been wrapped around the four pillars supporting the massive, vaulted ceiling, delicate arrangements of white flowers hung on the walls and at the end of the pews. A thick, crimson carpet smoothed the flagstones down the aisle that were as jagged and irregular as the day they were laid, the size of the congregation never sufficient to weather them despite centuries of foot traffic.

The smell of thick, melted wax filled the air. It made even the crisp, spring morning feel dense with heat between the church's great gray cool walls. To the front, a large, wooden, elaborately carved altar table draped in white linen stood beneath a huge stained glass window that featured pilgrims on horseback and on foot. Gently flickering flames from what seemed an infinite number of candles provided an aura of calm.

There was silence except for the occasional hiss from a candle, but when a side door opened, the draft made the flames dance erratically before they settled down again. Even the great chandelier that hung low on a heavy chain above the altar was filled with the unmistakable light of a hundred tiny flames, albeit they plugged into the mains. The atmosphere was calm, the silence almost complete. Everything was ready.

CHAPTER TWO

VILLAGERS HAD BEGUN to gather. They took their seats quietly, giving no more than a nod here or a hushed greeting there as they tiptoed across flagstones, grateful to reach the red carpet that would muffle their footsteps. Ville d'Eauloise was a God-fearing place and attendance at Mass was sacrosanct. All the villagers would be here for this most holy of days—Easter Sunday.

Off to one side of the church, close to the altar, there was a small, brown door, low enough to cause all but the shortest of adults to duck their heads. Behind the door, Father Julien stood in front of a small mirror adjusting his vestments around his ample frame. He smoothed his hair. It was so uniformly black that it was at odds with his skin, which despite his best efforts with creams and the occasional treatment, was showing signs of age. He coughed heavily and rubbed his forehead as he struggled to regain his composure. Whether it was the change of the seasons, the challenges of getting older, or the stresses and exertions required to prepare for today's Mass, he had recently begun feeling the strains of an aging body rather keenly. He closed his eyes and prayed that he would gather the strength to conduct the service—the most important of the Catholic year. As the senior clergyman, much was expected of him in terms of piety, devotion, and rituals. He needed a clear head, and the mild headache that was forming bothered him.

When Father Julien opened his eyes, his gaze fell on a small envelope lying on the simple desk that stood in the corner. He knew what it contained. A different, but identical one had been placed under the door of his office every day for the past week and for many weeks before that. After the second envelope arrived, he swore that he wouldn't open another, that he would discard any more that appeared, but his resolve had given way every time. And so it did again.

Father Julien roughly grabbed the envelope and tore it open, not caring whether he ruined it or its contents. As he had many times before, he pulled out the singular sheet of cheap paper he knew would be inside and unfolded it. There, pasted to the page, were a series of letters, each one individually cut from a different source—newspaper, magazine, or book—and arranged to form a most devilish message.

YOUR TIME IS RUNNING OUT. GOD WILL NOT HELP YOU.

The priest clenched the paper between his fists, ready to tear it to shreds, but he hesitated. His headache distracted him from properly considering whether this was the right thing to do. Instead, he leaned down to the small safe beneath his desk, and fishing for the key in his pocket, he opened it, struggling with the lock in his haste. After tossing the crumpled paper and its envelope inside, he slammed the safe shut with a bang.

As he straightened up, a pain shot across Father Julien's shoulder. Leaning over his desk, he cast around among books, correspondence, and other clergy detritus until he found a pill bottle. Quickly pouring some red wine into a gold chalice, the priest popped a painkiller along with a nub of bread into his mouth. He chased them with the wine.

A few moments later, he started to feel better, and after one more brief, but careful inspection of his vestments in the mirror, Father Julien left his office. He nodded at the junior priest who stood outside his door like a guard on sentry duty and walked to the altar, his eyes roving around the sanctuary. With his back to the burgeoning congregation, he began to check that everything was in place.

The assembled villagers had been subdued before, but at the entrance of their priest they grew even more so, calming their shuffling feet and restless bodies as they sat in silence. Many of them looked down in prayer as a group of nuns led by their Mother Superior filed along the red carpet to sit, as was customary, in the front pew that had been left empty for them. The light in the church dimmed as the big front doors were closed, and the shaft of light coming in through them was extinguished.

As Father Julien finished his pre-service checks, there was a creaking sound. The light in the church brightened briefly, there was an almighty bang from the doors, and the light in the church dimmed again. The organ stirred into life with a rousing chord. The sound reverberated around the impenetrable walls so powerfully that even the candles flickered a little.

The young woman who had rushed hastily across the threshold was beautiful. Her glossy jet black hair framed her face and accentuated the symmetry of her features while her big green eyes, strong cheekbones and neat nose were all underscored by her wide, full lips, and delicate chin. A small scar peeked out from below her eyebrow but did nothing to mar her beauty. She wore a plain white shirt punctuated by a large silver cross and a black A-line skirt with sensible shoes, the innocence of her young features affected only by the anxiety of her lateness. She slowed her pace and quickly trotted along the red carpet to the front pew where she slid in to her seat just as the organist began in earnest. Dramatic chords rang around the cavernous space.

The interruption had distracted everyone but now they dragged their attention back to the altar—and to Father Julien. He turned slowly, raising his arms wide to welcome his flock and envelop them in this celebration of the Resurrection of Christ. Everyone relaxed, preparing to be joyful—but only for a brief second. That was all it took for them to notice the strange look on Father's Julien's face, his open mouth and wide eyes, the shudder of his shoulders as if he were struggling for breath. He staggered and planted one foot forward, swaying weakly upon it. Then, he stopped, stiffened, and fell flat on his face.

CHAPTER THREE

MIKE NICHOLLS BROUGHT out his best pair of shoes from the closet and took them to his kitchen where he had laid out newspaper, a cloth, a brush, and black polish. He dabbed the cloth into the polish and started to apply it. It was Annabelle's big day, and while not much of a churchgoer himself, he wanted to support her as best he could.

As he pushed the polish into the leather, his fingers working in small circles, he thought about how his life had changed since he had met Annabelle. Fifteen years of police work that put him in direct contact, and often confrontation, with the most nefarious and duplicitous of society had given Mike an emotional spectrum that was limited and distinctly dark. Anger, frustration, disappointment, and dismay came easily to him—the best he could usually hope for being the brief sense of relief he felt when justice was served. For years, he had found it impossible to smile without feeling a tinge of sadness, laughter felt bittersweet, and he certainly had neither the time nor the inclination for silly jokes and trivial chatter. He was not a man accustomed to expressing joy.

So when he and Reverend Annabelle had begun walking their dogs together on Sunday afternoons—in the hours after her morning service and before Evensong—he felt as if it were a form of therapy. It was hard to remain gruff and cynical among the vibrant greens and somber browns of the Cornish countryside as the pleasing colors of the summer sunsets struck them with awe. When autumn came around and the days began to shorten, it was impossible for him not to beam with genuine pleasure as the lovely vicar's cheerful laughter pealed through the still, crisp air. By the time winter's cold snaps sharpened their pace, Annabelle had become a radiant presence in the inspector's life. She was like an electrical charge crackling with positive energy, and he was never more than a short glance away from an easy, comforting smile. The concerns and worries that plagued his thoughts—always on his work—seemed to melt away when he was with her. Her jovial manner and easy-going nature relaxed him, and for the first time in years, Mike found himself smiling and laughing like the young boy he had once been. And he simply could not keep a detached, apprehensive attitude when both of their young dogs were chasing and wrestling each other so playfully around them.

Annabelle and Mike's relationship had evolved slowly and gently. Mike had come across Annabelle many times in the course of his investigations, and although at first her propensity for getting in the middle of things had irritated his sense of proper police procedure, he had quickly realized that she was marvelously talented at getting to the bottom of things. Her sense of justice—albeit from a more pious source—was as ferocious as his own, yet she managed to unearth truths and right wrongs with a delicate, sympathetic hand. It had been a revelation to him that being able to act on strong principles while feeling a sense of deep compassion was possible, but over time, Mike saw that this was one of the most important lessons Annabelle had taught him. It was a lesson that made him a better detective, a better man, a better person. Though he was loathe to admit it in these terms, Annabelle had been good for his soul.

When they had met, the inspector had been deep in the throes of a contentious divorce, losing his beloved dog in the process. Thanks to his workload and his closed-off attitude, he hadn't noticed Annabelle's sincere—if somewhat clumsy—flirtations. Had one ever tickled the edges of his consciousness, he had deflected it with an angry swat. Yet, in the face of his determined grumpiness, Annabelle had been as dogged. It was she, recognizing a need in him, who had convinced him to take one of the pups she had rescued—the dog he was now impossibly attached to. He had been unable to resist Molly and with her entrance into his life, warm, tender feelings, feelings that had been long buried, started into being, giving him an outlook that was much more positive and optimistic. Annabelle had adopted one of Molly's brothers and as they schooled and enjoyed their dogs together, their relationship had matured. Now he came to think of it, as their dogs had grown, so had his and Annabelle's love for each other. Mike stopped polishing for a moment and tapped his temple. That was a profound thought, that was.

The shoes now matte with polish needed buffing. Mike stuck his hand inside one to get to work. He picked up a large soft brush, feeling the broad back of it against his palm as he prepared to put some effort in. He crisscrossed his shoe with quick, broad, soft brush strokes. The leather began to shine. When he was satisfied with the strength of the gleam he saw bouncing off the toe, he turned to the second shoe.

Mike now realized that Annabelle wasn't the enthusiastic proponent of gullible naïveté or unfounded faith that he had once thought, but rather someone who held deep, sincere beliefs about the fundamental goodness in people, and who, when that goodness did not readily spring forth, sought to understand instead of condemn. It was Annabelle's willingness to look beneath the surface that had helped him solve particularly difficult cases, ones that he nearly let slip through his fingers because of his tendency toward cynicism and mistrust. For that, he felt deeply indebted to her professionally, but he was also wildly impressed personally. Annabelle was a formidable woman. She was loyal, intelligent, and compassionate. Once they had overcome their mutual awkwardness, they had slipped into a relationship with the kind of easy contentment that made it seem strange that they had waited so long.

The shoes, now clean and shiny, sat side by side on the kitchen table, uniform and bright, the sight of them satisfying to a man like Mike who enjoyed order and routine. He went outside to get his walking boots and threw them into his car, along with his warm jacket. He whistled for Molly who was stretched out on her bed, and she came immediately. Mike bent down to scratch her head. "Right girl, time for the best part of the week. Are you ready?" Molly gave a little bark. She knew exactly what was up. She was ready. They both were.

CHAPTER FOUR

INSPECTOR CHARLES BABINEAUX was, above all else, a proud man. Proud of his achievements in the police force, proud of the effort he put into his appearance—his erect frame, his carefully styled moustache, and his firm jaw. But most of all, he was proud to be French.

This nationalistic pride was the reason his three-piece suits were exclusively tailored in Paris at a cost that far exceeded what was sensible given his detective's pay. It was why he reveled in the enjoyment of distinctive national dishes—snails, mussels, and *boeuf bourguignon*. It was why he made sure his meals were accompanied by mountains of fluffy white bread, lashings of butter, rounds of fragrant cheeses, and bottles of smoky red wine—all locally sourced, of course. His pride in his country did not stretch to car manufacturing however. German engineering was his preference there, but when the call had come in from *l'Église de Saint-Mathieu*, the station pool had been all out of Mercedes, and for his journey to Ville d'Eauloise, he had had to make do with that most iconic of French automobiles, a classic Citroen 2CV in pale baby blue.

"*Zut alors, Hugo!*" Babineaux exclaimed to the man beside him in the driver's seat, turning to him with small black eyes. They were like a bird's—sharp, observant. The inspector was in a bad mood. He had expected a quiet Sunday. A little bit of church followed by a sumptuous Easter feast that would have lasted well into the afternoon had been his plan. After that, a nap. Instead, he was now being jostled relentlessly inside a car with an infernally hard suspension on his way to a tiny village where the level of sophistication was likely to be on par with its medieval history. "We have been driving for over an hour, and there is still no sign of this Ville d'Eauloise! Are you sure this is not a prank call?" he said to his sergeant in rapid-fire French.

Sergeant Lestrange leaned over the steering wheel, his sharp, beaked nose only inches from the creased map propped on the dashboard. He frowned, studying it intensely as the 2CV rattled down the road. Lestrange was younger than Babineaux, still in his thirties. He possessed the persistently uncertain, slightly-confused demeanor of a man constantly out of his depth. His lack of authority was exaggerated by the fact he wore clothes that were two-sizes too big for his twig-like frame. The cuffs of his sleeves fell almost to his knuckles while a belt was essential to hitch up his trousers.

"The map says it is nearby," Lestrange said. "But I can't find the road to it—there is a crease in my map!"

"This is shameful, Lestrange!" Babineaux said, slapping his thigh and leaning over. "*Incroyable!* How can it be that we, two maintainers of the law, can get lost in our own country?"

"I'm sure I have been to the village once before," Lestrange claimed. "There is a track here somewhere."

"Well, I have never heard of it, let alone visited it. It must be a wonderfully peaceful, law-abiding village to have escaped my attention through all my years of police work."

"There is a church, and a convent. So I suppose it is quite a moral place, Insp...."

"Stop!" cried Babineaux. Startled, Lestrange slapped his foot on the brake and the 2CV skidded forward a full meter. "There! A track! The one we just passed!"

Lestrange wrestled the gear stick into reverse. It took him a couple of attempts and the engine whined in protest, but he backed up the car. He spun the steering wheel with more decisiveness than he was known for and revved the engine. The 2CV set off down the bumpy dirt and gravel track that led toward the oak trees, its unforgiving suspension delivering an even more uncomfortable ride for its two occupants.

"*Oof!*" wheezed Babineaux when his head hit the roof of the car with a thump. "Drive slower, Sergeant."

"But we are *le gendarmerie*, and there has been a suspicious death of a priest! There is no time to waste!" Lestrange replied, urging the car forward at an even more reckless pace.

"*Sacré bleu, non*! The deceased is already dead, and we cannot be of assistance if we do not arrive in one piece."

Lestrange took his foot off the accelerator and the car immediately slowed. Babineaux narrowly avoided another head injury as the windscreen came rapidly toward him.

Lestrange winced. "Are you alright, Inspector?" he said, pushing his superior back against his seat while keeping his eyes on the narrow road.

"*Oui, oui!*" Babineaux said, batting with both hands at Lestrange's efforts to help him. "Get off me!" He flicked an imaginary speck from his jacket. This inexorable journey felt like it was taking hours. He would be fortunate to arrive at all.

CHAPTER FIVE

THE REST OF the drive passed in silence. They drove through the tunnel of trees to emerge to the view of Ville d'Eauloise snuggled in the valley in front of them. Babineaux finally smiled as Lestrange glided the car along a mercifully smooth stretch of road down into the valley until they reached the outskirts of the village. There, to Babineaux's dismay, they resumed their juddering journey thanks to the ancient cobblestone lanes before finally reaching the church. It had been two hours since the emergency call to their police station had been made.

A large crowd was gathered in the square in front of the church when they arrived. The local café was doing a brisk business as, distracted now from the holy nature of the day, villagers drank coffee and ate pastries to fend off the shock of Father Julien's sudden death. As they attempted to calm themselves, they gossiped and discussed what had happened to their priest. Many could not believe that the venerable Father Julien was gone even though they had witnessed his passing with their own eyes.

The Citroen 2CV skidded to a halt in their midst, almost clattering into a group of elderly, slightly shabby men who demonstrated remarkable reflexes when they hopped aside in unison. Their hatted and well-dressed womenfolk remonstrated with them, speaking loudly in French, several attempting to smarten up their men with a tug of a lapel, or a smoothing of a jacket's shoulders, but it was mostly pointless. A group of children, bored by the adult's chatter and unconcerned about the priest's untimely death played a hopping game on the plaza while their parents huddled in groups nearby.

As it rolled to a stop, everyone turned toward the powder-blue vehicle. The police had arrived from the big city. A sense of anticipation in the square arose. The crowd wanted some kind of explanation or reason for this macabre turn of events. They were looking to the occupants of this quirky car to provide it.

The doors to the car flung open. From the driver's side, a red-faced and frightened-looking man emerged. The trousers of his brown suit creased over his shoes and the sleeves extended over his palms. His thick, chestnut hair was tousled as if he had just survived a hurricane. From the other side, a tall, slim man with long limbs and olive skin climbed out carefully. In contrast to his companion, his hair was oiled and perfectly-smooth. It gleamed almost as much as his shiny, expensive, heeled shoes. The man slammed the door shut, and cast his small, dark eyes around the crowd, assessing them as if they were exotic animals. He pulled a gold pocket watch from his waistcoat, checked it with a mild shake of his head, then looked up again and carefully drew his thumb and forefinger down the thin, sculpted mustache that sat above his top lip. The villagers looked at them warily as they conducted their own assessment of these two strangers. Was this pair up to the task that lay in front of them?

"Inspector Babineaux, I presume." A voice rose above the crowd, stern and uncompromising. The villagers stepped aside to let a nun through. Babineaux bowed his head graciously as she walked up to him. After watching Babineaux, Lestrange haltingly did the same, although there seemed something more reminiscent of a curtsey about his movement.

"I am Mother Renate, Mother Superior of the Order of St. Agnès. Our convent is located at the edge of the village. As the senior clergy of this parish, Father Julien and I knew each other quite well. Follow me." Mother Renate turned around briskly and led the two policemen through the crowd and up the church steps.

As Babineaux and Lestrange passed through the enormous wooden doors, their eyes were drawn to the flowers, candles, and other decorations that adorned the church. They seemed forlorn and jarring in light of the priest's death. Babineaux turned his head and said to Lestrange who walked a couple of paces behind, "A most wonderfully preserved church, wouldn't you agree, Sergeant?"

Mother Renate answered before Lestrange had a chance. "I did not call you here to admire our architecture, Inspector." She stepped up to the altar and turned back to face the two police officers, the prone body of Father Julien on the floor between them. "Here he is," she growled.

They all looked down at the priest lying on the floor in his ceremonial vestments. He had been rolled over onto his back and his mouth was slack-jawed, the color having faded from his skin. No one had closed his eyes, and he stared at ribbons that fluttered gently from a candelabra above him.

Babineaux noticed a small man standing off to one side of the altar. The man rubbed his face with a handkerchief, breathing heavily. "And you are?" he asked.

The man hurried over. He offered the policeman a palm that the inspector quickly realized was sweaty. Barely squelching a look of distaste, Babineaux dropped the man's hand quickly and reached for his own handkerchief.

"Giroux, the local doctor," the man said. "I was in the congregation when Father Julien fell... ill."

"He *died*, Giroux," Mother Renate said. "He collapsed before he could utter a single word."

Babineaux turned his beady eyes back to the doctor. "And what do you make of this?"

"It looks like a heart attack," the doctor said, in between heavy breaths. "He's a little overweight, a little arthritic, but he had no history of a heart condition. I have known Father Julien for years, as I have every person in this village. Aside from a little too much good living, he was in excellent health. This seems very... odd." Giroux looked at Mother Renate, presumably for support or reassurance, but her fierce eyes were fixed upon Babineaux. The doctor continued, "Which makes me think that... this might be due to... something untoward."

"He means murder, Inspector," Mother Renate said. The mother superior pursed her lips and continued to look down unflinchingly at Father Julien's body, her hands clasped in front of her.

The doctor bent down next to the priest's body and urged Babineaux to do likewise. "Look at him."

Babineaux flicked a quick glance over the dead man's face. He did not linger there but he noticed flecks of foam at the corners of Father Julien's mouth.

"And see his fists." Dr. Giroux indicated with his pen the curved, contorted nature of the body's hands, fingers curled in on themselves. "If we take off his shoes, I think we will find the same affecting his feet. See how his feet are pointed, the ankles stretched out? And here, look." Giroux lifted the sleeve of Father Julien's vestment to reveal a blackened patch of skin, around two inches long.

"But what is this? What does this mean?" Babineaux asked.

"These are signs of poisoning. I suspect that Father Julien died of a heart attack brought on by ingesting some kind of noxious substance."

CHAPTER SIX

BABINEAUX NODDED SLOWLY, turning to make brief eye contact with Lestrange, who gazed open-mouthed at the dead body. Murder wasn't a common occurrence in this part of France, and to the inexperienced sergeant, the murder of a priest was like something out of a novel.

"A murder..." Babineaux murmured, the glint of a sparkle in his dark eyes. "Lestrange," he barked suddenly over his shoulder, "please coordinate with the doctor here. We need a full post-mortem. Mother Superior, I would kindly ask that you provide me with the names of everyone who attended this morning's service. We shall want to interview each of them."

"There is no need, Inspector. They are already waiting for you." Mother Renate gestured down the blood red carpet in the aisle to the open doorway of the church. Babineaux turned to look at the crowd of villagers peering inside, unable to hear the conversation, but desperately trying to interpret the investigators' thoughts from afar.

"There must be a couple of hundred of them," he said.

"247 in total, soon to be 249. *Madame* Moreau will have her twins soon," Mother Renate confirmed. "I'm sure you and your sergeant here can manage."

"Oh, I don't interview witnesses, Mother Superior. My skills are more... deductive in nature." Babineaux stroked his moustache. "But my sergeant here will be happy to oblige."

The mother superior turned to a nun who stood at the brown door and whose arms were outstretched as she attempted to hold back the crowd. Strain etched her face. "Sister Dominique! Did you hear the Inspector? Organize the villagers so that the sergeant can interview them."

The crowd behind her stirred and a look of fear flashed across the nun's face. She redoubled her efforts to keep the crowd under control. "Yes, um, Mother Superior," she stammered as she wrestled with the swell.

"Véronique," Mother Renate called. Another nun emerged from a shadow in the corner. She was young and did not wear a habit. "Have you found Father Raphael? I'm sure the detective would like to speak with him."

"He is not here, Mother Superior," the young woman answered. She lifted her chin.

"*What?*" hissed Mother Renate.

"We cannot find him—no one knows where he is. He's not in the church, his rooms, or anywhere anyone can think of. He seems to have disappeared."

Babineaux raised a delicate eyebrow. "Who is this Father Raphael?" he asked.

"A young priest whose vocation Father Julien was overseeing," Mother Renate answered.

"Were they close?"

"I suppose," she sniffed. "He hadn't been here too long."

"Hmm." Babineaux turned around and walked across the front of the altar slowly. He held one hand behind his back while the other stroked his moustache thoughtfully. "A priest murdered at Easter Mass..." he said to himself. He now waved a loose index finger as if stirring his thoughts, "in front of hundreds... his young apprentice fleeing the scene of the crime... this is not a particularly complex mystery, *is it?*"

"That is *impossible!*" a thin, high voice shouted in English. Babineaux turned to see a nun, small and blonde, standing in the doorway of the office. "Father Raphael would not *do* such a thing!"

"Sister Mary!" Mother Renate shouted angrily. "How dare you speak so loosely? Leave this church immediately. Return to the convent for prayer. I shall deal with you later!"

Babineaux smiled softly as he watched Sister Mary hang her head and shuffle quickly away. "It is *plausible*," he said sadly. "It is always difficult to accept a friend is capable of killing."

"Inspector," Mother Renate said sternly, "in this instance, the young woman may be impudent, but she is also correct. Father Raphael is a holy man, and it is unthinkable that he might be responsible for such a heinous act. There may well be a reasonable explanation for his disappearance. I insist that you conduct a proper investigation before making assumptions as to his character."

"Yes," Doctor Giroux added, blinking owl-like behind his rimless round glasses, "and my early assessment is only a speculation. I don't want to condemn anyone based on a superficial examination."

Babineaux spun back around on his tall heels to face both of them, the smallest hint of a smile beneath that perfect moustache.

"But of course," he insisted, "we will investigate. We will do everything we can in order to verify what has happened here. But I warn you—my instincts are refined, and rarely incorrect. I am the best at what I do. I would be surprised if my conclusion varies greatly from my early supposition." Babineaux hummed slightly. "With all due respect, Mother Superior, persons of the cloth may be experts in forgiving wrongdoing, but they rarely have a sense for discovering it."

CHAPTER SEVEN

"SHALL WE TAKE the path through the woods?" Annabelle asked. "Or go over the hill by the lake?" It had been a busy morning. There had been the Easter Sunday service followed by the children's Easter Egg Hunt and then one of Philippa's tremendous Sunday roasts. It would have been easy to curl up on the sofa until Evensong, but her Sunday afternoon walks with Mike and the dogs were sacrosanct. Mike pursed his lips and thought the question over as if he were considering a dessert menu.

"The lake," he asserted eventually. "I'd like to see if there are any ducks about." He waggled his elbows and pulled a face. "*Quaaack.*"

"Oh, you are a silly sort," Annabelle laughed, taking his hand and bumping into him playfully. Mike smiled and squeezed her hand in return. He whistled to call the dogs.

Things had been discreet at first for Annabelle and Mike. Many of the villagers were accustomed to seeing the inspector visit on police business. And given that Annabelle was both a pillar of the community and compelled to right wrongdoings in the village, it was no surprise to see him make a beeline for her each time he arrived. As their relationship had deepened, however, the inspector became an even more familiar face around the village. Rumors began. They started as whispers passed over washing lines and store counters in hushed voices along with all the other gossip of the day.

"Mrs. Markham says she saw the inspector holding the Reverend's hand at the market yesterday!"

"No!"

"I tell you it's true! And Franny said she saw him going to her cottage with a heart-shaped box of chocolates under his arm!"

"Really?"

The rumors grew more sensational, spreading like wildfire, until the state of the vicar's and the detective's relationship became one of the village's major talking points along with the proposed pedestrianization of the village on Saturdays and whether shoppers should be charged for grocery bags or bring their own.

"So what do you make of all this talk about the inspector and the vicar, Fred?"

"Load of rubbish, if you ask me!"

"Why? Vicars can have their fun like anyone else!"

"Sure... But the Reverend's not exactly the flirty type, is she? Have you seen the shoes she wears?"

Annabelle and Mike remained oblivious. Mike continued to visit the village more often. He became intimately acquainted with the pubs as he undertook a thorough and methodical investigation of every local beer on tap. He put in a heroic performance when the tea tent collapsed during a downpour at the summer fête. He even indulged Annabelle by investigating a case of vandalism that caused a near riot when a local rabbit breeder's cages were broken into, unleashing a wave of long-eared, grocery-eating, vegetable-stealing destruction upon the village that peaked with the ruination of the flower show at the aforementioned summer fête. Many prize blooms had suffered an ignominious end after a nighttime attack by the nibbling predators. What with that, the rain, and the collapsing tea tent, it was a pretty disastrous village fête that year.

Discussions among the villagers about the relationship grew ever more heated, effectively splitting Upton St. Mary into those who believed that the rumors were true and those who refused to entertain them. Many believed Annabelle too lacking in the skills of romance and the inspector too scarred by his work for the idea to be plausible while others were convinced they heard the sounds of wedding bells when in the shower.

Wherever Annabelle and Mike went, people averted their eyes and hushed their voices. Upton St. Mary was a town well-versed in the dark art of gossip, as adept at concealing it as they were enthusiastic in engaging with it. Philippa, Annabelle's church secretary-cum-housekeeper, in particular, had enjoyed treating Mike to her famous Sunday roasts on the weekends, but even she, normally one of the main contributors to the village rumor mill, kept her thoughts to herself for fear that she might jeopardize... something.

Just as speculation reached boiling point, many of the villagers working themselves into a frenzy, one rumor away from marching up to the church and demanding an explanation, the question of whether Annabelle and Mike were a couple was settled definitively.

It happened at a birthday party for Barbara Simpson, the bubbly owner of the *Dog and Duck*. Annabelle and the inspector attended the packed pub, but spent much of the time engaged in conversation in one corner. This was enough, of course, to send many of the party-goers into a new tumult, but as they paused their whispers and nudges to sing "Happy Birthday" to Barbara, the diminutive, blonde, bee-hived, barnetted birthday girl, the question was settled once and for all. When Barbara bent over to blow out her candles, Annabelle and the inspector exchanged a kiss that was so tender, easy, and intimate, that all doubt was extinguished. Finally, the mystery had been solved, and it seemed to have the effect of the entire village, their curiosity satisfied, exhaling in unison. Finally they could stop watching, thinking, arguing, and speculating about the question that had burned so brightly in the minds of some that they were in danger of combusting and leaving nothing behind but a pile of ash.

But the calm didn't last for long. After a short reprieve, the population of Upton St. Mary switched tacks, and their interest in the relationship between their beloved vicar and her honest, down-to-earth police officer beau took on a different hue. With eyes only for each other, Annabelle and the inspector could not explain the sudden appearance of complimentary bottles of wine during candlelit dinners they enjoyed in local restaurants and free tickets to theatrical performances at the village hall that were pushed under Annabelle's door. Mike would find vast bouquets of flowers, red roses predominant, abandoned on the roof of his car. Baskets of local food ("to keep your strength up") would be left on the doorstep while a clergyman from a neighboring village offered to take Holy Communion one Sunday ("to give you a lie-in, Annabelle.") Bemused but delighted, Annabelle and Mike accepted most of the gifts, although the baby clothes ("thought they might come in handy,") were politely returned.

The increasing warmth that greeted their relationship only fueled Annabelle and Mike's deepening intimacy. In fact, as the bluebells poked their violet flowers above the surface in the woods through which they tramped, it was the case that if there was any contention or issue in their relationship, it was that the inspector wanted something even more serious, even more dedicated, even more committed...

CHAPTER EIGHT

"MIKE! LOOK!" ANNABELLE called, pulling herself close against his side and pointing at a tree in the near distance.

Mike leaned closer to her in order to gaze where her finger pointed.

"Do you see?"

He squinted and peered for a few seconds. "See what?"

"A kingfisher! There on the lower branches of that tree!"

"Ah! Yes, I see it," Mike said. "What's so special about it?"

Annabelle stood back and looked at him with a grin.

"You don't know much about birds, do you?"

Mike chuckled. "I live in a city. The only birds I'm familiar with are those that flock around breadcrumbs and make a right mess. Pigeons."

Annabelle playfully slapped him on the shoulder. "Well, we shall have to fix that," she said, turning and walking off as the inspector followed her. "I have just the book."

"Homework?" Mike smiled.

"Don't think of it like that," she said, threading her arm

through his as he caught up. "Think of it as another opportunity to spend some more time together."

"Bird watching?" he said. He raised his eyebrows.

"A wonderful way to spend a morning."

"If you say so."

"I do."

Mike gazed at her for a second as they walked. "You know, I can't imagine anyone else getting me to spend time on that sort of thing."

"I should hope not," quipped Annabelle.

They walked on a little further, Molly and Magic panting on either side of them. The dogs were getting tired now. But when they reached the crest of a hill beyond which a small lake glittered in the afternoon's fading light, the two dogs sprang forward once again.

Mike turned to Annabelle as she watched them run off. "You know..." he began. "I've taken this week off work."

"That's right, you told me. Do you have any plans?"

"Actually..." he said, his voice slow and steady, as if probing for the right words. "I was wondering if you might like to go somewhere. Together."

Annabelle's face froze for a second, before breaking into a blush.

"That sounds rather lovely. But it's short notice. And tomorrow's Easter Monday."

Mike nodded vigorously. "Of course, if you can't make it, I understand."

"No, no, let me think." Annabelle tapped her chin with her finger. "I'll have to make some arrangements."

"Uh-huh."

"And I couldn't leave until those were all set."

"Okay."

"Where did you have in mind?"

Mike inhaled. He hadn't got that far, most of his attention

being focused on the answer to the suggestion itself. He silently berated himself for not having thought further ahead.

"Um... The coast, perhaps? Brighton? Or maybe Salcombe?"

"Oh," Annabelle said, her blush fading. "That would be delightful," she added.

Mike frowned as soon as Annabelle looked away. Something wasn't quite right. He'd scored some moments in this relationship with his gestures for Annabelle—he'd flown to a remote Scottish island in a helicopter, he'd given her gold earrings in the shape of the cross, and got his sister, a master baker, to create one of her extraordinary cakes with the word "*Love*" written across the top of it—but this clearly wasn't one of them. His suggestion had fallen flat in a way that his cake had not. Annabelle might have taught him a lot in their time together, but when it came to being romantic, he realized, he would have to figure that out himself.

CHAPTER NINE

BY THE TIME they were in sight of the church, rain had begun to fall. Mike took off his jacket for Annabelle to huddle beneath as they dashed up the path that led to her cottage. When they arrived at the front door, eager to get inside, Annabelle reached for the handle, only for the door to open before she could grab it. "Oh!"

"Reverend!" Philippa said, her face full of concern, the whites of her eyes showing vividly as she opened them wide. The elderly woman wiped her hands down the front of her blue apron, a habit she had developed in those moments she felt most anxious. She glanced over Annabelle's shoulder. "Hello, Inspector," she said, bowing her head as if she were in the presence of royalty. The inspector eyed her carefully and nodded back not quite so regally while the two dogs scampered past Philippa to get out of the rain. She bent to catch them before they made it too far but she was much too slow for their youth and spirits. She pursed her lips and groaned.

"What's the matter?" Annabelle asked her.

Annabelle and Philippa spent many of their days together.

Having lived in Upton St. Mary all her life, Philippa was as much a pillar of the church and the local community as was Annabelle. Philippa ensured that St. Mary's bookkeeping was up-to-date, the church ran smoothly, and the various parish groups were disciplined and thriving. Leaders of vast global enterprises would be hard-pressed to out-organize Philippa. She also made sure that Annabelle was in peak condition, fortified by her delicious food, especially her cakes.

"There's someone here to see you," Philippa hissed in a low whisper, seemingly oblivious to the fact that both Annabelle and the inspector were still standing in the rain.

"Who?"

Philippa looked around, her eyes sliding from side to side. She leaned in closer to say something, before she suddenly changed her mind. The elderly woman stood up straight and folded her arms.

"Not someone we would expect here." Philippa pursed her lips and squinted as if she had the bitterest of oranges in her mouth.

"I'm sorry?" Annabelle asked. "Philippa, what are you on about?"

Philippa sighed and closed her eyes briefly. "She insists on speaking to you."

"Who does?" Annabelle asked again. "Who, Philippa?" She was still holding Mike's jacket over her head as raindrops dripped down her face. Mike stood behind her, fully exposed to the elements, but remaining stoic in the face of them. He appeared to be doing his British best to pretend that he wasn't really being drenched by a sudden rainstorm at all.

"It's just…"

"Just what, Philippa?"

"She's…"

"What?"

"She's…"

"What, Philippa!"

Philippa took a deep breath. "She's *Catholic*."

Annabelle growled and looked back at Mike in apology.

"Perhaps I should go," Mike said, feeling somewhat peripheral to this inexplicable drama playing out between the two women. He was starting to get cold, and he sensed that things weren't going to resolve themselves quickly, nor would they become clearer—to him, at least. He often understood the people he arrested better than he did members of the opposite sex. At least criminals usually had a strong motive for their behavior. Women were simply... unfathomable.

"Nonsense," Annabelle said, patting him. She shifted over and pulled him under the front door cover for shelter. "I must give you that book." Annabelle turned back to Philippa. "Can we come in, please?"

"Oh!" Philippa said, standing aside.

Annabelle and the inspector hurriedly took off their coats and shoes. Philippa brought them cloths so they could mop their hair and faces.

As she handed Annabelle a towel, Philippa whispered, "I don't know what she wants. She wouldn't tell me! She's very strange. If you ask me, she might be one of those door-knockers—the ones that pretend to be all nice and then once they've left your house, whoopsie, all your silver has gone. I mean, I wouldn't care to generalize, but I tell you, Catholics do have more than their fair share of..."

"Philippa! Will you *stop*," Annabelle said, glancing at her crossly as she slid her feet into her slippers. "I'm sure she's nothing of the sort. There's probably a completely innocent reason for her visit. Now, if you'll just let me find out what it is."

Annabelle pushed past Philippa and walked into the living room, leaving her housekeeper and the inspector standing in the hall, Mike still eyeing Philippa carefully. Neither of them spoke. Suddenly the silence was broken by a cry, and then a squeal.

They heard raised female voices talking over one another, chattering, laughing. There were more cries of delight. Philippa frowned. Mike relaxed. Perhaps this little drama would have a happy ending after all. He gave Philippa a sheepish smile and rocked on his heels.

Philippa, unable to contain herself, made a dash for the threshold of the living room to find out what all the fuss was about. Mike followed her. They discovered Annabelle holding a blond, curly-haired woman by the arms as she stood back appraising her.

"Mary!" Annabelle exclaimed.

CHAPTER TEN

ANNABELLE CRUSHED THE smaller woman to her in a fierce hug, and squeezed her eyes tight shut, a beatific smile on her face.

"Hello Annabelle!" Mary said, her words muffled by the press of Annabelle's shoulder. Mary's veil was now skew-whiff and in danger of falling off. She wrapped her arms around Annabelle's waist.

"But... but what on earth are you doing here?" Annabelle asked.

Strangulated sounds came forth, and Mary let go of Annabelle to flail her arms around.

"What was that?"

"Annabelle, I think you're, um, suffocating her," Mike said.

"What? Oh!" Annabelle released Mary who coughed lightly before brushing back hair that had fallen across her face. "Come, let's sit down." Annabelle led Mary to the sofa. "Philippa, Mike, this is Mary. We grew up together in London. She's my oldest friend!"

Philippa, mesmerized by the sight of an Anglican clergywoman embracing a Catholic nun, started with a jerk. Her mouth opened as her eyes flickered between the two. "Ohhhhhh," she said, releasing the sound like a puff of smoke. "In that case, I'm very sorry that I asked for proof, Sister."

Annabelle frowned at Philippa as Mary smiled awkwardly. "It's fine. I understand it's a shock turning up suddenly like this."

"Could we have some tea, Philippa?" Annabelle asked. It was not a question.

"Yes, yes of course. I'll go put the kettle on," Philippa said, spinning around. She scurried out of the room muttering. Annabelle wasn't paying attention, but Mike was pretty certain he heard the words, *"Barbara,"* and *"hearing about this!"* come from her lips.

"Philippa is my housekeeper and church secretary," Annabelle said, easing Mary back onto the couch and settling herself beside her. "And this is Inspector Mike," Annabelle said, waving to Mike who, still feeling surplus to requirements, was settling himself in the armchair in the corner beneath a giant aspidistra. He started to bat away leaves that kept falling in his face, an action he would soon come to realize was necessary every few seconds.

"Nice to meet you," Mary said in her delicate, fluttering voice.

"And you," Mike replied, gravely.

"He's a detective," Annabelle said, flashing her eyes at him and smiling, before turning back to her friend, her eyes resting dolefully on her friend's face. "What's wrong, Mary?"

As soon as Mary had sat down, her pretty smile disappeared. She looked nervously at Annabelle with large, watery eyes. Her hands twisted in her lap. She turned them over, interlaced her fingers, stretched them out, and released them to start the cycle all over again. "I don't know who else to turn to. I... I had to do something, but I just didn't know who could help me." Mary buried her face in her hands before slapping them down in her lap, finally managing to keep them still. "Oh Annabelle! I don't know where to start!"

Annabelle smiled warmly, sympathetically, and Mike watched with wonder at how patient and welcoming her expression must appear to her distressed friend.

"It's alright," Annabelle said gently, picking up her old friend's warm, small hand with hers. "It's wonderful to see you—even if you do seem terribly frightened!"

Mary laughed gently, and wiped her eyes with her free hand. "It's good to see you too, Annabelle. I'm sorry to spring myself on you like this. You must think me so rude."

"Of course we don't, but, but... I thought you were abroad."

Mary's laugh faded into a frown. "I was, until this morning, until..."

Mary looked like she was about to cry so Annabelle said. "Deep breath, Mary. Why don't you tell us what's been going on? Start at the beginning, or wherever you'd like. Don't worry about how long it will take. We're not going anywhere."

Mike had been planning on going home, but now realized he'd better get himself comfortable.

"You're too kind, Annabelle, Mike." Mary nodded at them both. She took a deep breath to calm herself, closing her eyes as she exhaled. After gathering her thoughts, she started to tell her story. "Six months ago, I took a break from nursing in Africa. I was feeling a—a little *unsure* about my vocation, and I needed time to contemplate, a simple life to give me the space to examine my relationship with the Almighty Father." Mary paused and shook a little. She gave Annabelle a small smile, her eyes a startling blue against her pink cheeks.

"Go on," Annabelle urged her gently.

"St. Agnès convent in northern France is a peaceful, fervent place. I've been happy there, but it hasn't been as restful as I'd hoped. When... when... *it* happened this morning, I had flashbacks to that time in London. You and me, together. Do you remember?"

"How could I forget?" Annabelle murmured. Some years earlier, before taking up her post as vicar of Upton St. Mary, her childhood friend had been framed for the deaths of two women. Annabelle had saved Mary by participating in a sting operation and unveiling the real culprit.

"I knew I had to do something, so as soon as I could I got a lift in one of the produce trucks out of the village. I was dropped in Reims, caught the first train to Calais, a ferry to Dover, and another train to Truro."

"But how did you get from there to here? Upton St. Mary is in the middle of nowhere and there are no buses today. It's Easter Sunday."

"Annabelle," Mary breathed. She stared at her friend, her eyes wide. "I hitched a lift! *Me.*"

CHAPTER ELEVEN

"I CAN SCARCELY believe it myself. But I—I was so confused and... I thought maybe... All I could think of was reaching you." Mary's voice gave out, and she sniffed suddenly. Not taking her eyes off her friend, Annabelle instinctively reached for a tissue from the box on the coffee table that sat there permanently for tearful situations just like this one. Well, not exactly like this one, but emotional ones of which, thanks to her calling and character, Annabelle experienced frequently when her parishioners came to visit.

"Thank you," Mary said, taking the tissue and burying her nose in it. She gave a delicate toot before lifting her eyes to Annabelle again.

"So what was it that prompted you on such an urgent errand? What happened?" Annabelle prodded.

"Annabelle, Father Julien is dead! And worse, no not worse, that sounds terrible, oh I don't know... But they suspect Father Raphael of killing him!"

Annabelle looked back at the inspector who was listening carefully in the corner. He had found an elastic band on the sideboard and with it had tied the aspidistra leaves back. He was now sitting squarely in his armchair, his feet planted firmly on the floor, his arms lying along the sides of the chair, his hands hooked over the ends of the armrests. He reminded Annabelle of a statue she'd seen in a book, but she couldn't place it. Mike flicked his eyebrows up and down. Annabelle turned back to Mary.

"I'm not sure I know who you're talking about," Annabelle said. "Who are Fathers Julien and Raphael?"

Mary once again buried her face into her tissue and exhaled loudly, but before she could speak, they were disturbed by the sound of clanging china being carried shakily into the room by Philippa. She was muttering and grumbling under her breath.

"These mutts are going to leave the house like a swamp!" Philippa said, as she deposited the tray onto the coffee table with a clatter. "I'm slipping and sliding all over the place. I've half a mind to knit them some bootees before their next countryside ramble!"

"Won't you join us?" Annabelle asked as Philippa turned to leave the room, courtesy overriding her need to hear out Mary without interruption.

"Oh no, thank you. I've got to give those mongrels a good rub down." Philippa left the room, closing the door behind her with a little too much force. Quiet descended on the room again.

Annabelle's lips formed into a little "O" and she exhaled slowly. She caught Mike's eye. He thought she looked rather attractive as she did that. She turned back toward Mary. "Please, carry on."

"My order is located in Ville d'Eauloise, a small village about 80 miles east of Paris. I, and my fellow sisters—there are 13 of us—were attending Easter Mass at the village church along with all the villagers. There are about 250 of them."

"That's a small village."

"It is. And it is a very, very big church. Anyway, that's not important. We had just arrived and were waiting for the Mass to begin when Father Julien—he's the senior priest—he... he...," Mary took another deep breath, "he collapsed in front of the altar! Just like that. Just like the woman at the café. Dead!" Mary looked wildly around at Annabelle, then Mike. "He had his arms out wide to welcome us. We were there for the resurrection, but what we got was a crucifixion!" Mary began shredding her tissue. "They think he had a heart attack. But he was in good health and there's talk he might have been poisoned, but that can't be! Not again!" Mary clasped Annabelle's hands and looked at her, imploring, her face pale now. "Can it?"

Annabelle squeezed Mary's hands. "I don't know, Mary, but why did this make you come to see us?"

Mary's stricken face colored, and she briefly looked down at her lap. "Because of Father Raphael. He's the junior priest at *l'Église de Saint-Mathieu*. After Father Julien collapsed, Mother Superior called the police. The local doctor told them that he thought Father Julien might have been poisoned and when they started insinuating Father Raphael might have something to do with it, I couldn't bear to listen. That's when I got the truck to the train station and I made my way to you."

"But why do they suspect this Father Raphael?" Mike asked, his investigative instincts taking over as he leaned forward to hear more of Mary's story.

"Because no one could find him after it happened."

"That looks pretty suspicious, don't you think?" Mike said.

"He didn't do it! Please, you must believe me," Mary pleaded with the inspector. She returned to wringing her hands, as if Mike too had condemned the junior priest with his words. "I know he didn't! Father Raphael is a good man. He's new to the church, but he's as devout as anyone I've ever met. He's good and loving. And he adored Father Julien for his teaching and guidance. There's simply *no reason* that Raphael would kill him!"

CHAPTER TWELVE

ANNABELLE RUBBED MARY'S back as she broke down once again into her tissue.

"Do the police have any other suspects?" Mike probed.

"None!" Mary said, laughing through her tears at the outrageousness of it all. "The investigation is being conducted by this awful man, an uppity detective called Inspector Babineaux. He damned Father Raphael before Father Julien's body was even cold!"

"Alright, alright, let's slow down. Perhaps you would tell us, in your own words, what happened," Mike said. "From the beginning to the end."

"Yes, Mary, do that," Annabelle said. "We'll just listen."

Mary took a shuddering breath and paused to calm herself before starting. "We had just arrived for Easter Mass. The entire village was there, of course. Father Julien was preparing for the service, one he has given many times before. It was all very routine, when just as he was about to start, and he'd opened his arms to welcome us, he pitched forward. He landed on the carpet with a loud thump." Mary closed her eyes to reimagine the scene. "There was this horrible sounding noise from the organist and then silence. For a few seconds no one moved. We expected him to get up and make some reference to the resurrection. Or to say he'd tripped. Or, or... something. But when he didn't, Mother Superior stepped up. She's a wonderful woman—stern, but fierce and righteous. Too experienced to be frozen with shock like the rest of us. She quickly made her way to Father Julien's side. She knelt down and pressed her fingers to his neck. We all waited for her to give us a sign." Mary opened her eyes. "It was horrible, Annabelle! Mother Superior raised her head and looked at us. We immediately understood what her expression meant. There was no need for words.

"After a second, people starting screaming and crying. It was terrible. It's such a big church that the sounds echoed all around making it worse. People were clutching their hands to their chests or fanning them in front of their faces. Some shielded their eyes from the sight of Father Julien's body. Some immediately kneeled to pray. Others, of course, peered over their neighbor's shoulders to get a better look, and some began to inch forward to assess the situation. But Father Julien was dead. There was no question. He was undoubtedly, indisputably dead.

"Then, Dr. Giroux came forward. He's the doctor in the village. He has seen everything. 'I am a doctor!' he called, but we all knew that. He ran up the aisle and up the steps to the altar. We craned our necks and leaned forward to watch as he knelt by Father Julien's side, desperately hoping that Mother Superior had been wrong, and Dr. Giroux would announce that he was still alive. It would have been a miracle, but it was Easter Sunday, and we were *so* hopeful. The good doctor examined him. He felt for a pulse, pressed his ear to Father Julien's chest, pried open his mouth, and put a finger on his tongue in order to gaze inside. I could tell the situation wasn't good when he pulled a handkerchief from his pocket and dabbed at his forehead. The church is freezing even in the middle of summer.

"Then I heard Dr. Giroux tell Mother Renate—Mother Superior—that he, Father Julien, appeared to have had a heart attack. Mother Renate was displeased, but then she is often displeased. She ordered everyone out except the nuns—we were to guard the doorways to make sure no one entered the church—and she commanded me to attend to her in the sacristy."

"Why you, Mary?" Annabelle broke in gently.

Mary shrugged. "I have no idea. I am not especially in Mother Superior's favor or confidence. No one is. I was in a bit of a dither to be honest. She made a call to the police station in Reims. 'Send an officer to *l'Église de Saint-Mathieu* in the village of Ville d'Eauloise at once!' she said, well, commanded really. 'What do you think has happened?' she said into the phone. That's how she is. 'There's been a death! A suspicious one!'"

"And where was Father Raphael all this time?" Mike asked.

Mary threw up her hands. Her eyes glistened. "He'd disappeared. He hasn't been seen since just before Father Julien died."

"That sounds awful," Annabelle said handing Mary a fresh tissue before deciding to offer her the entire box.

After another bird-like toot, Mary said, "I'm so sorry to arrive out of the blue like this. I feel ridiculous sitting here and telling you about it. I know you can't do anything. This is all happening in another country, in another language, in another branch of the church. I don't know what I expected really. I just needed to tell someone I could trust. I'm so convinced of Raphael's innocence. I'm *sure* he didn't have anything to do with Father Julien's death. Oh, I feel so helpless!"

"I'm so sorry, Mary. What a terrible thing to happen." Annabelle stroked Mary's arm as Mary shuddered and huffed next to her.

Mike looked at the two women. Between Mary's utter despair and Annabelle's slumped shoulders, he saw an opportunity. It was perfect. Before his thoughts were even fully-formed, words were leaving his mouth. "I know!"

Annabelle and Mary stared at him.

"You can go back to France, Mary, rejoin your cloister or whatever. And Annabelle and I will go with you!"

Annabelle and Mary continued to stare at him, now united in shock.

"I mean, we'll go to France, and see if we can help," Mike added.

Mary looked from him to Annabelle. "Would you really do that?"

"Well..." Annabelle began tentatively. "I suppose we..."

"We were already arranging to go *somewhere* together this week. Why don't we go to France with Mary?" Mike said, his enthusiasm for his idea gaining too much momentum to stop now. "We could take our holiday in France and while we're at it, we could offer our support to the investigation—within the bounds of what the French authorities would allow, of course. Annabelle, you and I could do some digging, look around for Mary's friend while we enjoy the delights of the French countryside, a few glasses of wine, some great food..."

"And some divine pastries!" Mary cried, suddenly catching on. She beamed so brightly at Mike's suggestion that her fair skin shone. Annabelle could see her reflection in it. The vicar fixed Mike with an expression of mild amazement. "Would you?" Mary said.

There was a pause as they waited for Annabelle's response but Mary and Mike could see her getting excited as the idea bloomed in her mind. A smile grew slowly upon her lips. "I think this could all work out quite conveniently," Annabelle said, slowly. "And if there is something amiss in the accusation of this Father Raphael..."

"Oh there *is*, Annabelle!" Mary insisted. "There *is*. I am absolutely positive! I would stake my life on his innocence!"

Annabelle looked from her to the inspector, and back again. "Then I suppose we're going to France!"

CHAPTER THIRTEEN

ONCE THE DECISION had been made, Mary relaxed slightly, and while she still seemed subdued and concerned, the three of them passed the time before Evensong preparing for their trip, drinking tea, and going over the details of the case.

There was a lot to do. Annabelle arranged for cover from Father Edward, an eccentric vicar from a neighboring parish ten miles away who spent hours writing elaborate sermons which he acted out using movie references and props in front of an audience of precisely three people every Sunday. He relished the opportunity to fill in for any vicar who needed help and had once made a sudden overnight trip to the north of Ireland in order to deliver his thoughts on the lessons that the movie *Avengers: Endgame* had to offer about conflicts of morality to an enormous (to him) congregation of twenty-four.

By 6 p.m. they had arranged almost everything. They'd found a dog-sitter for Molly, rescheduled the "oddly-shaped vegetable" competition, and postponed the parish council vote on whether to install a defibrillator in the red telephone box that stood at the corner of Lupin Lane and Swineshead Road. Once that was all sorted, they bought their ferry tickets online with the assistance of Sister Mary who seemed far too technologically savvy for someone who spent much of her time cloistered in the pious environment of a convent contemplating her vocation.

Then the phone began to ring. Continuously. Word had spread. Gossip flared across the village that Annabelle was going to France with the inspector. "Who on earth is ringing that phone off the hook?" Philippa asked as she walked into the living room with her hat on and her coat over her arm. In her hand she clutched a white rolled up umbrella with a wooden handle full of knots and gnarls, a gift from wood turner William Thomas in the village. Annabelle suspected he was an admirer of Philippa's, but Philippa shushed her away when she suggested it.

"News has broken out," Mike said. He made it sound like an announcement of war.

"What news?" Philippa asked.

"We're going to France!" Annabelle said, unable to conceal her excitement in. "We're going to help Sister Mary with something there. Will you take care of Magic and Biscuit while I'm gone?"

Philippa almost dropped her brolly. "France! I'd love to go to France! They have such wonderful pastry chefs there!" she said, her eyes shining. The Eiffel Tower was almost visible in her now big, child-like eyes. Quickly she snapped back to the present. "Yes, I'll take care of things, you know I will. Just make sure you come back with lots of tales to tell. Have a lovely time, won't you? Be careful what you eat. They might slip you a snail—or even a frog's leg!" She shuddered. "And don't drink the water!"

Even Mary laughed, and while Annabelle would have loved to sit and chat with her old friend, it was almost time for her final service of the day. Annabelle walked Mike to the door. He pulled on his boots, drew his jacket around him, and attached Molly to her leash.

"Oh!" Annabelle exclaimed suddenly, patting Mike affectionately on the chest before marching back into the cottage. After a few moments during which Mike waited patiently on the doorstep, Annabelle re-emerged carrying a book. "I almost forgot. Your homework."

"Ah," the inspector said with a smile, taking it from her and gazing at the blue bird on the cover, before sliding it carefully into his pocket. "I'll keep it for when we get back. I doubt we'll have much time for birdwatching in France."

Annabelle chuckled. "Well, we must make *some* time for ourselves while we're there. There's no chance I'm going to miss visiting a patisserie or two!"

"It might be difficult, what with conducting an investigation and all."

"Oh tish! We'll have that sorted in no time."

"I hope so," Mike said. He had hopes for the trip. Big hopes.

"See you tomorrow then," Annabelle said, planting a tender kiss on the inspector's lips.

"Can't wait," Mike said. He winked at Annabelle before turning and gently tugging Molly's lead as he stepped out into the rain, his hand inside his pocket tightly gripping the small, square, velvet box that he had kept close for weeks.

CHAPTER FOURTEEN

DESPITE THE FACT that the reason for their trip to France was to investigate the sudden death of a priest and the disappearance of another, Annabelle, Mike, and Mary couldn't help but feel excited as the French coast emerged on the horizon. Even Mary, who had spent much of the drive down to Dover wringing her hands, allowed herself a smile. As if pointing the way, early morning sunlight peeked through the parting clouds illuminating the comforting yellows and greens of the beach and the countryside beyond. The three of them stood on the bow of the ferry where they had stationed themselves to view the coastline. As the ferry got closer to Calais, when they looked past the port's containers and cranes, they could see the outline of sandstone buildings, orange-tiled roofs, and the gently undulating hills they would shortly be navigating in Annabelle's blue Mini Cooper.

To her right, Annabelle exchanged a smile with the inspector before turning slowly back to the view and extending an arm to her left around the much-smaller Mary's shoulders. It had been an awkward drive from home to the coast. Mary's concern for her missing friend had cast a gloom over the group and although Annabelle tried to jolly her along with some French jokes and terrible attempts to speak French, they mostly fell flat. Mary's anxiety was understandable, but what made things worse was Mike's equally fidgety, distracted manner. Annabelle had done her best to lift his spirits and stir up some enthusiasm, but Mike had mostly gazed blankly through the windscreen, apparently lost deep in thought for minutes at a time.

The British weather hadn't helped. A hazy, faint dawn fought with a light drizzle for most of the drive. As the sun steadily rose, the rain showed no signs of giving up, and Annabelle called it a draw until the reality of France cast itself on the horizon. In the promising light of the early morning, the fine drizzle that had shrouded them in a mist since they left home finally stopped, and as it did so, all three of them relaxed.

"A little bit more glamorous than when we were in Scotland, wouldn't you say, Mike?" Annabelle remarked.

"In the right company, anywhere is fine with me," the inspector smiled affectionately. He briefly distracted himself from his thoughts to put his arm around Annabelle's waist. Annabelle blushed. She still found herself disarmed by Mike's affection toward her. It was lovely but strange. The clouds parted even further and a welcome warmth crossed their faces. With Calais and the French countryside beckoning, they made their way back to the car parked in the ferry's hold.

Mike walked around to the driver's side, but before he could reach for the door handle, Annabelle clasped his wrist. "What are you doing?" she said.

"I'm going to drive," the inspector replied, casually. "You drove us down to Dover. It seems only fair that I drive the second half of the trip."

"Oh no!" Annabelle asserted, shaking her head. "No, no, no.

I've never driven in France before—do you think I would give up that opportunity?"

Mike glanced at Mary who stood on the other side of the car pretending not to notice. "Okay then, just remember that they drive on the right here," he said, as he retreated back around to the other side. He didn't really like being a passenger, but he had learned not to come between Annabelle and her steering wheel when she insisted.

Soon they were driving along the autoroute out of Calais and into the countryside to the east. As quickly as she could, Annabelle turned off the highway to travel more leisurely through quaint towns and villages, slightly regretting her decision to drive as she focused on the road while Mike looked out at the view. At a traffic light, she turned on the radio and pressed the buttons until a gentle, acoustic guitar-strummed song emerged from the static.

"Ah!" she said. "French is such a beautiful language, isn't it Mike?"

"Hmph," Mike grunted. He continued to stare out of the window.

If Mike had been a little agitated on the drive down to Dover, he was growing positively uncomfortable as they drove through France. The inspector was a sure man, confident, skeptical, and very rarely surprised. He had seen a lot in his time on the police force, and all of it had taught him what to expect, and what to do. There was rarely a situation in which he felt he couldn't draw upon his previous experience.

But that was in England, and as the small Mini Cooper whipped through France on the wrong side of the road with signs that seemed impossible to pronounce, an unknown, unintelligible singer on the radio, and an unfamiliar landscape around him, he began to realize how much of his confidence stemmed from his environment. He wrapped his hand around the furry box in his pocket. This was foreign territory for him.

"He's singing about a girl," Sister Mary said, poking her head between the front seats of the car, "about how he likes her too much to tell her."

"Oh!" Annabelle exclaimed with delight, turning to Mike. "Isn't that romantic?"

"Hmph," he grunted once again.

After almost two hours of driving, and with sharp, on-point directions from Mary, they found themselves on a bumpy, poorly maintained road that led between a mass of oak trees. When they emerged from the woods, Ville d'Eauloise appeared in front of them, just like it did for every visitor, settled comfortably in the valley, slate-covered turrets soaring above pointed roofs that jutted into the bright blue sky.

A sense of awe filled the small car. There was no need for Mary to direct Annabelle any further as the road down the hill and into the village led directly to the enormous, looming church at the village's center. "Whee!" Annabelle cried as they glided down the incline.

As she drove along the cobbled streets, they became acutely aware of the onlookers who turned their heads to stare at the unfamiliar blue Mini with white go-faster stripes. They passed an elderly woman carrying a wicker basket full of laundry on her head. Another man, just as old and wizened, rode a bike with a cage of chickens strapped to the back. Children playing in the streets with a bat and ball waved as they drove by, curious about the new arrivals and excitedly pointing at the unfamiliar car.

Once they reached the large plaza in front of the church, patrons of the café, shops, and businesses gazed at them, pausing as they brought their coffee cups halfway to their lips or placing their heavy bags of shopping on the ground as the Mini passed by. The looks grew more intense as the trio got out. Some of the onlookers sat up in their chairs. Others pulled down their sunglasses. A young child ran up to them and pointed. It was understandable. It's not every day you see a Catholic nun, an Anglican vicar, and a British police inspector step out of a small car with foreign number plates in a remote French village while going about your daily business. All before 10 a.m.

CHAPTER FIFTEEN

"WAIT HERE," SISTER Mary said. "I shall fetch Mother Superior and Inspector Babineaux. I've arranged to meet them here."

Annabelle nodded and walked around the car to join Mike, who felt distinctly overdressed in his customary trenchcoat. He was self-conscious now that the sun had warmed up and the focus of the village was upon him. They watched Sister Mary walk quickly up the steps to the enormous church. There was a French police car parked close by.

"Isn't this wonderful?" Annabelle said, paying the bystanders no mind as she spun around, wide-eyed, to take in the view. "It's like being transported back to the fifteenth century!"

"I suppose," the inspector murmured, glancing sideways at the people chattering to each other while nodding at them. He looked up at the church. Gargoyles and eerie ugly creatures carved into the stone walls peered down at him.

Annabelle stopped spinning and faced him, hands on hips, her lips pursed. "What on earth is the matter with you?" she said. "You've been acting strangely ever since we left home!"

Mike looked at her sharply as if he'd suddenly woken up. "Oh... um... I'm just concerned about the murder, if indeed it is one. Police instincts, you know. Difficult for me to relax when there's an investigation in the offing."

Annabelle smiled and stepped closer. "Well, I suppose we'll just have to sort it all out as quickly as possible then." She put her arm through his and leaned in for a kiss, causing a frisson of interest among the patrons at *Café Sylvie* a few yards from where they were standing.

A second later they were interrupted by the sound of footsteps pounding across the cobblestones. The tall figure of a nun bore down on them, briskly walking at a near jogging-pace with a long, stiff stride, her arms pumping. Following close behind trotted a much smaller, much more flexible Sister Mary, and behind her a well-dressed, tall, thin man strolled. His hair was glossy in the sunlight and his gait even and steady as he concerned himself with keeping his shoulders back and his chin up.

"Annabelle, Inspector Mike, this is the Mother Superior of St. Agnès, Mother Renate," Mary said, racing to catch up as the senior nun stopped abruptly before them. Mother Renate clasped her hands in front of her, the swaying crucifix that hung from her neck slowly coming to a halt. She offered only a stern, unsmiling expression and a quick nod as greeting. "And this is Inspector Babineaux—he's conducting the investigation into Father Julien's death," Mary added.

"A pleasure, *madame*," Babineaux said in English, offering his hand to Annabelle.

"Reverend Dixon is a priest in England," Mary added quickly, seeming a little alarmed at the French detective's behavior.

Babineaux's eyes widened fractionally at this information, and he ducked his head in acknowledgement. "Indeed?"

Annabelle accepted his hand and giggled in surprise when

the tall, languid man gently pulled her fingers to his lips and planted a soft kiss on back of them, his eyes never leaving hers. "Oh!" she said.

"Sister Mary told us zat we would be joined by a couple of England's finest detectives," Babineaux said, as he cast his eyes from Annabelle to the inspector, shaking Mike's hand a little more vigorously and to Mike's great relief making no attempt to kiss it. "We 'ave an interesting challenge."

"We're here on a break," Mike said. Mike made sure to grip the Frenchman's hand tightly for a couple of seconds longer than was necessary. "A holiday."

Babineaux raised a tweezed eyebrow as he looked them over. "Reverend Marple and Inspector 'olmes—it iz an interesting romance."

Annabelle giggled again. Even the policemen here were different! "Oh, I'm not a detective," she said, almost apologetically. "I'm just a friend of Mary's."

"Then why are you here?" Mother Renate cut in, almost angrily. Like Annabelle, the Mother Superior was tall. They looked each other directly in the eye. "We were told you have come to help."

"Mother Superior..." Mary began.

"We're here to enjoy the hospitality of your village," Mike said, suddenly feeling the urge to assert some authority. "We won't interfere with your investigation at all. But if you require our help, we'll be happy to assist."

The Mother Superior eyed Mike keenly, as if ascertaining whether his assertion was well-intentioned.

Babineaux had no such qualms. "*Absolument!*" he said, tilting his head theatrically. "I would welcome ze prospect of seeing what my British counterparts 'ave to offer. Maybe we can learn from ze other."

"Very good," Mike said formally. Mary, standing outside the Mother Superior's line of sight, beamed.

"I suppose you should come in then," Mother Renate said, the words flying from her mouth as quick and hard as bullets. "We will explain what happened."

She spun on her heels and began walking back to the church with no indication that she expected them to do anything other than follow. Sister Mary quickly bowed her head and chased after Mother Renate. A second later Mike did likewise but not before realizing that Annabelle and Inspector Babineaux were walking side by side in front of him. The French detective's hands were behind his back, as if they were out for a stroll rather than embarking on an investigation into a suspicious death. Mike scurried along behind them, his frown deepening when he heard Annabelle giggle yet again.

Mike was so flustered that he nearly missed noticing the truck that was parked outside the café, its rear doors open to reveal trays full of bread. A nun flicked her skirts aside and clambered inside the truck. She handed a tray of loaves to the café owner who stood waiting patiently. Several others formed a line behind him.

"What's happening over there?" Mike called out to the others ahead of him.

"Our convent makes bread," Mother Renate said after stopping and turning to see what he was looking at, "and has done for over one hundred and fifty years. St. Agnès is situated outside the village. We have fields where we grow wheat, a mill where we grind it into flour, and a bakery from which we supply the whole village and all those as far as Reims."

"It iz a wonderful bread," Babineaux called back over his shoulder, "I 'ad some this morning, so soft—'ow do you say it, melt in ze mowff. Ze taste, texture iz very refined—if you 'ave ze palate for such zings." He looked at Annabelle as he said these last words, and Mike almost lost his train of thought when he saw her blush for apparently no reason at all.

CHAPTER SIXTEEN

ONCE ANNABELLE AND Mike were inside the church, Babineaux embarked on a dramatic retelling of the events of the previous day. As he did so, Mother Renate tightened her lips even further, only opening them when necessary to correct salient details that the French inspector embellished in his attempt to make Father Julien's death appear as interesting as possible to their international visitors.

"... at which point I made my wise deduction," Babineaux concluded, swiping the air with an exaggerated gesture, "zat zis was murder! And zat Father Raphael was ze killer! Ze only question is..." he said, pausing for effect. He leaned in, staring at them, "*Why?*"

"No!" Sister Mary cried, her eyes pleading. "You're wrong! He's innocent! Father Raphael is innocent!"

Mother Renate frowned. "Sister Mary, please!" She turned to Annabelle. "I don't approve of histrionics. They are unbecoming and undignified. Please excuse Sister Mary."

"It's quite alright, Mother Superior. I have known Mary a

long time, and I know how much she believes in truth and justice. If she feels so strongly, there must be a good reason."

"What do you know about the two men?" Mike asked.

"Ze Father was a priest who 'ad been 'ere for nearly twenty years. He rarely left ze village. What zere is to know, we all know. Ze junior father, he arrived 18 months ago. What did 'e do before? 'e lived a regular young man's life. Apparently 'e was a model before attending seminary and being assigned to Father Julien for mentorship. 'e graced ze catwalks of gay Paree."

Mother Renate harrumphed at this piece of information. Seeing that Mary was about to protest again, Annabelle jumped in quickly, "Right, well, do you mind if we take a little look around?"

"But of course!" Babineaux said, raising his chin and standing to attention. He gestured with his arm across the expanse of the large church like he were a ringmaster at the circus.

"You may," Mother Renate said. She glared at Babineaux. Murder investigation or not, permission for their visitors to tour the church was not his to give.

Slowly, Annabelle and Mike began to wander around. Acutely aware of their hosts' watchful gazes, they whispered softly to each other.

"What do you think?" Annabelle hissed, glancing back at Mother Renate, Babineaux, and Mary. Sergeant Lestrange had joined them. They stood as if awaiting a ceremonial visit from a local dignitary.

"I've never seen a detective relish talking about a case so much—you'd think he *wanted* it to be murder!" Mike said, offering a placating smile at the line-up in the distance. "Ridiculous way to conduct an investigation. And talk about jumping to conclusions!"

Annabelle widened her eyes and raised her eyebrows a little at this last statement. "Really? I don't know any detectives who might do that, do you?"

Mike looked back at her, his eyes narrowing. Annabelle meant something but he wasn't quite sure what. She did that sometimes.

"But no, you're right, jumping to conclusions simply won't do, will it?" she added.

There was a clang, then a bang, followed by the sound of a rush of water. A nun came out of a side door, wiping her hands. When she saw the pair, she blushed and ran away giggling.

They stepped up to the altar and looked down at the spot where Father Julien had collapsed.

"Are you sure he died from a heart attack?" Mike called across the pews.

"Yes, the doctor has confirmed it," Mother Renate said.

"But couldn't his death simply be the result of natural causes?" Annabelle asked.

"Zer is no 'istory! 'e was perfectly fine until 'e died!" Babineaux countered. "We are awaiting ze results of ze post-mortem. But it looks very, 'ow do you say, *fishy*. 'e was tortured."

"*Contorted*," Mother Renate corrected.

After examining around, on top, and behind the altar, Annabelle and the inspector found themselves at a small door. "Allow me," Babineaux said, suddenly springing to their side and opening it for them.

"Ah, his office," Annabelle said. "It is very similar to my own."

"You've seen a few of these in your time. What do you make of this one?" Mike asked.

"It's on the sparse side," Annabelle said, taking it in slowly, "but nothing out of the ordinary."

Mike strode over to the desk, and tapped his foot against a safe that sat on the floor. "What's in the safe?"

CHAPTER SEVENTEEN

BABINEAUX SHRUGGED. "WHO knows?"

"You haven't opened it?" Mike frowned.

"A man's private affairs are private—even after 'is death."

Mike breathed in deeply. "But according to you, this is a murder inquiry. There may be items pertinent, if not *central* to the investigation in here."

"Father Julien was ze victim—not ze murderer. A Frenchman is entitled to 'is privacy. It may be all 'e 'as."

Mike spoke again. "And I'm sure if it *were* murder, the murderer would be just as keen to keep such things private. Look, so far you have nothing, only conjecture. No motive or apparent understanding of the lives of either Father Julien or Father Raphael. You need all the information you can get. You can't condemn a man without knowing everything you can. You're putting the cart before the horse."

Babineaux squinted, his beady, black eyes getting beadier and blacker, a challenging look appearing on his long, slim face for the first time. He didn't exactly understand what the inspector was saying, but he suspected that the English policeman wasn't in awe of his deductive reasoning.

"Why don't we allow ze *Révérend* to decide," he said, turning slowly to Annabelle. "Should we examine ze inner workings of ze man's life? Should we unveil 'is secrets, 'is little *peccadilles* to ze world? Should we... expose 'is inner soul, hmm?"

With both men staring at her expectantly, Annabelle gulped and considered the problem. She could see both sides and hated to pry, but she couldn't help feeling that they needed to know more.

"I know that under normal circumstances it would be considered terribly inappropriate, but on this occasion, I do think Inspector Nicholls is right," she said. Mike grinned broadly at this before catching Annabelle's eye and quickly rearranging his features to a more serious expression. "We should try to learn as much as we can about Father Julien *and* Father Raphael, and I think opening this safe would help. It can't be difficult. It has a lock. Just needs a key."

"Very well," Babineaux said, haughtily tilting his head as he conceded defeat before walking to the open doorway. "Lestrange!" he called out loudly. He barked some instructions in French, causing the hapless sergeant to run so quickly out of the church his footsteps echoed around the enormous interior long after he had left.

Annabelle and Mike continued to poke and peer around the small, stone-walled room for a few moments longer, opening the cupboards and scanning desk drawers mostly filled with writing equipment, paper, communion supplies, and boxes of candles.

"Par for the course," Annabelle said. "There's nothing unusual here except for how tidy it is." They returned to the sanctuary.

Mother Renate stood still, as if she were built of the same stone as the walls around them. She had watched them poke around while Mary shifted anxiously from foot to foot, wringing her hands. Babineaux sat down, crossed his long legs, and draped his arm nonchalantly over the end of a pew. He appeared indifferent.

"Well," Babineaux said, "what iz your conclusion?"

Mike answered curtly, "Our *conclusion* is still a long way off. There is much more to do, to *investigate*."

"Would it be possible to talk with your sisters?" Annabelle asked Mother Superior.

"The sisters?" Mother Renate said incredulously, her hard emerald eyes glinting like rocks. "Why would you speak to my nuns? This is a matter of priests!"

"Yes," Mike said, "but one of them is dead, and the other has disappeared. And your sisters were there when that happened."

Mother Renate pursed her lips while she thought about this. "Very well. Shall I fetch them?"

"No," Annabelle answered quickly, glancing at Mike, "we've just arrived, and we would like to find somewhere to stay and settle in. Tomorrow, perhaps, once we've got the lay of the land. For now, maybe we can retire to our rooms and have a think."

Mother Renate paused before bowing her head, acceding to Annabelle's request. "We will see you tomorrow, then."

"Allow me to walk you to your car," Babineaux said, stepping forward and offering his arm.

"You are most kind, Inspector." Annabelle accepted Babineaux's offer, and they left the church, trotting down the steps to her car. Mike and Mary walked behind.

"Ze Mini Cooper. Quite an interesting car. Very 1960s, Carnaby Street. Mini skirts. 'ot pants. I take it, *Révérend*, zat you are as proud of your nation as I am of mine."

Annabelle chuckled. "Oh, I just like the way it looks. Small cars are easier to park."

Babineaux smiled as if this was the wisest thing ever said. "Indeed, *Révérend*."

Mike huffed a little as he made his way to his side of the car before seeing his French counterpart graciously open the driver's door for Annabelle. She smiled broadly and blushed once again while Mike grumbled to himself, irritated that he had never considered doing that. He tried to make up for it by opening the passenger door for Sister Mary, but it wasn't quite the same.

"If you need anyzing, please call. 'ere is my card. I am staying in ze village while we conduct ze investigation. *Au revoir*." Babineaux closed the car door with a click.

"That Inspector Babineaux is such a gentleman!" Annabelle said. She turned the engine on with one hand and waved at Babineaux with the other.

"Hmph," Mike grunted. "Incompetent, too."

"Can we give you a lift back to the convent?" Annabelle asked Mary's reflection in her rear view mirror.

"No, it's alright, Annabelle. I have arranged for you to stay at an auberge a few minutes away. Drop me off there, and I'll walk. It's not far."

"Very well. A guesthouse in a lovely picturesque French village. I can't wait!"

CHAPTER EIGHTEEN

FROM THE BACK seat of the car, Mary guided them to a beautiful, old villa with a lichen-covered roof. Thick vines curled its green fingers across the stonework as if comforting the squat, two-story building. Up close they could see buds of wisteria hanging from the green leaves like bunches of tiny purple grapes. The buds would wait for the warmer weather to arrive before opening to reveal long fronds of lilac flowers. Embedded in the walls of the building, large windows sat behind window boxes full of small spring flowers—crocuses, snowdrops, bluebells, and primroses—that gave color and life to the plain, ancient, weathered stone that was cracked in places and from which the villa had been built centuries ago.

"Oh, it looks lovely," Annabelle breathed as she stared up at the building. "Doesn't it, Mike?"

Mike, still cross, grunted.

"I'll see you tomorrow then, Annabelle," Mary said as they got their luggage from the car.

"Yes, about 11 I should imagine. I doubt I'll be rushing through my breakfast. I want to savor such a divine place."

Annabelle beamed at Mary and gave her a hug. "Don't worry, we'll find Father Raphael, I promise. I'm sure it will all work out."

"Oh, I do hope so, Annabelle. I am so worried."

They said their goodbyes and Mary turned to hurry back to the convent while Mike pulled the rope next to the wooden front door. They could hear a bell ringing a low note somewhere inside the auberge.

"Oh, isn't this delightful!" Annabelle squealed, her eyes wide and her mouth open as she looked from side to side. Clay pots with more colorful spring flowers were dotted around the entrance. She bent over to smell a bright pink hyacinth. "And it smells so wonderful!"

"It certainly looks promising," Mike admitted, finally finding cause to relax a little. "But no one is coming to the door."

"Look, there's a path that goes around to the back here. Let's follow it."

The path led around the side of the building, past a lawn of almost impossibly bright green grass. It was enclosed by shrubs and a stone wall that looked even older than the auberge. A wooden table stood on a patio partly in the shade of a lattice frame over and through which more wisteria vines formed a ceiling of lush, green leaves. It was past lunchtime now and the sky was the color of Inspector Babineaux's 2CV, a bright clear blue. Mike yawned.

"C'mon, slowcoach," Annabelle called out to him and as usual, her enthusiasm put a zing in his step. Mike picked up their bags and followed her.

Around the back, they found a door slightly ajar. Annabelle knocked. Not waiting this time, she pushed the door open and the pair went inside. They found themselves in a beautiful living room with oak-paneled walls and aged leather furniture. Shelves of books lined the walls. Directly in front of them was a narrow desk upon which the inn's guestbook lay. There was also a bell.

Annabelle hit it smartly with the heel of her hand. "I've always wanted to do that!"

After a few moments, an elderly man with sun-browned skin and thick, grey-black hair shuffled through a door toward them. He was slight and stooped and wiped his hands on a towel as he walked. The door was completely surrounded by bookshelves. There were even shelves above the frame. Each one was crammed with books, many of them old.

"*Bonjour!*" he said, his voice a little hoarse.

"*Bonjour!*" Mike responded in such a bad accent that the man immediately switched to English.

"You are the English visitors."

Mike swung around to look at Annabelle and back to the old man. "I guess we are. I believe you are expecting us?"

CHAPTER NINETEEN

THE OLD MAN assessed the pair in front of him. Annabelle was wearing her civvies—a pair of jeans and a sweater on this occasion, but her dog collar peeked over the crew neck of her light green pullover. Mike was less distinguishable in a button down shirt, his collar undone and open, his favorite trenchcoat over his arm. "We only have single rooms. We are redecorating the suite now."

"Perfect!" Annabelle said. "That would be fine, thank you."

"*Bon,*" the innkeeper said, "Follow me. *Je m'appelle Claude.*" He lifted two sets of keys from a board full of them and turned to lead the pair, very slowly, to their rooms. They traveled up a set of stairs and along a landing, stopping in front of an old oak door. The elderly man unlocked it and pushed it open. *"Révérend."*

"See you in a bit, Mike," Annabelle said as she wheeled her case through the doorway. "Meet you downstairs in ten minutes?"

"Right you are," Mike replied easily. He had realized long ago that being around Annabelle required him to suspend his expectations and roll with whatever presented itself. This was one of those times. He turned to follow the old man down the landing.

With a lot of banging and huffing, Annabelle wrestled her case through the door and stepped foot inside her room. "Ohhhh..."

The room was magnificent. Early afternoon sunlight streamed in through the large arched windows lighting up the room, the ends of the beams falling on an enormous mahogany four-poster bed covered in cream silk bed linen. Vines of ivy were carved into the posts which rose up to support an intricately folded canopy of cream lace. Above waist high, duck egg blue wooden wall panels, pink roses and more vines decorated mustard yellow wallpaper. A matching chaise longue sat opposite the bed and to one side a small table laden with fruit, madeleines, pain au chocolat, and orange juice beckoned.

Annabelle, unable to resist and feeling a little peckish after their long morning, picked up a madeleine and nibbled it as she made her way over to test the bed, slipping off her shoes as she walked across the dark stained wooden floor. She bounced gently. The bed was as soft and light as the sponge in her little cake. She flopped backwards, feeling the silkiness of the quilt against her cheeks, the sunbeams that crossed her chest warming her. She closed her eyes and sighed. She couldn't think how life could get any better.

After he'd thrown water on his face and changed his shirt, Mike went downstairs. He browsed the bookshelves for a while and studied the old black and white photographs on the walls that appeared to be scenes of the village from around a century ago. After a few minutes he went outside and looked around at the walled garden until he heard a noise behind him. "*Monsieur?*"

Mike turned to see Claude advancing. "May I offer you and your, er, lady friend some wine?"

"That would be delightful, thank you."

Shortly, the hunched innkeeper returned carrying a bottle of wine and two glasses on a tray. The tray shook as he walked, the glass tinkling. Without saying a word, he pointed at the wooden table on the patio. Mike dutifully sat and the elderly man with the ease of an action performed a thousand times efficiently uncorked the wine and poured a small amount for Mike to taste. "Good, no? It's made with grapes from a local vineyard. It has won awards. We are very proud of it here in Ville D'Eauloise."

"Delicious."

Claude filled Mike's glass, leaving the opened bottle on the table. He went back inside but momentarily returned with a basket of fresh bread, a dish of olive oil, and some blue veined cheese.

Mike dipped some bread in the oil and chewed it lazily. He sipped some of his wine. He looked at his watch. There was no sign of Annabelle. He finished up his glass and poured himself another. He could get used to this.

CHAPTER TWENTY

"MIKE! MIKE! WAKE up!" Annabelle shook him gently. "You won't sleep tonight if you're not careful."

"What? Oh." Halfway down his third glass of wine, with his arms folded across his chest, Mike had fallen asleep in the sun. He was now sporting a pink nose.

"What's been going on here?" Annabelle looked a little sleepy herself, like she'd also just awoken from a nap. She had changed into a sundress and plonked a straw hat at an awkward angle on her head.

"Claude made us lunch. I ended up eating and drinking most of it, sorry."

Annabelle laughed and picked up the bottle. It was still a third full.

"Mind if I do?" she said.

"You go ahead," Mike said, struggling to sit up. "I think I've had quite enough."

"Ah, just have a little. Keep me company." Annabelle sloshed a small amount into his glass and a significantly larger amount into her own before breaking off a chunk of the cheese and ripping off a piece of bread. "Mmmm," she murmured as she closed her eyes. "This is heavenly. Would you like some?" She offered some of the bread and cheese to Mike but he waved it away.

"It isn't really my cup of tea."

Annabelle shrugged. "You're missing out. Once you've tried a really good smelly cheese, you'll never go back. It is simply divine." Annabelle turned her face to the sun, savoring the taste of cheese on her tongue and the warmth on her cheeks. "Oh! You should see my room! There's a four poster bed and a chaise longue."

"Not a single room then."

"Oh! No." Annabelle giggled. "My bath has feet and there are all these fabulous patterns in the floor tile. My, my, I feel like Marie Antoinette at the court of Louis XVI. Except of course, I wouldn't tell anyone to eat cake."

Mike laughed. "Marie Antoinette? You? Hardly. Joan of Arc, more like."

Annabelle was unable to reply to this having just popped another mouthful of bread and cheese into her mouth. She chewed, gesticulating with her hands until she swallowed. "What about you? What's your room like?"

"Um, truth be told, I didn't notice. It has a bed, a bathroom. You know, the things you need." Mike had had other things on his mind. "I thought the owner said he had only single rooms."

"Hmm, I think he was protecting my virtue." Annabelle grinned and snorted at the same time. This culminated in a coughing fit. Mike patted her on the back.

It was late afternoon now, and they were bathed in a sunny warmth that was in stark contrast to the showers and cool temperatures they had experienced earlier in the day.

Annabelle held up her wine glass. "To a wonderful trip!" she said.

Mike clinked his glass against hers, and they sipped in unison. Annabelle savored the ruby-colored liquid.

"Rather good, isn't it?" Annabelle said.

Mike watched her lean her head back and breathe in the fragrant air around them. After a while she looked at the inspector, her eyes soft, her mouth curved gently into a small smile.

"What?" Mike said, looking down at himself in case there was a stain on his shirt. "What is it?"

"We should really get you a decent coat," she said. "Something more suitable than the one you've got."

"What's wrong with the one I've got?" Mike said. He liked his trenchcoat. He'd had it for years.

"Oh, nothing," Annabelle said. "I just think you'd look rather dashing in something more stylish."

Mike grunted. "More like Inspector Bambino, you mean."

Annabelle chuckled. "*Babineaux*," she corrected. "He is rather elegant, isn't he?"

"Pfft. He looks ridiculous—you know he combs that moustache don't you?"

"You're just jealous," Annabelle chided, smiling as she sipped her wine.

"Of *him?*" Mike exclaimed. "A man who looks like he spends more time putting God-knows-what in his hair than he does doing police work?"

"God probably does know what he puts in his hair, actually. Shall I ask him?"

The inspector growled. "Don't worry," Annabelle said reassuringly after a pause. "I'm not about to run off with a French detective."

Mike broke into a smile, unable to be irritable any longer. "I doubt it would work anyway. Joan of Arc meets Inspector

Clouseau—hardly a match made in heaven, is it? His magnifying glass versus your sword? It would be off before it even got started. His head, I mean. I may not know much but I know when to let you have yours."

CHAPTER TWENTY-ONE

"OH YOU ARE naughty, Mike!" Annabelle laughed.

Mike laughed with her before pouring her some more wine. "But if the post mortem results come back positive and the priest didn't die of natural causes, I do think he might be right about the killer, however."

Annabelle frowned. "That Father Raphael did it?"

"Yes, unfortunately. I hope he's wrong, for Mary's sake, but the circumstances are pretty damning. He must have known all Father Julien's little habits, foibles, and customs. He's outside the priest's office as they prepared for the service, then he scarpers when he dies."

"Hmm," Annabelle said into her glass, "I know it doesn't look good, but I'm sure there's more to it than that. I mean, what motive could Father Raphael possibly have?"

"We need more information."

After a minute's thought, Annabelle stopped frowning and leaned over the table, putting her hand over the inspector's to draw his attention away from the small bird that was feverishly investigating the wisteria.

"But," she began, "why would you commit a murder and make yourself the number one suspect by running away? Surely you wouldn't disappear from the crime scene as soon as it occurred. It would make you look incredibly guilty."

"Fleeing the scene of the crime is common."

"But not when you're poisoning someone," Annabelle said. "Poisoning implies forethought, calculation, subtlety. A mind that is careful, strategic, deliberate. I can't imagine Father Raphael putting in all that effort only for his exit strategy to be to get away as fast as possible."

Mike thought about this. "Possibly. But then we have to consider something else. If Raphael isn't guilty, why would he disappear the moment Father Julien collapses? If Father Raphael were innocent, his reaction would be to go to Father Julien's side."

Annabelle hummed. "Perhaps he knows something, but didn't actually commit the murder. Or perhaps he's attempting to take the blame for someone else? Perhaps he's been kidnapped. Perhaps he tried to stop the murder, and when he couldn't, he fled the scene, traumatized. Perhaps he's wandering about the countryside dazed and exhausted as we sit here drinking wine and eating smelly cheese." Annabelle's voice rose an octave as she ended her sentence. She half stood up in her seat, stricken at the thought of Father Raphael wandering the fields alone and confused.

"Calm down, Annabelle. We're straying into wild speculation territory now." Mike took Annabelle's hand and pulled her down into her seat. He sat rubbing her fingers while she settled herself. They sat in silence, enjoying the sound of the gentle breeze through the leaves of the trees, and the birdsong that trickled in from the distant fields.

"There is one interesting thing about this," Mike said.

Annabelle raised her eyebrows in expectation.

Mike pointed to the bread. "This."

Annabelle smiled. "It certainly is interesting," she said, tossing another ball of the fluffy white bread into her mouth.

"No," Mike said, "I mean the fact that the convent makes bread. Seems a rather unusual thing to do. All that heavy fieldwork for a dozen or so nuns."

"Oh, it's fairly typical for orders to produce things. It's how many of them survived throughout history. Farming isn't so common, but they seem to make it work."

Mike nodded and leaned back. "You should still talk to the nuns though. See what they have to say. There might be some clues there. I could try talking to the locals."

"That's a good idea, but how will you communicate? I doubt they speak English, and well, I've heard your French."

"I'll point, wave my hands about like they do. Maybe I'll get Bambino to translate for me."

"*Mike*. Stop calling him that. You'll forget and say it in front of him."

As small smile crept across Mike's lips. "Yes, I might, mightn't I?"

CHAPTER TWENTY-TWO

ANNABELLE JUMPED UP. "Come on! Let's go for a walk. We should explore this place, get our sea legs."

Mike groaned. "Oh, alright." He pushed himself to standing and followed Annabelle down the path and past the Mini to the lane beyond the walled garden. He looked up and down. Ville d'Eauloise was certainly a curious place. The ancient cobbled streets were so narrow, Annabelle had had to use all her Cornish driving skills to navigate them. Used to tiny, curving, undergrowth-lined lanes, she had handled the village streets with aplomb but unlike back home, she'd run the risk, not of landing in a ditch, but of scraping all the blue paint off her car. Like the garden at the auberge, the lanes were walled on either side. Buildings loomed, casting the lanes mostly in shadow at this late stage of the afternoon, and making them appear mysterious and a little creepy. And they were quiet, oh so quiet. Where were all the people?

Hand in hand, Annabelle and Mike wandered leisurely down the lanes that meandered throughout the village. The hills were steep, and they had to be careful not to slip on the stone surface. A few of the homes had raised terraces nearly all of which were covered with garden pots full of flowers and always, always tables and chairs. Every so often there were patches of raised lawn held in place by the ubiquitous stone retaining walls that were everywhere providing verandahs, flowerbeds, and even stages. A few of the lawns were scattered with bluebells. Along the way, they came upon a surprising array of animals. Chickens, goats, a couple of cows, and even a pig seemed to have free roam of the village.

"So they go in for containing their plants, but they don't seem so keen on the concept for animals," Mike said.

"Right, isn't it marvelous? Free range in the truest sense of the word." Annabelle was charmed.

"One might think the two concepts were at odds with one another."

"How so?"

"The free range animals eating the contained, immoveable flowers."

"Hmm, true."

A lone elderly woman in a floor-length dress and brightly colored crocheted shawl passed them. She nodded. Annabelle and Mike nodded back. Annabelle attempted some French. *"Bonsoir, madame."* The woman mumbled indistinctly back.

"Where do you think she's going? It's only 5 p.m., and we haven't seen anyone except her," Annabelle said when the woman was out of earshot.

"I don't know. Perhaps they're all inside minding their own business."

"Doesn't seem quite right to me. I would expect them to be outside on a lovely evening like this. Especially as it is still Easter."

"Perhaps they're in mourning for their priest."

"Maybe. Let's go to the square and see if anything is going on there."

When they got to the plaza, the church now casting a shadow over it making it cold and dark, it too was empty. No children were playing games, no one sat outside *Café Sylvie* drinking and chatting, and there were no passersby.

"Huh, what shall we do now?"

"I'm a bit peckish. Fancy something to eat?" Mike said.

Annabelle thought back to the crumbly, heavy cheese she'd eaten earlier. "Oof, I'm not very hungry."

But Mike wouldn't be dissuaded. "Come on, try something. Some snails or frog's legs. Isn't that what we're here for? To try out the local delicacies. You can't go home and not tell Philippa you've had snails! Look, there's a restaurant just over there."

"Oh, alright. Just something small though—and you have to help me."

The sign above the awning announced the name of the restaurant: *Chez Selwyn*.

"Funny name. And I thought France was all about outdoor dining," Mike wondered aloud. There was no one sitting at the tables outside the darkened frontage.

"It does seem strange. Perhaps it's closed?"

"*Ouvert*. That means open, doesn't it?" Mike pulled on the door handle. "Here we go."

The clamor that erupted from the open doorway evaporated immediately the pair went inside. Faces, open with curiosity, turned to them, eyeing the two British visitors with interest.

"Oh!" Annabelle breathed, a smile fluttering on her lips, unsure.

"Well, I guess we've found where all the people are," Mike whispered in her ear. He felt a bit hot under the collar, but he hadn't seen any threatening faces in those staring back at them. No one seemed pitching for a fight. The place was packed.

"*Bonsoir à tous*," Annabelle tried. Silence greeted her words. No one moved. When Mike told Annabelle later that she'd bobbed a little curtsey, she had no memory of it.

There was a shout from the kitchen, then another, before a full-bloodied tirade commenced. Heads turned again as the kitchen door opened and a short, red-faced, round-bellied man in chef's whites stormed into the restaurant, flicking a tea towel over his shoulder like he was swatting a fly.

"Watch-oo lookin' at?" the chef said to his patrons as he passed. He spoke in English. On catching sight of Annabelle and Mike, he stopped in his tracks. He lifted his chin and stared down his nose at them pugnaciously. It looked like it was the *chef* who was fixing for a fight.

"Yeah?" the man said.

CHAPTER TWENTY-THREE

"UM, WE WONDERED if you had a table. For two?" Annabelle said.

The man blinked and stared at them. You'd have thought he'd come across a talking donkey rather than a vicar asking for a table in a small restaurant in an out-of-the-way tiny French village.

"English!" he exclaimed. He walked up to them. "So this is what you look like these days. I haven't ever seen one in this village. And I've been here since 1991."

Annabelle was flustered. The people in the crowd were murmuring to each other now. It seemed as though the entire village were there—elderly people, young people, children and their parents. All ages were gathered together at tables full of bottles and glasses and plates of food.

"Well, if you don't have room, we can j-just leave. It's n-no problem."

The man kept staring at her. His face was ruddy, curls of his wiry, red hair peeked from beneath his tall white hat. His eyes were a sparkling blue and framed with white eyelashes and white eyebrows. Annabelle thought she detected traces of a Welsh accent.

"Leave? *Leave?* You're not going to leave." He took Annabelle's arm and gestured with a thick meaty hand covered in freckles and coarse white hair to a table for two by the window, the only one available. "I haven't spoken English outside of yelling abuse for thirty years. You, my dear, are going to sit right here and have whatever you want on the menu. On the house!"

"Oh, right, um, thanks. That's jolly good of you, but there's no n..."

"Thanks, mate," Mike interjected. "Very decent of you."

"Not at all, not at all." The chef clicked his fingers at a beautiful dark-haired woman who was hovering at the back of the restaurant. He wiggled his hand. The woman nodded in response and disappeared. The villagers seemed to have got over their shock and were now returning to their conversations, although judging by the glances cast their way, it looked as though they'd exchanged curiosity about Annabelle and Mike for talking about them.

"I'll send you my specialty for you to try."

"That would be lovely, Mr...,"

"Oh, what am I saying?" The man held out his hand. "Selwyn. Selwyn Jones. From the valleys of beautiful Wales originally."

"Pleased to meet you, Mr. Jones. You're a long way from home," Annabelle said.

"Ah well, it's a long story, but it involves a gorgeous French girl and a youth hostel. Swept me fair off my feet she did, but wouldn't leave her family, so I had to come to this forsaken place. She's long gone now, but this is my daughter Françoise."

The tall beauty who Selwyn had been signaling to earlier, floated over with a bottle of wine. Annabelle and Mike looked from the short, red-faced chef to the tall, graceful woman with big brown eyes and long dark eyelashes.

"Yeah, I know what you're thinking. How did an ugly mug like me end up with a daughter like her? Everyone does. She a dead spit for my wife. But she's got her daddy's temper. There's fire in them veins so watch out." The Welshman laughed, his smile making his otherwise threatening face far more congenial.

"Are you looking into Father Julien's death?" the chef asked.

"Just helping out, you know, asking a few questions," Mike replied.

"Well, if you need any help, you just let me know." He lowered his voice to a whisper. "They're not too bright, this lot, and very close knit. Suspicious of outsiders, you know how it is."

"We'll be sure to remember that, Mr. Jones," Annabelle said tactfully.

"And now, I'll get you your dinner."

"I hope it won't be frog's legs or snails," Mike hissed to Annabelle across the table when the chef had disappeared into the kitchen.

Selwyn reappeared carrying two plates. Mike's eyes lit up. "Sausages and chips! Now that's what I call a specialty."

"Ah, but not just any old sausages. *Andouillette de Troyes*, a traditional dish of our region. Enjoy!"

"Hmm, they're very good, Annabelle. Try one."

"Just a bite, I'm not very hungry."

"Well, give me yours then. I'm starving." Mike switched plates with Annabelle and tucked in.

"Did you like?" Françoise said as she came to clear their plates.

"It was delicious," Mike said enthusiastically, wiping his mouth on his napkin.

"Have you always lived here, Françoise?" Annabelle was curious that a lovely young woman would wish to live in such an out of the way, isolated village.

"Yes, always. Like many of the people here, I can trace my ancestry as far back as the fifteenth century, and even though many of the younger generation leave for Paris and other cities, they almost always return. We have a saying, 'Wherever you go, Ville d'Eauloise will find you.'"

Suddenly, the sound of chairs being dragged across the floor started up, the big screen TV above the bar flickered into life, the noise of restaurant chatter dying away to almost silence.

"Oh! What's happening?" Annabelle wondered.

"We're going to watch *The Life of Brian*," Françoise said.

Annabelle and Mike stared at her.

"What? Monty Python?" Mike said.

"Yes, we do it every Easter. It's a tradition. My father introduced it when he moved here. It's his favorite film."

"Blimey," Annabelle said.

"We talk along with it too," Françoise continued. "Everyone knows the words. The children learn it at a young age."

"In English?"

"Yes," Françoise said, as though it were the most natural thing in the world for two hundred plus French people to recite the dialog of a British comedy film in a language they didn't understand every Easter Monday.

"Well, this should be a treat," Mike said, and he wasn't referring to the crème brûlée Françoise had just laid in front of him.

🌑

"They really get into it, don't they?" Annabelle whispered a short while later. The villagers were entranced. All of them from the oldest to the youngest were focused on the screen, shouting out the dialog in perfect time with the actors, clearly well-practiced, many of them assigned roles into which they threw themselves with hand gestures, funny voices, and even props.

"Do you think they know what they're saying?" Mike asked Annabelle.

"Do you?"

"No, I think they are just having a rollicking good time." Mike was agog, he had never seen anything quite like it. "And it is very weird and strange. And I think we should get out of here before we get roped in."

Annabelle giggled. "Are you sure?"

"Quite sure. Come on, let's go."

And so quietly, with everyone absorbed and without anyone noticing except perhaps Françoise, Annabelle and Mike slipped away into the night.

"What do you think was in those sausages?" Annabelle asked Mike as they walked back to their auberge.

"Pork, I assume. They were very tasty."

"Hmm." Annabelle wasn't so sure. But she decided not to say anything. It had been a strange enough evening as it was.

CHAPTER TWENTY-FOUR

THAT NIGHT, ANNABELLE slept like a log—one packed with full-bodied red wine, some sausage, and a variety of French cheeses. Mike, however, barely slept at all. He paced around his room, performed sit-ups, showered three times, and as he sat on the edge of his bed, he turned over in his hands the tiny box he'd been carrying in his pocket.

"Annabelle, I'd like to ask you something," he said into the bathroom mirror, his voice low in case the walls were thin. He did *not* want to be overheard. "I know this might seem a little sudden, but I've given it a lot of thought, and considered all the angles. It makes sense logically to me, however surprising it may seem to you. And I know there might be issues, but if you can think of no objections then—*Damnit!*" He banged his forehead with the heel of his hand. *"Too formal!"* He settled himself and tried again.

"Annabelle, I've had the time of my life since I met you. It's been really good. Really, really good. Would you—*No! It needs to be romantic!*" He shrugged his shoulders, stretched his neck, first one side then the other. He bobbed on the balls of his feet like he was about to enter a boxing ring. "Deep breath. Come on, Mike, you can do it. Annabelle, your hair is as brown as burnt chestnuts, and your eyes remind me of the headlights on a perfectly-restored 1961 Jaguar E-type—*Oh bloody hell*—Why are proposals so hard? They make it look so simple on television."

Mike had been through a proposal before, but last time was almost an accident. He'd been very young and a lot of alcohol had been involved. This time, proposing was an altogether different proposition. He had to get it right. Mike wracked his brain as he tried to recall his favorite movies for inspiration. Very quickly, he realized there was a distinct lack of romance in John Wayne and Clint Eastwood films. Even his hero Humphrey Bogart failed him.

"Frankly Annabelle, I just don't give a damn. Let's bloody well just get bloody married—bloody, bloody, bloody." He sighed once more before throwing himself on his bed and attempting to sleep again.

CHAPTER TWENTY-FIVE

MIKE AWOKE QUITE late, late enough to find Annabelle already sitting in the sunny courtyard with a cup of coffee and a plate of croissants in front of her. Groggy and grumpy, he squinted in the painfully bright morning sunshine.

"Morning," she smiled, as he leaned down to swap a quick kiss before sitting down, "did you sleep well?"

Mike groaned. "No. I think the sausages disagreed with me."

"Hmm," Annabelle had spent some time looking up what exactly was in *Andouillettes de Troyes*. Somehow she didn't think Mike would appreciate what she'd learned.

"Did you?" Mike asked. "Sleep well in that big four poster bed of yours, I mean?"

"Beautifully," Annabelle said, before winking at Claude who was hovering in the doorway. "Could we have some more coffee, please? For my friend here." She turned to Mike, "Would you like to take it easy today? You do look rather tired."

Mike gave a wry smile, his grumpy mood dissipating in the

face of Annabelle's concern. "I would hate to miss out on anything," he said. "And we've got plenty to do."

Annabelle chuckled and pushed the remaining croissants toward him. "These are simply delicious, but I do believe I've had as many as I can manage. You finish them up. They'll make you feel better. After that, why don't we take those bikes for a spin?" She nodded at two bikes propped up against the wall of the auberge. "It's a bit chilly this morning, it'll warm us up."

"Bikes? I haven't been on one in 20 years."

"Well then, it's about time you refreshed your memory. Come on, chop, chop."

Mike stuffed a croissant into his mouth and grabbed another "for energy," and once more found himself trailing Annabelle who was already astride her bike enthusiastically checking out the gears.

"Let's ride to the plaza, it's all downhill," she cried.

Mike refrained from pointing out that it would be all *up*hill on the way back and cautiously tried out his bike with a couple of circuits of the path around the garden. "Okay, I think I've got it. After you," he said.

They sailed down the hill to the village center, parked their bikes at the back of the church, and strolled arm in arm through the narrow, cobbled streets. Annabelle laughed and smiled like an excited child, pointing out interesting aspects of the architecture, even the quite grotesque gargoyles that were carved into the sides of the stone buildings, and delighting over the names of the shops. Mike did his best to match her mood and as he listened to her bright, cheerful voice, he kept wondering if perhaps now was the moment, but he kept deciding against it. Not when they still had a death to figure out. And not before he'd got his speech sorted.

After an hour spent exploring and visiting the shops in the village, Annabelle, charmed by the exquisite handiwork of the village's craftsmen, bought herself an elegantly-carved and painted figurine of a dog that looked rather like Magic. After that, she was satisfied enough to retreat to the auberge. They returned to their bikes. Strapped to the back of Mike's was a cage with two live chickens inside.

"What the..." Mike said. He looked around. Two young women were standing in the shadows, laughing. He pointed at the chickens. This only made the two women laugh even more before they scurried away.

"They mean for you to take them to your auberge, Inspector." It was Selwyn. He was polishing the tables outside his restaurant. "That's how we do things here."

Mike stared at the chickens. They looked at him without blinking. One let out a cluck. The other bobbed its head. "Are you sure?"

"Quite sure, boyo."

"What will happen to them then?"

Selwyn stared at him, then drew his finger across his neck. "Go on, it won't kill you."

Mike looked at Annabelle. She shrugged. He blew out his cheeks. "Okay, okay, if you can't beat 'em, join 'em, I suppose, but don't you tell anyone about this back home. Promise?"

Annabelle ducked her head. "Yes, sir!" she said, gravely.

"Are you taking the mickey?"

"No, no, no." Annabelle looked over at Selwyn. He winked.

And so Mike got on his bike and wobbled off, sending the chickens into a bobbing and clucking frenzy that lasted all the way up the hill to the auberge.

Mary was waiting for them. "Annabelle, Inspector—I'm sorry I left you to yourselves. I had meant to come and meet you earlier this morning but things have been chaotic at the convent and..."

"It's alright," Annabelle reached out to gently rub her friend's arm, her soothing voice calming Mary. "We went for a lovely bike ride and walk around the village. I got this dog figurine and Mike got these... chickens."

Mary smiled meekly, her face strained with anxiety. "I see..." she began slowly. "Would you like to do something with them? Before you speak to the nuns, I mean. I can take you to the convent and introduce you. We were all there when Father Julien... when, you know." Mary's voice trailed off to a whisper.

Mike and Annabelle looked at each other. "We'd very much like to do that," the inspector said. "And take a look around the convent, if that's alright."

"I'm sorry." Mary held up her hand like a policeman directing traffic. "It's not." Her voice was sharp. Mike blinked in surprise. "No men are allowed at our convent. Mother Superior is adamant, even our plumbers and repairpersons are female. They're called in from outside the village if necessary. We've even had women from the village learn trades more usually performed by men because they know they can count on us as customers."

"Oh, that's quite alright," Annabelle said. She looked at Mike. "I can go along on my own. You could talk to the villagers like we discussed?" Mike looked at the chickens.

Before he could answer, Mary spoke again. "Inspector Babineaux would like to see you, Inspector. Apparently he has some news." Mike suppressed a deep groan, squeezing his eyes tight to avoid expressing how he felt.

"Perfect!" Annabelle said. "You meet with Inspector Babineaux, and I'll go speak to the nuns."

Mike opened his eyes. "Yes..." he said slowly. "Perfect." He took the cage containing the chickens from his bike and carried them inside to Claude.

CHAPTER TWENTY-SIX

SET AGAINST THE medieval charm of the sleepy village, St. Agnès convent fit right in, but as Mary led her along the winding path toward it, Annabelle was no less impressed. Like the church in the center of the village, the building stood large and proud reflecting the importance placed on religion in the region. Also like the church, the convent was made of old blocks of stone, darkened and cracked with age and carpeted in places with moss.

There were wings on either side of the main building, like an "H" if viewed from above. Covered archways ran around the outside. A pair of heavy, arched black wooden doors were set into the building, and small, barred windows peeped out from the thick stones as though shrewdly keeping an eye on things. A path ran past flourishing vegetable and flower gardens and through a gap in a hedge to the open fields in the valley beyond.

Annabelle found herself gawping as she neared it, full of awe at the stark contrast of the solid, dark stone building against the light, vivid greens and yellows of the rolling hills behind it. The surrounding countryside was brightened by a morning sun that was slowly heating up the atmosphere. She could see the dew from the ground evaporating into the air forming a mysterious, romantic haze.

"That's remarkable," she said, almost to herself.

"What is?" Sister Mary replied. "Oh, yes, it's beautiful, isn't it? And so restful, contemplative. It's been good to be here. I have been able to... well, think."

Annabelle turned to look at her friend. "Are things alright, Mary? I mean, from even before this latest business. You seem a bit out of sorts."

"Oh, that's just because of what has happened. I'm fine, otherwise. Perfectly fine." Mary swung her arms before forcing them still. "It's quiet here. We are fortunate that we are off the beaten path. It would be terrible if we became a tourist hotspot. We occasionally get the odd artist dropping by—female of course, but that's about it. The convent was formerly a monastery, and many say it was the second building constructed in the village after the church. The village arose around it to farm the land and serve the monks. But, well, it has quite a gruesome history..."

"Tell me."

"Not here exactly, but not far from here, sometime in the 5th century, a young woman named Agnès was killed quite brutally on the instruction of a Roman Emperor. She wouldn't stop performing miracles, or so the story goes. On her death she became a martyr and relics that are supposedly her remains are tucked away at the church. They are considered very valuable. Pilgrims drop by to see them sometimes."

"Interesting," Annabelle said, "if a bit morbid. What are those buildings over there?" She pointed to a huge stone barn alongside which ran a small river. A huge wheel hung off the side of the building. A short distance away, surrounded by weeds and overgrowth, was a large wooden shed.

"The one on the left is where we work."

"Making the bread?"

"Yes. There's a mill, a granary where we store our flour, and a bakery. We work shifts, taking turns to get up early. We are on a strict rota."

"Hmm."

"The other is just a shed where we keep all our bits and bobs."

"Like what?"

"Spare parts for our machinery, bikes, ropes, the normal things you keep in a shed, really. And over there are our wheat fields and orchards. Apple and fig trees. Oooh, we make the most wonderful jam. It's sold in some of the most expensive shops in Paris."

Mary waited for a response, but Annabelle was deep in thought. They walked across an old bridge that passed over the river. Annabelle gazed around. There was a feeling of peace and holiness about the convent and its grounds, something Annabelle knew well. It immediately made her think of the Mother Superior's hard eyes. Protecting her territory seemed very important to the convent's most senior of nuns.

"Are you sure it's alright for me to just walk in like this?" she asked Mary.

"Oh yes, Mother Superior knows you're coming."

"And the other nuns?"

Mary sighed. "They're fine with it."

Annabelle stopped and placed a gentle hand on her old friend's shoulder to compel her to do the same. "What *is* the matter, Mary?"

Mary stopped, turned, and looked up at Annabelle. "It's nothing," she said.

"Come on, Mary. This is me, you're talking to. Annabelle."

Mary pulled a face. "I'm fairly new here, just a few months. Some of the nuns have been here for decades."

"And?" Annabelle asked, sympathetically.

"I'm just being silly."

"No. Go on."

Mary breathed deeply. "I'm not really close with the other nuns. They're perfectly polite to me, and friendly enough…"

"But you're not having wild parties every weekend?" Annabelle chuckled.

Mary looked sad. "Or even friendly chats. They really are wonderful… I just haven't found it easy. I don't have a single friend here except for Raphael. Oh, Annabelle, I miss you more than ever. I've never been lonely before. Up until now, when I've been troubled, I've always had God, but even he seems to have abandoned me."

Annabelle put her arm around Mary's shoulder and gave it a squeeze.

"But loneliness is a small thing," Mary said, smiling as if she had released some personal burden. "And this is a place of contemplation and devotion. It's not really important. My feelings will pass."

"Everything is important in the eyes of the Lord," Annabelle said softly.

Mary ducked her head under Annabelle's chin gratefully. They stood admiring the view of the countryside, the rolling hills, and a chateau that stood many miles away on the crest of a hill. After a minute, they turned to walk back to the convent.

CHAPTER TWENTY-SEVEN

"SO MUCH FOR a romantic getaway," Mike grumbled as he pounded the cobblestones on the way to *Café Sylvie,* the café to which Babineaux had summoned him. He'd decided to walk this time. The French inspector had turned a table at the café into his "office."

"Second day here, and I'm spending it with a pompous French twit who wears two-inch heels."

"'Allo!" called a distinctive voice from a table on the café terrace. "*Inspecteur!* Come! Come!"

Mike looked up and saw the lounging frame of Babineaux beckoning him over like Mike were a child to whom he was about to give a few euros. His beleaguered colleague, Sergeant Lestrange, sat beside him with his legs crossed and his hands clasped in his lap. His thumbs fidgeted with one another.

"Good day, Inspector," Mike said, shaking hands with Babineaux before offering his hand to Lestrange who had to hold back his cuff in order to take it. "Sergeant."

"'Allo," the younger man said. Mike realized now that the confused expression on the sergeant's face was permanent.

"Sit! Sit!" urged Babineaux, patting the chair beside him. "Where iz *Révérend* Annabelle, may I ask?"

"She has gone to the convent. She's currently talking to the nuns."

"Aha!" Babineaux said, pointing his finger into the air. "Very good! Two amateur detectives separating in order to cover more ground! Clever!" He slapped Mike on the shoulder hard.

Mike closed his eyes. "I'm not an amateur, and I can assure y..."

"You are in an amateur *capacité, Inspecteur*."

Mike bristled. "What did you want to talk to me about?" he asked impatiently.

Babineaux delicately sipped from his coffee cup before placing it back on the saucer. He squinted mischievously and rubbed his palms together.

"It iz very interesting," he said, pronouncing his consonants in the slow, drawn-out way Mike already recognized as one of the French inspector's mannerisms. "First of all, we confirmed ze death was caused by ze poisoning. Ze signs were all zere. It was definitely a murder."

"Okay, good. Progress. What's the interesting part?"

Babineaux smiled and leaned in slightly, sliding a slim finger across his even slimmer moustache. "It was a gradual poisoning!"

Mike waited. There was more to come, he knew it, but he would not give Babineaux the satisfaction of asking what it was.

Babineaux leaned forward even further. Instinctively, Mike sat back. "Ze poison was not given in one killing dose," Babineaux continued, as if reading a horror story, "but in small pieces!"

"How is that possible?"

"I am told zat if tiny amounts of ze poison are given in zis manner *régulièrement*, ze probability of ze death increases until it iz *inévitable*!" Babineaux widened his eyes and exaggerated the last word like he was telling a story to a child. "But almost undetectable. Death comes from ze secondary problem like an 'eart attack, as in Father Julien's case."

"What kind of poison?"

"We don't know. Zey cannot find it. Zere is nothing in Father Julien's stomach except for ze rye bread and ze red wine and some over-ze-counter painkiller. Zeems 'e 'ad an 'eadache."

Mike leaned back and folded his arms. He scanned the great plaza in front of the church before turning back to the French detective. "There's more, isn't there?" Mike asked.

"Oh yes!" Babineaux replied, jabbing his finger in the air. "Zat iz just ze beginning, my friend. Zis iz a very curious case indeed."

CHAPTER TWENTY-EIGHT

AFTER AN HOUR at the convent, Mary had shown Annabelle almost every part of it; the spartan rooms, the gardens, and the efficiently-run farming and milling operation. Annabelle found herself impressed, not just by the peaceful environment but by the organized daily routines by which the nuns lived. With Mary as translator, Annabelle spoke to the sisters as she came upon them, but she found, much as Mary had described, that the nuns, while polite and welcoming, were distant. The sisters spoke quietly, mostly to each other, and once they had offered a polite greeting and confirmed they had no information that would help the investigation into Father Julien's death, they quickly disappeared to carry out their duties.

"I wish I were so disciplined," Annabelle said to Mary. "How many of you are there?"

"Including Mother Superior, 13. A baker's dozen." Mary smiled at her little joke.

"We've talked to eight. You and Mother Renate make ten. Just three more left."

"Okay, we'll find them, but I need to hang laundry in the yard. Would you like to have a cup of tea while you wait for me?"

"No, I would like to help you with your laundry."

"Oh, there's no need, Annabelle."

"I insist. Look, we haven't talked to *that* nun." Annabelle pointed over to a tall, young woman who was pegging out undergarments. "You never know what might come up. I bet many a secret has been shared across a line, a few pegs, and a row of freshly washed knickers."

"Alright, if you insist." Mary handed Annabelle a basket of laundry and she set about pegging cotton sheets to a washing line that zig-zagged its way between posts stuck into the ground next to the orchards where fig and apple trees spread out in rows as organized and structured as the nuns' daily lives. A set of posts over, the tall nun was shaking out a vest.

"Annabelle, this is Véronique. Véronique, this is Reverend Annabelle. She's from England. Véronique speaks English, Annabelle," Mary said.

"Pleased to meet you," the nun said, quickly pegging her vest to the line before offering her hand, her head hung low so that Annabelle couldn't quite tell if she was even looking at her. She took the young woman's thin, soft hand in hers.

"Véronique is relatively new here," Mary added.

"Hello Sister," Annabelle said to the young woman.

"Oh, I am not a sister. I am merely an aspirant."

"Ah," Annabelle said, swinging her eyes to look at Mary for an explanation.

"Véronique is trying us out for size, Annabelle. To see if this is the life for her, and for us to see if she would fit in."

Slowly, Véronique raised her eyes to meet Annabelle's, and the Reverend found herself almost stunned by the beauty of the young woman. All the nuns possessed the fairness of features that came from pure living, clean air, and fresh food, but Véronique was even more striking. Her cheeks were rosy, and a pale scar below her eyebrow stood out, but what made her attractiveness even more noticeable was the deeply sad expression she wore. Her big green eyes were luminous and moist, her full red lips parted slightly. As befit her status as a temporary member of the order's community, Véronique wore street clothes—a button down shirt underneath black dungarees. "I have been looking around the convent and spending my time here working and praying. It's a wonderful, holy place and so very productive."

"It certainly appears a hive of industry," Annabelle replied. "You all seem very gainfully employed.

"We are doing God's work. Are you here to find out who killed Father Julien?" she asked, her voice still soft, yet rising with hope.

"Not exactly," Annabelle said. "But I am doing my best to help."

Véronique nodded, before lowering her head again.

"Perhaps you can tell me what Father Julien was like?" Annabelle asked.

"Father Julien was a wonderful priest," Véronique began. "He was wise, loyal, and generous. He was private, but he always had time for those who needed him. He would mentor me about the life of a nun and help me explore if it was for me. I had several private audiences with him."

Véronique's features glowed, her eyes shining as she spoke of the priest. Annabelle caught a glimpse of her beautiful almond-shaped eyes brightening before they were weighed down by sorrow once more. The young woman looked down at the grass again and said more softly, "He was a Godly man. It is unspeakably terrible what happened to him."

"And what about young Father Raphael? Did you know him at all?"

"Oh no, I didn't know him to speak to. Just by sight and to say 'hello,' that's all."

"How do you like it here? Do you think you will stay?"

Véronique looked from Annabelle to Mary and back again, a little alarmed. "I do like it here. Mother Renate is a wonderful Mother Superior, so kind and strong. But I have no decision to make. My prayers are very consistent. I am waiting for God to instruct me. As yet, I am still waiting."

"Véronique!" A cry came from a few yards away. Another nun, around the same age, but shorter and plumper, came striding toward them. She said something in fast French that Annabelle didn't catch.

"Excuse me, Reverend. I have to go to the bakery. It was nice to have met you. *Au revoir.*"

"*Au revoir*, Véronique," Annabelle replied, watching as the beautiful aspirant seemingly floated across the grass despite her dungarees.

CHAPTER TWENTY-NINE

THE OTHER NUN arrived, panting, to take over Véronique's task. A sheen of sweat was apparent on her forehead where it met the white coif to which her black veil was attached. She wore thick glasses that magnified her eyes to an improbable size.

"Annabelle, this is Sister Josephine." Mary proceeded in French to introduce Annabelle to the new nun.

"I know who she is, Mary," Sister Josephine snapped. She spoke perfect English. Mary stopped as though she had been slapped. She colored before raising her palm to her cheek to cool it.

"Pleased to meet you, Sister," Annabelle said. She inhaled slowly to calm herself.

"I hear you're asking about Father Raphael."

"Among other things, yes."

"I have some information for you."

"Oh?"

The nun thrust her chin out. She flashed her eyes at Annabelle and nodded in Mary's direction.

"I shall continue this while you talk," Mary said. Her lips pinched, she picked up her basket of damp laundry and moved off to the other end of the washing line.

Annabelle watched Mary walk away, dignity etched into her posture, and then turned her attention back to the nun whose breathing had eased now.

"That Father Raphael was not what he seemed," Sister Josephine hissed. "He wasn't always a priest, you know."

Annabelle smiled evenly. "Of course not. None of us were."

"But some come to it later than others, if you know what I mean."

"How so?" Annabelle kept her expression measured, determined not to feed this insensitive, over-excitable nun further.

Sister Josephine took a deep breath, glancing toward Sister Mary once more.

"Father Raphael led an *interesting* life before he joined the priesthood. He grew up in Paris. He drank. Lived decadently, so I've heard." Sister Josephine hesitated, before continuing. "He was a..." She looked around to check that no one could hear. "He was a *model*. On the catwalk. On the front of magazines. And you know the lives those kinds of people live." She folded her arms. "Then suddenly—he became a priest! That's strange, don't you think?"

"There are many paths upon which to find the Lord," Annabelle said. "His is not new."

"Father Raphael had a long way to go on his *path*," Sister Josephine replied.

Annabelle paused for a moment. "What do you mean?" she asked. She clenched the inside of her cheeks with her teeth and tilted her head back, waiting for the nun to enlighten her.

"He was still a junior priest, an apprentice to Father Julien," Josephine explained, her French accent more prominent now as she spoke louder and with more confidence. She leaned in and shielded her mouth with her hand. "Despite how it might seem, I do not wish to speak or think ill of anyone."

"Sister Josephine, if what you know might help find whoever killed Father Julien, then it is a greater ill to keep it to yourself."

The sparkle in Sister Josephine's eyes got brighter. She looked up at Annabelle, then again at Sister Mary who was busy pegging more wet clothing to the line.

"They were close, you know."

"Who? Father Raphael and Sister Mary?"

"Yes."

"What's wrong with that?"

"Nothing," Josephine responded. "At least, not for those who haven't devoted themselves to God. But Father Raphael is a priest, and Sister Mary is a nun."

Annabelle scowled a little as she tried to wrangle some sense out of what she heard. "Let me get this straight. You think that Sister Mary and Father Raphael's relationship is untoward?"

"Correct."

"But what does that have to do with the murder of Father Julien?"

Sister Josephine sighed deeply. "I don't know. I only speak of what I have seen. And that things are not *what* they seem." She leaned in again. "Secrets are afoot," she hissed before taking a step back and speaking more loudly. "My thoughts now are only with Father Julien, God have mercy upon his soul." She crossed herself before turning around to walk off toward the bakery.

"Wait!" Annabelle called. But Sister Josephine disappeared, and Annabelle's shoulders slumped as she sighed.

Mary walked up to her. "What did she have to say?"

"Not much, to be honest. Self-important nonsense."

"She doesn't like Father Raphael and hasn't been terribly nice to me since I got here," Mary said. "I don't know what I did wrong."

Annabelle looped her arm through Mary's. "Probably nothing. Some people are just like that. Inexplicable," she said. "Let's go and have that cup of tea, and hope that Mike is having more luck than us."

CHAPTER THIRTY

MIKE SAT AT the table in the café, a half-drunk cup of coffee in front of him beside the small bowl of snails Babineaux insisted he try. Mike had eaten one, it wasn't bad, but he had other, more pressing things on his mind than indulging this pompous nitwit. He had done everything he could to turn the conversation back to the investigation, but Babineaux seemed determined to quiz him about British police work. It felt, to Mike, like a form of assault.

"Do ze English spoil ze crime scenes often...? Are ze regular police as incompetent as ze shows on TV make zem seem...? Would zey ever actually consult a person like Sherlock 'olmes...? How do ze English treat crimes of passion...?"

Once Mike's temper was wound as tightly as the threads in the French detective's smart suit, he held up a large palm to stop further questioning. He was pretty sure this, and the snails, were a set-up. "Enough," he commanded, in the low but authoritative voice he used with truculent prisoners. "I don't have time for this now. Perhaps when we've made some progress, eh?"

Babineaux raised his eyebrows. "Huh?"

"Let's get back to the cause of death. You said that Father Julien was poisoned gradually rather than with one lethal dose, but that there was more to it than that. What did you mean?"

Babineaux leaned forward and smiled conspiratorially. "Look at zis," he said, pulling a stack of envelopes from inside his navy blue, double-breasted jacket. He placed them on the table and slid them slowly toward Mike as if he were conducting a card trick, one eyebrow raised.

"What are they?" Mike said, ignoring the envelopes. He figured the safer option was to keep his eyes on the French inspector. There was no telling what he would do, or say, next.

"Ze safe. We cracked it open..."

"It only required a key."

"Well, yes, but zis is what we found. I must admit, a clever decision on *Révérend* Annabelle's part."

"They should be in evidence bags. Fingerprints, man!"

Babineaux's face froze for a second, his mouth open, as the implications of what Mike was saying sunk in. "*Oui!*" he said, nodding as confidently as he could. "Well-observed, *Inspecteur*. Of course, I knew zat. Just a little test for you."

Slowly, holding only the edge, Mike picked up the top-most envelope from the pile Babineaux had placed in front of him and using a fork levered out the sheet of paper that was inside.

"Unmarked," commented Babineaux. "Probably placed under ze door."

Mike scanned the letters that were pasted haphazardly onto the cheap paper.

"What do they say?"

"*WATCH YOUR BACK... WE KNOW WHAT YOU DID... YOU CAN'T RUN...*" Babineaux translated for him.

"Then these are death threats!"

"*Mais oui!* From our murderer, no doubt!" Babineaux tilted his head and nodded nonchalantly, his hands steepled in front of him.

"Do you have any idea what they might be in connection with?"

"Absolutely none. But it adds to ze mystery, does it not?"

"It most certainly does. I wonder what he was hiding."

"He must have been receiving zem for quite some time." Babineaux nodded at the pile of envelopes. "Zere are at least zirty 'ere."

"Have you tested them for a poisonous substance?"

"Ah, *non*." Babineaux pursed his lips and squinted. He wagged his finger at Mike. "But zat is a very good *idée, Inspecteur*."

"It's detecting basics is what it is," Mike said. "And we need to talk to people to find out what was going on in the priest's life that might have caused these to be sent."

"We 'ave spoken to everyone. We did it as soon as ze priest was killed. Zey know nothing. We 'ave reached a dead end, *Inspecteur*."

"Someone must know something. As you say, they're not postmarked, so someone in the village must have sent them. Someone is lying. We need to delve deeper." Mike threw his head back to drain the last of his coffee. "And I need another drink."

Babineaux watched the inspector as he disappeared into the café before slapping Lestrange on the shoulder. "Put those letters in a bag and get them tested. *Non!* Not with your hands! Use a napkin!" he growled in French.

CHAPTER THIRTY-ONE

ONCE THEY HAD drunk their tea, Mary took Annabelle on a walk around the orchard. Along the way, they came upon nuns wrapping the trees in nets.

"What are they doing, Mary?"

"They are protecting the trees from pests," Mary explained. "We don't use any pesticides or chemicals. This is an area of natural beauty and habitat for a number of protected wildlife so we use environmentally-friendly methods to protect our crops."

"That looks difficult and labor-intensive."

"It is harder to protect everything, and we haven't always been successful. Apparently the grain crop got contaminated with a fungus once, and it was all lost that year. But overall it is the right, sustainable thing to do. We must protect all God's creatures. Come late summer these trees will be brimming with fruit."

Annabelle nodded at the working nuns as she passed by. Everything seemed pleasant enough. The sisters were devout, took pride in their work, and followed their routines. They enjoyed basic comforts and a focus on simplicity—and yet when she had spoken to them earlier, Annabelle felt a lingering sense of uneasiness long after their conversations finished.

"Mary, it feels a little strange here."

"Really? How do you mean?"

"Well, when we speak to the nuns, when I mention Mother Superior to them, I feel a change. It's difficult to put my finger on the source, but I feel it keenly nonetheless. They talk of Mother Superior with an undercurrent of awe."

"She's an impressive woman, Mother Superior."

"She certainly is, and formidable." Even in the short time she had spent in their company, Annabelle could see how much authority Mother Renate had over the women who were, due to their age and their lack of worldliness, highly impressionable.

"I think she's rather wonderful in her own way. She's not soft and cuddly like you, Annabelle, but she has a certain… something."

"She does that."

As the light of the day began to fade from bright mid-afternoon sunlight into what would become a more subdued, deliciously-rich burnt orange of sunset, Annabelle realized that while she had spent a wonderful, eye-opening, spiritual time at the convent, she had made very little progress with respect to Father Julien's death.

"Mary, there's one more nun I'd like to speak to."

"Yes, Sister Simone. She's Mother Superior's second-in-command. She's in charge of farming and production. She'll be in the bakery, setting up for tonight."

"Show me."

***

Sister Simone's lined and wrinkled face appeared to pop out from her traditional wimple, the white cloth that wrapped around her head, the sides of her face, and her chin. She blinked owl-like from behind thick glasses and was clearly older than any nun Annabelle had met that day. Nonetheless, as Annabelle and Mary entered the building, they saw the elderly woman lift a bag of flour easily onto her shoulder. Annabelle found herself pleased to be looking at a soft-faced woman with intelligent light-brown eyes who seemed incapable of deception, dishonesty, and pettiness. Simone had the look of a person who had seen much throughout her lifetime, not all of it pleasant, but who was better prepared than most to accept it.

"It's very nice to meet you, Sister Simone," Annabelle said.

"Welcome, Reverend," the senior nun said in English. "Please, come in."

Annabelle gazed around the big, well-equipped room. There were shelves full of flour, long tables down the middle of the room, a large thermostatically controlled proofing cabinet in the corner, and at the end, huge ovens, which despite having finished baking bread hours earlier, still emanated a warmth that Annabelle could feel yards away. Bench scrapers, lames, serrated bread knives, weighing scales, loaf pans, and cooling racks sat on a counter against the back wall.

"This looks complicated," Annabelle said.

"It's not, not really," Sister Simone replied. Her voice was soft and calm. "It's an entirely natural process that we simply encourage. We try to use the old ways where possible—these are linen proofing cloths we use for the baguettes—but as you can see we aren't adverse to modern technology." Sister Simone nodded toward the tall glass-fronted proofing cabinet.

Annabelle smiled. "That's a rather nice way of looking at it."

"It is the simplest way. We like simplicity here. Routines we repeat continually. It helps calm the mind and enables us to focus on our Lord and his work."

"Sister Simone is one of the wisest women I know," Sister Mary said, smiling.

"That's a polite way to say that I'm old," Simone replied, straight-faced.

Sister Mary laughed, long-since used to the woman's dryness.

"We've been making bread for centuries, as long as the convent has been here." Sister Simone stroked the worn tabletop. There were cuts, knots, even burns ingrained into its surface. "These tables where we knead our dough are even older than me, if you can believe it. The crop logbooks go back to the seventeenth century. Ville d'Eauloise is a place where you hold on to the past."

Sister Simone's soft, calm voice made her words sound like poetry and Annabelle nodded with respect. She would love her sermons to take on such gravitas so effortlessly. Something brushed her legs. "Argh!" Annabelle looked down and saw a big grey cat sitting at her feet. Black fur wound around its eye like an eye patch. It was the biggest cat Annabelle had ever seen.

"That's Poupon. Eats as much as a horse, but we do love him. He keeps the mice down," Simone said.

"He's a big chap, isn't he?" Annabelle said, eyeing the cat carefully. He looked like a giant beast compared with Annabelle's cat Biscuit, who was no doubt currently fast asleep back in Upton St. Mary. "Is the village as sleepy as it looks? What about crime? Do you need much security?"

"No, we're a convent on the outskirts of a tiny village hidden beyond a forest in a valley with one road leading to it—burglary is not a problem with the exception of the odd few apples stolen by the local teenagers a few times a year. Our biggest problem is stopping the thieving birds. At least, that is, until Father Julien's death and Father Raphael's disappearance."

Sister Simone broke into a small smile. "Even a so-called 'wise' woman like me can't know everything. But generally speaking Ville d'Eauloise feels like the safest place on earth. It's why this sudden death is so shocking. We are not used to such things here."

CHAPTER THIRTY-TWO

THAT EVENING, ANNABELLE and Mike quickly got ready and went out again, strolling to the plaza to have dinner at *Chez Selwyn* again. It was the only restaurant in town. It was much emptier than it had been the previous night, and everyone was behaving normally this time. For their part, the villagers seemed to have grown accustomed to the sight of the tall, imposing man and his equally tall, cheerful lady-friend, and paid them no mind.

As soon as Annabelle and Mike sat down, they began recounting to each other what they had learned during the day. They were so involved in their stories, they barely stopped long enough to place their orders. After Françoise, Selwyn's beautiful daughter, had taken their order, Annabelle and Mike continued to try and fit their individual pieces of the jigsaw together. They leaned over the table, waving empty forks in their enthusiasm. They jabbed at invisible threats floating in the air and jousted with butter knives to make their points. Annabelle nearly stabbed Françoise when she returned to the table to uncork their wine.

"So the death threats sent to Father Julien had something to do with his death?" Annabelle said.

"We don't know that, it's supposition only at this point, but I'd bet my coat on it."

"I wish you would bet your coat on something!" Annabelle joked. Mike groaned. What was wrong with his coat? Was it really that bad? "So we can assume that the person who sent the letters killed him then?" Annabelle added.

"Right. There were dozens of them. He must have been receiving them for weeks, months," Mike said.

"Golly."

"And what's more interesting were the messages in the letters. A lot of stuff about *'knowing what you did'* and *'time running out.'*"

"What do you think it means?"

Mike paused as he considered Annabelle's question. "Sounds like Father Julien had a dark secret—or at least, someone thought he did."

"Interesting... But it only raises more questions," said Annabelle. She sighed and propped her elbows on the table, resting her chin in her hands.

"Right."

"What about the poison? Anything on that?"

"They've confirmed he was poisoned, but they can't identify what it was. Only rye bread, a painkiller, and red wine in his stomach, so perhaps he didn't ingest it. He could have inhaled poisonous fumes or absorbed it through his skin. Crucially, it seems he was poisoned over a long period of time. Not a one-time dose but lots of micro-doses that built up over time and eventually caused his heart attack. They're testing the letters to see if that was the source, but who knows how long that will take? It's like time has barely moved on here from when dinosaurs roamed the world."

"And a lovely place it is, too."

"What did you learn at the convent?"

"Nothing."

"You must have learned something."

"I learned that Mary is lonely there, that the nuns are a bit strange and unforthcoming, that they revere Mother Superior, that they make a lot of bread, and that they have a huge, gray cat named Poupon that even Biscuit would take notice of. I learned that one of the nuns has it in for Father Raphael, but it didn't seem to be much more than idle gossip. Oh, and the village has something of a macabre history. Seems there is a relic stored in the church."

"A what?"

"A relic. The remains of a girl who was killed for her 'witchiness' back in the 5th century and who was subsequently made a martyr. Agnès. St. Agnès."

"Lovely."

"A relic like that, true story or no, will be considered a precious artifact imbued with massive amounts of symbolism. We should check it out."

"I can't wait." Mike sighed and leaned back, crumpling his napkin in frustration.

"What now?" Annabelle said. "We've run out of ideas, it seems."

"We need to find Father Raphael," Mike said, determinedly.

"But how? He could be anywhere by now." Annabelle put her elbows on the table and rested her face in her hands. "Mary is still very hung up on his disappearance. She's convinced something bad has happened to him."

Mike looked out onto the plaza. Highlighted by the moonlight, a few couples strolled across it. It seemed virtually everyone walked or cycled everywhere here. They had only seen a couple of vehicles in the two days since they had arrived. "I don't think so. I think he's still here, in Ville d'Eauloise."

"Why would you say that?" Annabelle cried, astounded at

Mike's assertion. "How would he go unnoticed in such a small village? Everyone knows him. It would be virtually impossible to hide here."

"I don't know, just a feeling."

"Just a feeling? That's not like you."

"You just said that Sister Mary was hung up on him."

Annabelle lowered her eyes and started pleating her napkin. "Yes."

"What do you mean?"

Suddenly reluctant to talk about her friend, Annabelle talked slowly and carefully. "I don't know for sure, but the way she... I might be wrong but... I've known her for a long time... And I think she might be...," Annabelle cleared her throat, "in love with him."

"Really?" Mike said.

Annabelle looked at him and blinked. "Perhaps he feels the same."

"But... but she's..." Mike trailed off before starting up again. "And he's..."

Annabelle patted a fingertip against her lips and blinked again. "It happens. It did in *The Thorn Birds*."

"That was a work of fiction, Annabelle."

"It happens, Mike," Annabelle insisted, her voice harder now, her eyes defiant, her tone earnest.

Mike softened. He gave Annabelle a look of such tenderness, her cheeks went a deep shade of red. "Then he's here. And if I know anything, it's that a person will do whatever they need to, to stay close to the one they love."

CHAPTER THIRTY-THREE

THE VILLAGE OF Ville d'Eauloise was small, but it felt never-ending as Sister Mary ran through its cobbled streets. As she lifted her habit around her knees so as not to get it caught under her feet, tears streamed down her face. She scrubbed them with her sleeve. She battled against a strong wind, but nothing would stop her.

It was early by anyone's standards. Only the nuns were up, the sun having risen just a few minutes ago. No one was around to help Sister Mary when she stumbled. Tripping on a curb as she tried to take a corner at breakneck speed, she tore her habit when she trod on it, the hard cobblestones grazing her knee badly. She needed no help to get to her feet again, however. She was powered by adrenaline, shock, and desperation as she continued on, pushing herself to run even faster toward her destination. Finally she reached it, yanking the gate open and running up the path to hammer on the door, sobbing loudly and uncontrollably as her small fists pounded on the wood.

Claude opened the door quickly, scowling. He was wearing blue and white striped pajamas and a matching nightcap, the end of which was topped by a fluffy bobble. He even carried a candle. He looked like Wee Willie Winkie, or perhaps, given the expression on his face, Ebenezer Scrooge. He was cross, a state that didn't change even when he saw the disheveled, tear-stained nun standing in the doorway.

"Why are you banging so loudly at this time of the morning?" he asked Mary in French. "It's not even 6 a.m. yet!"

Mary answered by pushing past him as if he were a feather. She began rushing about crying "Annabelle! Mike!" every few seconds until they emerged, groggy and yawning, to see what all the fuss was about.

"Sister Mary?" Mike said, incredulously. He rubbed his sleepy eyes and then opened them wide to check they were working correctly.

"What is it, Mary? What has happened?" Annabelle cried, more alert to her friend's anguish. "Oh! And you're hurt!"

Sister Mary came to a stop in front of them, bending over to put her hands on her thighs. She gasped for breath. It was the first time she had paused since rushing out of the convent.

"Mother... Renate..." she said between pants and sobs. "Mother... Superior..." A deep breath. "Dead!" A few more pants. "Hung... herself..."

It was as though saying the words out loud made the tragic event occur all over again. Sister Mary gathered some oxygen from somewhere and wailed dramatically before beginning to cry violently. Annabelle pulled Mary to her chest, looking back to see Mike's reaction. He stood dumbfounded. He was certainly awake now. Annabelle took her friend to her room, and after giving her a cup of sweet, strong coffee, they met Mike downstairs. Annabelle drove the three of them to the convent, she and Mike listening as Sister Mary told the astonished couple what had happened.

"All the sisters gather every morning at 5 a.m. to pray together," Mary said, her sobs soft and stuttering now. "And Mother Renate always led by example. She was the first in the prayer room, and I've never known her miss morning prayers except for one time when she got the flu. So when she didn't arrive this morning, we knew something was wrong.

"We assumed there had been some emergency that she needed to attend to so we went to look for her to see if we could help. Some of the sisters went to check the kitchen and common areas. Some went to the orchards. We knew she wasn't in the bakery as the nuns had just come from their shift. Sister Simone, Sister Josephine and me, we went to... went to..." Mary was sobbing too hard to continue. Mike shifted in his seat to pull his handkerchief from his pocket and hand it to her. "Thank you," Mary said, comforted by the kindness. "We went to her room, and then we saw her... hanging there."

Mike and Annabelle swapped frowns.

"I screamed," Mary continued, "and then, I don't know, I just ran—all the way to you. I didn't know what else to do..."

"It's alright," Annabelle said, glancing at her friend in the rear view mirror. "We'll find out what happened."

When they reached the convent a few minutes later, Babineaux's distinctive Citroen 2CV was already there. Annabelle quickly parked her Mini beside it.

Even under the gathering light of dawn, the dark atmosphere that cloaked the convent was palpable. It was as if the calm, order, and solemn devotion that Annabelle had witnessed the day before had been tossed out and replaced by a force of chaos and fury. A trio of nuns stood outside consoling each other, crying into their hands while attempting to pray. Empty flour sacks blew about in the swirling wind that whistled as it flew around the corners of the building and through the covered archways while lights inside the convent intermittently turned on and off.

Annabelle and Mike passed the nuns outside, acknowledging them with a nod. Sister Mary led the pair inside the building, the "women only" rule abandoned. They marched along a long, empty corridor that reverberated with disembodied sobs and wails that echoed off the medieval walls yet they saw no one.

"Stay here," Annabelle said to Mary, taking her friend's hand. They saw the figure of the experienced, calm, but pale Sister Simone coming toward them. "We can find our way to Mother Renate's room from here. There's no need for you to go through all that again."

Sister Mary looked up sheepishly for a moment, before nodding with relief. She turned to Sister Simone, who wrapped an arm around the distraught nun's shoulders and led her away.

Annabelle took Mike past another cluster of crying nuns as they headed toward the door at the end of the corridor, voices beyond the door growing audible as they got nearer. She stopped and cast one more look at the inspector before knocking and pushing the door open.

CHAPTER THIRTY-FOUR

MOTHER RENATE LAY on the floor. She'd been covered with a sheet, a frayed scrap of twisted heavy rope visible at one end, the tips of her toes peeking out at the other. Inspector Babineaux stood to one side. He turned his face slowly to the newcomers. Even the French detective's typical theatricality was dulled by the specter of a second sudden death. He was solemn. Behind him stood Sergeant Lestrange, his perpetually alarmed eyes darting around, his mouth open. His lips quivered as though he were talking to himself while across the room was Doctor Giroux. He had his back turned to the room as he put his instruments into his doctor's bag.

They all nodded and mumbled brief greetings before gazing at the central figure like it were some foul museum exhibit or an inexplicable piece of art. Instinctively, Mike stood next to Babineaux—the events at hand causing him to dismiss his previous reservations about the French detective.

"What do you think?" Mike asked, without taking his eyes from the figure on the floor.

"What can I zink?" Babineaux replied with a Gallic shrug. "She 'anged herself from ze 'ook. It iz obvious."

Mike nodded and folded his arms. He looked over at the large iron hook above the fireplace around which a short piece of rope was still wound. "What's that used for? Normally, I mean."

"No *idée*. Probably for 'anging saucepans and zings in ze 15th century." As Mike had done, Babineaux folded his arms and the two men stared down at Mother Renate's sheet-draped body, united for once in investigative camaraderie.

"One never knows what goes on in another's mind," Mike said, after a contemplative pause.

"*Oui*, she must 'ave been devastated by ze death of Father Julien and tells no-one. Then, she 'angs 'erself."

"Yup. Seems an open and shut case."

"Really? But how can that be? It is impossible! Do you hear? *Impossible*. She was Mother Superior! She wouldn't hang herself!" Annabelle exclaimed, barely managing to respect the solemnity of the situation and contain herself. She took a breath and continued more calmly. "Mother Renate lived a life of devotion, of peace, of Godliness. Why would she commit a mortal sin? She simply wouldn't have been able to do it no matter how upset she was."

Mike gently placed a hand on Annabelle's shoulder. "That's not how this works, Annabelle," he said. "I see it all the time. People in authority, people with responsibilities, they lose their minds. Things get too much for them. They can't think straight. They lose all perspective and the ability to reason."

"Mother Renate was a competent, capable woman," Annabelle insisted, shrugging off his hand. She was seething.

"They're always the ones who don't show it," Mike replied. "The ones that others look up to. You yourself said the sisters are in awe of her. Those who do this are often the ones with nobody to turn to, confide in, when they really need it."

Annabelle huffed, unwilling to relinquish the point. "She had

God to turn to," Annabelle said, defiantly. "*I think she was murdered.*"

Mike, lacking an answer and suspecting Annabelle wasn't his number one fan right at that moment, turned back to Babineaux. "Inspector, what would you say?"

"We are all sinners, *Révérend* Annabelle," Babineaux said apologetically. "Perhaps ze Mother Superior expected a special *pardon*."

Annabelle put her hands on her hips. She stared intensely at the covered body on the ground, her horror and revulsion overwhelmed by the frustration she felt at the two policemen's resistance to her theory.

"I understand your willingness to find an explanation, *Révérend*. It iz awful. It iz shocking. *Terrible!*" Babineaux said, his shoulders level with his ears. He stepped closer to Annabelle, his heeled shoes clicking on the hard floor. He looked at Mike then back at Annabelle sadly. "And as a respected woman of ze church, you seeing another respected woman of ze church... Well, I cannot imagine ze effect zis must 'ave on you, *Révérend*." Babineaux put his hand gently on Annabelle's arm.

Mike felt something rise within him, that same feeling that occurred when he saw how easily Babineaux spoke to Annabelle. But this time, it quickly passed. He didn't want to, but on this occasion he agreed with the French detective. And for once, Annabelle didn't seem charmed.

CHAPTER THIRTY-FIVE

ANNABELLE TURNED FROM Babineaux. She looked past the body to Doctor Giroux who had finished putting away his medical instruments and was now standing in the corner looking very much like he'd prefer to be far from this morbid room and its occupants, both the dead one and the ones very much alive.

"What do you think, Doctor Giroux? Do you think it's possible that this wasn't a suicide?" Annabelle asked, trying to keep the pleading tone out of her voice and failing only slightly.

Doctor Giroux snapped to attention at the sound of his name. When he saw the expectant look on Annabelle's face, he took his glasses off his nose, fumbling with them as he did so.

"Ah...it is difficult..." he mumbled. "I am not experienced with such things. I have called for a pathologist from Reims. They should arrive this afternoon."

"But in *your* opinion," Annabelle said, "as a doctor, did Mother Renate hang herself?"

Doctor Giroux began breathing heavily, rubbing his glasses

on a handkerchief as he considered Annabelle's question. He glanced a few more times at the body on the floor. Eventually he shrugged and said, "Yes."

Annabelle sighed. Her shoulders slumped.

"All the signs," Giroux continued, "are that she hung herself. There is no sign of a struggle. Not on the hands, not on the face. The discoloration of her cheeks—it is distinctly suffocation."

Babineaux and Mike looked at Annabelle, expecting her to be satisfied with this expert explanation, and ready to offer sympathy once she accepted the unanimous verdict of the others in the room. But Annabelle wasn't yet done. She wandered over to Mother Renate's desk. Papers were strewn over a blotter. There was a wooden desk tidy, a pen with its cap off, a pencil sharpened to a fine point, and a cup and saucer. The cup was overturned, pale yellow dregs of tea tipped into the saucer, long cold. Annabelle idly picked up the cup. She sniffed before putting it down again.

"And as man, a human being?" she asked Giroux coolly, her composure intact now. "I mean, that's your professional opinion as a doctor, but personally, what do you think?"

Doctor Giroux breathed so heavily the sound filled the room. His lips quivered. He seemed almost frightened by the question. He looked down at the glasses he held in his hand and lifted them to his face, winding the wire arms around his ears.

"I am very God-fearing," he said, looking at Annabelle directly now. "I never miss church. I confess twice a week. I have spoken with Mother Renate many times and… and… I cannot believe she killed herself." He paused but then quickly continued on, "But please! Please. Wait for the pathologist. I don't know! Really. I don't know. I am not an expert."

Sergeant Lestrange walked over to the doctor and said something in French that seemed to calm him. Babineaux turned to form a tight circle with Mike and Annabelle.

"*Révérend*," Babineaux said, keeping his voice just low enough so that his words could be heard by only the three of them, "*Inspecteur*. We waste time on ze 'if' when we should examine ze 'why' ze good Mother Superior killed herself."

"Do you think Mother Renate's death could be linked to that of Father Julien?" Annabelle asked the two men.

"Perhaps," Mike said. "If they were close, his death might have pushed the Mother Superior over the edge."

"I don't zink so. From what I understand, ze Father and ze Mother were not very close. From what I have 'eard, zey seemed to keep much distance between zemselves." Babineaux stroked his moustache with an elaborate flourish, ending with his finger pointing up into the air.

"Perhaps there was something else then. Money worries? A secret illness? Guilt?" Mike added.

Annabelle frowned and opened her mouth to say something before closing it again.

"We're all speculating wildly," Mike said. "We need more information, more evidence. We need to learn about the histories of Mother Superior and Father Julien. Inspector Babineaux, may we read your file on Father Julien? And Mother Renate's too, as soon as you have it."

Babineaux opened his eyes wide. "Ze file?"

"Yes," Mike said, his expression growing incredulous as his suspicion grew. "The files. Surely you compile files on your victims? Their personal histories, places of residence, bank accounts, work details, health records, that sort of thing."

"Um..." Babineaux trailed off, rubbing his thumb and forefinger as if still interpreting the request. Slowly he turned to Sergeant Lestrange who was still talking to Giroux. He said something in French that caused the sergeant to look over and shrug, his angular shoulders lifting his jacket a full three inches before slumping down. Babineaux's tone grew tense and curt.

The sergeant snapped to attention and made a beeline for the door suddenly displaying more speed and coordination than he had in the entire time Annabelle and Mike had been in the village. Once Lestrange had made it safely out of the room, Babineaux turned to smile at the inspector. He rubbed his hands together. "Ze files are on zeir way."

CHAPTER THIRTY-SIX

ANNABELLE AND MIKE bid a sympathetic farewell to Sister Mary who insisted on staying at the convent alongside the other nuns. They went back to the car. When they got inside, Annabelle simply sat, staring forward.

"What's wrong?" Mike asked slowly, gazing at her resolute profile.

After a moment's pause, Annabelle sighed and looked down. "I'm sorry, Mike."

"*Sorry*? What for?" A stream of ice stole across Mike's heart.

Annabelle turned to look at him. There was remorse in her eyes. "I thought this would be such a lovely trip. Quiet, inspiring, *romantic* even. And instead it's become more like a busman's holiday for you. If you drove a bus, it wouldn't be so bad. But your work is quite horrific."

Mike smiled easily. "Oh, it's no problem. It was my suggestion to come here."

"I know..." Annabelle sighed. "But it was for my friend. And I'm starting to think I should have stopped you."

"Annabelle," Mike said, stroking a stray hair from her face.

"There will be plenty of trips, plenty of quiet, romantic experiences in the future. I care about making you happy, and if that means we have to solve this case together, then that's what we'll do. Lord knows that that blustering baby baboon Babineaux isn't going to."

The words slipped out easily, without any of the usual awkwardness Mike felt when he spoke so earnestly. Annabelle smiled at him warmly, and they leaned in for a soft, loving kiss. As they pulled away, Mike heard the small voice that was persistently nagging at him. *Now?* It was followed by another voice, just as persistent. *With a body just a few feet away? Don't be daft.*

"What should we do?" Annabelle asked, breathing out. She still found it strange, a relief, glorious, to have Mike by her side. She loved being a team. She'd been alone, besides God of course, for so long, having someone trustworthy to lean on was a new, refreshing, uplifting experience. She didn't ever want it to end.

"Breakfast. Obviously," Mike replied.

"At the auberge?"

Mike frowned. "The church square," he said, as Annabelle revved the Mini's engine. "I'd like to check something out that's been bothering me."

By the time Annabelle and Mike were settled in *Café Sylvie* directly opposite the imposing church steps, the mid-morning sun was high and hot. Now that the shock of the morning's ghastliness had passed, a steely determination to answer the many questions swirled in their minds. As they picked at the last of their light brunch—perfectly-soft croissants, lightly scrambled eggs with smoked salmon and dried figs—and drank some strong coffee, they gazed silently across at the church. Both were lost in their thoughts.

"What do you expect to find in the files?" Annabelle asked, breaking the silence.

Mike breathed heavily through his nose and wiped crumbs from his hands.

"Clues to a secret, perhaps? Reasons as to why someone would send death threats to Father Julien? A hidden shame that caused Mother Renate to kill herself? A link. Something. Anything. In my business, when you've been doing it as long as I have, you get a nose for these things."

"Hmm."

Mike wiped his mouth briskly and tossed the napkin onto his plate. "But that birdbrain Babineaux!" he said, glaring across the square at a plant pot. The French inspector wasn't standing next to it, but given the stare Mike was aiming in that direction, Babineaux would have burst into flames if he had. "How could he not have compiled files? I would expect better from an amateur!"

Annabelle put a calming hand over his. "It makes sense. They were both high-ranking members of the church, and they take their faith very seriously here. No one would have suspected them of anything, certainly that they might have secrets. They probably still don't."

"The cleaner they look, the harder we scrub," Mike grumbled. "That's what my inspector used to tell me when I was a sergeant. I don't care if they were living saints. If you ask me, the church is full of people with secrets..." Mike stopped himself, suddenly turning back to Annabelle. "Oh, I'm sorry... I didn't mean... You know... I just..."

"It's alright," chuckled Annabelle. "I know what you mean."

Mike grunted apologetically.

Annabelle squinted. "How do you see me, Mike?"

"What do you mean?"

"Well, do you see the clothes, the ritual, the life of my calling? Or do you see me, Annabelle, the person, the woman?"

Mike looked at her, puzzled. He had no idea what she was talking about, but he had a sense he was being tested. It was disconcerting. What was the right answer? He looked into his coffee cup as though he might find it there. He felt the small velvet box in his pocket poke him in the thigh. *Now?* "You're simply Annabelle to me," he replied. "My girlfriend with a funny job."

Annabelle blushed and looked away. Mike looked to see if he'd passed. He thought he had. Not failed anyway.

CHAPTER THIRTY-SEVEN

"WELL," ANNABELLE SAID, changing the subject, "what can we do now? Apart from wait for the pathologist's results and perhaps those files? You mentioned something you wanted to check."

"Oh, yes," Mike said, looking immediately at the church. An old man was dragging a brush slowly across the top step. "I'll pay the bill, and we can go."

"Do you think the church will be open?" Annabelle asked.

"Why not? St. Mary's always is."

"Yes, but St. Mary's wasn't the site of a recent murder. I think they've kept it locked up if no one in an official capacity is in attendance."

"Well, we're in our official capacities. Come on, let's find out."

Mike led Annabelle toward the giant entrance of the church, the sight of the hunched figure of the old man performing his steady sweeping motions across the steps in front of the giant oak doors seeming like the tableau of an elaborate life-size cuckoo clock.

"Excuse me," the inspector said, gaining the old man's attention. "I'm Inspector Mike Nicholls, British police, and this is Reverend Annabelle Dixon."

The old man's round, dark eyes blinked at them.

"*Oui, je te connais,*" the old man said, nodding slightly.

"Ah, right." Confused, Mike turned to Annabelle.

She whispered in his ear. "He knows who we are."

"Okay, yes. *Door? Open door?*" Mike said, pointing at the lock. He made turning motions with his hand.

The old man spoke a little more hurriedly in French before looking at the entrance, then mirrored the inspector's hand gestures.

"Yes!" Mike said. "*Oui!*" It sounded more like "wee."

The old man spoke in French some more, clasping at the ring of keys hooked onto his belt.

"*Wee!*" Mike called out again, even more loudly, as if volume would make his effort to speak French sound more authentic.

Eventually, the old man pulled out a great iron key and unlocked the door. He pushed it open and the door gave a long, low, whine as it swung on its huge hinges.

Mike and Annabelle nodded gratefully as they passed.

"*Ten minutes!*" Mike shouted. He flashed all his fingers and pointed at his watch.

The old man nodded again, ushering the two inside with a flap of his hands as if already weary of the inspector's attempts at communication.

Once inside, Annabelle chuckled.

"What?" Mike asked.

"Nothing," Annabelle said, still laughing as she turned to take in the giant room. "So what is so important, it would cause you to put on such a display?"

Mike stepped forward slowly, treading lightly on the balls of his feet so as not to make a sound. He held up a palm to request

Annabelle's silence. He slowly crept up the aisle, Annabelle following him with the same, soft footsteps. The inspector's expression grew even more strained as he neared the altar, until eventually he sighed with exasperation and shook his head.

"The first time we were here," he said, "I heard a noise. Sort of like a distant knocking." He ran up the steps and stood at the altar table, the flickering candles warming his cheeks.

"You think it came from inside the church?" Annabelle sat herself down in the front pew.

Mike looked up and pursed his lips. "I don't know, the acoustics in here make it difficult to tell."

"What do you think it was?"

Mike frowned as he continued to listen.

"It sounded like plumbing, but I've lived in enough rundown places to know that banging pipes have a certain rhythm to them. This was sort of... random."

"How do you mean?"

Mike shrugged. He started to walk backward to get a better view of the sanctuary and altar. He looked up into the high vaulted ceiling of the church. "I don't know... But we've been here a few days now, and I've listened for any other sound like it. There's been none."

Annabelle strained to listen some more.

"Gah!" Mike exclaimed, balling his fists in frustration. "Another dead lead! Another stupid idea! I'm doing the very thing I hate to see in other detectives now—grasping at straws—whoa!" he shouted suddenly. He crashed backward down the steps.

"Mike!" shrieked Annabelle, running quickly to his side. "Are you alright?"

Mike lay spread-eagled across the stone steps like a stricken sacrifice. He pointed a finger in the air. "There it is!" he cried. "There's the sound!"

Annabelle froze mid-motion as if his words had turned her to stone. She was bent over the inspector, her arms out in order to help him.

"Do you hear it?" he whispered forcefully.

Annabelle gritted her teeth and wrinkled her nose as she struggled to make out any noise. Apart from the sound of a distant passing truck, she heard nothing. She looked down at Mike's pleading face, suddenly aware of how the scene of a fallen man and a helping hand from above must look in such holy surroundings. After a few more seconds, she shook her head. "I'm sorry," she said softly. "I can't hear anything."

"There! There! That was it, I'm sure! Quieter than last time, but I heard it!" Mike looked up at Annabelle's blank face. "Oh, never mind!" Mike took Annabelle's hand and made to get up but instead pulled her down on top of him.

"Oh!" Annabelle cried as she tumbled. Mike grabbed her around the waist and together they rolled down the steps, laughing as they landed at the bottom.

"Mike!"

"What? It's just a bit of fun."

"We're in a church."

"No one's here."

"God is. God's ev..."

There was a creak from the back of the church and the doors swung open. In crept the old man, his broom in his hand. He stared as he looked ahead and saw the couple lying in a heap at the bottom of the altar steps, Annabelle splayed on top of Mike, her hair over her face.

Mike twisted his head to look at the old man and waved. *"Bonjour, Monsieur. Comment allez-vous?"*

Annabelle stifled a snigger as she pushed herself upright. She helped Mike to his feet and dusted herself down. Mike grinned and took her hand, squeezing it gently as he led her toward the open door, the old man staring at them the whole while. The irony of the situation wasn't lost on the inspector, however. *Typical, I'm leading her the wrong way down the aisle!*

CHAPTER THIRTY-EIGHT

THE NEXT DAY, Mike was up early. Earlier than Annabelle, earlier even than Claude. He always got this way when he was at a vexing stage of a serious case, and although the officers at Truro police station joked he had some vampiric qualities that enabled him to go without sleep beyond which seemed humanly possible, none of them really understood the agitation that prohibited him from a good night's rest when he felt he had work to do.

After pacing up and down his room, flicking through a book he'd hastily thrown into his bag before he left home, and checking the clock every thirty seconds in the hope that time had progressed to a more acceptable hour, Mike finally got dressed and silently left his room. He moved carefully through the hotel and out toward the table in the courtyard. The early morning hours were pleasing to him. It was still dark and stars twinkled brightly in a velvety-black sky. No one was about. The auberge looked even more appealing under the shimmering half-moon.

The temperature was much warmer than in England. Warm enough that he needed no jacket to sit outside, and yet the air was crisp and fresh. It was filled with the fragrance of flowers around him. He inhaled deeply, savoring the aromas of refreshing mint, pungent hyacinths, budding wisteria, and finding a touch of cherry blossom layered on top. *No wonder the French have such a nose for wine.*

But the peacefulness of Mike's surroundings couldn't calm his racing thoughts. The case was troubling enough. It had been four days now since Father Julien's murder, and they had few leads, no idea where Father Raphael was, and now another death. His hopes of solving the case quickly and enjoying the rest of the week alone with Annabelle, building-up to his pitch-perfect proposal and an unqualified acceptance, were quickly fading.

He pulled the small ring box from his pocket, flipped it open, and set it on the picnic table. He gazed at it lazily, the gentle moonlight amplifying the diamond's perfectly-cut dimensions. When it had come to selecting it, money had been no object. The inspector was frugal but not ungenerous. He had learned long ago that purchased items brought him little joy so he had plenty of money to spend on an engagement ring for his beloved. The tricky part had been choosing the right diamond. And keeping it a secret.

There was a jeweler in Upton St. Mary who was highly regarded, but had he gone there, he might as well have taken out an announcement of his intentions in the parish newsletter. Instead, following weeks of consideration, after visiting every single jeweler in Truro, and with the patient help of a kindly shop assistant who had, she told him, overseen thousands of similar purchases in her thirty years of service, he had picked out a brilliantly cut, sizeable but not ostentatious, solitaire diamond ring. As he regarded it in the early morning darkness, he thought it beautiful. If the response to a proposal were based on the ring alone, acceptance would be guaranteed. But there's only so much a ring can do. And Annabelle would not be swayed by a mere bauble.

For the first time in his life, the inspector was genuinely afraid. He had faced down entire gangs of criminals by himself. He had taken blows during arrests, had risked his entire career on hunches, and had even gone toe-to-toe with a fellow detective during a corruption scandal that had almost torn the station apart. But all of that paled in comparison to the challenge he was facing now.

What if she says no?

Mike forced himself to think about this for a moment. *She'd probably let me down gently, be kind about it, tell me to wait a year.* Gazing into the sparkling reflection of the diamond's multi-faceted surface as if it might reveal the future, Mike turned his thoughts inside out, knotted them up, and threw them over his shoulder before retrieving them and starting the process all over again until the diamond began glinting even brighter in the light of dawn.

Through a window, Claude caught sight of Mike sitting forlornly in the yard. Shortly afterward the aroma of brewing coffee mixed with warm brioche filled the auberge. Annabelle emerged, Pavlovian-like, her nose wrinkled in anticipation and an expectant smile on her face, unaware of her beloved's anxiety.

"Morning, Mike," she said, leaning over to kiss him before sitting at the table.

"Morning, Annabelle."

"We're like an old married couple, aren't we? Sitting down to breakfast like this every day."

"Not really, we emerge from different rooms."

"Apart from that."

Mike wasn't sure how to take this exchange so he decided to focus on his breakfast. Halfway through their breakfast of cheese, brioche, soufflé, and coffee, Claude appeared at their table.

"*Inspecteur? Révérend?* Inspector Babineaux has just called. He says you are to meet him at his office. He says the files have arrived!"

"About time too," Mike said.

Annabelle looked at him like she would a naughty child. Mike quickly finished swallowing a mouthful of soufflé. "Thank you for passing on the message, Claude. Much obliged."

"Detective Babineaux has an office here?" Annabelle asked when Claude had left.

"Oh yes," Mike said drily. "It serves snails."

CHAPTER THIRTY-NINE

AS THEY DROVE through the streets of Ville d'Eauloise toward the café, Annabelle and Mike noticed that the villagers seemed unusually low-key. There was a sense of sadness that seemed at odds with the gloriously warm sun that was set in the clear blue sky. Father Julien's death had been public and dramatic, causing shock and grief. But as news of the Mother Superior's apparent suicide spread, the locals had become a lot more withdrawn.

Father Julien had walked the streets, given sermons to the villagers, and had known many of them well. He had his foibles, such as his penchant for pastries at all times of the day and the way he would palm his hair back with the care of a young man about to hit the town. But he had also been present in the lives of the villagers at their most intimate points—not just their births, deaths, and marriages, but via the confessional, their scandals, their money woes, and their darkest thoughts.

By contrast, Mother Renate had been a stern, imposing personality, more akin to a force of nature than a mortal woman. When she walked through the streets it had always been with a destination in mind. Passers-by would not call to her but simply nod respectfully, expecting no more than a mere flicker of an eye in return. Children stopped their mischievous games in her presence. Adults refrained from small talk, jokes, and village gossip when she was near. Under her guidance, the dozen or so nuns at the convent led lives of selflessness, simplicity, and industry. And despite praying for many hours a day, they still managed to farm their land and bake enough bread to supply the village and those nearby. This was down to Mother Renate's leadership.

As they arrived on the plaza, Annabelle and Mike bumped into Selwyn, the Welsh chef.

"Morning, Selwyn," Mike said.

"Mornin' boyo."

"Everyone seems very subdued," Annabelle said.

"Aye, they are troubled by the deaths, for sure," Selwyn responded. "This latest one has fair taken the wind out of their sails. To their minds, Mother Superior was too firm and forthright to die. To hear that she has passed is strange. To hear that it was by her own hand is unbelievable."

Annabelle and Mike went to the cafe and greeted Babineaux and Lestrange quietly, but warmly. Well, Annabelle did. Mike simply nodded. Babineaux used his old-world charm on Annabelle once again and kissed the back of her hand. Mike suppressed an eye-roll but he wasn't about to be out-maneuvered twice in a matter of seconds and quickly won the race to pull out Annabelle's chair before Babineaux could do it for her.

After exchanging polite small talk about the weather, Babineaux reached into the tasteful, aged-leather satchel at his side and pulled out three folders.

"We 'ave the pathology report for Mother Renate. It confirms she suffocated. 'er death is consistent with 'anging." Annabelle frowned at this news. "And 'ere we 'ave ze victim's files," Babineaux said. He placed the files on the table, and pushed them toward Annabelle and Mike. "I 'ave 'ad zem translated for you."

"These are the case files on Father Julien and Mother Renate?" Mike said, picking up one folder as Annabelle took the other.

Babineaux shrugged. "*Oui*. Please, read. We shall wait." He crossed his long legs and sat back.

Mike opened his folder to begin, glancing over at Annabelle, who was already halfway down the first page in hers.

They passed the next few minutes in silence, broken only by the occasional sip of coffee, the rustling of a flipped page, and the exchange of folders. Babineaux sat patiently, quietly exulting in his ability to produce something he was sure would impress the English detectives. Eventually, Annabelle and Mike set the folders down quietly, and all three of them exchanged glances. The contents of the folders had certainly given them food for thought.

Annabelle broke the silence. "So Father Julien was born to a working-class family in Nice in Southern France. There wasn't much on his early adulthood, but we know he held odd jobs as a laborer which must mean he was a strong, healthy, young man. He entered the priesthood at 28, studying in a seminary on the outskirts of Nice and then performed missionary work in Asia, before returning to France and being appointed to the parish of Ville d'Eauloise."

Mike continued. "Right, and like Father Julien, Mother Renate was also born in Nice, but to a wealthy family. Her father was a major Catholic benefactor, donating huge sums after parts of Nice cathedral were destroyed in a fire. After she finished school, Renate left Nice to study chemistry at the university in Reims. Soon into her studies, she abruptly left and travelled to Switzerland where she became a nun. As Mother Renate, she spent two decades travelling the world doing humanitarian work before eventually being assigned the role of Mother Superior at St. Agnès convent a few years ago."

There followed several moments of thoughtful coffee sipping before either Annabelle or Mike spoke again.

"They were from the same city," Annabelle mumbled.

"And they ended up in the same village," Mike added.

"A coincidence?"

"Don't believe in them," said Mike.

CHAPTER FORTY

MIKE OPENED HIS folder again to check the dates. "Look here, they grew up in the same place. Then, twenty-something years after they leave, after all sorts of adventures, they both end up as Catholic clergy in the same, out-of-the-way, medieval French village miles from where they grew up. And they end up dead within a couple of days of one another. What are the chances of that?"

"So..." Annabelle began, drawing her words out slowly as she continued to think, "you think there's some connection between them, something related to their earlier lives that is behind their deaths? Perhaps they knew each other? When they were younger, I mean."

"Hmm, maybe. And why would Renate go all the way to Switzerland to become a nun?" Mike asked. "Why not train, or whatever it is you do to become a nun, right here? There are plenty of convents in France, aren't there?"

Babineaux nodded. "Indeed, zey are all over."

Annabelle shrugged. "There could be lots of reasons for it—space, fit, location. It's a decision that encompasses an aspirant's entire existence. And it's expected to last a lifetime! Perhaps she wanted to see a little more of the world and this particular order in Switzerland could provide that."

"But then why end up in Ville d'Eauloise?" Mike asked, butchering the village's name with his impatience and poor French accent. He didn't need to say the words "sleepy backwater," but they were there in his tone.

"A recommendation, maybe," Annabelle said. "If they did know one another previously, Julien might have known the convent was looking for a Mother Superior, and suggested Renate for the position."

"Is that how they do it? They apply for promotions and transfers like anyone else?"

"Of course. And just like secular organizations, they often promote from within. But if that isn't possible, they will look to another."

"Hmph, not that much different from the force." Mike slapped his file down on the table and folded his arms.

"*Pardonnez-moi, Révérend.* But you are saying zat zis information is completely irrelevant?" Babineaux said.

"No, but it raises more questions than it answers," Annabelle said. She gestured at the folder. "This all seems quite normal to me. Nothing extraordinary. Coincidences and similarities, but that's all. We are using supposition to connect the dots. We need more."

"Look," Mike said adamantly, placing his palm flat on the folder in front of him. "There's a connection here. Two people who died under strange circumstances in this village grew up only a few miles apart, before travelling the world, and being drawn to the same place years later. I've got a hunch there's something in this."

Babineaux raised one of his fine eyebrows so high, Mike wondered if it were caught on a fishing line. "Ze mind goes to ze romance, does it not?"

"Romance?" Annabelle said, incredulously.

"*Mais oui.* Father Julien was young once, as was Mother Renate. Zey were ze right ages for ze love to 'ave blossomed. 'e was an 'andsome young man with muscles from ze 'ard work 'e did, and ze 'air 'e kept to ze end. Ze Mother Superior was most likely a girl of intelligence and wit before she added discipline and righteousness to 'er character. She 'ad fine bones, she could 'ave been a beauty when she was younger. These qualities are magnetic, zey draw zem to each other. Somezing rare among zeir peers, somezing only zey can understand. Zey walk along ze Côte d'Azur, talking to each other of ze divine beauty and poetry in ze Bible, sharing zeir thoughts zey never told anyone else, until it is impossible to imagine being with anyone else." Babineaux squinted and looked at his rapt audience, his eyes shining. "Zey discover zat they both feel a deep, devout love for not just ze Lord, but for each other. But 'er family doesn't approve. A working boy and wealthy girl. Zey are separated, and she is sent away, but not before zeir passion overcomes zem and..."

"Okay, okay!" Mike exclaimed. "We get the idea." He glared at Babineaux.

Mike turned to Annabelle, waiting for her response, but she seemed lost in the scene that Babineaux had painted. She had a small smile on her face, and a distant look in her eyes. "It's possible," she said dreamily.

"It would explain much," Babineaux said, adding a smoky mystery to his voice.

"Like what?" Mike asked.

"Like why she killed 'erself," Babineaux said.

"I don't follow," Mike said.

Babineaux grinned knowingly and leaned back in his chair, shaking his head slightly. "Ze love of 'er life was murdered. Ze man she came 'ere to be close to."

"Hold on!" Mike said, waving his palms. "You're telling fairytales now. There's no room for that in police business. There's no evidence." He rocked back on two legs of his chair, his lips pursed.

Babineaux continued to look amused at this uptight Englishman. "All romance is a fairytale in a sense," he said.

"Even *if* they were a couple *once*," Mike said firmly as he glared at Babineaux, "there can't have been anything between them now. It's ridiculous! I mean, we're talking about *a nun* and *a priest* here!"

"You are not well-acquainted with ze facts of ze romance, are you *Inspecteur*?" Babineaux's wry grin taunted Mike.

"What on earth does that have to do with anything?" Mike slammed the front legs of his chair on the ground and banged his hand on the table loud enough to turn heads.

"Calm down, both of you!" Annabelle said. "You're police detectives—not children!"

Mike hung his head. Babineaux offered a nod of apology.

"We don't know much," Annabelle continued, "so anything is possible. Yes, they might have been romantically linked at some point—however I have to agree with Mike, it doesn't seem likely to me. We do have some kind of connection to work with though." Annabelle sighed and pushed her chair back to stand up.

"Where are we going?" Mike said, beginning to rise. Annabelle pressed a hand on his shoulder and pushed him back down.

"*I'm* going to meet Mary. *Alone.*"

"Oh, well... What about me?" Mike asked, suddenly feeling like a ditched pet.

"*You* should get back to finding Father Raphael," Annabelle said. "I believe he's still the key to all of this, and he's still very much missing." She looked at Babineaux. "He's *your* main suspect," she said, before turning to Mike again, "and he's the reason *you're* here in the first place. But there's absolutely no sign of him. So I suggest you two stop your bickering and use whatever on earth they teach you in detective school to try and find him!"

Without a word more, Annabelle walked briskly across the plaza to her car, and slamming her door hard, she drove off, watched with a sense of awe and admiration by the detectives she left behind.

CHAPTER FORTY-ONE

ONCE ANNABELLE DISAPPEARED from sight, Mike noticed with some alarm that Babineaux was eyeing him keenly.

"What?" Mike asked quickly.

Babineaux chuckled lightly to himself. "You are besotted, are you not, *Inspecteur?*"

Mike cleared his throat awkwardly and sat upright. "I don't see what that's got to do with..."

Babineaux chuckled again. "In France, we often talk of ze love. We feel it strongly, and we like to share our love with ze world."

"Well, I don't feel like sharing anything, thank you very much."

Babineaux performed his signature move. He leaned back in his chair and crossed one long languid leg over the other, bringing his coffee cup to his mouth in a smooth, delicate movement. He kept the glint in his eye focused upon Mike, however, even as he set his coffee cup down.

"'ave you decided 'ow you will do it?"

Mike frowned. "Do what?"

"Propose, of course."

Mike's frown fell away, along with his jaw. He looked around furtively, checking that no one was listening before leaning forward across the table. "How did you know that?" he hissed in a low whisper.

Babineaux shrugged. "I am not as incompetent as you zink, *Inspecteur*. Ze British always assume others are not as observant as zey are."

"Okay, but *how?*" insisted Mike. "Did you go through my things and find the ring? Do you have spies listening to me at night? Did Claude say something to you?"

Babineaux laughed, and looked across at Lestrange, but his sergeant was busy solving a crossword. The older detective turned back to Mike and brushed his moustache, reveling in the other inspector's confusion.

"*Mon Dieu!* You are so typical of ze English detectives! Always looking for ze misplaced scalpel or ze stained 'andkerchief. It is a wonder zat two British people ever fall in love with such logic at zeir core! I suppose zat is what makes your fictional detectives so interesting to read. A French Sherlock 'olmes would simply look into people's eyes and see all zat 'e needs."

"Are you going to answer my question?" asked Mike impatiently.

Babineaux brushed his moustache again, as if considering the request, before tilting his head. "You are agitated. Agitated, despite 'aving a wonderful woman by your side. A woman who is kind, compassionate, and devoted to you. You are in a picturesque village among beautiful countrysides with much to share with such a woman, and yet you act as if zere is some immense chore you must carry out. I do not believe ze murder is ze cause of your frustration—you are too experienced for zat. So what is zis *task* zat bothers you so?"

Mike breathed heavily through his nose, but he could think of no response.

"For a man like you, marriage iz not a choice—it iz an *inevitability*. You are not reckless or overwhelmed by your passion. You are cautious and careful. You are British through your very core. Like, what is it you say? Ah yes, like a *stick of rock*. And especially when your lover iz a priest, zer iz little room for ze *living in sin* as it is called in your language, but is called *love* in mine. Yes, *Inspecteur* Nicholls, marriage was on your mind from ze very first time you kissed *Révérend* Annabelle, of zat I am certain."

Mike huffed and folded his arms. "I could sit back and make a few observations about you too, you know," he said, grudgingly.

"But zer iz a *problème!*" Babineaux said, plowing on. "You speak directly, and plainly. Everyzing from your language, to your clothes, to your choice in *café*," Babineaux said, gesturing at the black, unsweetened coffee that sat in front of the inspector, "indicates zat you 'ave little time for ze details, ze small pleasures, ze frivolous, zings zat are not, 'ow do you say, *pratique*. And to propose is ze opposite. It iz ze ultimate romantic gesture."

Mike sat quietly. He grew hot as he listened to Babineaux. He was conflicted. He wished he could conjure up a withering put-down, but at the same time he felt relieved that the problem that had plagued him for so long was now shared with someone. Even if that someone was a tall, poncy Frenchman who looked like he wore mascara.

"Well, either way," Mike said finally, "don't tell anyone about this, okay?"

"*Bien sûr!*" Babineaux said, opening his arms wide. "I intend to '*elp* you cultivate ze fruits of love, *Inspecteur*, not destroy zem!"

"*Help?* Oh, heck no. What are you talking about?"

Babineaux chuckled and kept Mike waiting as he sipped from his cup before answering. "I am offering my assistance, in order to make your proposal ze perfect one."

"I don't want your assistance."

Babineaux laughed again. "I am certain you don't *want* my 'elp, *Inspecteur,* but I am also certain zat you *need* it!"

Mike looked down. For a moment, he considered the idea. Annabelle certainly seemed taken with Babineaux. She was often charmed by the Frenchman's way with words and manners. He tapped his thumb against his knee. But no, the idea was preposterous, ridiculous—a grown man, a respected police detective, taking advice from a lithe, lofty lothario who probably wore moisturizer? His pride would never allow it.

"No," Mike said, flatly.

"*Non?*"

"No," Mike said, once again. "It's a silly idea. I'm not a teenager who needs tips on how to conduct himself. The notion is ludicrous."

With a customary tilt of his head, Babineaux shrugged, and returned his gaze to the comings and goings of those on the plaza. "It iz wise to know when you don't know zings," he said softly, offering his words to the air and letting them fall where they may, like someone blowing on a dandelion clock.

Mike frowned. He wanted to get up and leave, but found himself unable to do so. The men sat in silence, Mike still banging the side of his thumb against his knee, distinctly more agitated than his companion. Finally, he could contain himself no more. "Okay, what exactly are you suggesting? That Annabelle will say no if I don't present her with the right flowers? Or if I don't say the right words? It's just a marriage proposal, you know. A simple question with a yes or no answer. I'm positive she'll say yes."

Babineaux turned slowly toward him, that fishing line tugging at his eyebrow again. He looked amused, as if surprised to find the inspector still sitting there, let alone venturing to talk.

"I have a ring." Mike continued. "I'll pick a good moment, and I'll simply ask the question. That's all there is to it. People propose all the time. Not all of them are grand gestures. What are you trying to do? Make me think there's more to it than that? You're just trying to make me second-guess myself, Bambino. I'm not having it!"

Slowly, Babineaux set his cup down, uncrossed his legs, interlaced his fingers, and leaned forward across the table. As always, he placed a dramatic emphasis on his words by pausing before uttering them. "It iz not about ze yes or ze no, *Inspecteur*. You are right. She will say yes. Of zat, I am sure."

Mike tried to hide a smile. He felt relieved and he didn't want the French detective to realize how much his words reassured him. "Good," he said. "I'm glad you agree."

Babineaux shrugged. "But it iz a shame, iz it not?"

Mike frowned some more. "What do you mean?"

"To a man," Babineaux said, pointing his finger in the air, "ze proposal is as you say, 'a yes or a no question.' Were it up to us, we would ask it at ze breakfast table, in between ze conversation about ze weather and ze latest football results, *non*? But to a woman... To a woman it is an *event*, a *moment*, somezing to be remembered. It is a symbolic gesture of ze love up to zat point, a story to be told to friends and future children, a representation of everyzing she 'olds dear. Zis is how a woman zinks, in symbols and moments. You leave ze toilet seat up, it iz not a simple mistake, it iz a sign of how much you don't care about 'er. You buy 'er chocolates at ze gas station on ze way 'ome, it is not about ze cost or ze quality, it iz a symbol of 'ow much she is on your mind."

Mike found himself laughing. "That's rather stereotypical. And sexist. Annabelle would have your guts for garters if she heard you."

Babineaux chuckled, leaning back in his chair and opening his arms wide. "We are detectives, are we not? We, of all people, should know 'ow much truth zere is in ze stereotypes."

"I still don't need your help," Mike said, gulping down the last of his coffee and getting up.

"Zink about it, *Inspecteur*," Babineaux said. "When she tells ze story of 'ow you proposed, will 'er eyes light up and 'er 'eart skip a beat? Will she feel a warm glow, a deeply moving reminder of what a wonderful man she committed her life to? Or will she simply say: ''e asked me over dinner—I 'ad ze chicken'."

CHAPTER FORTY-TWO

ANNABELLE FOUND MARY in the convent's vegetable garden. She watched her friend for a few moments. Mary was digging furiously, turning over dark soil with a fork that was almost as large as she was. On the ground next to her was a bag of manure. Annabelle could hear Mary pant and grunt with effort and saw her wipe her brow before she plunged the fork into the dirt again. With a stamp of her foot, Mary thrust the tines in further, and pushing down with her entire bodyweight, levered the soil up. She gave the fork an angry twist. Fresh soil dropped on the ground next to her, and the tiny nun raised the handle above her head, preparing to pitch it into the ground again.

"Mary! Yoo-hoo!"

Mary looked up. Annabelle showed her the two mugs she held in her hands. Her friend tossed down her fork and marched over to her.

"PG Tips," Annabelle said. "From a little stash I brought over with me specially."

"Thank you." Mary took the mug from Annabelle gratefully, wrapping her hot, pulsing palms around its sides.

"You look like you've been busy." Annabelle nodded to the bed that Mary had been working over. Half of it comprised dark, steaming, fresh soil while the other half was dry and compacted.

"I'm preparing it for planting. I'll work in the fertilizer when I've loosened up the soil. Bit of a smelly old job, but someone has to do it. And today I felt like it should be me." Mary wiped her brow.

The two women strolled over to where an old wrought iron bench sat overlooking the vegetable garden. It was surrounded by overgrown shrubs and flowers left to grow wild.

"Hmm, what's that smell?" Annabelle lifted her nose to the air and closed her eyes.

"Mint, probably. From our herb garden behind you." Annabelle turned to see a profusion of plants, all various shades of green and distinctly different from one another. "Ah yes, I recognize the mint. And there's rosemary, and chives, and dill. And what's that? Cow parsley?" Annabelle pointed to a bush with tiny white flowers.

Mary turned to look. "Yes. Mother Renate likes a cup of cow parsley tea before bed."

"Huh, I thought cow parsley was a weed." Annabelle saw another patch by the hedgerow that ran alongside part of the vegetable garden. She turned back to Mary. "So what's got you into such a mood? I thought you were going to murder that soil the way you were stabbing it with your fork."

Mary immediately banged her mug down on the bench, sloshing her tea over the sides. She folded her arms. "I'm angry, Annabelle." She twisted in her seat. "I'm angry—with God, with Raphael for disappearing, with myself. I don't know what to do."

"You are being tested, Mary."

Mary threw herself against the back of the bench, sloshing more of her tea. Annabelle took her hand. Her touch seemed to calm the nun. Mary closed her eyes and turned her face to the sun, exhaling deeply.

"Yes... yes, you're right. I'm in such turmoil. I want... *this* to be over. I keep waiting for a sign. I think I get one but then another one, a contradictory one, pops up. Then some time goes by and I get yet another sign. More contradictions. Oh, I'm just so confused. I don't know *what* is expected of me." Mary started to cry. "And I feel so ashamed."

"Ashamed? What do you have to feel ashamed of?" Annabelle was aghast. She reached into her pocket and pulled out a packet of tissues.

"I've broken my vows, Annabelle. To God. I have sinned."

"I'm sure it's not that bad, Mary. Tell me, you'll feel better if you do."

Mary shook her head.

"Is it to do with Father Raphael?"

Mary didn't reply. She stared down at her lap.

"Whatever it is, Mary, God will forgive you."

Mary nodded and started to blub again. Annabelle put her arm around her friend's shoulder and hugged her.

"Will you forgive me, Annabelle?" Mary said through her tears.

"Me? Of course I will, Mary. I'd forgive you anything."

CHAPTER FORTY-THREE

"IS THAT COLOGNE you're wearing?" Annabelle said as she sat down for breakfast.

"Um...just a little," Mike mumbled, shuffling in his seat as Annabelle took hers.

Annabelle closed her eyes and smiled warmly. "I like it." She opened her eyes again and appraised him. "You know, I think the French sense of style is rubbing off on you," she said.

"Really? How?"

"Those cufflinks for a start." Annabelle grinned.

"You don't like them?" Mike said, fingering the silver and blue cufflinks he'd bought at a jewelry store on the plaza the day before. He might have seen Inspector Babineaux wearing some very similar.

"No, I do like them. They are very stylish. Style makes you look even more handsome." Annabelle lifted her coffee cup to her mouth and wrinkled her nose flirtatiously.

Again, Mike tried to quell the small smile that threatened to telegraph his feelings. *Damn that Babineaux! His advice on women is as good as his investigative instincts are poor!*

"How did you get on with Babineaux after I left yesterday?" Annabelle asked, as she plucked a croissant from the table. "You came back late. I was so tired when I returned from the convent, I went straight to bed."

"Oh...well...you know, we had a lot to go over—about the case, I mean. Babineaux prattled on a lot. We disagree on many things."

Annabelle nodded, satisfied with his explanation.

"How did you and Mary get on yesterday?"

Annabelle sighed. "Mary is having a crisis of conviction. It's quite common. She's not sure she's cut out for the sisterhood. We had a long chat."

"Huh, but hasn't she been a nun for years now? Why is she suddenly having second thoughts?"

Annabelle smiled. She leaned over and ruffled Mike's hair. "Why indeed?" She didn't elaborate, and Mike decided not to probe further.

"We're over halfway through our trip now. We've only got a few more days left," he said, changing the subject.

"Yes. I'm still sorry this hasn't turned into much of a break for you."

"It's alright," Mike said, shrugging. "Even an investigation can be satisfying when I'm with someone I respect."

Annabelle eyes widened. She smiled. "Respect? That's so... nice."

"That we spend time together is the main thing."

"You're right, that's the main thing."

"Annabelle," he said deliberately, causing her to raise her eyes from her croissant expectantly, "the French sunlight really brings out the beautiful shades in your eyes."

It wasn't quite what he meant to say, but Annabelle immediately went red and beamed. "*Mike!*" she said, reaching her hand across the table to take his. "What a sweet thing to say!"

"Just stating the facts," Mike said, gruffly.

"It's just so... unlike you." Annabelle retained her glow for several more moments. They continued to eat their croissants, Annabelle's eyes bashfully glancing up at the inspector every so often.

Mike stared down at his plate. *Now?* Here they were, the bright yellow morning sun filtering through dancing leaves, the sounds of small birds chirruping their mating calls to one another, the smell of cherry blossom mixing with the rich buttery aroma of a delicious breakfast; it was perfect. Or at least, it would have been, were it not for the darkness of two deaths hanging over their thoughts like a heavy, velvet cloud.

"That's it!" Mike said, slamming his palm on the table, ruining the romantic mood, and causing Annabelle to snap to attention. "I'm going to solve this murder today! We've only got a few more days left, and I intend to enjoy them with you."

Annabelle leaned back, eyebrows raised. "How do you intend to do that?"

Mike's face was determined. "The pieces are all there: Julien and Renate's histories, the death threats, Raphael's disappearance. The one thing that bothers me, a hunch I never should have left hanging, was that sound at the church. I'm going back there, and I'm not leaving until I figure out what it is—even if it does turn out to be just some plumbing that's as old as the building. I'll ask Mary to come with me. She might have some insight I've missed." He bit off a mouthful of croissant like a lion tearing meat from a carcass.

Annabelle smiled, her face going red once again. "You know, Mike, you're terribly attractive when you're determined to do something."

Mike looked up. He gave her his best thousand-yard-stare, but found it rather difficult with his mouth full of soft, fluffy, buttery pastry.

CHAPTER FORTY-FOUR

WHEN MIKE ARRIVED at Babineaux's café-office, the French inspector greeted him with a wry grin. Before Babineaux could say anything or discomfort him further though, Mike took charge of the conversation.

"I'm going to investigate the church one more time. Sister Mary is going to join me there."

Babineaux's smile turned to a shrug of acquiescence. "Come, I will walk with you." The tall detective got out of his chair.

"I assume by ze fact you say nothing of it, zat my advice worked, *non?*"

Mike huffed a little. "Well... she noticed the cologne."

"*Bien!* Scents are very important to a woman."

"And the cufflinks."

"Ze details make ze man!"

"And she seemed to like those flowery words..."

"*Fantastique!* A man is only as good as 'is words," Babineaux said, misinterpreting the saying but making his point nonetheless.

"But I feel such a fool saying them!"

"*Mon ami!* Love is foolish! And to love is to embrace being a fool!"

"But there are still two massive problems," Mike said. "The first one is this bloody murder investigation. How can I be romantic when there's death and suicide and conspiracy everywhere?"

Babineaux offered a Gallic shrug. "We must do what we can," he said, sympathetically. "What is ze other *problème?*"

Mike sighed and huffed, as if needing to expel air before more words would come out. "I have no idea what to say!" he blurted. "Complimenting her over breakfast is one thing, but asking her to be my wife is quite another!" Mike ran his hand through his hair. "I have to face it, I need help, Bambino, help!"

"Hmm," Babineaux stroked his moustache thoughtfully. "Come, come, *mon ami*. We will consider zis together. What does Révérend Annabelle like? What *moves* her? Is it music? Art? Poetry?" They were crossing the plaza now.

"Cake. She likes cake."

Babineaux raised an eyebrow and continued. "Well, we have plenty of zat 'ere. Sweet zings and sweet nothings make an excellent *combinaison.*"

Mike blew out his cheeks. Together, the two men noticed Sister Mary emerging from a side street.

"Do not worry," Babineaux said, patting the inspector's arm. "We will come up with somezing. Ze proposal will be sweeter zan any cake Révérend Annabelle ever ate!"

CHAPTER FORTY-FIVE

THE CONVENT FELT eerie as Annabelle traipsed up the worn path in the early morning light. She had decided to come back while Mary was gone in order to further probe the goings-on there. She hoped that Mary's absence might make the nuns open up more. She noticed a couple of black-clad figures silently conducting their work in the orchards, and a nun hurriedly making her way toward the barn, a basket in her hand. As Annabelle drew near she noticed the stocky figure of Sister Josephine coming toward her.

"*Bonjour*," Annabelle said, cheerfully.

"Good morning," the nun replied, her French accent making her English words sound complex and exotic. "Sister Mary isn't here at present. She left fifteen minutes ago."

"That's alright, Sister. I just came by to see how you were doing following Mother Renate's death."

"We are doing well, Reverend," Sister Josephine replied, crisply. "Thank you." The nun bowed her head slightly. She seemed more reticent than the other day when she had been only too happy to dish on Father Raphael.

"Oh," Annabelle said. "That's good." She said nothing more. Sister Josephine looked at her expectantly.

There was an empty pause as both women waited for the other. Sister Josephine blinked first. "You are welcome to come inside, of course," she said. "Or you can wander around the grounds."

"Thank you. Is Sister Simone here?"

"Yes. But I'm not sure where."

"No problem, I'll walk around, see if I can find her."

Sister Josephine bowed politely and swooped off like a bird taking flight, her veil rippling like a stingray wafting through water searching for its prey. As she watched her, Annabelle was reminded again of what Sister Mary had said concerning the nun's coolness toward her.

Turning, Annabelle made her way to the big barn beside the river where they milled the wheat and baked the bread. She pushed open the stout, aged-oak door and walked inside. The small vestibule was in darkness. It led to the milling operation in one direction, and the bakery in another. Propped against one wall beneath some empty shelves, Annabelle could just make out a workbench.

"Baking must be over for the day," Annabelle murmured to herself.

Only a thin beam from a small high window provided any light, and just a square foot of the floor could be seen with any clarity. Annabelle groped for a light switch, but before she found it the silence of the convent was broken. Annabelle heard a hard clang in the dark, the loud crash of something heavy falling, a low rumbling that got louder and louder. There was a huge crash and a door burst open. Annabelle's eyes didn't need to adjust to realize there was something heavy thundering in her direction. She quickly leapt onto the workbench, banging her head hard on a shelf as she did so. "Aarghh!" Ignoring her pain and lightheadedness Annabelle desperately perched herself on her hands and knees on top of the bench and squeezed her eyes tight. She felt a rush of air as something huge and heavy trundled past her followed by another almighty crash and then silence.

Annabelle sat back on her heels and rubbed the spot on her head where she had hit the shelf. She waited for her heartbeat to return to normal. The outside door opened, and she squinted into the light. There was a flurry of moving figures silhouetted in the doorway. Alarmed voices spoke quickly in French.

Two nuns fluttered up to Annabelle and helped her down from the bench, while another opened the door to the bakery. Daylight filled the room—and shone a light on what had just happened.

"I am so sorry, Reverend!" one of the nuns said in English. "Please forgive us!"

"There's no light! The bulb is broken!" the other explained.

Still dazed and rubbing the crown of her head, Annabelle looked beyond the nuns at the giant millstone that had ended its journey by crashing into the vestibule wall. It had proved no match for medieval stonemasonry, however. It now lay in three pieces on the floor.

CHAPTER FORTY-SIX

"WHAT HAPPENED?" ANNABELLE asked, drowsily.

"We were switching the millstones over. We use a pulley on the outside of the building," one of the nuns explained. "The handle slipped in my hand, and it got away from us. We're so sorry."

Annabelle gave them a wan smile through a slowly receding throb of pain. "It's alright," she said. "My fault. I should have let you know I was coming."

"Come outside," the nun said, gesturing for the others and Annabelle to join her. "Let me see the bruise."

Annabelle made her way into the daylight—almost blindingly bright after the darkness of the mill. Several pairs of hands compelled her to sit on an old bench against a wall while one of the women parted Annabelle's hair to look at the injury.

"Perhaps some tea?" the English-speaking nun suggested.

"*Oui!*" another replied. She scurried off.

A few moments later, an old wooden cup was thrust into Annabelle's hand. Bits of crushed leaves sat at the bottom in yellow water. "Cow parsley tea. It is good for healing. Mother Renate, God rest her soul, used to swear by it."

"Thank you," Annabelle said. She was becoming bothered by the fussiness of the nuns. It was a bit early in the day for such a lot of attention.

"Drink."

Annabelle brought the cup to her lips. "Arghh!" A stab of pain shot through her shoulder. She flinched. The cup went sailing through the air. It landed a few feet away, spilling its hot contents on to the soil floor outside the barn.

"Oh!" Annabelle exclaimed, clutching her shoulder.

"Are you alright?"

"Yes, yes," Annabelle said, holding up her palm to protest against any further ministrations. "Just an old hockey injury flaring up. I'll be as right as rain in an hour or so."

The nuns nodded, shrugging and muttering in French. "Would you like some ice?"

"No, no, I'll be fine. But would you be so kind as to fetch Sister Simone?" Annabelle said, still rubbing her shoulder. "If she's free."

"Of course," the English-speaking nun said, quickly leaving. The other two stayed behind watching Annabelle curiously from a few feet away as though she were an alien being of a kind with which they had had little contact. Which indeed they had not.

"I'll be fine, really," Annabelle said to them. "Please, continue with your work." The nuns, getting the gist, wandered off wordlessly, and Annabelle sat for a while, raising her face to the sun and letting the warmth comfort her after her shock. She rolled her shoulder gently, easing away the dull ache, and gingerly brought her other hand to her head again to feel the swell of the emerging bruise.

Sitting there, soothing her injuries, alone in the vineyard of a convent in a strange place, Annabelle felt, for the first time, out-of-place. What on earth was she doing? She had intended to have a pleasant—perhaps romantic—week with Mike, and instead, she was off on her own chasing a killer, maybe two. She loved Mary dearly, and could never have said no to her request for help, but she wondered now if perhaps they could have helped in some smaller sense and left the thrust of the investigation to the appropriate authorities without compelling Mike to use his week off searching medieval churches for clues or requiring her to dance with death in a grain store.

Just as she was considering how she might show her appreciation to Mike for his sacrifice, her thoughts were interrupted by Sister Simone, who appeared from around the corner of the building, squinting and wrinkling her nose like a mole who'd just breeched the surface.

CHAPTER FORTY-SEVEN

"ANNABELLE, HELLO." SEEING Annabelle holding her head with one hand and rubbing her shoulder with the other, Sister Simone said, "Are you are alright?"

"Sister Simone," Annabelle replied, getting up from the bench to greet her. "It's wonderful to see you again."

The elderly nun offered her right hand, but Annabelle grimaced and pointed to her shoulder. "Sorry," she explained, "I had a little accident."

"What happened?"

"Didn't the nuns tell you? A flying millstone almost flattened me!" Annabelle chuckled.

Sister Simone frowned and marched toward the open barn door, peering in to look at the aftermath. She shook her head almost imperceptibly.

"My fault," Annabelle explained, "I arrived unannounced."

The sister glowered at Annabelle. "No. The nuns know how to work a pulley. They've had lots of practice. I train them myself. They probably weren't paying enough attention to what they were doing. And what is this?" the elderly nun said, noticing the wooden cup on the ground. She picked it up and lifted it to her nose, immediately grimacing. "Ugh," she said, tossing what was left of the tea out toward the fields and placing the cup back on the bench. "Do you think you can walk? It will help if you keep moving. You won't become too stiff."

Sister Simone helped Annabelle up and slowly they walked away from the building.

"The investigation is not going well?" Sister Simone asked.

"What makes you say that?"

"If you are back here so soon, you must have made little progress."

Annabelle couldn't argue with that. As they walked, they passed the large wooden shed. Most of it was surrounded by weeds, but the undergrowth had been beaten back around the door.

'Mary said you keep machinery, ropes, you know, 'shed things' in there."

"There? Yes, a whole lot of things we have little use for but which might be useful one day. We also store our surplus threshed wheat—the wheat we don't have room for in the other building.

"Can I take a look?"

"Of course!" Sister Simone reached to unlatch the heavy door.

"How have things been since Mother Renate... passed?" Annabelle asked.

"The only thing to live beyond death is a legacy," Sister Simone replied, "and Mother Superior's legacy was one of routine and obedience. The sisters have that still. We can carry on for a while until a new Mother Superior is appointed." Annabelle stepped into the dusty, dim interior of the shed, while Sister Simone placed a rock in front of the door to keep it open. Slowly, Annabelle's eyes adjusted to the darkness, the small amount of light reflected a million times in the floating dust particles. The shed was as Sister Simone had described it—full of old, unused things. Curious, rusted machines; boxes and containers with layers of dust so thick they obscured the labels; a few old bicycles in the corner among a pile of wood, metal sheeting, and rope, cobwebs binding them all together in a messy, angular parcel.

"Here is where we keep extra bins of threshed wheat," Sister Simone said, pointing to big plastic bins stacked on top of one another.

Annabelle peered at them. "So these are all full of grain?"

"That's right. When we need them, we bring the bins over to the other building to be milled."

Annabelle nosed about examining the other items but not finding anything of particular interest. There were some old kitchen cupboards mounted on the wall. "May I?" Annabelle said, reaching a hand toward them.

Sister Simone shrugged gently her permission. Annabelle opened and closed all the doors but the shelves were empty except for one. In the last cupboard was a bottle of molasses, some olive oil, and an old ice cream tub. Fingerprints marred the otherwise perfect layer of dust on the tub's lid.

"What's this?" Annabelle murmured. She lifted down the tub and opened it. It was full of soft, gray powder.

Sister Simone walked over. "That? That's rye flour. We haven't baked with that in years." She took the tub's lid from Annabelle and snapped it firmly back on. "I should throw it away." She tucked the tub under her arm. "Anyhow, does any of this help you?"

Annabelle looked around the shed and frowned. "Not really. The ropes," she said, walking toward the heaped pile that lay on the floor beside the bikes, "presumably Mother Renate took the ones she... used from here."

"It would have been rare for her to come into the shed. She hated dust," Sister Simone said, "but yes, I suppose she must."

Annabelle prodded the ropes with her foot. "Do you really think Mother Renate killed herself?" she asked, more out of dead-end desperation than genuine curiosity.

Sister Simone pursed her lips. "I am not a fortune teller, unfortunately. I really couldn't say."

"But you must have an opinion?"

"Renate was a devout holy woman. She went by the book. Suicide would be anathema to her, and she seemed fine when I brought her tea that evening, but who's to say what was in her mind. That is between her and our Lord. We cannot know."

Annabelle sighed again. "Did you know there was a connection between Father Julien and Mother Renate?"

"Connection?" the old woman asked.

"They both come from Nice, miles away from here and yet decades later, they end up in this tiny village together."

"Hmm," Sister Simone mused. "I never had any idea. But I would say it is coincidence. The world of all things holy is a small one these days."

"I know," Annabelle said, "but then Father Julien dies, and days later Mother Renate appears to hang herself. It's a bit, well..."

Sister Simone allowed herself a mild laugh. "You've been reading *Romeo and Juliet*, I see."

Annabelle matched the nun's chuckle. "There doesn't need to be romance at the heart of it but... well, it was a thought."

Sister Simone shrugged. "I would be surprised if he were her secret."

"But you think she had one?"

Sister Simone paused, her face falling.

"What?" Annabelle said. "What is it? *Did* Mother Renate have a secret?"

CHAPTER FORTY-EIGHT

FOR A FEW seconds, Sister Simone looked at Annabelle, studying her, weighing her options. Eventually, she seemed satisfied, and after a deep breath, began talking.

"When I was a young novice, important considerations were not part of my experience. I liked to gossip, to giggle at saucy jokes, to play silly games. It took much more than a habit and a vocation for me to become worthy of God's love. One of the games I played with the other equally childish novices alongside whom I served the Lord in those early days was to guess the motivation behind other nuns' decisions to take their vows. While we all say we are called by God, the stories behind our choices are often mundane and not at all spiritual.

"Many of the reasons are as you might expect, some young women feel blessed by the Lord and seek to honor that. Others crave a sense of importance, of greater meaning in their lives. A few simply struggle to function anywhere else, and want a place of safety. But sometimes there's a more complex reason, a life-changing event, perhaps some trauma, or some illuminating experience.

"As I matured, I lost interest in those juvenile worldly distractions that had so held my interest. I stopped devouring magazines that had handsome movie stars on their covers, I stopped lingering at shop windows full of glamorous clothes, and I refrained from gossiping with the other nuns. But I could never stop wondering why my sisters had decided to take this path. It was an almost unconscious habit, a bad one. When I said my prayers and lay down to sleep, my mind would often drift, and I would wonder about a new sister I had just met. The reason for their decision would nag at the fringes of my mind, and I would speculate almost without realizing it."

"And you think there's an extraordinary story behind Mother Renate's decision to join the church?" Annabelle asked.

Sister Simone sighed. "I have an idea." She quickly held up a finger. "I have no evidence, mind you."

"Tell me."

"I believe she may have had a child."

Annabelle gasped, her hand jumping to her mouth as her eyes opened wide.

Simone nodded at Annabelle. "And her shame and despair drew her to a life serving God."

Sister Simone sat on a grain bin and continued. "Over the years, I have noticed many things. There was a sad, longing look in Renate's eyes whenever there was talk of children—particularly girls. The only time you would see her smile was during visits by local schoolchildren; she insisted upon taking them around the convent herself. Her manner was quite different at those times. She was softer than normal. She even smiled. Her sorrow was most noticeable, however, when a child appeared on our doorstep."

"Lost?"

"Not exactly. One morning, we found a baby in a basket left

at our door. Just a few hours old, it was. It doesn't happen much these days, but years ago it wasn't so unusual for unwanted children to be given up in this way, secretly left at the doors of a convent where the mother could be sure that their baby would be taken care of and raised in a godly manner, a life from which she may have fallen."

"How awful!"

"Yes. It was very sad, but with the Lord's blessing we were usually able to make a childless couple very happy and give the child a home with love and consistency. Nevertheless, when it happened here, Mother Superior found the situation very difficult. She was distraught. I had never seen her like that. She couldn't be in the presence of the child as we took care of it. She delegated the arrangements for the adoption to me. She spent three days locked up in her quarters praying obsessively when it was time for the baby to leave. I would go to her door to bring her food, and almost every time I did, I heard the sound of weeping that would abruptly stop when I knocked. It was the only time I saw her feelings get the better of her."

Stunned, Annabelle breathed in deeply and shook her head in an effort to process what she was hearing. "And you think this was because she had had a similar experience years before? She had a child that she gave up for adoption? You think that's why she was so affected?"

"Maybe. Or the baby died." Sister Simone shrugged and stood up to wander to a shelf where she fingered some bottles. "Let's stop this talk. I am telling you what I observed, and I am speculating like I used to when I was younger. This is not useful nor is it in the service of our Lord. Come, let us leave here and turn our minds to other matters."

As she said it, there was a long, slow creak followed by a click. The shed went dark. Annabelle gasped, unable to see a thing. Her heart skipped a beat. She heard Sister Simone tut under her breath and her feet shuffle toward her.

"What's going on?" Annabelle exclaimed.

"The rock must have slipped from the door."

"But we can open it, can't we?"

Annabelle heard Sister Simone walk past her then grunt a little as the door gave a tiny creak.

"The latch has fallen. We're locked in."

With her arms out in front of her, Annabelle moved through the darkness toward the sound Sister Simone's voice.

"Careful!"

"Oof! Sorry," Annabelle said, bumping into her. "Do you have a lighter of some kind?"

"Good lord, no. I stopped smoking years ago."

"Matches? Candles?"

"No."

"Hmm." Annabelle ran her fingers over the door. "Perhaps we can yell for help?"

"These walls and the door are three inches thick. We are well away from the main paths. No one would ever hear us."

"I know! There's a sliver of light coming in. Perhaps we can slip something between the door and the frame? We might be able to lift the latch."

"*Bonne idée!*" Sister Simone exclaimed. "But we need something slim, and we need some light to see by." There was a pause. "Wait!"

Annabelle felt the small, determined frame of the nun push past her.

"What are you doing?" Annabelle asked.

There was some rattling and clanging and a grunt. "There's a bicycle light here attached to the wheel by a dynamo, so if I just..."

Bright, white light flared, blinding Annabelle for a few moments until she caught sight of Sister Simone in the shadows. She was lifting a bicycle by its handlebars with one hand and spinning its front wheel with the other.

"Quick!" Sister Simone said, her voice tight with effort. "I can't do this all day!"

Annabelle sprang into action, her head spinning rapidly as she searched the cluttered shed for something thin enough to slip around the door. After picking up a piece of plywood and quickly discarding it for being too thick, she found an offcut from a sheet of aluminum and rushed over to the door.

"Does it fit?" Sister Simone asked, struggling under the weight of the bike and the awkwardness of her task, the bicycle light flickering as she grew tired.

Her answer was a click. Annabelle slid the aluminum into the crack around the door and pushed it up to dislodge the latch. The door popped open, first a little and then a lot as Annabelle leaned her shoulder, her good one, against it. Then, misjudging the effort required, the door burst open and Annabelle pitched forward, tumbling onto the ground outside.

"Ow!" she cried as she hit the dirt. Despite her pain, she stood up quickly and held the door open for Sister Simone, before allowing the door to slam shut again under its own weight.

"What is going on, Sister Simone? I doubt that rock moved by itself," Annabelle said, rubbing her shoulder. Now she had injured them both.

"I agree with you," Sister Simone replied, scanning the outside of the shed. "It is very odd."

CHAPTER FORTY-NINE

MIKE, BABINEAUX, AND Mary marched up the church steps together like superheroes. There was a sense of purpose about them, the English detective spearheading the group, the other two trailing slightly in his wake. Mike was frowning, his lips pressed into a thin line, hands thrust into the pockets of his trenchcoat. They stopped at the doors, and Lestrange, who was trotting behind stepped forward to unlock them. Silently and respectfully, they crossed the threshold and began to move around the huge space, taking slow, deliberate steps between the pews and scanning the walls around them carefully as if they had never seen them before.

After Father Julien's death and Father Raphael's disappearance, there had been few visitors to the church. Without services, confessions, and random prayers, it hadn't taken long for the church to feel disused. As if yearning for its past, the church felt like a relic, and the effect on the visitors was profound.

"There is nothing sadder than an unused church," Mary said softly, almost to herself. Nobody responded, their silence agreement enough.

Not one of them failed to notice the small changes in the church's interior since Father's Julien's murder. Spiders had been busy weaving large cobwebs in its nooks and crannies, the pews had a sprinkling of dust along their dark oak surfaces, the air was as musty as that of a crypt.

Halfway up the aisle, Mike stopped and turned around to face the other three, his eyes fixed keenly on Mary.

"Okay," he announced, with the voice he used to command his officers, "tell me again what happened on that day. From the top."

Mary nodded quickly, and began. "We were all here for Easter Sunday Mass..."

"'We?"

"The nuns, the entire village, and those who live in the countryside around."

"Where were you specifically?"

Sister Mary turned to the pews on the left hand side of the church.

"Here, near the front, on the same side as the office."

Mike looked at the spot she pointed to, envisioning the scene.

"Where was Father Raphael at this time?"

A quick blush flashed across Sister Mary's face. "He stood by the door, waiting for Father Julien."

"I see," Mike said. "So you could see him clearly from where you sat?"

Mary flushed again. "Yes."

"What happened after you arrived?"

"Well... Father Julien came out and walked to the altar. He had his back to us as he prepared to conduct the service. He likes to look everything over, check everything is in place. There was nothing unusual about any of it."

"Father Raphael was still standing to the side?"

"Yes," Mary said. "The music started and everyone went quiet. The service was about to start. That's when Father Julien turned around, took a step, and... fell. Everyone gasped, stunned! Sister Josephine started screaming. Sister Simone was quietening her. Mother Renate ran up the aisle. I looked back to where Father Raphael had been standing, but he had gone!"

"Hold on," Mike said, raising a large palm. "Sister Josephine started screaming?"

"Yes!" Mary said, confounded by the inspector's question. "Father Julien was dead!"

"But you didn't know that—not yet," Mike replied. "All he'd done was fall over. He could have fainted or had a heart attack. He could have simply tripped over. Bit of an overreaction to start wailing straight away, isn't it?"

"*Inspecteur,*" Babineaux interjected. "She is young. Of course ze young woman was distraught. Even if 'e did, as you say, 'trip over.'" The Frenchman shook his head slowly and muttered something that sounded to Mike suspiciously like *"Ze British and zeir upper stiff lips..."*

"Perhaps," Mike said, putting the point aside but not conceding it. He looked at the door to the office, screwed his face up in thought for a second, and then marched toward it. The others quickly followed. "So Father Raphael was standing here, right?"

Mary nodded.

"Father Julien walks past him toward the altar," Mike said, moving his hand as if pushing an imaginary Father Julien in that direction, "then everyone waits for the Mass to start."

"Yes," Mary said.

"We 'ave gone through zis a million times," Babineaux sighed.

"So everyone was looking at Father Julien," Mike continued. Abruptly, he spun around and pushed open the door to the office, stepping inside quickly as the others filled the doorway behind him. Mike's eyes went immediately to the small, head-height window. There were two bars across it. Mike grabbed one firmly, shaking it a little before turning back to

Mary. "Tell me, could Father Raphael have gone through this window?"

"It iz too small!" Babineaux said, causing Mike to scowl at him.

Sister Mary considered Mike's question for a full four seconds before answering. "He's very athletic, and slim... but... perhaps. I don't know."

"Okay," Mike said, "I'm going to dismiss the window then."

He marched back out of the office, the others quickly moving aside out of the determined inspector's way, before filing in behind him as he passed. After a few steps, Mike stopped abruptly. His companions banged into him and each other.

"Father Raphael couldn't have moved from his post *into* the church," Mike said, recovering quickly and ignoring the others as they straightened their clothes and hair and rubbed their bruises. "You would have seen him. That leaves only one way he could have gone."

Quickly, Mike moved down the side of the sanctuary toward the very front of the church, one palm brushing against the wall, until he came to another door hidden by a velvet curtain that matched the red carpet that ran down the main aisle. Mike pushed the curtain aside and rapped his knuckles on the door behind it. "What's this door?"

"It leads to the confessional," Mary answered.

"Why is it so small?" The door was at least six inches shorter than was typical.

Mary turned down the corners of her mouth. "Discretion? Age? People were smaller in the 15th century."

Mike glanced at Babineaux.

"*Lestrange!*" the Frenchman said. He held out his hand and clicked his fingers without taking his eyes off Mike.

CHAPTER FIFTY

L ESTRANGE STEPPED FORWARD, plucking the huge bunch of keys from his pocket and trying several until he found the right one.

Beyond the door, they found themselves in a tall, wide, but short corridor. At the other end was another small door, and to the side a couple of ornately-carved booths. Mike stopped a few feet into the corridor, taking in as much of it as he could. Here, the space was different. The walls had wood paneling and the floor was made of varnished oak slats. Another thin red carpet ran down the center of the corridor. Babineaux walked past Mike, brushing his moustache as he peered at the confessionals like an art critic, one hand behind his back.

"This other doorway?" Mike said, his eyebrows high in his forehead. He pointed to the door at the other end of the short corridor.

"It's for people who want to slip in and out," Mary answered. "Anyone can confess during certain hours or at a prearranged time. They can enter here from the alleyway behind the church. It's much more discreet."

Mike nodded and took a few careful steps forward, scanning the room.

"Mary," he said slowly, his eyes still steadily considering his surroundings.

"Yes, Inspector?"

"Does the church have problems with its plumbing?"

There was a pause before Mary spoke. "I don't think so. How do you mean?"

"Noises. Rattling. You know, the kind of sound you get when plumbing is old. Air gets in the pipes."

"Noises? Not at all. I often come to the church to just sit and contemplate. It's one of the most profoundly quiet places I know. Even when there's a market or some kind of fair in the plaza, if the doors are closed you would think the church was in the middle of nowhere."

"Hmm," Mike said, frowning a little. "What about this?" He pointed to a recess built into the wall. There were three more, but this one was different. It was empty. Each of the others contained an artifact stored inside a glass case—a box, a goblet, a clock—all of them antique, ornate, and gold. On the wall was a large piece of artwork depicting *The Last Supper*. "Why is this one empty?"

"Oh!" Mary exclaimed. "It's missing! I hadn't noticed." She walked up to the blank spot in the recess and stared as if by doing so, she could conjure up the missing item.

"What is? What's missing, Mary?"

"St. Agnès. Her remains are stored in a tall gold box and kept behind this glass. The box is missing!" Mary turned to look at Mike, her eyes wide with horror. "This is terrible. They are sacred!"

Suddenly, they were distracted by the sound of the two French policemen talking animatedly. Babineaux was waving his hand at Lestrange, dismissing him.

"What is it?" Mike asked, walking toward them.

"Nothing! Lestrange used to be a carpenter's apprentice—'e iz obsessed with wood!"

Mike looked at Lestrange. He was pressing his foot slowly but firmly on a spot in the carpet. Mike ran then. He crouched down quickly, gesturing for Lestrange to move out of the way. He grabbed the carpet and flung it aside. There, set into the floorboards was a small iron ring. Mike didn't even look up to get the reaction of the others before yanking at the handle.

"*Mon Dieu!*" Babineaux said, peering into the black hole that appeared.

"Anyone got a light?" Mike asked.

Lestrange opened his roomy jacket and like a magician pulling a rabbit from a hat, he produced a flashlight. Mike quickly put the end of it into his mouth and slid himself through the opening. He let go of the sides and a second later, the sound of his shoes landing on the hard stone reverberated around the walls. Babineaux, Mary, and Lestrange knelt to peer down into the hole, their mouths open, waiting for the inspector to tell them what he could see.

"My God!"

"What iz it!?" Babineaux shouted excitedly down into the cellar.

"There's a man down here!" came Mike's startled response.

It took a second or two for things to click, but when they did, strong instincts took over. Mary hitched up her habit and leaped down into the hole, her skirts acting like a parachute, her veil like a sail. She landed precisely and lightly on the stones below. She ran toward the beam of light, slamming into the inspector.

"What are you doing, Mary?" Mike exclaimed.

"Where is he?" Mary instructed, her voice gruff and uncharacteristically low.

Mike cast the flashlight's beam to illuminate a dirty thin figure slumped against the wall in the corner of the chamber.

"Oh!" Sister Mary said, as if days of hurt and pain were being experienced all at once. She threw herself down next to the figure who rolled his head at the sight of her. "Raphael! Raphael! You're alive!"

The young man raised a weak smile. He looked a sight. His lips were chapped, his face gaunt. Dust had mingled with tears to leave his skin streaked with dirt. And yet, despite his suffering, it was still possible to make out Raphael's chiseled cheekbones and strong jaw, the handsome features that had paraded along the catwalks of Paris. Mike walked over to the opening and shouted up. "Water!!" he yelled. "Quickly!"

Once again, after some rummaging, Lestrange and his jacket came to the rescue. He passed a bottle of water to Babineaux who tossed it down to Mike.

"He must have been here since everything kicked off. He's in pretty bad shape," Mike said to Mary, crouching next to her and handing her the water. "Look, he's been knocking on the pipes with that piece of wood. That was what I could hear."

"Raphael," Mary said, "drink this." She gently tipped the water between his parted lips. The man closed his eyes as the cool liquid moistened his dry mouth.

"It's alright," Mike said, gently pressing a hand on Raphael's shoulder. "We're here now, and you're alive. We'll get you to a hospital."

"What iz 'appening?" Babineaux's voice wafted into the cellar from the trapdoor. "Iz everyzing okay?"

"Yes!" Mike said, standing up and walking back to the opening to see the long oval face of the French detective peering down at him like a full moon. "We've found Father Raphael. It looks like he's been trapped here since the murder."

"Sacré bleu!" Babineaux cried. "We must arrest 'im!"

"Are you insane?"

"It iz ze perfect crime! 'e killed ze priest and 'id 'imself away where no one could find 'im!"

Mike rubbed the bridge of his nose and shook his head. "For

crying out loud, what are you talking about? Get a doctor, you fool!"

Mike looked back at the couple on the ground. Mary was kneeling on the floor offering Raphael some more water. She was tenderly wiping his face with a white handkerchief when she stroked Raphael's face. "I'm so sorry Raphael... I've thought so much about what you said... I haven't thought about anything else. And then, I thought you were... The answer's yes. Of course it is! Yes, Raphael! I will marry you. Nothing would make me happier! I'm just so sorry I had to say it like this! Please forgive me for making you wait so long!"

Mike's eyes widened. He almost dropped his flashlight. *Father Raphael proposed to Sister Mary? How can a half-dead priest who's spent days trapped in a cellar be doing better than I am?*

CHAPTER FIFTY-ONE

THAT EVENING, WHILE Father Raphael recovered at Doctor Giroux's cottage hospital, Sister Mary a constant presence at his side, Annabelle, Mike, and Babineaux had dinner together at *Chez Selwyn*. On the way to the restaurant, Mike had told Annabelle about Mary's acceptance of Father Raphael's marriage proposal. Annabelle had smiled serenely. "I'm sure they will be very happy," had been her only comment.

The meal lasted five hours, and everything about it was intense and passionate. Only a third of the time was spent eating. The rest was spent debating, talking over one another, and occasionally listening to various points and counterpoints. Halfway through, even Mike began gesturing with his hands. Their fellow patrons around them in the restaurant ate in silence, listening intently to the talk of murder, conspiracy, and other nefarious acts until toward the end of the night, they too had formed their opinions and began to argue among themselves.

"It doesn't make *sense*," Annabelle said, waving a piece of wine-infused beef on the end of her fork. "Why would Father Raphael lock himself up in a secret cellar?"

"But do you not see, *Révérend*," Babineaux answered, opening his arms wide imploringly. "To make 'imself look like ze *perfect victim*."

"No," Mike said gruffly, shaking his head. "You're wrong. You saw the rug placed over the trapdoor. Father Raphael couldn't have got himself down there *and* pulled the rug into place."

Babineaux shrugged and waved Mike's comment away. "A passerby, or ze nuns, perhaps—zey see ze rug, zey fix it! You are focusing on ze details *too* much!"

"He nearly *died!*" Annabelle exclaimed, through a mouthful of beef.

"Not every criminal iz a competent one," Babineaux replied quickly. "Maybe 'e intended to 'ide and zen found 'e couldn't get 'imself out of ze predicament 'e got 'imself into."

"You've been barking up the wrong tree from the start, Bambino," Mike said.

"I do not know what zat means—but I assume by your tone it iz not a compliment," Babineaux said, with a tilt of his head. "If not ze Father Raphael, zen who? You are very good at dismissing my instincts and you 'ave spent much effort in exonerating ze priest," Babineaux admonished from behind a waving finger. "But you 'ave offered me no other suspect. So I ask you, if not ze Father Raphael, who? Me? Ze waiter? Ze ghost of Moriarty?"

Mike sighed and looked at Annabelle, deferring to her. She furrowed her brow.

"Father Julien and Mother Renate had a connection…"

"Oh! Again with ze *connexion*! We do not even know if ze Mother Superior was murdered! It is still officially a suicide, *Révérend!*" Babineaux said, stopping as Mike glared at him to allow Annabelle to finish.

"And I've been thinking. What if… what if they had a child

together? A child they gave up for adoption before Mother Renate joined the church."

"*Sacré bleu!*" Babineaux said, fanning himself with a napkin. "And you accuse *me* of fairytales. You are going from A to P to Q and back to A again! *Révérend*! I must say, ze English seem to 'ave a better grasp of concocting mysteries zan zey are at solving zem!"

"But you see, today I was at the convent, asking questions. Strange things kept happening. Dangerous things. Things designed to scare me, put me off, even harm me. Someone didn't want me there. I don't think that convent is the pure, devotional, holy place it is purported to be. I think they are hiding things."

"*Quelle imagination! Imaginations fantastiques!*" Babineaux scoffed.

"Are you alright? Are you hurt?" Mike asked. This was the first he'd heard of Annabelle's challenging day. He put a hand on her arm, his eyes full of concern.

"I'm fine. But it was disconcerting. I think we need to look further into the goings on there."

"Zere iz another possibility..." Inspector Babineaux said slowly.

"Oh? What other possibility is that?" Annabelle asked.

"Well..." he began, before stopping himself and sighing heavily.

"Go on! What is it?"

"*Révérend*, you know 'ow I respect you. I 'ave seen many times 'ow intelligent and insightful you are..."

"What are you on about, Inspector? Please, spill the beans!"

"Somezing else I do not understand but I zink you mean me to 'urry up. One person brought you 'ere with ze sole purpose of exonerating Father Raphael. Ze same person who does not get along with ze other nuns. Ze same person who keeps inviting you to ze convent where strange zings 'appen to you."

Mike looked at Babineaux, then back at Annabelle. He fiddled with the stem of his wine glass.

"Inspector, you can't...!" Annabelle was breathing so heavily her shoulders rose and fell despite the weight of Mike's heavy hand he placed there to calm her. She opened her mouth several times to start speaking, but couldn't find words to express herself. After one more deep breath she finally said in a strangled voice, "I have known Mary since I was a baby."

"Iz she loyal? Would she do anyzing for you?"

"Of course!"

"Zen I imagine she would do just zat for Father Raphael too. She is madly in love with 'im."

Once again, Annabelle found herself stunned into silence. "I can't believe what you're saying," she said eventually, shaking her head vigorously.

"We cannot ignore ze facts. Inspector Mike keeps saying so."

"You think Raphael killed Julien, and that Mary has been protecting him all along?" Pink spots appeared on Annabelle's cheeks.

Babineaux pursed his lips and turned down the corners of his mouth. He gave a little shrug and crossed his legs. He placed his hands crossed at his wrists over his knee. "Maybe."

"Mary would never be involved with anyone who had committed such a terrible crime."

"Perhaps you don't know your friend as well as you thought. Before you arrived 'ere, did she tell you she was in love with a priest? Zat 'e 'ad proposed marriage to 'er?

"Well, I..."

Babineaux tapped the side of his nose. "It iz best to keep an open mind, no?"

"Well, yes, but..."

"Zen we shall. We will open our minds, and," Babineaux leaned toward Annabelle, smiling now, "our 'earts."

The three diners went back and forth long into the night. The sun set over the church, and eventually the only light left was the flickering candles at the table and the old-fashioned lamps that hung in the church square. After a dessert of cheesecake topped with figs and honey (Annabelle had seconds) and unable to agree on anything at all, they took their leave of one another, sufficiently comfortable now, having drunk enough wine, to exchange kisses on the cheek before departing. Even Mike submitted.

CHAPTER FIFTY-TWO

THE NEXT MORNING, Annabelle was first to breakfast. She felt down and discouraged as she rifled among the books looking for something to pass the time while she waited for Mike. She eventually settled on an English magazine and got stuck in to an interview with the star of a British period drama that was winning awards on both sides of the Atlantic. She quickly became engrossed. Claude brought her some coffee and pastries. "Would you like some eggs, *Révérend?*" he asked her, "Or cheese and some freshly baked bread?"

Annabelle looked up from her magazine and beamed at him. "Yes, please."

When he had gone, Annabelle stared across the lawn, her interest in her magazine taking second place to her thoughts for the moment. Babineaux's comments about Mary the previous evening were gnawing at her. Not for one moment, did she believe that Mary had anything to do with Father Julien's death, but Babineaux was right about one thing. Mary had kept a secret from her. A big one. And while Annabelle understood why Mary had done so, it made her heart break just a little. Over time, things changed. Alliances shifted. That's just how it was. They weren't young girls anymore. They were adults with big grownup issues to navigate. Annabelle shook herself and picked up her magazine again.

Claude returned as Annabelle was flicking through pages trying to find the conclusion to her article.

"Claude, you've been here since...?"

"1964, *Révérend*."

"So since before Father Julien arrived?"

"*Oui*, our previous priest died. He was very old. It was rumored he was over a hundred."

"Gosh, that is old. So you first met Father Julien what, sixteen years ago? That's when he took up his post here, isn't it?"

"Oh no, I met him for the first time several years before that. He was doing construction work in the village. He moved on to become a priest and later returned here to serve the Lord. He always said he liked the village so much, he found a way to come back. Many people feel that way about this place." Claude wrinkled his forehead as though he couldn't understand why.

"Interesting!" Annabelle looked at the tray Claude was carrying. "What examples of heavenly deliciousness have you brought for my breakfast today?"

Claude didn't smile at Annabelle's playfulness. Claude never smiled. Solemnly, he recited the tray's contents. "I have cheese soufflé, warm fruit compôte, pain au chocolat, ham and cheeses with some rye bread."

"Rye bread?"

"*Oui*, it is particularly good with the ham. Did you see a pig as you went about?"

Annabelle thought back to her first stroll around the village. She nodded.

"Well, you won't see it anymore."

Annabelle shut her eyes for a long moment. "That's nice, how very... rural."

"Rye was Father Julien's favorite bread. He had some every day." Claude deposited the food on the table and shuffled away. Annabelle ignored the ham and pressed some brie onto the bread and took a big bite.

She chewed slowly, her thoughts turning to the case and her experiences of the past few days. She felt forlorn. Guilt for dragging Mike on this trip to nowhere, a feeling of sorrow around her altered relationship with Mary, and frustration that there was still no solution in sight to the mystery of Father Julien's murder. She gave a great sigh and pressed more brie onto her bread.

"What's up?" Mike said when he arrived a few minutes later, finger combing his wet hair into a modicum of order. Annabelle was flicking the pages of her magazine back and forth furiously. Finally, she slapped it onto the seat of the chair next to her. "I do hate it when they do that."

"What?"

"Put the end of an article at the back of a magazine where you can't find it. Never mind, it's nothing."

Mike sat down and forked a piece of ham onto his bread. "Listen, I forgot to tell you last night what with all the kerfuffle about finding Father Raphael and Mary, and... you know. Anyway, before we found him, we discovered that a gold box containing the relic of St. Agnès is missing. It's normally kept in a recess in the back room where the confessionals are, but it's disappeared. Mary said this was a big deal. Is that right?"

"It is. I wonder where it might have gone."

"Who would want such a thing?"

Annabelle thought. "I can't imagine. People used to believe that relics were capable of performing miracles, many still do. It's not that unusual."

"Hmm, they're not short on unusual people in this village, that's for sure. But maybe the relic wasn't the target. Would the box have been valuable? If it were stolen, the thief might have taken it for its resale value and not have known about the relic, or cared."

"Then they'd get a nasty surprise when they opened the box."

They heard footsteps and Mary appeared around the corner of the auberge.

"Mary!" Annabelle cried. "How lovely to see you. What are you doing here so early?"

CHAPTER FIFTY-THREE

"MORNING, ANNABELLE, MIKE. I'm so sorry to interrupt your breakfast," Mary said sincerely, wringing her hands. "But I thought you'd want to know as soon as possible."

"It's fine Mary," Annabelle said, rubbing a hand on her friends arm. "What is it? Not more bad news? How is Father Raphael doing?"

Sister Mary took a few breaths and nodded. "Better. He's in a state of shock—delirium. Doctor Giroux says he'll sleep it off, and with plenty of rest he should be fine in a few days."

"That's good to hear," Mike said.

"And how are *you* doing?"

Mary gave a little smile. "I'm fine. Lots to do, you know. People to tell. But that's not really what I came to say," she said, growing anxious again. "Raphael woke up—only for a brief moment—but he said something."

"What?"

"He just said... It was ever so strange... '*The nuns*'."

"The nuns?" Mike repeated.

Mary nodded. "I wanted to ask him more, but I didn't want to stress him, and he fell back asleep right away. It could have been a dream, or something... I don't know. Annabelle, Mike, you don't think it could mean that... well, um, the nuns put him in there? Down that hole?"

Annabelle sighed sympathetically and looked at Mike.

"After what happened to you yesterday... all those 'accidents'...?" Mike said.

Annabelle knit her brows and waggled her lips back and forth as she thought.

"I should go back to Raphael," Mary said. "I just thought you'd want to know."

"Okay, Mary, we'll see you later," Annabelle said, patting Mary's arm as she nodded and hurried away. "Oh! Mary! Wait!"

Sister Mary stopped and looked back at them.

"Just out of curiosity, are there any nuns in the convent that are in their mid-twenties? Twenty-four or twenty-five?"

Mary brought a finger to her lip as she considered the question.

"I'm not sure... Véronique, perhaps. Sister Josephine, for sure. Her birthday was just last month. I don't think there are any others. Not that I can think of off the top of my head, sorry." Mary left, leaving Annabelle and Mike to look at each other with thoughtful expressions.

"That was an interesting question," Mike said. "Why did you ask that?"

"Just something I've been thinking about."

"And...?"

"It's just wild speculation. I have no evidence and I know how you are about evidence." Annabelle was idly spreading more brie on her bread. It was thick and creamy, and she left butter knife marks in it as she pressed down.

"Alright, but you clearly have a theory."

Annabelle sighed and put down her knife. "Claude just told

me that Father Julien worked in the village before he was a priest. He did some construction here."

"Okay."

"Well, that would put him in the village when Renate was at university in Reims not too far away. It strengthens the idea that there was something between them."

"And you think if Mother Renate did have a secret child, that child, now grown, might be at the convent?"

Annabelle shrugged. "It's a possibility."

"But why would you think that?"

Annabelle leaned on the table, her shoulders slumped. "No reason, just my fanciful imagination. You're right. And really, if Renate and Julien did have a child, why would the child track them down by pretending to be a nun? I'm just letting my imagination go wild. Too many romance novels, I suppose. Forget I said anything. It's a silly idea." She picked up her butter knife again and started bouncing it on top of the brie. It made a pleasing thumping sound.

"Interesting that Sister Josephine is the right age, though," Mike said.

"How so?"

"I had a thought when I was at the church yesterday. Mary said that as soon as Father Julien fell to the ground, Sister Josephine started crying."

"That's plausible."

"Not really," Mike said. "All he did was fall. Everyone was shocked, yes, some people rushed to his side—but to just start crying? No one could have known he was dead at that point."

Annabelle's eyes widened.

"What is it?"

"What if Father Julien and Mother Renate were in a relationship while she was at university and he was working in the village. She found out she was pregnant and went to Switzerland to have her baby. After secretly giving up her child, she entered a convent, perhaps out of shame. And then that child sought them out. A child seeking to wreak revenge on those who abandoned her!"

Mike huffed the way he sometimes did when he was considering a possibility with huge ramifications. "Perhaps you *have* been reading too many romance novels."

"That's what you said before about Mary and Raphael. And I was right then. Do you think we're getting warm?" Annabelle added when there was no response from Mike.

"Well, it's a theory, certainly. But...." If he were honest, Mike thought the reality of this was about as likely as him adopting Babineaux's grooming habits. But this was Annabelle talking... He grabbed her hand. "Oh, come on. There's only one way to check it out. Let's go!"

CHAPTER FIFTY-FOUR

IN A CLOUD of dust, Annabelle drove the Mini to the convent. Her hands and feet pounded and pummeled her gearstick, brakes, clutch, and accelerator as she manipulated them all with the coordinated skill and precision of a rally car driver while Mike held on to the dashboard, eyeing Annabelle warily while being shaken to a frenzy from which he wondered if he'd ever recover. When the convent buildings came into view, the car skidded to a halt on the loose dirt. Annabelle turned the engine off sharply and was out of the car in a flash. Mike matched her for timing and pace even though he didn't quite know where Annabelle was headed.

The sounds of doors slamming caught the attention of a nun who seemed to have a cold. She blew into a handkerchief as Annabelle called to her, waving.

"Hello? Sister Colette?"

The nun glanced around anxiously before trotting over to them. *"Bonjour?"* she said. Her nose was red, her eyes watery.

"Hello," Annabelle said once again, trying to smile through her panting.

The nun gave Mike a quick glance before looking away. "*Pardonnez-moi, s'il vous plaît,* no men allowed," she whispered to Annabelle.

"That's okay," Mike said, quickly offering a placating palm. "Is Sister Josephine around? Perhaps she can come out to talk to us."

"Josephine?" the nun said. Behind her, the bakery truck emerged from the back of the convent and rumbled slowly past them.

"Yes. Josephine," Annabelle said. "Here?" She pointed to the ground then to her open mouth. "To talk?"

"Josephine? No, Josephine not here," the nun said, her eyes anxiously moving to the departing truck.

Mike tugged on Annabelle's arm. "Annabelle," he said.

"Hold on, Mike." Annabelle pulled her arm away and looked back at the nun. "When will she be back? Erm... *Quando... Ici... Zurück?*"

On hearing a French word among two unrecognizable ones, the nun launched into more than a few sentences of fast, complex French, replete with gestures, shrugs, and even a little giggle at the end.

"*Pardonnez moi, mais...*" Annabelle stuttered as Mike continued to watch the truck speed up as it trundled down the track.

"Annabelle, I think..."

"Mike! Please! Erm... *Quelle heure...*" Annabelle said, tapping her watch in front of the nun. "Josephine come back *ici?*" she said, making swirly gestures with her hands before pointing down at the ground.

The nun continued to talk in complicated, frenetic French. Annabelle didn't understand a word.

"Annabelle!" Mike barked suddenly. "She's in that truck!"

Annabelle looked behind her quickly to see the vehicle crest the brow of a hill and disappear. She looked at Mike, then at the nun, and back to Mike again. "Blast!" she said. She sprinted to the Mini.

Annabelle had the car in motion in seconds, the inspector flailing to close his door as she reversed. After she'd spun the Mini like a pro, she revved the motor as they zoomed down the dirt track away from the convent.

"Are you sure?" she shouted to Mike over the noise of the roaring engine.

"I don't understand French, but I understand body language—and that nun was stalling," came Mike's reply. He held onto the dashboard again, this time for dear life.

As they sped along, they passed Babineaux and Lestrange lounging next to their 2CV parked on the side of the track. Lestrange watched them drive by while Babineaux leaned against the car smoking a thin cigar.

Ignoring them, Annabelle pressed on. She caught sight of the truck just as it reached the end of the track. To the right was the road that led to the village. To the left was the wood and beyond that the highway to the rest of France. The truck turned... left. Annabelle sped up. She took the turn with the inch-perfect racing line of a Formula One driver and gained plenty of ground on the truck just before it turned a corner and disappeared from view. Annabelle raced to the corner and threw the car into it, dropping down a gear with a deft flick of her wrist almost without slowing. Mike braced himself against his door and the dashboard. He correctly anticipated a fearsome pull of gravity as Annabelle negotiated the adverse camber of the road surface. She turned the car so sharply that the Mini rode on two wheels for several yards before righting itself, causing Mike to suppress a shout of fear that they would tip over. Once all four wheels were back on the ground, they looked ahead for signs of the truck, but it was nowhere to be seen. It had disappeared. Annabelle slammed on her brakes and stopped the car, their seatbelts the only thing keeping Mike and her from flying through the windshield.

"Where did they go?" she said, scanning the horizon.

"There's only one way *to* go. They are heading for the highway. She's escaping!" Mike replied.

Annabelle didn't need to be told twice. She plunged her foot down again on the accelerator, causing the Mini to shoot forward, not thinking twice now about two-wheeling it around corners in pursuit of the truck. Her sole focus was to chase it down that long, rough road that was the only way in—and out—of Ville d'Eauloise. And yet despite her efforts, when they reached the hill that led up through the woods, the truck was a mere dot disappearing into the shadow of the dense trees.

"Damnit!" Mike said, as Annabelle built up momentum to attack the hill. "By the time we reach them they'll be on the highway!"

Annabelle answered by gritting her teeth and pressing down harder on the gas pedal. "Not if I have anything to do with it!" she cried as the car powered up the hill. "My Mini is a nippy little thing, and we can catch up to a rumbling old truck, no problem." She gripped her steering wheel until her knuckles were white. If she could drive the car up the hill using nothing but her determination, she would. Her lips pinched and her eyes narrowed with effort. The road was still rough, and she and Mike bounced up and down inside the small car like a couple of pieces of popcorn at the bottom of an empty bag, but they were too focused to be concerned. With their eyes fixed ahead, they slipped under the canopy of the oak trees. There was no sign of the truck. They ploughed on.

"Look!" Annabelle said.

"What? I don't see anything!" Mike cried.

"Exactly! We should be seeing the truck. It's disappeared. Where's it gone?"

Mike peered around. In the distance, in the midst of the oak trees, he saw the truck lumbering away from them, weaving around tree trunks and fallen branches as it attempted to get away. "There!" he pointed. "It's gone off-road."

Annabelle spun the steering wheel and once again set off after the truck. As she eased her beloved car across country, wincing as she jolted the underside against debris and rock, another vehicle appeared among the trees ahead of them.

"Don't tell me they've got an accomplice!" Mike exclaimed, just before he bashed his head on the car roof.

His answer came quickly. With a precision and a maneuverability that impressed even Annabelle, the other vehicle approached the truck from the side, gained speed to overtake it and then dramatically swerved in front of it to cut it off. It slid sideways, cutting lengthwise across the truck's path, causing the driver to slam on the brakes, stopping mere inches from the other vehicle, as Annabelle's Mini pulled up and pinned it from behind.

"It's Babineaux!" Annabelle exclaimed.

"Well, well, well..." Mike said.

But it was not Babineaux who quickly and purposefully got out of the driver's seat, whipping out his police badge and wielding it in front of him as he walked toward the truck. It was Lestrange.

By the time Annabelle and Mike clambered from the Mini, two nuns had climbed out of the truck and were remonstrating loudly with the sergeant. Inspector Babineaux was slower to emerge. His door flung open and after two long seconds, he staggered out of the 2CV groaning slightly, his burgundy three-piece suit creased and a little dusty in a way that obviously displeased him.

CHAPTER FIFTY-FIVE

ANNABELLE AND MIKE eagerly jogged toward the fracas. As they ran up, Babineaux was yelling in French at Lestrange who yelled at the nuns, who yelled at both of the policemen seemingly indiscriminately. Annabelle suspected that even a fluent knowledge of French wouldn't help her understand what on earth was happening. The four furious French people were so passionately engrossed that they barely noticed the two English visitors.

"Everybody!" Mike shouted, in his most vehement crowd-control voice. "Calm down!" His tone was loud and forceful, causing them all to spin around and stunning them into silence. "What the hell is going on here, Bambino?" Mike said.

"Lestrange has gone mad!" Babineaux said, throwing his hands up in the air then gesturing down at his dirty trousers as if they were proof of his sergeant's compromised mental health. "We were sitting on ze side of ze road one second, and ze next second, 'e seizes ze car! I tried to stop 'im but all I could do was jump in ze passenger window! 'e starts driving through ze fields and through ze trees! 'e drove through ze forest with my legs dangling on ze outside! 'e could 'ave killed me!"

Babineaux turned to glare at Lestrange who quickly began explaining himself in French. His superior officer was having none of it, and off they went again gesticulating and explicating.

"One at a time!" Mike shouted, stopping the chaos before it got dug in too far. "What is Lestrange saying?"

Lestrange launched into a monologue neither Annabelle nor Mike could understand.

"Oof!" Babineaux cried out. He threw his hands up in the air and walked off a short way, his hands on his hips. "'e iz crazy! 'e iz talking nonsense!"

"But what is he saying?" Annabelle asked insistently.

Babineaux took a deep breath, looked at Lestrange who was still talking, then turned back to the English visitors.

"'e says zat when 'e saw ze truck leaving ze convent, 'e knew somezing, 'ow do you say, was *up*. Zat zey 'ad no reason to leave today..." Babineaux paused as Lestrange continued to talk. "'e says 'e 'as been observing zeir delivery schedule and zat since Mother Renate died zey 'ave not produced any new batches of bread, and zat zere is no reason ze truck should be leaving... Zen 'e says zat... *Mon Dieu!* But it is too *stupide!*"

"Tell us," Mike growled.

With another sigh and a melodramatic shrug of his shoulders, Babineaux continued. "I am sorry to translate such idiotic zings—even in translation I feel a fool for letting zem pass my lips. My sergeant says 'e zinks ze nuns are 'iding somezing. Zat..." Babineaux stopped to laugh, rub his face, and shake his head despairingly. "Zat you were chasing zem, so 'e thought 'e would 'elp. *Quelle bouffon!*" He turned to glare at his hapless sergeant.

Mike and Annabelle exchanged a quick glance. "He was right. We were chasing them," Annabelle said.

Babineaux's eyes went wide with shock, before he slapped a hand to his face and looked up to the heavens imploringly.

"We think Josephine might be the love child of Father Julien and Mother Renate and that she murdered both of them as revenge for having abandoned her," Annabelle informed him.

Mike raised his eyebrows, his eyes widening fractionally at Babineaux who looked at him incredulously, man to man, detective to detective, for confirmation. Mike looked down at the ground briefly. Suddenly, there was a clanging at the back of the truck. The gathered group moved as one to stand behind it as the doors swung open, revealing the figure of the nun that was hiding in there.

"Véronique!" Annabelle cried.

The young, shy nun, the aspirant that was trying on the sisterhood for size, looked out at them. She was no longer dressed in her demure clothes but in a pair of jeans and a pink t-shirt. There were tasseled, suede ankle boots on her feet. She looked no less beautiful than earlier, but there was a serious, hard expression on her face as she stepped down from the truck with the grace and poise of a queen descending her throne.

Her audience was speechless. Véronique stood in front of them, her shoulders back, chin raised, proud and defiant. All traces of the hesitant young woman she had been were gone. "Very well," she said, her voice firm. "I suppose this is the end."

CHAPTER FIFTY-SIX

IT WASN'T THE most conventional place to conduct an interview. In fact it wasn't conventional at all. They had considered the office of Doctor Giroux, but with Raphael recovering there, it had seemed inappropriate. Annabelle had suggested the auberge, but eventually they had settled upon Babineaux's 'office' after the café owner agreed to shut the blinds and close for several hours while they interviewed Véronique.

At a round table in the corner, a single lamp above them illuminating it, Véronique sat with her back to the wall, her hands clasped in front of her, and her back ramrod straight. Detective Babineaux and Annabelle sat opposite her, while behind them Lestrange and Mike leaned against the café counter.

Babineaux had changed his creased, dusty suit for a fresh, navy-blue pinstripe and felt all the more composed for it. With a flamboyant flourish, he plucked his phone from his pocket, set it to record, and placed it in the middle of the table.

"For ze benefit of our foreign friends," Babineaux said, gesturing to Annabelle, "please conduct zis interview in English."

"Alright," Véronique said, swiveling her eyes to Babineaux

while keeping her head fixed forward in an upright, regal position.

"So, I assume you wish to confess," Babineaux announced, "and I suggest we begin with your death threats to Father Julien. Ze motive behind zem."

Without flinching, Véronique said, "I don't know what you are talking about."

"You wish to pursue zis charade? We found you in ze back of ze truck, I remind you. Dressed in..." Babineaux waved at Véronique's clothes, *"vêtements civils."*

"I wished to run away from the convent," Véronique said. "I didn't like it there. I do not want to become a nun. That is my confession."

There was a pause. Annabelle and Babineaux exchanged apprehensive glances.

"Véronique," Annabelle said, putting her hand on the table between them as if offering something, "as an aspirant, there's no need to run away. You weren't being kept there against your will. Simply notifying Sister Simone would have sufficed. Something else is going on."

Annabelle was interrupted by a haughty snort of derision. *"Ridicule,"* Véronique said.

"It's only a matter of time before we find out, Véronique," Mike said wearily, walking over. "I know you want to keep your dignity, but you're not doing that by delaying the inevitable."

"I am being dignified because I am innocent!" the young woman offered angrily.

"Listen to me," Mike said, crossly, "you can confess now and your sentence will probably be lenient. But if you don't, you will certainly be punished harshly. DNA tests will be run to confirm your parentage. Fingerprint testing will be performed on the death threats. Searches of your room will be performed for traces of the poison and the glue used in the letters. Interviews will be conducted with the other nuns and the chances are that at least one of them will tell the police everything. But even without that, we will dredge up enough evidence to convict you during a trial. It will be long, painful, and humiliating for you—so I ask you to do this for your own sake. Confess and face the consequences under an umbrella of truth, rather than fighting hopelessly."

Véronique's head turned by only a few degrees, her green eyes—now so obviously reminiscent of Mother Renate's—piercing the assembled congregation.

"Quite a speech," she said. "I imagine it would work—*if* I were guilty."

Mike sighed loudly and went to the counter to grab a coffee. "This could last well into the night."

"Very well," Babineaux said slowly, stroking his moustache, "if you do not want to tell a story, I shall tell one myself. Let's presume ze first zing you ever knew was ze inside of an adoption center. Was it an expensive one? Or a poor one?" Babineaux dismissed his idea with a flick of his wrist. "It doesn't matter because of course, soon a family took you. 'ow could zey not? So beautiful! With such *belle* green eyes and thick raven 'air. Such a sweet *bébé*! And zey spoiled you, indeed. You bear all ze signs of a girl flattered. Look at you!"

Véronique's nose twitched. Everyone noticed it. Silently, Mike brought over his coffee cup without a saucer from the bar, his shirt sleeves rolled up, sipping it slowly as he watched what was unfolding. Annabelle leaned her forearms on the table, her hands clasped.

"You do not bear ze subdued manner of one who 'as been bullied," Babineaux said with a wry smile and a wave of his hand. "*Non*, rather, you 'ave ze cunning way with ze words and ze self-control of one who iz a very clever bully 'erself."

Véronique cleared her throat and looked away. Babineaux glanced quickly at Annabelle, smiling and giving her a quick wink before continuing. Véronique shuffled her shoulders, her face tense. The French detective had taken away her one defense. He could see under her skin.

"But to 'ave everyzing only reminds us of ze one zing we are missing, does it not? For you, zat was your birth parents. You were so wonderful, so *special*. 'ow could zey abandon you? *Alors*, 'ow zat question must 'ave burned! Was zere somezing wrong with you? Somezing you did not realize? A young girl growing up must lie awake every night wondering such zings. Ah! But zere was an answer! You just needed to find zem.

"But 'ow did you do zat? No doubt through a *combinaison* of your charm, beauty, and intelligence—information, 'ints your adoptive parents gave you. You came to zis small village, tucked away in ze valley of ze French countryside, to find zat both of your parents 'ad become leading figures in ze church! Ze gall! Ze audacity! Two people who 'ad committed ze terrible sin of abandoning you were now masquerading as pure devotees of ze good Lord! But *ma cherie*! Why did you simply not tell zem? No doubt zey would 'ave taken you in zeir arms and expressed ze love for you zat you felt you deserved?"

Véronique's face contorted into an expression of utter disgust. "I would have spit on their *love*! They are not worth the ground they will rot within!" Annabelle quickly sat back in her chair in the face of this sudden vitriol. Véronique was clearly done holding back.

"Yes! I hated them! And I am not sorry they're dead. And you may condemn me for it, but they tossed me aside like some unwanted gift. How long did they suffer? The priest, hardly at all? Mother Superior, a few seconds? *I've* suffered from the moment I was born!"

"But Véronique," Annabelle said slowly. "You could have shouted a bit, even thrown some things. Why did you have to kill?"

CHAPTER FIFTY-SEVEN

VÉRONIQUE PURSED HER lips tightly, her chest rising and falling with hot breath, her eyes closed until she eventually spoke, her words hard-edged and taut.

"I didn't kill anyone!" She pointed at Babineaux. "He's right! It *was* outrageous for them to claim to be so holy, so divine. I would have preferred it if Julien were a criminal and Renate a drunk; I could have understood then. I would have been able to explain why they abandoned me. But they were upright, thriving, and devout. There was nothing stopping them from raising me as their own—nothing but their own selfishness.

"I came here, and every week I would watch Julien lecture people on serving the Lord, on morality, on doing good in the eyes of God—all while he had committed the sin of abandoning me to an unknown life. And Renate? Mother Superior? Ha! It's ironic to call her that, isn't it? To see her, every day, commanding the other sisters, telling them what to do, acting like the ultimate wise woman, a voice of supreme guidance. And yet she couldn't, wouldn't, face censure and raise a tiny, defenseless baby. She was a coward. For shame. She *sickened* me. But I was simply curious.

I wanted to find out about them, so I posed as a wannabe nun so I could see them up close." Véronique grabbed a glass of water from the table and gulped hungrily from it as the others exchanged glances.

Annabelle tried a different tack. "Let's move on. What about Father Raphael being found in a cellar in the church? Did you have anything to do with that?"

Véronique laughed, seeming to relish the explanation of her deeds now, as if reliving them. "Do-gooder Father Raphael," she said slowly. "Always in the way. So pure, so perfect, so respected. But he was dishonest, too. Just like the others. I saw how he looked at Mary. I saw them in the orchard once, heard them professing their love for one another. They were just as bad as Renate and Julien. Lying, cheating, dishonest. Yes, I had something to do with that. But it was just a bit of fun."

"Bit of fun? He would have died if Mike hadn't found him!" Annabelle cried.

Véronique shrugged. "But he didn't, did he?"

"How?" Mike asked. "How did you trap Father Raphael in the cellar?"

"Perfect planning, of course," Véronique said, as if they were merely making small talk. "I knew that all eyes would be on Julien at the front of the church as he said Easter Mass. I told one of the nuns to call Raphael to the confessional booths the moment Julien went to the altar. The nuns did whatever I asked and believed anything I told them. They were in thrall to me, so naïve, so gullible. A few stories, some chocolate, and a magazine or two, and they are anybody's. The nun told Raphael a story about noises coming from the cellar. The silly man trusted her enough to go down there himself. You can guess the rest. It was just a coincidence that Julien chose that moment to die. I knew you'd find Raphael eventually."

Annabelle shook her head and looked away as Babineaux let

out a brief sigh of disgust. Only Mike kept his eyes steadily on the young woman.

"And what of Mother Renate," he said. "What do you have to say about her death?"

Véronique shook her head. "She was no loss. No one will miss her. The other nuns hated Renate almost as much as I did. Do any of you even know how much of a slave-driver she was? Sometimes the nuns would only sleep three hours a night. She would have them doing the work of farmhands in the daytime, expect them to pray half the night when they were almost dead from heat and exertion, and then get up in the early hours to bake bread! If she was killed, take a hard look at the nuns. Renate was a control-freak. A tyrant."

"I guess that's where you get it from," Mike quipped.

Véronique ignored him. "I also enjoyed making things difficult for you too, *Révérend*, but you were a slippery fish."

"The millstone," Annabelle said slowly. "Locking me in the shed."

Véronique shrugged and chuckled lightly to herself. "You were just too good. Pitiable attempts, I know, but that's what you get for telling the thick-headed nuns to 'think' for themselves. They couldn't think if their lives depended on it. All they can do is follow orders, routines, daily devotions. Spare me." Véronique looked at her nails and gave them a quick buff on her t-shirt before fixing Annabelle again with her emerald green eyes. "Listen, I may have played around, but I didn't kill anyone."

"I don't believe you," Babineaux said. "I zink it was time for you to make a stealthy departure from Ville d'Eauloise before our investigations led us to you," he added. "You figured zat if you left quietly, you would 'ave been long gone before we knew about it. Zat was why you were in zat truck."

Véronique sat back and folded her arms. "You are quite wrong, Inspector. I wanted out and knew that if I left publicly I would be subject to a whole lot of questioning that I didn't have the patience for. I decided to slip away. It was easy to convince the nuns I was the victim, and they offered to help me. Once Renate was dead, they were rudderless. They were, I believe the English call it, 'like putty in my hands.'"

"I don't believe you." With one final, dramatic, gesture, Babineaux reached over the table, turned off the recorder, and secreted his phone into his pocket once more. "I 'ave 'eard enough!" he said. He turned to Lestrange and said something in French, prompting the sergeant to take out his cuffs and lock them over Véronique's wrists. Babineaux got up. "Take 'er away and charge 'er!"

"With what?" Annabelle asked.

"Conspiracy, kidnapping, attempted murder! And we shall zink of more, no doubt. You may be beautiful *mademoiselle*, but zere is no beauty in your 'eart. And 'ow you got those nuns to 'elp you, I will never know." Babineaux flicked his head dismissing the young woman. Lestrange led Véronique away.

Babineaux sat back and slapped his thighs, exhaling deeply as he let the tension of the interview evaporate. With a clap of his hands, he made a proposal. "Shall we take some afternoon tea, *Révérend*? I zink we are done 'ere."

When there was no reply, he looked over. Annabelle wasn't paying attention. She was scrolling on her phone. Suddenly she grabbed her purse and her car keys and ran outside. Once again, Mike and Babineaux found themselves watching Annabelle race to her car. A moment later, all that was left in her wake was exhaust fumes.

CHAPTER FIFTY-EIGHT

"WHERE IS SHE going?" Babineaux cried out.

"I don't know, but wherever it is, she's not going there for fun," Mike replied. They ran to the 2CV.

"*Allez, allez!*" Babineaux cried out to Lestrange. The sergeant stopped reading Véronique her rights and looked up. After a moment's indecision, Lestrange handcuffed Véronique to a lamppost, and jumped into the car after the other two men.

"I bet she's going to the convent," Mike cried from the back as Lestrange turned sharply out of the plaza and up the hill out of the village. Mike was hanging on to the back of both front seats as he tried to prevent himself from being tossed about like a lettuce in a salad. When, oh when, was he going to get a decent ride?

Lestrange powered the car as fast as he could along the road to the convent just in time to see Annabelle climb out and run into the big stone barn next to the convent.

"What should we do?" Babineaux asked Mike.

"She won't want us following, she would have taken us with her if she did. But she might be in danger." Mike hesitated for a second. "Let me go. I'll see what's what and step in if I have to." He sprung out of the car and ran to the barn, quickly opening the door and slipping inside.

He looked around. There was no sign of anyone, but in the distance he heard voices, women's voices. They were low, calm, quiet. He tiptoed toward them and flattened himself against the wall next to a doorway. Peering around the doorframe, he could see Annabelle sitting at a table. Her back was to him, obscuring the person to whom she was speaking.

"Tell me what happened. I know it was you who poisoned Father Julien. But I don't know why." Annabelle shifted in her seat and for a quick second, Mike caught a glance of who sat on the other side of the table. Sister Simone!

"You poisoned him with that spoiled rye flour, didn't you?" Annabelle spoke sympathetically. "From the tub in the shed. You knew it was toxic and that over time, in small amounts, the stress on his body would eventually kill him. You essentially tortured him. Why did you do it, Simone? Why, after all these years of being faithful to the Lord, did you feel the necessity to take a life? And in such a way? How did it feel knowing that he would be stealthily poisoned without realizing that this elderly nun who went out of her way to bake him his favorite rye bread was really intent on killing him?"

"It wasn't terribly difficult. Julien was a vain man and a glutton." Simone spoke softly. Mike could hardly hear her. "He wouldn't question why I might bake him, and only him, a loaf of rye bread several times a week for months on end. He wasn't very bright either. He probably assumed the bruising on his arms and legs were the result of clumsy knocks or old age. His creaking joints, arthritis. The sore throat that came and went the result of a virus." Sister Simone took off her glasses and gave them a polish before putting them back on. "But it was his heart that was my target, literally and figuratively. I knew it would give out in the end. It took time and patience, but the plan worked perfectly. It wasn't my intention for him to meet our Lord during Easter Mass but it was as good a time as any."

"But why? Why did you do it?"

Simone nodded sadly. She looked at the table she and Annabelle were sitting at, examining the cuts and knots and the burns on its surface. "They were very discreet and clever, but I knew. They didn't know I knew, but I saw them together after Mass one evening. Renate was laughing. Renate never laughed. I knew then."

"And you didn't approve?"

Mike saw Simone flash an angry look at Annabelle. "Of course I didn't approve. I couldn't stand it. I hated them both. There's a very fine line between love and hate, Reverend, and I couldn't distinguish between the two. They had broken their vows. I saw no reason why I shouldn't too."

"So you hatched this plan to poison Father Julien?"

Sister Simone had a mug of hot tea in front of her. The nun had her hands clasped around it. Now she twisted the mug between them. Mike could see steam rising from it. "I just wanted to hurt him at first, but as time went on, I couldn't stop. I became obsessed with him. I knew the fungus would kill him eventually, but I didn't care. I wanted him to die. With Julien gone, I thought my path would be clear."

"Clear to what?"

"To Renate, of course.

"Renate?"

"Yes, Renate. Dear, sweet, sad Renate." Tears welled in Simone's eyes. "I loved her from the moment I saw her. I faithfully served her all these years. She was my soulmate. Don't you see, I could have made her whole again? I would have wiped away her tears for that spawn of hers, given her anything she wished for. Nothing would have made me happier than to devote myself to her for the rest of my life. But she wasn't interested. After Father Julien died, I told her how I felt..." Sister Simone faltered, and looked sadly down at her mug. "She laughed. I lost my mind. That's when I decided to deliver the same fate to her."

"You poisoned her with the tea?"

"I brought it to her before bed that evening except I switched her usual cow parsley for hemlock. They look almost identical, you know? Yes, of course you do, that's why you're here isn't it? You are very astute, Reverend."

"I learned that at one of Jessica Sparrow's bushcraft talks in my village. Never thought it would come in useful."

"I kept a small bush of it in one of our hedgerows, separate from the cow parsley in our vegetable garden. Anyhow, it was very quick. The hemlock caused respiratory failure, suffocation basically. It was easy to disguise as a hanging. Once she was dead, I lay her on the floor, tied the rope around her neck and another shorter one on the hook above the fireplace.

"But *why* did you make it look like suicide?"

"To throw you off. Or at least to throw off those idiot policemen. I knew they would think she'd killed herself and not pay attention to the tea. I didn't think you'd be so stupid, but they outnumbered you and delayed things for a while. You were right, Renate would never have killed herself."

"So you found out that Father Julien and Mother Renate were having an affair, so you set about poisoning Father Julien with the rye bread. You hoped people would believe it was a heart attack, and then when you told Mother Superior what you'd done and why you'd done it, you killed her with hemlock tea and made it look like a hanging?"

Sister Simone sighed. "Yes, that's right." She twisted the mug in her hands again. "I don't regret it, you know. There was always going to be someone in pain, no matter what. At least now, they are together in God's arms for all eternity. Renate is finally at peace. Killing her was my final kindness."

"What about God, about love for him?"

"God? He left me years ago."

Mike shifted his weight and hit a small stone with his shoe. It made a clinking sound.

"You can come out now, Mike," Annabelle called. And then, more quietly, "It's all over now."

Sheepishly, Mike appeared around the doorjamb. Annabelle stood to face him. Sister Simone blew her nose, and drained the dregs of her tea.

"I think Sister Simone is ready to face the consequences of her actions," Annabelle said.

There was a gurgle behind her. Mike's face froze. Annabelle whirled around in time to see the elderly nun slump over the table.

"The tea!" Annabelle cried. She leaned over to shake Simone, but it was too late.

CHAPTER FIFTY-NINE

"Z AT IS ZAT, zen. A most intriguing case," Babineaux said.

"A horrific one," Mike said.

"A tragic one," Annabelle added. They had returned from the convent to *Chez Selwyn* for a debrief, leaving Sergeant Lestrange and Doctor Giraud to process the tragic scene of Sister Simone's suicide.

"'ow did you know it was Sister Simone, *Révérend*?"

"I must admit, I thought at first it was Véronique, but after she denied she was the murderer, it all fell into the place. First of all, the bread. Rye poisoning was common in the Middle Ages. The rye would develop a fungus, and if eaten, would cause bruising, twisted limbs, and ultimately death. It was called *St. Anthony's Fire* back then. Sister Mary, or Mary as I should call her now, told me about a crop that was destroyed by the nuns after being contaminated with fungus. And later I found a tub of rye flour in the shed. Sister Simone said they hadn't baked rye bread for years, but she was lying. There were recent fingerprints all over the tub. Everything in the cupboard was thick with dust but the dust on the tub was smudged."

Babineaux nodded. "Clever, *non?*"

"And as you know, I couldn't believe that Mother Renate killed herself. For one, it would be against her beliefs, and two, her desk was a mess. She was such an orderly woman, she would never have left it like that. I would have expected a note, too. But the clincher was that Sister Simone brought Mother Superior her tea on the night she died. Cow parsley and hemlock look very similar, but one is harmless, beneficial even, and the other is deadly. But when I realized the murderer had to be Sister Simone, I was stumped. I couldn't think of a motive."

"So you went to track 'er down to get it out of 'er," Babineaux said.

"When I went to the convent, I thought that if I put what I knew to her, she might unburden herself. I think she had had enough of all the lying, death, and chaos. She knew the game was up and had decided confession and death was the only way forward for her. And so it was."

After dinner, the three of them left the restaurant and walked into the cool night air, the sun having long disappeared. The orange-tiled roofs of the buildings that were lit up in daytime were now in shadow. Daylight had been replaced by the warm glow of the moon and supplemented by street lamps around the plaza that reflected the jewel-colored stained glass of the church in pools of light that lay directly at the base of each lamp.

Babineaux sighed. "Sometimes, I zink zat a criminal is just a normal person with a twisted outlook," he said.

"It is often the case, Inspector," Annabelle responded, solemnly.

"But we still don't know who was ze poison pen writer," Babineaux lamented.

"I would have a chat with Claude if I were you," Annabelle said.

Babineaux's eyes widened. "*Non!*"

"Ask him why there are pages missing from his magazines."

"Well, I'm going to leave that one up to you, Babineaux. I'm finished thinking about criminals," Mike said, as he stretched, his arms aloft. "I've got one day of my holiday left, and if you don't mind, I'd like to completely ignore the existence of crime for the duration of it."

Babineaux nodded graciously. "A fond farewell zen, my English detective friends. It was a pleasure to work beside you. I must admit without your 'elp it would have taken me a little while longer to solve zis mystery."

Annabelle and Mike exchanged smiles with the Frenchman. "Good luck, Inspector," Mike said, offering his hand.

Babineaux shook it and then embraced Annabelle with a kiss on both cheeks. "*Révérend*, it was a unique and delightful pleasure."

"Likewise," Annabelle said.

"Maybe we'll see you again before we leave," Mike said.

"Quite so," Babineaux said, smiling broadly.

CHAPTER SIXTY

IF THE DAY had been long and chaotic, the night was dark and ethereal. Annabelle was exhausted. Arms intertwined and in comfortable silence, Annabelle and Mike walked up the hill to a bench that overlooked the village. Neither of them needed to say a word, their relief evident as they strolled slowly through the cobblestone streets. They passed a few villagers walking in the opposite direction who nodded at them as they passed, unaware of the dramatic day the pair had had.

"Well," Mike said, as they reached the bench, "I suppose we'd better find something to do tomorrow, or we might get bored."

Annabelle chuckled and leaned her head tenderly on his shoulder. "I'm so sorry we ended up spending your week off running around investigating gruesome murders."

Mike wound his arm around Annabelle's shoulders. "I keep telling you, Annabelle, it's quite alright. That we've spent it together is enough. And we've had some good times, haven't we? We certainly gave that old man at the church something to talk about."

Annabelle looked up at him, a mischievous glint in her eye.

"Perhaps we could go wine tasting or find someone to give us a French cookery lesson," she said, with a wink. "Perhaps Welsh Selwyn would do it. Or we could go roaming around the beautiful countryside on bikes."

"As long as there aren't any chickens on the back." Mike nodded approvingly, then quickly frowned as he foraged in his jacket pocket. He pulled away from Annabelle, patting himself down hurriedly, then frantically. "Damnit! I don't have my wallet."

"Are you sure?"

"I had it in the restaurant. My police badge is in there!"

"Oh no!"

"I'll go get it."

"I'm coming with you," Annabelle insisted. "I'm sure it'll still be there. No one in this quaint little village will pinch it."

They stood, re-threaded their arms, and began walking back the way they had come. It wouldn't take long, it was downhill all the way. As they neared the plaza, a low humming rose into the air around them as if the atmosphere were vibrating melodically.

"That's strange," Annabelle said.

"What is?"

"That sound. I thought I was imagining it at first, but I'm not. There must be a particularly deep, sonorous wind chime somewhere."

"Must be," Mike replied. They turned another corner.

"Do you hear it, Mike? Now sounds like human voices, a choir!"

Mike turned to her and frowned, straining to hear. "Oh yes, I can hear it... vaguely. Oh well, I suppose they're just practicing."

"Hmm." Annabelle lifted her face to the moon. "It sounds lovely."

"Yes," Mike said. "It does."

"Reminds me of St. Mary's. Makes me a little bit homesick."

At the end of another bumpy, narrow street, the plaza came

into view. "Oh!" Annabelle exclaimed as she noticed the crowd filling the square. A glow surrounded the crowd like a warm halo. Every single person was holding a flickering candle. "Something's happening! Look! What do you think it is?"

"It looks like some sort of ceremony."

They walked over to the crowd in front of the church. Old wrought iron lanterns lit the steps up to the church illuminating baskets of flowers linked together with large ribbons. A red carpet strewn with purple petals led up to the door of the church that had been decorated with a huge arch of white and purple flowers. Children wearing red cassocks sang a psalm, their pure high voices ringing out in the still night air. Annabelle slowed her pace, as if she were entering a dream. The voices and the flames of the many candles seemed to make the air shimmer with hope and expectation.

As Annabelle and Mike got closer, the crowd in the square noticed them. Every head turned toward the couple. Annabelle stopped and gasped, bringing a hand to her mouth as she noticed them looking at her and smiling. Mike took a step forward before looking back at her.

"Is this for me?" she whispered.

CHAPTER SIXTY-ONE

MIKE REACHED FOR Annabelle's hand and led her forward, the crowd parting to create a path that led to the church steps.

Wide-eyed and stunned, Annabelle allowed Mike to lead her through the crowd, the people closing in as they passed them. There was no escape from what was about to come. Annabelle noticed the faces around her, smiling, their eyes glittering with excitement. There in the crowd was everyone they had met in the past few days.

Babineaux tilted his head as they walked past. Lestrange said something in French. Sister Josephine peered through her thick glasses. Mary seemed to have tears in her eyes, and beside her Raphael leaned on a walking stick, beaming happily, much of the color having returned to his face. Even Selwyn's elegant daughter, Françoise, was there.

At the bottom of the church steps, Annabelle looked up to see a small table set in front of the church door. It was draped with a red cloth and decorated with more purple and white flowers. Mike and Annabelle walked up the steps toward it before turning to face the crowd, which was by now, entirely still.

For a moment they looked at each other, Mike smiling, slightly tense, and Annabelle still in a state of shock, unsure about what was to happen, but quite certain it was going to be momentous. The choir came to the end of their psalm and stopped singing, leaving a delicate quiet hanging in the cool night air.

Annabelle's eyes were fixed on Mike as he took a small box from the table, and brought it carefully in front of him. He opened it slowly, and once Annabelle found the strength to peel her eyes from his, she looked down to find a glorious shimmering diamond ring, sparkling like the stars in the sky above her, its light hypnotizing her further.

Mike gracefully got down on one knee, proffering the diamond ring in front of him. He looked up at Annabelle who with one hand was clutching the crucifix she always wore as though it might hold her up if her knees failed her.

"Annabelle," Mike said, his voice low and tender, yet seeming to flow through the clear, light, cool air, "every second I spend with you makes my world come alive. Before I met you I felt as if there was nothing more for me to see and nothing more for me to do. The world seemed full of darkness. But then you made me laugh, you showed me joy, you gave me a new lease on life, you showed me a whole new world. You taught me what true love is. You are a wonderful woman, worthy of far more than I could ever give you, but I want to promise that I will do my best, that I'll never stop doing my best to make you as happy as you have made me. I love you, Annabelle. Will you marry me?"

During this speech, Annabelle's eyes got wider and wider. Her hand went to her open mouth. Her eyes slowly moved between the sparkling diamond and the inspector's bright eager expression as she looked for confirmation with her eyes of what her ears were hearing. Seconds passed. Everyone, from the youngest babe in arms to the most wizened, world-weary elder was fixed upon Annabelle, their faces full of hope. In those seconds, dry lips were licked, heads craned forward, breaths were held.

"Annabelle?" Mike whispered.

At the sound of his voice, Annabelle started. Slowly, she removed the hand from her mouth, a realization dawning on her face, her mouth breaking into a huge smile, her eyes welling with joyful tears. "Oh Mike! Yes! Yes, of course! Of course, I'll marry you!"

The next moments were chaos. Annabelle threw herself at Mike who, rising quickly, caught her just in time to grab her in a tight embrace. The choir started singing "Hallelujah," the children's voices full of light and hope as they threw handfuls of rose petals over the couple, their high young voices offset by the deep baritone of Selwyn Jones who had sprinted up the steps to join them. The crowd cheered and then applauded before their claps morphed into chants of *"Les Anglais, Les Anglais,"* as Mike and Annabelle turned and waved to the crowd.

In the excitement, everyone missed Babineaux giving Lestrange a quiet, discreet nod. But they didn't miss rockets of bright colors that began shooting into the air above the church shortly thereafter, crackling and exploding into incandescent flecks of trailing, swirling, soaring light. The crowd cooed and gasped as the display continued, coloring the night sky in a rainbow of patterns and fire. Annabelle and Mike parted to cast their eyes overhead, transfixed by the flashes of colored lights that glowed against the darkness.

"Oh Mike," Annabelle said wistfully as she once again leaned her head on his shoulder, "how on earth did you manage all this?"

Mike chuckled lightly. "I had a little help," he said, casting his eyes down onto the square. He exchanged a glance with Babineaux, who stroked his moustache and with a smile flickering on his lips, nonchalantly turned to look up at the fireworks exploding in a dramatic climax above him.

Later, as Annabelle and Mike walked back to the auberge, Mike's phone pinged.

"Huh, looks like we'll be making our own breakfast in the morning. Claude has admitted to sending those poison pen letters. He was warning Father Julien off. Seems like the priest had money problems. He pawned the gold box with the relic of St. Agnès at a shop in Reims. Claude saw him do it."

"Well, well, who would've guessed?"

"Unbelievable." Mike had had his views of the priesthood and those living a religious life utterly shattered in the past few days. He felt like he would never be able to look at a nun in the same way again.

They heard a cry behind them.

"*Attendez! Attendez!*" A young mother pushing a child in a buggy ran up to them. She wordlessly pressed a bag into Annabelle's hands. After performing a curious action resembling a curtsey crossed with a bow, the woman ran off again. Annabelle peered into the bag.

"What is it?" Mike said. Annabelle didn't answer. "It's baby clothes again, isn't it?"

"Yes." Annabelle wrinkled her nose at him and smiled coyly. "But let's keep them this time."

EPILOGUE

THERE WAS A slight drizzle as Annabelle's Mini Cooper rolled off the back of the ferry onto British land. The droplets that immediately landed on the car windshield made Annabelle and Mike smile. They were a subtle reminder that they were home, a final confirmation that the events of the previous week were behind them. And they were a signal that their new lives started now—or at least as soon as they got home.

It was an overcast day, a slight wind picking up the gentle downpour, making it seem more fearsome than it really was. As they drove back to Upton St. Mary, a sense of anticipation and excitement about what awaited came over them.

During their last evening in Ville d'Eauloise, they had learned that the French were rather good at goodbyes. They took the words *au revoir*—"until we see you again"—literally. Everyone seemed entirely sure that they would meet the English couple at some point in the future. They had all turned out to greet them on their last evening at *Chez Selwyn,* and mercifully, in Mike's opinion, had left the comedy sketch recitals for another time.

"Sometimes," Annabelle mused, as she eased the car through the streets toward her church, "I think the best part of a holiday is coming home and appreciating everything you've missed and that you have right at your own front door."

Mike chuckled. "I would agree with that," he said warmly, gently thumbing the lapel of his new coat. "While I enjoyed the pastries and the wine, and the French food, even the snails, what I'm really looking forward to now is a good pie and chips."

Annabelle brought the car to a stop in the church courtyard, and they both got out, Mike walking around the car to wrap Annabelle in his arms and plant a loving kiss on her lips.

"Cup of tea?" Annabelle said. "If you're not too eager to get home!"

"I'm already missing you!" Mike said, taking her holdall as they turned to walk up the cottage path. With smiles they couldn't wipe from their faces, they stopped in front of the door and with a sense of ceremony Annabelle lifted the large knocker.

After a few moments the door opened. When she saw who was standing there, Philippa gasped and put her hands to her cheeks. "Oh! You're back!"

"We certainly are," Annabelle said, as Magic ran up for some attention. "I know it's my home, but I thought I'd knock rather than surprise you by entering unannounced."

"How lovely to see you. How was it? Was the food as good as they say? Were your rooms warm enough? And what happened with the Catholic business? Did you solve the mystery?" Philippa asked in a rush.

"I'll tell you everything over a cup of tea," Annabelle said.

"Let me go put the kettle on," Philippa replied.

Annabelle and Mike made their way to the living room and stood there listening to Philippa hurriedly clattering teacups and saucers onto a tray.

"We should tell her now," Mike said. "She might spill her tea down herself if we wait."

Annabelle nodded. "Philippa! Would you come in here a moment, please?"

Philippa emerged from the kitchen, her eyebrows high in expectation. "Yes? Is anything the matter?"

"We have some news," Annabelle said, glancing quickly at Mike, who squeezed her waist against his. Annabelle took a deep breath.

Philippa tilted her head slightly, looking back and forth between them. "Yes?"

Annabelle couldn't hold the news in any longer. "Mike proposed!" she said suddenly. "And I said yes! We're getting married!"

Philippa's face went rigid. Her cheeks turned a deep shade of rose-red. She didn't say a word. Annabelle and Mike waited for a reaction, shooting each other a quick, confused look, before looking back at the elderly woman.

"Philippa?" Mike asked. "Are you alright?"

No sooner had he said it than Philippa, stiff as a board, face-planted onto the carpet.

"Oh my!" Annabelle quickly rushed to the fallen woman's side. "Philippa?"

She rolled Philippa onto her back. She slapped her cheeks gently. "Philippa?" Annabelle looked up at Mike. "She's out cold."

Mike crouched down next to her. "Quick, where are your smelling salts?" he said.

"Smelling salts?" Annabelle replied in a panicked tone.

"Yes! Something to bring her back!"

"I haven't got any smelling salts! Who has smelling salts in this day and age?"

"Maybe we should splash some cold water on her?"

"No, too shocking! We might revive her only for her to have a heart attack."

"Well, what then?"

Annabelle gazed down at her friend's pale, placid face with concern. "The holdall!" she said suddenly.

Mike flung the bag open and foraged inside it, tossing aside various garments in search of the carefully wrapped gourmet cheese they had brought back with them. He tore open the soft, waxy covering and rushed to Annabelle's side, breaking off a piece so that she could waft it under Philippa's nose.

"Blurgh!" Philippa said, gasping and smacking her lips as she regained consciousness, shaking her head and paddling the air with her hands as she sought to get herself away from the obnoxious smell.

Mike began laughing. Annabelle joined him. Philippa blinked herself awake.

"Are you alright?" Annabelle asked.

After a short pause during which Philippa looked from Annabelle, to Mike, and back again, she smiled and sighed deeply as though waking from a long, deep, restful sleep. "Did you just say you're getting married?"

"Yes!" Annabelle exclaimed.

Philippa staggered to her feet and hugged both of them with all her tiny might, her eyes glistening with tears. Wordlessly she moved to the coat rack in the hall, put on her hat, and her coat. She pulled her brolly from the umbrella stand. Annabelle and Mike looked on in confusion.

"Um... Philippa," Mike asked, "what about that tea?"

"Yes," said Annabelle, "we were going to tell you all about our trip!"

"Pfft!" came the older woman's dismissive response. She moved to the door. "I've no time for tea!" She grasped the door handle. "I've got to get on." Philippa turned to look at Annabelle and Mike. "Haven't you heard? I've got a wedding to organize!"

Thank you for reading this omnibus edition! I will have a new Annabelle adventure for you soon! To find out about new books, sign up for my newsletter: https://alisongolden.com

If you're looking for a detective series with twisty plots and characters that feel like friends, binge read the *USA Today* bestselling Inspector Graham series featuring a new and unusual detective with a phenomenal memory and a tragic past. Get your copy of the omnibus edition comprising books 5-7 from Amazon now! This omnibus is FREE in Kindle Unlimited.

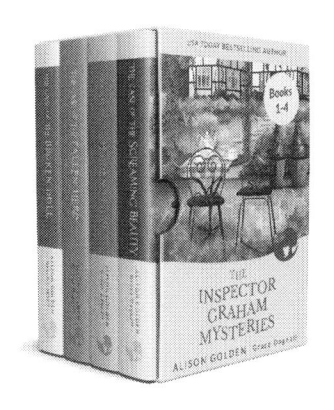

And don't miss the Roxy Reinhardt mysteries. Will Roxy triumph after her life falls apart? She's fired from her job, her boyfriend dumps her, she's out of money. So, on a whim, she goes on the trip of a lifetime to New Orleans, There, she gets mixed up in a Mardi Gras murder. *Things were going to be fine. They were, weren't they?* Get your copy of the Roxy Reinhardt trilogy here. Also FREE in Kindle Unlimited.

If you're looking for something edgy and dangerous, root for Diana Hunter as she seeks justice after a devastating crime destroys her family. Follow her journey in this non-stop story of suspense and action by purchasing the omnibus edition featuring the first four books in the series. This omnibus is FREE in Kindle Unlimited.

I hugely appreciate your help in spreading the word about this omnibus edition, including telling a friend. Reviews help readers find books! Please leave a review on your favorite book site.

Turn the page for an excerpt from the first book in the Inspector David Graham series, *The Case of the Screaming Beauty*...

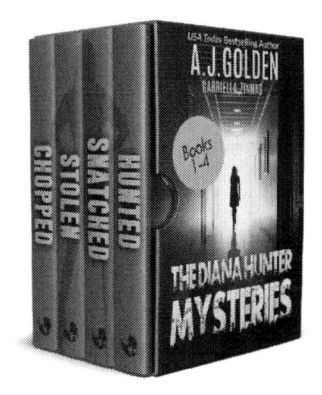

AN INSPECTOR DAVID GRAHAM MYSTERY

USA Today Bestselling Author

THE CASE OF THE SCREAMING BEAUTY

ALISON GOLDEN Grace Dagnall

THE CASE OF THE SCREAMING BEAUTY

CHAPTER ONE

AMELIA SWANSBOURNE STRAIGHTENED up, wincing slightly, and admired the freshly-weeded flower bed with an almost professional pride. It was, she mused, as though she were fighting a continuous, low-level war against insidious intruders whose intentions were not only to take root and flourish, but whose impact on the impeccably arranged beds and rockeries of her garden was as unwelcome as a hurricane. Amelia was ruthless and precise, going about her work with a methodical focus that reminded her of those "gardening monks" she'd once seen in a documentary. Perhaps, she chuckled, moving onto the next flower bed, weeding would be her path to enlightenment.

As she knelt on her cushioned, flower-patterned pad and began the familiar rhythm once more, she let her mind go where it wanted. How many other women in their early sixties, she wondered, were carrying out this basic, time-honored task at this very moment? She pictured those quiet English gardens being lovingly tended on this very temperate Sunday morning, silently wishing her fellow gardeners a peaceful and productive couple of hours. It must have been true, though, that she faced a larger and more demanding test than most. The gardens of the *Lavender Inn* were spread over an impressive and endlessly challenging four and a half acres.

Guests loved walking in the gardens. They had become a major attraction for many of the city folk who retreated from London to this country idyll. Among the visitors were those all-important ones who checked in under false names, and then, after their visit was over, went back to their computers to write online reviews, the power of which could make or break a bed-and-breakfast like the *Lavender*. The gardens appeared often in comments on those review websites, so Amelia knew her work was an investment, however time-consuming it could be. Keeping the gardens in check—not only weeded but watered, constantly improved, pruned, fed, and composted—would have been a full-time job for any experienced gardener, but Amelia handled virtually all of the guesthouse's horticultural needs on her own. She preferred it this way, but it did take its toll. Not least on her aging knees.

The gardens had proved such a draw and the satisfaction of their splendid appearance was so great that Amelia had long ago judged her efforts to be very much worthwhile. Besides, it was a fitting, ongoing tribute to her late Uncle Terry, who had bequeathed Amelia and her husband this remarkable Tudor building and its gardens. The sudden inheritance had come as quite a shock. Cliff, in particular, was worried that he was entirely unready to be the co-host of a popular and high-end B&B. However, Terry had no children and had been as much a father to Amelia as had her own. It made her proud and happy to believe that the place was being run well and that the gardens had become the envy of the village of Chiddlinghurst, and, judging by those reviews, beyond.

A bed of roses formed the easterly flank of the main quadrangle, within which Amelia had spent much of the morning. They were looking particularly lovely; three crimson and scarlet varieties found their natural partners in the lily-white species which bloomed opposite on the western side. By the house itself, an imposing Tudor mansion with all its old, dark, wood beams still intact, there were smaller beds and a rockery on either side of a spacious patio with white, cast-iron lawn furniture. Further over, against the western wing of the inn, was a bed of which Amelia was particularly proud: deep-green ferns and low-light flowering plants, their lush colors providing a quick dose of restful ease among the brighter hues around them. Amelia took a moment to let the greens sink into her mind, soothing and promising in equal measure. She indulged in a deep, nourishing breath and began truly to relax and enjoy her morning in the garden. Which was why the piercing scream that burst from the open window of the room just above the bed of ferns turned Amelia's blood as cold as ice.

Dropping her trowel and shedding her heavy work gloves, Amelia dashed across the immaculate lawn of the quadrangle and up the four stone steps that led to the patio. Peering through the conservatory doors, she could see nothing out of place. She was quickly through and into the dining room and then the lobby. She took the stairs as fast as her ailing knees would allow, and within seconds of hearing the scream, she was knocking at the door of a guest room.

"Mrs. Travis? Can you hear me? Is everything alright?" Amelia panted, her mind already racing ahead to the horrors that might accompany some kind of tragedy at this popular house.

"Mrs. Travis?" she repeated, raising her hand to knock once more.

The door opened and Norah Travis was smiling placidly. "Hello, Amelia. Whatever is the matter?"

"You're alright!" Amelia observed with a great sigh of relief. "Good heavens above, I feared something awful had happened."

"I'm sure I don't know what you mean," Norah assured her. "It's been a pretty quiet Sunday morning, so far."

There was nothing about Norah which might raise any kind of alarm. As usual, there wasn't a blond hair out of place, and her bright blue eyes were gleaming. If anything, Amelia decided, she looked even younger than her twenty-seven years.

"I could have sworn," Amelia told her, gradually regaining her breath, "that I heard a scream from the window there," she pointed, "while I was outside in the garden. Clear as day."

"Oh, I've nothing to scream about, Amelia," Norah replied. "Could it have been someone else? I don't think I heard anything."

Cliff won't let me hear the end of this. He'll say I'm losing my marbles, that I've finally gone loopy. And who's to say he's wrong?
"It must have been, my dear. I'm so sorry to have disturbed you."

Amelia bid Norah a good morning and returned downstairs, distracted by the chilling memory of the sound, as well as its mysterious origin. She could have sworn on a stack of Bibles....

To get your copy of The Case of the Screaming Beauty and three further books in the Inspector Graham series, The Case of the Hidden Flame, The Case of the Fallen Hero, and The Case of the Broken Doll, visit the link below:

https://www.alisongolden.com/graham-boxset-paperback

REVERENTIAL RECIPES

CONTINUE ON TO CHECK OUT THE RECIPES FOR GOODIES FEATURED IN THIS BOOK...

ANGÉLIQUE APPLE & FIG CHEESECAKE

For the sponge base:
2 oz. butter at room temperature
2 oz. self-raising flour, sifted
½ teaspoon baking powder
1 egg
2 oz. sugar or caster sugar
6 oz. apples, peeled, cored, and sliced
2 oz. figs chopped

For the cheesecake filling:
12 oz. fromage frais
3 oz. sugar or caster sugar
½ oz. powdered gelatine
3 tablespoons water
1 teaspoon vanilla extract
⅓ pint double or whipped cream, whipped
3 egg whites, stiffly whisked

To decorate:

1 tablespoon sifted icing sugar
3 fl. oz. double or whipped cream, stiffly whipped
A few slices of apples
Chopped figs
Caramel sauce

Preheat the oven to 180°C, 350°F, Gas Mark 4. Grease and line a 7 inch sandwich tin. Place the butter, flour, baking powder, egg and sugar in a mixing bowl and whisk until light and fluffy. Cook for 20 minutes, Turn out on to a wire tray to cool.

Mix the fromage frais with the caster sugar. Dissolve the gelatine in the water over a gentle heat and add to the cheese with the vanilla extract. Fold in the whipped cream. Lightly fold the whisked egg whites into the cheese mixture.

Lightly oil the sides of a 6½ inch loose-based cake tin. Cut the sponge in half horizontally and place the bottom half in the tin.

Lay the apples on to the sponge base. Sprinkle the figs evenly over them. Pour in the cheesecake mixture and top with the reserved sponge. Chill until set.

When set, carefully remove from the tin. Dust the top with sifted icing sugar. Decorate with whirls of cream and apple slices and figs. Drizzle with the caramel sauce. **Serves 4-6.**

Variations:

Cheesecakes make a very versatile dessert with many variations. There are many types of soft cheese now on the market and most are suitable for cheesecakes. Curd cheese, cottage cheese if sieved and skimmed milk soft cheese are all good for keeping the calories down. If full-fat soft cheese is used, half the cream in the recipe can be substituted with plain unsweetened yogurt.

The strawberries in the recipe can be substituted with any other soft fruit or to make a lemon cheesecake omit the vanilla essence and add the grated rind and juice of two lemons but add a further ½ teaspoon of powdered gelatine.

If a biscuit crumb base is preferred rather than the sponge base, crumble 6 oz. digestive biscuits or graham crackers, mix with 2 oz. sugar and 2 oz. melted butter. Put half the mixture into the base of the tin then sprinkle the rest over the top.

CHÉRISSABLE CRÈME BRÛLÉE

1 pint fresh double or whipping cream
4 egg yolks
3 oz. sugar or caster sugar
1 teaspoon vanilla extract

Put the cream in the top of a double boiler or in a heatproof bowl over a pan of hot water and bring to just below boiling point.

Meanwhile, put the egg yolks, 2 oz. of the sugar and the vanilla extract in a mixing bowl and beat thoroughly. Pour in the cream and stir to combine. Pour the mixture into a shallow baking dish and place in a roasting tin half full of hot water. Bake in a cool oven (150°C/300°F or Gas Mark 2) for one hour or until set.

When set, remove from the tin and leave to go cold. Chill in the refrigerator for several hours, preferably overnight.

Sprinkle the top of the crème brûlée with the remaining sugar and put under a preheated hot grill until the sugar turns to caramel. Leave to cool before serving.

This sumptuous dessert is at its best served chilled with fresh raspberries or strawberries steeped in vanilla sugar - these contrast well with the richness of the crème brûlée.

DÉLICIEUSE DRIED FRUIT AND SPICE COMPÔTE

4 oz. dried figs
4 oz. dried apricots
2 oz. dried apple
4 oz. dried prunes
2 oz. raisins
2 oz. sultanas
2oz. currants
1 teaspoon mixed spice
3 tablespoons cooking brandy
¼ pint strong black coffee
⅓ pint water

This dish is full of nourishment and may be served with a little cream for a lunch or supper dessert or warm it up for comforting breakfast.

Place all the ingredients in a large saucepan and bring gently to the boil. Simmer for 5-6 minutes.

Turn the contents of the pan into a large mixing bowl, cover with a clean tea towel, and allow to go quite cold.

Turn the compôte into a large glass or earthenware pot, seal, and allow to stand in a cool place for at least 12 hours before using. **Serves 4-6.**

Note:

The compôte may be heated if you wish, but never return any hot leftovers to the main compôte, as all will go bad. If it is properly stored in a cold place, you may add more fruit, cold liquid and brandy (which acts as a preservative). If well sealed, it will keep for more than 2 weeks.

QUALITÉ QUICHE LORRAINE

4-6 oz. unsmoked streaky bacon, rinds removed and chopped
Shortcrust pastry flan case
2 whole eggs
2 egg yolks
¼ pint fresh single cream
Approx. ¼ pint milk
Salt and freshly ground black pepper
2 oz. Gruyére cheese, grated

Fry the bacon over gentle heat in a small frying pan until the fat runs and the bacon becomes golden brown. Put the bacon into the flan case. Beat the whole eggs, egg yolks and cream together lightly in a bowl and pour over the bacon. Stir in enough milk almost to fill the case. Season to taste with salt and pepper and sprinkle with the grated Gruyére.

Bake in a fairly hot oven (190°C/375°F or Gas Mark 5) for 25 to 30 minutes or until the filling is set and the pastry is golden. Remove from the oven and leave to rest for 10 minutes before serving.

SACRÉ STRAWBERRY SOUFFLÉ

¾ lb. fresh strawberries, hulled and washed
5 oz. caster sugar
3 eggs, separated
1 tablespoon gelatine powder
2 tablespoons lemon juice
Red food coloring (optional)
¼ pint fresh double cream
1 oz. finely chopped hazelnuts or walnuts or crushed ratafias to finish

First prepare a 1 pint or 5 inch soufflé dish; cut a strip of doubled greaseproof or parchment paper long enough to go around the outside of the soufflé dish (overlapping by 1-2 inches) and 2-3 inches higher than the dish. Tie this securely around the outside of the dish with string. Brush the inside of the greaseproof paper above the rim with melted butter.

Pureé the strawberries in an electric blender or work through a sieve, reserving a few whole ones for decoration. Stir in 2 oz. of the sugar.

Put the egg yolks and remaining sugar in a heatproof bowl and stand over a pan of hot water. Beat with a rotary beater or whisk until thick. Remove from the pan and continue beating until the mixture is cold. Fold in the strawberry pureé.

Sprinkle the gelatine over the lemon juice in a small heatproof bowl. Leave until spongy, then place the bowl in a pan of hot water and stir over a low heat until the gelatine has dissolved. Leave to cool slightly, then stir into the strawberry mixture. Add a few drops of red food coloring if the mixture seems rather pale. Whip the cream until it is thick and stir into the strawberry mixture, making sure that it is thoroughly blended.

Beat the egg whites until stiff then fold into the strawberry mixture. Spoon into the prepared soufflé dish and chill in the refrigerator for at least 4 hours or until set.

Before serving, carefully remove the greaseproof paper. Decorate the top of the souffle with the reserved strawberries and press the nuts or ratafias around the edge.

All ingredients are available from your local store or online retailer.

You can find printable versions of these recipes and links to the ingredients used in them at https://www.alisongolden.com/fireworks-in-france-recipes/

For a limited time, you can get the first books in each of my series - *Chaos in Cambridge, The Case of the Screaming Beauty, Hunted, and Mardi Gras Madness* - plus updates about new releases, promotions, and other Insider exclusives, by signing up for my mailing list at:

https://www.alisongolden.com/annabelle

BOOKS BY ALISON GOLDEN

FEATURING INSPECTOR DAVID GRAHAM

The Case of the Screaming Beauty

The Case of the Hidden Flame

The Case of the Fallen Hero

The Case of the Broken Doll

The Case of the Missing Letter

The Case of the Pretty Lady

The Case of the Forsaken Child

FEATURING ROXY REINHARDT

Mardi Gras Madness

New Orleans Nightmare

Louisiana Lies

As A. J. Golden

FEATURING DIANA HUNTER

Hunted (Prequel)

Snatched

Stolen

Chopped

Exposed

ABOUT THE AUTHOR

Alison Golden is the *USA Today* bestselling author of the Inspector David Graham mysteries, a traditional British detective series, and two cozy mystery series featuring main characters Reverend Annabelle Dixon and Roxy Reinhardt. As A. J. Golden, she writes the Diana Hunter thriller series.

Alison was raised in Bedfordshire, England. Her aim is to write stories that are designed to entertain, amuse, and calm. Her approach is to combine creative ideas with excellent writing and edit, edit, edit. Alison's mission is simple: To write excellent books that have readers clamoring for more.

Alison is based in the San Francisco Bay Area with her husband and twin sons. She splits her time between London and San Francisco.

For up-to-date promotions and release dates of upcoming books, sign up for the latest news here: https://www.alisongolden.com/annabelle.

For more information:
www.alisongolden.com
alison@alisongolden.com

facebook.com/alisongolden.books
twitter.com/alisonjgolden
instagram.com/alisonjgolden

THANK YOU

Thank you for taking the time to read books 5 through 7 in the Reverend Annabelle Dixon series. If you enjoyed them, please consider telling your friends or posting a short review. Word of mouth is an author's best friend and very much appreciated.
Thank you,

Printed in Great Britain
by Amazon